Sweetness *from* Ashes

Marlyn Horsdal

BRINDLE
& GLASS

Library and Archives Canada Cataloguing in Publication
Horsdal, Marlyn
Sweetness from ashes / Marlyn Horsdal.

ISBN 978-1-897142-43-1

I. Title.

PS8615.O777S94 2010   C813'.6   C2009-906894-X

Editor: Rhonda Bailey
Cover image: Alf Ertsland, istockphoto.com
Proofreader: Heather Sangster, Strong Finish
Author photo: Wendy Hilliard

Canadian Heritage	Patrimoine canadien	BRITISH COLUMBIA ARTS COUNCIL	Canada Council for the Arts Conseil des Arts du Canada

Brindle & Glass is pleased to acknowledge the financial support for its publishing program from the Government of Canada through the Canada Book Fund, Canada Council for the Arts, and the Province of British Columbia through the British Columbia Arts Council and the Book Publishing Tax Credit.

Mixed Sources
Cert no. SW-COC-001271
© 1996 FSC
FSC

The interior pages of this book have been printed on 100% post-consumer recycled paper, processed chlorine free, and printed with vegetable-based inks.

Brindle & Glass Publishing
www.brindleandglass.com

1 2 3 4 5 13 12 11 10

PRINTED AND BOUND IN CANADA

Only connect!

—E.M. Forster, *Howards End*

CONTENTS

PROLOGUE: Last Wish

It is mid-afternoon on a clear day. City streets are lined with dazzling tall buildings, and sunlight bounces off the glass facades to brighten the asphalt below. Images of blue sky and clouds and neighbouring skyscrapers reflect down into the eyes of passers-by on the sidewalks. Mountains with snowy peaks are visible, due north among the towers. Ornamental cherry trees bloom pink and white, their fallen petals piling up in pastel drifts along the curbs.

In an office on the twenty-first floor of one gleaming building, two people stand looking down.

"I love Vancouver in the spring, don't you?" says the lawyer, instantly feeling guilty and awkward. What a cruel thing to say.

"I do," says the person who has come to sign the will. "It still delights me, after all my years out here, that spring stretches out for such a long time."

The lawyer, who has grown up on the West Coast and knows no other climate, nods in agreement anyway. "Would you like to sit down and read over the document? Make sure the last changes you requested are all correct?"

"Yes." The other person sinks carefully into a soft-bottomed chair and picks up a small sheaf of papers.

"I would have been happy to come out to you with these," the lawyer begins but is interrupted.

"No, no." A dismissive wave of a hand. "I'm still getting around and I like a reason to come downtown. Can't just sit around the house and wait, you know."

Silence, while the visitor examines each page and the lawyer gazes out to the west, fingers fiddling with a pen.

Finally, "This looks fine." The client picks up the pen on the desk and writes initials and a strong signature in all the places indicated. The lawyer signs as witness.

1

Rising slowly, the visitor also looks away to the west but is visualizing a scene in the not-too-distant future:

It is the middle of the night. On a quiet, tree-lined street the warm air is fragrant with the unseen presence of a few night-blooming flowers, leaves, freshly cut grass. Most of the big houses are in darkness.

In one of them, the tall bay windows on the second floor show the faint and spectral green glow from a nightlight. Two large easy chairs face the windows; a person might survey the garden from there. Behind the chairs, head against one wall, a narrow hospital bed is dwarfed by the room's generous proportions. The person lying in the bed is breathing in a soft, slow rhythm. Apart from these gentle exhalations, the room is still.

The bedroom door is opened. Light from the hall streams in and the door is quickly shut again. Footsteps cross the floor. The newcomer leans over the bed, hesitantly, in a flood of mixed emotion: hope and terror, regret and—with any luck—love.

"Well," says the visitor, "it would certainly be interesting to see what comes of this." A pause. "I won't, of course," briskly.

The lawyer, a kind young person unaccustomed to thinking about death, says, "I'm terribly sorry. I . . ."

"I know you are, and thank you. Everybody is. I am too, naturally. But—you never know what life is going to throw at you, and you just have to deal with it." No quaver in the voice. "Thank you for all your help with this will business. I should have done it earlier."

"Not at all, that's fine, you're most welcome. I'm glad that I could be useful and I'm—I'm honoured to have met you."

A firm handshake and the appointment is over.

ONE: A Sugar Maple

"Why don't you just mail it?" asked Sheila, chewing her lower lip and gazing dubiously at the urn in the centre of the coffee table. "I'm sure it'd get through all right." She was curled up tightly in Jenny's recliner chair, clutching her knees.

"Or courier it, if you're nervous about the postal service." Chris lounged on the chesterfield, arms crossed behind his head. "Though there's no problem about the contents going stale, of course."

"Oh, Chris," Jenny said, half annoyed, half laughing guiltily. "No, the will explicitly says 'take.'" She waved the paper at them. "It says, 'I direct that my ashes be taken back to Juniper Farm, to be interred in the high (that is, southeast) corner of the field we used to call Deer Field, and that a *sugar maple*'—it's italicized—'be planted on top of them. And it is my wish that Sheila, Chris, and Jenny take them there.'"

"Why a sugar maple?" Chris disregarded the main issue for the moment.

"I don't know. Maybe there's something in the papers that'll explain it. I haven't gone through everything yet."

The condo was tiny but bright, its outside wall floor-to-ceiling glass. Mirrors on the back wall reflected the light, as well as the disconcerting impression of the freighters moored in English Bay crouching in the corner. Jenny loved the little space, though friends sometimes wondered aloud how she could live in eight hundred and fifty square feet. "Because it doesn't feel small. And because I'm neat," she would tell them, which was not really the case. Her Murphy bed folded up behind mirrored doors, and facing it across the room was a matching large closet that she called "the media room." Computer, television, desk, stereo, and telephone lived in a constant clutter of papers, but when those doors, also mirrored, were closed, the main room was immaculate.

"Imagine remembering the farm so well that you could pinpoint a corner like that after all this time, without ever going back." Sheila shook her head, indicating amazement. After her years on stage, she was good at gestures.

"Have you ever been there, Sheila? You must have been near it often on tour."

"No, Chris, I haven't," irritably. "It's probably a bit of a drive out of Ottawa, and it never occurred to me to go."

"Why not? Weren't you curious?"

Sheila raised her eyebrows, shook her head again, hard enough to make her glossy black hair swing, and took a sip of wine. Clearly not to be drawn. Chris shot her a level glance but did not repeat his question.

"Well, when shall we go?" Jenny looked expectantly from Sheila to Chris.

"I'm not going," Sheila declared. "And why should Chris go? It's not really anything to do with him. I mean, directly."

Jenny gaped at her, blue eyes wide. "But, Sheel, Chris was as much a part of Pat's life as me. *Before* me! And it says right here that we're all to go."

"No, it doesn't. It says 'wish'—it doesn't say we *have* to go. It's not like 'unless you all three go you won't get your inheritance.'"

Shocked, Jenny turned to Chris. "Chris, you'll come, won't you?"

"Yes, I'd like to. I'm very interested in where Pat came from."

"So, Sheila, you have to."

"I do not."

"But why," Jenny wailed. "It's what Pat wants. Wanted." She put the will down on the table and picked up her glass.

"I've lived my whole life perfectly content without delving into any of that stuff" —she paused for a second as if expecting a challenge on this— "and I'm damned if I'm going to start now. You guys can go and I hope you have a great time." Sheila tilted the recliner farther back and turned to examine the view.

"Okay—you don't *have* to come." Jenny was reluctant to provoke Sheila's wrath but she persisted. "But you should. It's not right to ignore the provisions of a will."

Sheila glared at her. Chris, keeping out of the crossfire, unfolded himself to his considerable height and wandered over to the windows. The glass gave onto a generous terrace, colourful with tubs of flowers and evergreens—Alberta spruce, marigolds, pansies, impatiens, a Japanese maple—and on over the harbour to the North Shore mountains. Later, the lights of West Vancouver would twinkle like a curtain of fireflies.

Jenny tried a different tack. "We'd have fun! We haven't been on a trip together since before Sandy died. It's time we did."

"You want us to go off and *bond*," Sheila snorted.

"What's wrong with that?" Glad to have elicited even a minimal response. "At least think about it."

"When do you want to go?" Chris asked.

"Soon. I don't know if I like the idea of living with these ashes very long." Inoffensive in itself, the urn dominated the little room.

"I have a friend whose father was cremated a couple of years ago, and he and his brothers can't agree on where to strew him so he's keeping the ashes till they decide. He brings them out for occasions, like Father's Day, or Christmas. Everybody says, 'Hi, Ralph' and goes on with dinner."

"I think that's excellent, Chris. Why don't we keep the ashes in Vancouver and share them around? The urn could board at each of our places in turn," Sheila suggested.

"Ugh. No. You're just saying that to annoy me." Jenny's red curls fairly bristled. "The will says take them to the farm, and that's where they're going."

"Fine. You two can take them."

Jenny contemplated Sheila's set face. Why is she being so stubborn about this? She has always done things her own way, of course, has always been self-centred, and her single-minded determination has served her well in her career. You don't get to the top of any profession if you dissipate your energies. But this is about *us*, however oddly connected we are. Sheila had a much more strained relationship with Pat than I did, but still. And then another thought slid into her mind: Should I tell them everything now? I have to do it at some point—Pat was adamant about that. Will it make any difference to Sheila's decision? I'd better give it a try.

But before Jenny could speak, Sheila did. "If we're done with the will—I mean, for today—I'm going. I presume we'll be getting together again about the house and all the furniture and things like that."

"Oh yes, it's bound to take a while. But Pat was very organized."

"I'll go too, Sheila. But Jenny" —Chris turned to her with concern— "do you really not feel comfortable with the ashes? Do you want me to take the urn home with me?"

"No, no, I'm fine. But thank you—that was a nice thought."

After the others had left, Jenny thumped down on her recliner, tilted it back, and looked glumly at her view. Usually it cheered her up, but now she glowered out at the mountains. "Why are you the executrix?" people had very sensibly asked, since she was the youngest, and "Because I'm so responsible," she had quipped. But that wasn't why. She frowned at the urn. Why didn't I tell them the whole thing now? This was the perfect time. What an ass I am. When will there ever be a better time? Much as she loved her home, on occasion it did feel too small and this was one of those times. She grabbed a thin vest and headed out the door.

Two blocks from English Bay, she let herself into Elise's Victorian cottage. Mostly surrounded by newer buildings that towered over it, the little green-and-white house sat composedly on its lot, exuding gingerbread and the sense of a gracious past. A relief for the eyes, Jenny thought, compared with the severe vertical lines of its neighbourhood.

Molly had heard Jenny's footsteps crossing the veranda and was waiting just inside the door, tail waving, fat front feet dancing.

"Hello, sweet pea. Ready to go walkies?"

"Woo-woo-woo," answered Molly, which Jenny took to mean, "What a silly question, you pleasant but idiotic human." If she could, she would have met Jenny with her leash in her mouth, but bassets weren't built for leaping up to snatch things off hooks.

Jenny got the leash as Molly pranced and exclaimed in the front hall. Out the door they rushed, down the steps, turn left, canter along the sidewalk, "Woo-woo-woo!" ("Hurry up, Jenny, this is fun!"), across the street and into the park.

The gardeners had just been in, and the air was full of the delicious, fresh-watermelon aroma of cut grass. After the first hundred excited yards, Molly usually slowed down, sniffing busily, piddling, gazing soulfully around. In search of what? Jenny wondered. Badgers—or whatever prey animal bassets were intended to chase? Other dogs? Food? Did she slow down because she liked the feel of the grass under her pudgy feet and wanted to get the pavement parts over with quickly? They almost invariably took the same route, so presumably Molly knew where they were going.

They both enjoyed these walks enormously—Molly swaggering along in her comfortable basset waddle, sensitive nose a-twitch, observing her world happily from a foot above the ground, Jenny strolling in the same world but absorbing different elements, content with the cloudy coastal greyness, the mist in layers on the North Shore, the flat silver sea and the warm, moist air. Her partner, Nick, loved bright sunshine and cloudless blue skies, and seriously disliked this sort of weather, especially in the summer, but Jenny thought of it as soothing, pearl-like and comforting. Trying to explain this to one of her authors, transplanted from the East, she had said, "Maybe it's the idea of nourishing—the rain is replenishing, softening, encouraging growth. As long as it's not absolutely pissing down rain, I go out every day." "When is it ever not pissing down?" grumped the author. But he wrote about economic trends, and was often grumpy.

Such shades of greys and beiges, Jenny exulted. Must be my North European heritage. Who needs brilliant colours? Look at the extraordinary range of hues and textures. The shimmer on the water—mauve, platinum, charcoal, steel-blue—there's no single tone of grey. Rough boulders, smooth pebbles—the colours change with the surfaces, and whether they are wet or dry. And the wealth of wood—the rich dark browns of bark, the wheat and oatmeal of scuffed driftwood, the yellows, almost gold, of the smooth, peeled logs, more recent escapees from booms. I've even seen streaks of pink and green. It depends on the light, and whether there's a glisten of rain over everything.

Bored with non-action, Molly lolloped up to a woman jogger, who stopped and squatted to greet her.

"You're so lucky," she said, stroking the appreciative Molly. "I used to have a basset. Aren't they wonderful?"

"They are," replied Jenny, "but she's not exactly mine. She's my foster dog. I'm not allowed to have a dog in my building, so I walk Molly whenever I can. Her owner is a friend of mine."

"What a neat idea." The jogger gave Molly a final pat. Molly gave her departing back an earnest gaze for a few seconds, whuffed gently and headed in the opposite direction.

Jenny followed, grinning at Molly's rocking-horse gait. The basset gambolled up to a dog they both knew, a blond collie-shepherd cross with a sweet face.

"Hello, Hannah," Jenny said as the dogs sniffed and wagged. "Who're you with today? Uh—hi, Andrew. Haven't seen you for a while. How're you doing?"

"Pretty well, thanks. In fact, I just had a check-up. My T-cells and viral load are in very good shape." He fell into step with Jenny. "And how's the gorgeous Nick?"

"Oh, fine. Busy. I'm so glad about your good news! And Bruce?"

"Right as rain. If that's not an oxymoron out here."

"Not by me. I like the rain."

"You've been here all your life. Softening of the brain."

"Yeah, yeah—webbed feet, moss in the armpits, all that. But I notice you guys are staying," she teased. "Not hopping on the next plane back to Toronto."

"Absolutely not."

"I was just thinking about Toronto, actually. I've had a job offer there so I was sort of idly considering it."

"I gather in your line of work Toronto's the hub. All the biggest publishers and so on. Is it more money? If you don't mind me getting down to brass tacks."

"No, I don't mind. Yes, it's more money. But they want me to live in Toronto. And how could I replace all this?" She waved expansively at the trees, beach, ocean and mountains. "I've come along here some days and seen seals and herons and eagles, all on the same walk. And the air's so clean."

"Is the work more interesting?"

"It might be, a bit, but it's basically the same. Editing nonfiction. I'd get to work on 'bigger' titles, so to speak, I suppose."

"Maybe you'd get trips to New York. Or London. Work with big-name international authors. Sounds like fun. But then you'd have to buy clothes, Jenny." He laughed. "Get an actual wardrobe."

Jenny laughed with him. "And there'd go all that extra money! I think you just helped me decide. I wasn't seriously considering it—just one little part of me was thinking, 'Career move!' A faint quiver of ambition."

"Oh, good. Hannah's doing her thing." Andrew pulled a plastic bag from his pocket and went over to collect the deposit. "Come on, Hannah, short walk today."

"Thank you for picking up after your pet," Jenny called after him, and he waved. It was one of their routines. Positive reinforcement, Andrew called it. Whenever you see somebody scooping the poop, give praise.

Jenny ambled along in Molly's wake. People often smiled and stooped to talk to her, so going walkies was not a matter of brisk exercise. She picked up the pace. "Come on, Moll. Even a basset can go faster than this!" Challenged, Molly obligingly shifted into a slow gallop.

On their way down the street after the reading of the will, Sheila and Chris stopped for another drink.

"I think you should come to the farm, Sheila. It might be a bit harrowing for Jenny, and I'm not likely to be much help."

"Why not?" Sheila lifted her wine. "You're very supportive. And it'd be good for Jenny to be in charge. Why on Earth does the will say we should all go?"

"I have no idea." Chris took a sip. "Did you get the feeling that something was bothering Jenny? I mean, even before you announced that you don't want to come? She didn't seem as cheery as usual."

"Good!"

"That's not very nice."

"Oh, I don't really mean it, but sometimes I get a little tired of her bounciness. Well, Jenny's probably feeling the saddest of all of us about Pat, so of course she'd be more subdued than usual."

"I'm sure she's sad, but I get an undertone of something else."

"Hm." Sheila looked at him. Should I tell him what I think it is? No. That has to be up to Jenny. She changed the subject. "Did you streak your hair?"

"Yes. Just to emphasize the blond. It seemed to be fading."

"It was so light and bright when you were younger."

Chris sighed. "Weren't we all, princess, weren't we all." Ever since a reviewer had called Sheila "Canada's princess of song," Chris had adopted the label.

"Don't get maudlin on me. Do you want to go to Ontario?"

"Yes, actually, I do. I feel very curious about it. And you should come too."

"No."

"Okay," calmly, "let's think about this. Why are you so determined not to come?"

"Oh, Christian," Sheila said crossly. "I've got a goddamn therapist. I don't need *you* to go all analytical on me." She only used his whole name when she was seriously annoyed with him.

Sheila's and Chris's lives had merged when they were both nine. Each had been an only child, with all the problems and privileges of that position, and they had instantly engaged in a struggle for dominance in their newly enlarged family. Chris was older by three months, so to Sheila's eternal annoyance, he could play the seniority card. They had scrapped and clawed through their teenage years, when Chris's growth spurt allowed him to tower over Sheila, another source of fury for her, but as adults, they had come to value each other. Chris no longer claimed elder status, but he had developed a clarity of insight, an ability to grasp the whole picture that was often as intensely irritating to Sheila as his youthful bossiness had been.

"Maybe you do. Maybe you and your therapist haven't dealt with all your family background issues. Have you?"

"Of course we have." A toss of the sleek head. "Well, quite a lot."

"Oh yeah? Both sides?"

"Why are you suddenly pestering me about my mental health?"

"You're not answering my question. But why now? Because now it's relevant to taking the ashes back East the way Pat wanted. You'll have to face up to it sometime. And I've had enough therapy myself to know how important it is to face your demons if you're going to have a happy life."

"I have a happy life already, thank you very much. I don't need to delve into a lot of murk to make it happier."

"There's always something gold hidden in the murk, you know."

"Oh, stop. What a cliché."

"Okay," smiling, "but I'm right. Denial and avoidance aren't good for you. It was wrong of Pat to encourage that."

And the worst thing, Sheila thought, was that it was true. She should have explored her heritage in depth, long ago. In fact, despite her avowal to Chris, she hadn't been to her therapist for ages. She probably wasn't even "her" therapist anymore. Her marital woes had been what sent Sheila to counselling, not her complicated family, but she was not about to admit that to Chris.

TWO: A Ghastly Split

Faint streaks of light began to brighten the late summer sky to the east; the fields and encircling hills gradually revealed themselves, wisps of mist clinging to the trees. This was Ben's favourite time of day. With his hand curled around his first cup of coffee, always the most delicious, he gazed out upon the beloved farm and the contours of the landscape that were indelibly printed in his mind, wherever in the world he might be. It was too early in the day for colour—the treed hills merely looked dark, the fields light. Later, the same scene would be all rich greens and golds, with splashes of crimson, under a bright blue sky, but at dawn, softer shades prevailed, between the silver of the pond and the sky.

The view was not a dramatic one: he looked over the field that sloped gently down and away from the house, across the creek and up again to the forest. The pond, a wide part of the creek above the dam, lay placid in the still air, the bulrushes at one end quietly upright. The farther fields shouldered each other in gentle folds, and trees climbed up the rise. Carved out of the endless woods generations before, the farm represented a long-ago victory over the assertive and encroaching pines and maples. From upstairs, where Grace was serenely asleep, Ben would be able to see more, but he liked this vantage point: the cozy feeling of the home fields, the lower angle on the pond, the old maple tree beside the house, and right in front, the dogs on the broad veranda outside the kitchen.

Sitting close to the window, grinning, ears pricked, they were looking in at him now. They knew his routines. They would patiently let him finish his coffee before they moved around, stretching and whining, eager to get on with the chores. Ben examined them, his assistants and pals, the children and grandchildren of dogs who had lived on this farm for many dog generations. The original sire, a border collie from Scotland, had belonged to his own great-grandfather. For this lineage of dogs, Juniper Farm was the world. They weren't inbred, because Ben, like his father and grandfather, was careful to bring in good new blood, but the line of descent from that first Juniper dog was clear. Was the farm's very landscape bred into their genes by this time?

And what about the people? Had he been born imprinted with that skyline of treed hills? Was it hard-wired into his son and daughter? Smiling at the thought, Ben drained his cup and got up. Time to see to the cows. Immediately, the dogs leaped to all fours and capered gleefully on the wide old boards, heading for the back door. They were quiet—wise enough not to bark, especially at this time—but Ben could hear the thumps and scratches of their feet as they bounced and bumped each other. He opened the solid, ancient door and went out through the mudroom into the freshness.

"Morning, guys," he greeted the dogs in a low voice, squatting down to scratch ears and stroke backs, as the three frothed around him. "Everybody ready for a new day?"

They loved the sound of his voice, pushing to get closer, rubbing against him like cats, tails whisking in delight.

"All right then." Ben straightened slowly, pushing off his knees, a tall, freckled man with wavy red hair, clad in old jeans. "Away we go," and the little band trooped off down to the barn.

The sky was bright when Grace awoke. She squinted out the window to gauge the time and nestled into the pillow for another two minutes. The regular tonk of a cowbell was the only sound, the birds having long finished their pre-dawn racket. She rolled over, stretched hugely, threw off the covers, and padded naked across the creaking floor into the bathroom. What luxury it seemed, having their own bathroom. She could hardly imagine, now, how they had all managed with just one, especially when the kids were teenagers. The jostling in the mornings, the knocking on the bathroom door, the shouts ("You've been in there for hours!"), the rush to get ready for the school bus ("Finish your breakfast, Elly." "Mum, I'll be late!"). Fun to look back on, but now it was a treat to walk around in a morning-quiet house and enjoy a bathroom to yourself.

After her shower, Grace pulled on pink sweats that were comfortable on her sturdy body and went down to organize breakfast. Ben always left coffee in the Thermos jug for her, so she could have a cup right away, and like him, she took it over to the old oak table in the windowed corner. The farmhouse kitchen was too large to be efficient, but she had come to love it.

In a modern kitchen you were supposed to be able to whirl from stove to fridge to sink in a couple of steps, not walk clear across a room, but Ben's forebears hadn't known that when they built the house more than a hundred years ago. The cupboards were so tall you had to get onto a chair to reach the top shelves. They'd been put up by men, of course. Big men. Changes had been made—indoor plumbing, more and bigger windows, a trim electric stove beside the huge black wood stove—but the dimensions of the kitchen were the same, high and handsome, and the warm brown of the tongue-and-groove pine walls still provided a rich background to family gatherings. In the old days, the table had been pulled out to its full length and presided in the middle of the room. Ben and Grace had taken out the centre leaves and moved the less-intimidating span into the corner, under the large new windows. It was more comfortable for the two of them, but it made the kitchen look even bigger.

Grace opened a window beside her and let in the warming air, heavy with the scents of grass and leaves. They hadn't turned the furnace on for months, but soon the mornings would be uncomfortably chilly without it. She sipped the strong coffee with appreciation and sniffed the sweet air. This was joy. Time to sit, the house quiet, the coffee rich and the air divine. How wonderful that we've reached this state in our lives. Who would have predicted it, when we came here? She shook her head, recalling her arrival with Ben at the front door, baby in arms, meeting his family for the first time, the old man pounding his cane and bellowing from the parlour, "Bring her in! Bring her in! I want to see my granddaughter-in-law and my great-grandson!" They said he'd mellowed a lot by that time, but nevertheless, his mouth had dropped open at the sight of them, and he hadn't said another word for quite some time.

Boots sounded on the veranda, startling Grace out of her reverie. She turned, a wide smile dimpling her round cheeks, as Ben came in. "Morning, darling!"

He bent to kiss her. "Morning, sleepyhead. What were you looking so amused about just now?" He took the can of coffee out of the freezer to start a new pot.

"I was just remembering the day we arrived here, with TK in his little bunting bag, and how we managed to shock your grandfather into silence, for once in his life."

Dumping the old grounds into the compost pail, Ben smiled. "We did that, didn't we? My folks tried to prepare him but he'd assumed I'd married another Canadian volunteer."

"And remember how TK was so fascinated by Granddad's beard? He was just itching to grab it."

"That would have really finished us. Out in the cold. 'Never darken my door again,' and all that. And now look at us," with a sweeping gesture. "Two happy farmers on their happy little farm."

"With time to sit and realize it," Grace added. "That's the miracle, to me. Especially looking at this lovely view."

"I'm glad you think so."

"Finally, you mean." Grace laughed up at him, her brown eyes crinkling. "You're thinking, 'Finally, she sees it the way I do. After all these years, the Canadian Shield has won her over.' Aren't you?"

"I probably am. Maybe I've been afraid, at some level, that the pull would be too strong and you'd have to go back."

Grace considered, her scrutiny on his face, her inner eye seeing the village of her childhood—the beaten red earth swept clean of twigs and leaves, the generous mango trees casting wide patches of dark shade, herself as a small child in a blue school uniform, pattering barefoot between the low houses. After a moment she sighed. "The visits back have been wonderful. And I'd always have loved to stay longer. But no. Strange, isn't it, how it's the old pattern of the wife following the husband. Biblical. Your granddad would actually have approved, if he'd thought of that."

"He was fond of you and the kids, eventually. You know that. He just could never admit it."

"Because of Pat?"

"Maybe that, but also, did you ever hear him admit he was wrong about anything? Even if you proved something, right before his eyes?"

The coffee machine chuffed softly to itself and the faint cawing of crows drifted in the window with the soft air. The sun shone golden on the far fields.

Then, "What's your plan for today?" Ben poured the coffee.

"Letters and petitions and phone calls to catch up on. I'll have to spend a couple of hours in the office. But I almost sound like a lady of leisure, don't I?"

"Compared to earlier times in your life, you do. Granddad would have been happier about this arrangement. He liked his women at his elbow."

"Making his sandwiches, pouring his coffee." Grace chuckled. "Why are we dwelling on him? I haven't thought of him so much in years."

"Because we heard from my cousin, I suppose. Peculiar about the ashes. Well, these are my relatives, even if I've never met them." Ben fell silent again for a moment. "I wonder if they'll feel any connection with the farm. It's in their blood too."

"It may be in their blood, but I doubt that genes carry that kind of information." Grace got up, carrying her cup, to start their breakfast.

"Funnily enough, I was thinking about that earlier. About the dogs. So many generations of them have lived on this farm—by now do they have an inherited memory? And then I started to think about me, and the kids. Are we programmed to run this farm?"

Grace was getting butter out of the refrigerator, ready to slap it immediately on the hot toast the way Ben liked it. "You may be, hon, but I wouldn't count on the kids. It doesn't look to me as though either of them is going to come back here to live."

Ben smiled ruefully. "No. I never expected it." He turned to look out the window.

At the view that's carved in his heart, Grace thought sympathetically as she concentrated on poaching the eggs. How he'd love to keep it in the family. "Do we know how many cousins will be coming?"

"Not exactly. There are three of them—Jenny, Sheila, and Chris—well, Chris's not technically a cousin—but Jenny said Sheila might not come." A long pause and a sigh. Then, just as the eggs were ready, Ben asked, "Are you still convinced this is a good idea?"

"To have your cousins come here? Of course I am! Don't tell me you're having second thoughts." Grace stalked across the room with the eggs and toast, placed a plate in front of Ben and stood, fists on hips.

Ben poked into the rich yellow yolks and frowned. "Not exactly. It's just that—after all these years—to think of total strangers, who are also my cousins, coming here, with Pat's ashes . . . Don't you find it—unsettling?"

"I absolutely do not!" Grace exclaimed. "I find it a wonderful chance to end this ghastly split in your family, and you should be grateful that they're taking the will seriously enough to come all this way. Honestly, Ben, I can't *believe* this."

Ben chewed and swallowed before he spoke again. "I'm only . . ."

"You're only uncomfortable because it's something you haven't faced before."

"It troubles me. I'm going against the way the family's been for . . ."

"There's nothing worse than not knowing your own family!" Grace plunked herself down in her chair and pushed her plate away. "We had all this out the night Jenny phoned."

"I know." Ben dragged his gaze from his eggs to Grace's face. "And I'm not changing my mind, really." A slow smile. "I have faith in that African wisdom."

"Good." Grace reached for her plate. "Then I can eat my eggs before they get cold."

The coffee machine fell silent and after a short pause, Ben got up. "More coffee?" It sounded like a peace offering.

"Yes please." As Ben filled her cup, Grace looked up at him. "Don't worry about it, hon. I'm sure they're lovely people. I don't know anything about Jenny or Chris, but I would certainly like to meet Sheila. I hope she'll come. I've always liked her music. It's odd that we've got quite a few of her CDs, but we've never gone to a concert. She's in Ottawa every now and then."

"It is odd, now you mention it," Ben mused. "I wonder why it never occurred to us to go see her. I always knew she was my cousin—just not how close. I'm still awfully programmed by Granddad."

"Not anymore, because the cousins will actually be here. He may roll over in his grave, but it won't bother us. We'll have a wonderful time with whoever comes." Grace sounded completely confident.

"I hope you're right." Ben spread bright red jam over the peanut butter on his toast. "You've always wished we had more family around."

Grace nodded. "Wasn't it lovely, the year we had Joseph here?"

"It was. I'll never forget his first sight of snow. Remember—he thought it fell all at once, like a blanket, and stayed for the whole winter, because he'd only ever seen it in pictures. He was so excited—he ran around outside catching the flakes in his hands."

"But he sure got tired of the cold."

"Now that's in the genes." Ben laughed. "Somebody else I know gets tired of it by about December." When he had finished his breakfast he kissed Grace's forehead. "On with the day, before it gets too hot." And went whistling out the door.

Grace sat a while longer, pondering his nervousness about the upcoming visit. It wasn't like Ben to worry. As long as she'd known him, he had been calm and thoughtful and decisive, but confronting the gulf in his own family was disturbing him deeply. Well, they were committed now; it should have been arranged long ago. She gathered the dishes beside the sink and headed upstairs. The old kitchen was left to its high, woody silences.

THREE: Coping

For a Sunday afternoon symphony, Sheila saw no need to dress up. Why get fancy and then sit squashed in the dark for two hours? So she usually wore elegant pants (not jeans, because people who recognized her might think jeans disrespectful) and a sweater. The day was warmish, so she put on a pretty sweatshirt painted all round with large and lovely flowers. Lots of pink ones, which she liked. Why was she suddenly keen on pink? It somehow made her feel lively and energetic. Energizer Bunny Sheila. Thump, thump, thump.

She got to the concert hall early because she liked to read the program notes thoroughly, and she loved listening to the orchestra tune up. She thought of it as batting practice. There was a wonderful sense of anticipation about watching as the audience filtered in, greeting, chatting, stumbling over knees, and listening to the musicians do their final checks, the discordant squeaks and trills and rasps sounding chaotic and free, compared with the later discipline and beauty of the planned music.

The thought of the proposed junket to the farm with Pat's ashes kept pushing itself into her mind. What was the point? She and the others had got on fine all these years, ignoring that side of their history—in fact, honouring Pat's wishes to do so. But had Pat's death changed things? Was it time to face the Eastern Past?

As it got closer to "O Canada!" time, the seat on Sheila's left remained empty, and she began to hope that nobody would show up to fill it. It was nice to have a bit more space. But no—a short old woman with grey hair cut bluntly at ear level came stumping along the row. Sheila stood up politely to let her by, and she plopped down loudly.

"Made it," she muttered, apparently to the audience in general. "Not a bad seat. Of course, this orchestra isn't what I'm used to. The London, the Cleveland, Berlin. You can't match them."

Sheila stared straight ahead, concentrating on the stage and thinking what a snob the old bird was. She didn't come to concerts to chat. The lights dimmed; the concert began.

First, a modern, amusing piece, Stravinsky's "Circus Polka," intended for fifty ballerinas and fifty elephants!! according to the program notes. Sheila's ear was a little confused by some of the chords but it was interesting music. Sitting in the warm dark, watching good musicians intent on their work, with wafts of scent—some expensive perfume, some cheap, some lavender, the occasional fart—drifting through the air, was all such a joy to her that she could overlook the inevitable crackling of cough candies being unwrapped and the flipping of programs by people who should have done those things before the conductor raised his baton. Then came the Dvorak cello concerto, which was the reason Sheila had chosen this concert. She always looked for cello soloists and she was particularly fond of this dramatic work. She sighed happily as the lights came up for the intermission.

"Decent," commented the short old woman, who had hummed annoyingly during the first half.

Sheila got up and escaped to the lobby. She ran into a few acquaintances who were pleased to be seen talking with her, had a glass of wine and smiled at two men who peered at her in some awe. When she returned to her seat, her neighbour was sitting in lonely splendour. Probably tried talking to the man on her other side, thought Sheila, and he left too. The house lights began to dim, so she hoped that there would be no time for any conversation. In vain.

"My grandfather was the organist for our church," the old lady started right in, "and I used to turn the pages of his music for him. Great education, great education," she muttered in what Sheila now realized was an English accent. "People today have no respect for great music." Out of the corner of her eye, Sheila saw the woman turn to look her up and down. "Look at you," she pronounced. "You aren't dressed very well for the symphony. And you're old enough to know better."

Realizing that everyone within twenty feet could hear this opinion, and that at least some of them knew who she was, Sheila could maintain her focus on the stage no longer. She swivelled to peer coolly down at the irritating old body.

"You hum too loudly," she said. "Nobody with respect for music does that." Take that and shut up, she thought gleefully, as the woman's mouth fell open. Subdued delight rippled out through the audience around them. The concertmaster, with perfect timing, trotted out onto the stage.

After the concert, Sheila walked over to her favourite pub, thinking about her first husband, Steve, a fine cellist himself. He had left suddenly, although his unhappiness had been evident for some time. It reflected hers.

"You don't want me around anymore," he had shouted, several times.

"I do, I do," Sheila had cried. And when he was gone, she could hardly bear the emptiness.

But the truth was, she hadn't wanted him around—not all the time. There were times when she needed to be alone, and things she wanted to do by herself. But she was too young, then, to know that that was all right, even healthy, or to disagree when Steve insisted that they were a couple now and should do everything together. So they shopped for groceries ("Shall we get a couple of avocadoes?" "Is this the kind of soap we like?") and cooked dinner together and went to bed at the same time. Steve always wanted to help Sheila with her songwriting ("Two heads are better than one") and picked her up from her work, three days a week in a music store, as if she were too fragile to get herself home through the streets of Vancouver. She had expected to enjoy living with him and had delighted in all the arrangements for the big wedding Pat and Sandy had given her. But the reality—"He's always there," she had moaned to friends, who had replied, "Well, that's the point of getting married, isn't it?"—was that encouragement and care came to feel like suffocation and, unable to explain this to Steve, who adored her, Sheila grew grouchy and hostile.

Steve was observant; he noticed the fleeting frowns, the tightening of Sheila's lips and the impatient tossing of her head when she turned to answer a question. Later, she could understand that he admired her talent and didn't feel competitive; he intended to be her support and foundation while she went off to well-deserved stardom, and he would have been happy in that role. He couldn't understand why she was closing herself off from his unwavering assistance, but at the time she felt hemmed in.

And then, when Sheila had the apartment and all her time to herself, she missed Steve, and wept and hated herself, knowing she was guilty of giving pain to a good man. What an awful person I am, she bitterly berated herself. How can I be so selfish?

After a year or so, she saw the situation more clearly, and understood that it was a question of balance. "How do you do it all?" she asked friends, awed by lives filled with husband, careers, children, book clubs, cooking classes, gym time, volunteer work.

"You know," replied one friend, who had given this a good deal of thought, "you can do it all—you just can't do it all at the same time."

"You make it sound so easy," Sheila mourned.

Steve was happy, she was glad to report when anyone asked, though it was now many years ago, and fewer and fewer people remembered that she had been married to him. "He got married again—not to a singer, I guess he'd had enough of that!—but still, another musician, a violinist. We're good friends. I make a better friend than a wife, it seems."

Thinking about all this, Sheila was feeling sad when she reached the pub, but she cheered up at the sight of Kate, her manager, sitting at a table with four chairs and eating nachos. Sheila reached for a section that had mostly escaped the cheesy goo.

"I've had a query from Newfoundland," said Kate, getting directly to her agenda before the others arrived. "Three venues. They like you there," in response to Sheila's down-turned mouth.

"I like them too. It's just so far."

"What does it matter, once you're on the plane?"

This was old ground. "It's not the plane. It's all the changes. You can't go direct from Vancouver to Saint John."

"St. John's. Saint John is in New Brunswick. You never get them straight."

"I know. But it's so hard, two places with the same name. Almost the same name," she amended hastily, as Kate's mouth opened. Geographers were so picky. How did a geographer get into the music business, Kate was sometimes asked, in tones of disbelief that irritated her. She would reply, huffily, "Who has a better idea of the world? I don't plan tours for my people that are impossible, bouncing back and forth across the country like a yo-yo, like some so-called managers."

Kate was also Sheila's good friend from their high school days, her most acute critic and listener, the first to evaluate a new song, a new backup musician, a new lover. "I should have taken psychology," she once complained to Sheila. "I'm turning into your therapist." And Sheila had said, "I don't need another therapist. And even my therapist told me that an hour with a couple of good women friends is better than two with a therapist."

"Anything in between here and Newfoundland?" Sheila crunched into more tortilla chips.

"Mm-hm. Sudbury, Brandon, and Fort McMurray."

"I'm working harder for less money. Nowhere really big wants me anymore."

"Not right away," Kate agreed with characteristic bluntness. "I'm telling them all that you're not touring till next year. But as soon as you get the new CD out, even the big guys'll be interested. And you know what? People do still want to know what you're doing, and that's a big plus. I often get 'Where's Sheila Muir been? Haven't seen her for ages.'"

"They probably all think I had a drug problem and went to the Betty Ford."

"Who's at Betty Ford?" Eyes gleaming with curiosity, Sally, the expected third, a large woman in a brightly coloured cape, plumped into a chair. "Get some more beer, Dave," she said to the younger man with her. "A jug of the Granville Island Lager, it looks like," casting a knowledgeable glance at the glasses on the table.

"Okay." He trotted off to the bar.

"You really shouldn't order him around like that." Kate shook her head reprovingly.

"Please!" Sally yelled at Dave's back. "So," turning around, "tell."

"Nothing to tell. Sheila was gloomily saying that people probably think she's been to Betty Ford because they hadn't seen her in a while."

"Oh. No gossip." Disappointment. "So how was Betty Ford?" She grinned.

Sheila started to protest, saw the grin, and subsided.

"What did the will say?" Sally was quickly on to another topic. Always a vibrant presence in any group, she was a strikingly lovely woman: coffee-with-cream skin, huge brown eyes and a mane of hair in a near-Afro. "Did you get piles of moola?"

"Well, yes. We all got the same. I'll be able to pay back what you loaned me."

"That wasn't why I was asking. I never had any worries about you paying me back. It's fun being part of it. Thanks, darling," as Dave placed a jug and two more glasses on the table.

"Kate'll cook up a tour for me when I get the next CD done. Shall I be mother?" Sheila lifted the jug and looked inquiringly around.

"One of her get-to-know-your-country-better tours? If it's Tuesday, we must be in Thunder on the Tundra?"

"You got it."

"Hey, you guys! You go where the market is, you know. And they love Sheila everywhere."

"Is there any place that'll get me into trouble?"

"You mean like Clayoquot?"

"Yes."

"No."

"Trouble?" Dave sounded surprised.

"Sheila was part of a benefit for environmentalists at Clayoquot Sound a few years ago, and got banned from some gigs later, in logging towns."

"Politics meets art," he said, understanding.

"But they do love her in most places," Sally amended. "They think she's exotic. Isn't that what one of the papers said? In some place like Let's-All-Leave-This Landing?"

"Yes. Exotic. And my eyes are really quite round, don't you think?

More walnut than almond, I'd say. How can a multi-generational Canadian be exotic!"

"That's just on the one side, ducky." Sally reached over to pat Sheila's cheek. "My family's been here since the 1860s on both sides, and people still look at me as if I'm a tourist. From Alabama, usually."

"That's not why they're looking at you, you idiot." Sheila was smiling. "It's because you're so gorgeous. It's nothing to do with the colour of your skin."

"Ha! Much you know about colour of skin. I'm 'other.' I could be as plain as a post and they'd look at me the same way."

"Not a chance," Sheila maintained stoutly. "And what about all the whistles?"

"The whistles, okay. I'm not ugly. The eyeballing—it's the colour. Remember the time we all went to Saltspring? Where my family'd been for all those generations? And the gal at the craft show asked me where I was visiting from?"

"Yes, but that was the middle of summer. Everybody on the island's a tourist then."

"Did she ask you where you were from, Sheila?" Triumphantly.

"No. But she knew who I was, so that doesn't prove anything."

Another of Sally's lightning switches in topic. "So, back to the will. Was it painful? Reading it?"

Sheila thought. "No, it wasn't actually painful. It was—weird. It was all so quick. And final. After this person has been around your whole life—whether it was good or bad—poof! They're gone."

"Is it a relief? I mean, I was at the funeral and everything, but that's basically theatre. What does it feel like now you're back to real life?"

"A relief?" Sheila repeated slowly. "Yes. Because Pat had been sick for so long and nobody would want to prolong it. But also, there's a big hole in the background." She took a pull on her beer. "I don't think Jenny and Chris have quite the same reactions as I do."

"No, of course they wouldn't. It was different for both of them. How are they doing?"

"Okay I guess. The will says we're to take the urn back to Ontario."

"When are you going?" Kate asked.

"I'm not."

Kate looked carefully at Sheila. "Do you not have a sense of duty to go, because of being the cause of the—what could we call it— exile? I don't mean you *should* feel that—I'm just wondering if you do."

"I wasn't actually the *cause* of it," Sheila retorted. "But I see what you mean. No. I don't feel it's a duty of mine at all. Jenny and Chris can go. I have no intention of getting into any of that."

Kate and Sally exchanged glances.

"What are you supposed to do with the ashes when they get there?" Sally asked.

"They're to be buried in an amazingly specific place. In a particular corner of a particular field. And then a sugar maple is to be planted on top of them."

A brief silence. "Now, what about this new guy, Sheila?" Sally kept conversations lively.

"Oh." Sheila shrugged. "Don't know yet. We've been out a few times—nice dinners, a baseball game—he's fun, he's got lots to say— we'll see. Maybe I'm learning not to get my hopes up too early."

"Doesn't sound exactly thrilled, does she?" Sally inquired of Kate.

"No, but I like it better. It's too tiring when she's thrilled at first. She gets so down when it ends."

"Yeah, but her downs make for some great songs. Remember the ones she wrote after Hugo?"

Sheila made a wry face at Dave. "You'd think they were my great-aunts or something wouldn't you, the way they go on about my love life?"

Dave smiled but said nothing. Smart of him, Sheila thought.

Hugo, Sheila's second husband, hadn't left, but when it became clear that he never would, she had. By the time she tried marriage again, she was well known, her career horizons steadily broadening, and Hugo had been very pleased with his position at her side. An older, wealthy businessman, he had surprised her with his courtship—giving her a weekend at a spa after a long and tiring tour, arranging to have her windows washed when she was out of town, sending her gift baskets of, not chocolates and wine, but different kinds of peanut butter and olives.

"He's so original," Sheila crowed happily to friends. "Not just wine and flowers."

"Or boring old diamonds," agreed her accompanist as Sheila waved a giant ruby engagement ring.

Hugo bought a big house out near the university and Sheila had, for the first time, a room specifically for practising. "My music room," she would proudly open the door. "It's soundproof."

But she confused space with time, assuming that since she had one, the other was hers as well. More confident now, Sheila had explained to Hugo that she needed certain hours alone each day, for songwriting and for exercising her voice—quite a few hours, as it turned out—and Hugo never understood that. He was respectful— he always made sure to knock before entering the room—but he liked to be there. Even when he sat entirely still behind her ("I'm just a little mouse in the corner, pay no attention to me"), holding his helpful comments till later, his was an intrusive presence. Why did he have to come in so often?

He liked to joke that he was checking on his investment, after he had bought into the company that recorded Sheila, and in the beginning, she had appreciated his intense interest, to say nothing of his financial support. She marvelled at his unconcerned spending on clothes and food and travel, not because she hadn't been around money but because Pat and Sandy bought art and property and books. They enjoyed those things as much as Hugo did his silk shirts, and since paintings and books were more lasting, they seemed to Sheila to be of higher intrinsic worth. Just my snooty value system, she would think, drinking a glass of Château Margaux with her filet and feeling hypocritical.

One evening, in a bid to give herself some solitude, she gently proposed putting a lock on her music-room door. Hugo responded coldly with "Fine. You put one on the inside and I'll put one on the outside." Aghast, Sheila stared at him with her mouth open, absorbing the implications.

A few days later, when she said crossly at the end of an exchange, "You don't own me, you know," he just gave her a flat, patient look, as if she were a little dim, and she knew the relationship was over. This time, there was less pain, but the guilt was still strong.

It's my fault, Sheila kept thinking. I put myself first again, I don't consider other people enough, I'm mean, I'm too focused on my work. Why do I think my songs are so important? I should have been more flexible; it wouldn't have killed me to play Trophy Wife a little more often; I should have retired and volunteered with the symphony. At this last picture of herself she laughed, and the other little voices took over.

You *do* have to work, you undeniably have talent and it would be an unconscionable waste not to develop it; if you don't concentrate you'll never know how good you could be; you don't want to be an old woman croaking about what might have been. Here Sheila laughed again and felt more cheerful. Still, she went off to have a heart-to-heart with Sandy.

They sat in the easy chairs in the bay window of Pat and Sandy's upstairs bedroom, looking down at the garden.

"It was so odd, Sandy. He was attracted to me in the first place because of who I am, but then it was like he didn't want me to go on *being* that person. It doesn't make sense."

"You mustn't expect men to be rational," Sandy said comfortably. "Everybody thinks men are so linear and such problem-solvers, but it's just a myth. I'm sure Hugo loved and admired you, but I could tell from the start that he also saw you as an asset."

"Why didn't you tell me?!"

"You were in no state to hear it, Sheila dear. You were enjoying his courtship way too much."

"I was, wasn't I," ruefully. "And he's not a bad person, so I feel really guilty. Relieved, in a way—but then I feel guilty about feeling relieved."

"Wallowing in guilt, in fact."

"Yes. I know in my head that it's not all my fault, but I'm still drenched in guilt. Why is that?"

"I could venture a guess," Sandy proposed, "that four thousand years of social conditioning might have something to do with it."

"How do you mean?"

"I mean that, ever since the male gods came down out of the mountains and took over from the Great Mother, women have been supposed to put their families' and husbands' interests first. You didn't. You put your career first. You're the 'Uppity Woman,' so you're feeling the weight of community disapproval that's been around since the Neolithic era."

"But nobody I know has been criticizing me."

"Of course not. I'm talking about your subconscious. There's all sorts of stuff roiling around down inside that we're not aware of. Here's an exercise for you—imagine yourself not feeling guilty. Carrying on proudly, not caring, head held high." A pause. "How did that feel?"

"I cringed a bit."

"You see? Even the word you picked implies surrender. Bowing your head."

"But still, I should have made more room for him in my life."

"Nonsense," briskly. "It would never have ended. He'd have expected more and more."

"Until my career went down the tube and he went looking for someone younger and better looking."

"Now you're seeing clearly. Let's go down and have a drink."

Sheila stood up. "No more on my romances. Dave needs a break. I'll get a refill."

When she was out of earshot, Sally leaned over to Kate. "How's she doing?"

"Coping—not bad. I think it'd be good for her to go the farm with Jenny and Chris, but we shouldn't mention it again today. You know how mulish she gets if she's pushed."

"It would be closure, you mean? Taking the ashes back would complete the circle."

Kate nodded. "Something like that."

Chris examined another martini glass, holding it up to the light and squinting. Okay—crystal clear. He hung it back on the rack and picked up the next one. Even though people couldn't smoke in bars these days, the glasses still got dirty and he liked to make sure they were all brightly clean. It wouldn't get busy until just before lunch, so he had time for a thorough check, and martinis were big with the power-lunch crowd. Flavoured martinis. Which weren't really martinis at all. What a purist I am, Chris thought in amusement.

"What are you grinning about, like the proverbial thingamy cat?" asked Wendy, straightening a knife on the table nearest the bar. Then she frowned and refolded the linen napkin.

"Cheshire. The cat. I was thinking what a snob I'm becoming about peppermint martinis. And cranberry. They just aren't martinis."

"I know, I know." Wendy was used to Chris's pet peeves. "But you're fighting a losing battle. It's like your shtick with 'hopefully.' It's part of the language now. Maybe you should go back to being an English teacher."

"Nope."

"But bartending isn't a career. Most people are bartenders just for a little while because they really want to be doing something else."

"Like acting. Yeah. But I've had a career. Now I'm going to live. This job is fun. It pays enough to give me a roof over my head and keep me fed, and it lets me do things I want to do." He shrugged. "What else do I need?"

"But you're a smart guy. Don't you want to be getting somewhere in your life?" Wendy's youth was showing.

In an earlier version of this conversation she had once protested, "You don't do anything. You just come to work and go home."

"What's wrong with that?"

"Why don't you take courses in something? Or volunteer somewhere? A soup kitchen, for instance?"

"Sweetie, I have an MA—I don't need to take more courses. And I've done my community thing—I spent more than twenty years teaching. I read. I listen to music. I ride my bike. I go to parties. I see my friends and my family. I stay home and reduce my carbon footprint. It's a nice life and I like it.

"You know," Chris continued as he moved on to the highball glasses, "the difference between us is that you subscribe to the great modern myth of 'Progress.' You believe that life has a purpose and that everything's getting better, even if slowly, and that we're all supposed to be going onward and upward, toward some goal." He put a glass down and gave her a straight look.

"Well, of course I do." Wendy regarded him seriously. "If I didn't think that, what would be the point of living? Oh. I see what you mean." She turned toward the windows, a faraway look on her smooth face. Slender, tall and sunny, she was a great favourite with the bar's patrons.

Chris knew that one of the courses she was taking this semester was philosophy. He kept quiet, polishing a glass that had failed inspection.

Wendy came over to sit on a stool, smiling broadly. "I like that 'myth,' as you called it. It gives me hope."

"Sure it does," Chris agreed. "That's why it was invented. But it's a very recent notion."

"You may be right." Wendy did a full circle and then hopped off her stool. "But enough with the intellectual chit-chat. We'd better get ready for the hungries." Her pet name for the movers and shakers who were regulars for lunch at Jason's Grill Room was two-edged: hungry for food and hungry for influence and recognition. She was an innately skeptical observer, Chris had noted approvingly, despite her youthful approach to life.

"I love this room when it's quiet." She walked among the tables, making sure each one was perfectly set. "It's so beautiful with nobody here."

True, thought Chris, casting a glance around. The exquisite proportions, the thick carpet that kept noise to a minimum even on Friday nights, the comfortable chairs, upholstered in a warm cherry red, the generous tables, widely spaced, the shining mahogany bar with its glittering glasses and the huge mirror behind its full length. And the view: the glory of Vancouver Harbour and the North Shore mountains, basking bright blue and green in the sun, lay beyond the glass wall. It's why the designer had used the red inside, Chris knew: as a counterpoint to the cool colours of that view, and to cheer people up, when the outside prospect was all in shades of grey.

"It feels like a church." Wendy was standing near the door, looking back across the whole lounge. "It's the hush, I expect. And the high ceiling."

"The Church of Money."

Wendy shook her head at him and pivoted gracefully, just in time to greet the day's first patron.

"Hi, Mr. Baxter," she said cheerfully. "How many today?" reaching for menus.

"Four, honey. Window table, please. Out-of-towners. Got to dazzle 'em with the setting."

And the lunch flow began. Stockbrokers, celebrities, movie producers, politicians, developers, journalists, occasionally tourists. By now Chris recognized a lot of faces, both local and international figures. Sheila turned up now and then, in one group or another, always with a big wave and smile, and a chat, if she could manage it, for Chris. He didn't think she ever explained their relationship: people probably just assumed that she knew all the bartenders in town.

If Wendy liked it quiet, Chris liked the hum of a happy bar. When the tables were full, he and Wendy worked smoothly to keep the drinks flowing, and the food waiters threaded their way through the room with practised grace. Handshakes, smiles, sincere or not, conversation, the odd loud laugh, decibel levels gradually increasing, the clink-clink-clink of silver on china. Chris was never so busy that he didn't know what was going on around the room. Champagne for that table from the recording company—must have agreed on a release. A Hollywood actress in town for a shoot getting up to leave too early, her lunch unfinished—uh-oh, bad news there. Loud laughs and cheers over in the corner—action in the mining stocks.

A reporter Chris recognized was hovering in the doorway, craning her neck and trying not to look obvious. Who could she be looking for? The provincial cabinet minister whom Chris had heard asking if the salmon on the menu was wild or farmed? ("Wild," the waiter had told him in no uncertain terms. "We don't serve farm fish.") The renowned scientist who was in town speaking at the AIDS conference? If it was the movie star, the reporter was out of luck—she had already made that dramatic exit. Oh—it was the stock promoter. Question answered, Chris turned his attention to other action.

"What do you say to that, Chris?"

He looked across the bar at the woman who had spoken. She was sitting with her lawyer. They never took a table; maybe they liked to keep their backs to the room.

"Sorry, Ms. Mortimer. I wasn't following what you were saying." She had never invited him to call her by her first name, though he knew perfectly well, by this time, what it was.

"Always pay attention to what the lady says, Pedersen." The lawyer gave Chris a sly wink. "That's my advice."

"Is that 'lady' as in me, Glen? Or do you mean all ladies?" Flirtatiously.

Chris could see the calculations behind the blue legal eyes. "Both. But you in particular, my dear." He leaned closer to nudge her shoulder, and winked again at Chris.

The woman smiled. The case must be going well, Chris thought. A settlement in her divorce? "Well, if that son of a bitch had paid attention to what I said years ago, he'd be a lot better off now." Yes, probably a very big settlement. "Just as well for me that he didn't." But she didn't look all that happy about it. Chris poured her another gin and tonic. Her third. Definitely not happy.

The lawyer looked at his watch. "Come on, milady. Time to go." And to Chris, "I know the food's good here, but we've got a reservation at Lindsay's."

A tête-à-tête restaurant; small, quiet, costly. Chris glanced around the room, half-wondering if the soon-to-be-much-poorer ex-husband was here.

"Bye, Chris."

"Bye, Ms. Mortimer. See you again."

The intriguing thing about being a bartender was that you were here but not here. You observed and listened and drew conclusions, but to most of your customers you were a piece of furniture. People discussed the most astonishing subjects at a bar, as if it were an extension of their living rooms. Or maybe it was just the liquor, freeing their tongues. It was a fascinating job, and after the hours of noise and rush and constant, fleeting impressions, Chris could go happily home to quiet and calm.

Lunch had peaked, and tables were emptying, the noise level dropping. "I forgot to ask you before" —Wendy had slowed down enough to pause at the bar, though she was keeping a watchful eye on the room— "about the will. Did you inherit oodles of money?"

Chris gazed at her blankly for a moment. "Oh. Yes, I guess so. There's a portfolio of investments."

"And how are Sheila and Jenny feeling?"Wendy was very impressed by Sheila. "I hope Sheila's not going to retire, with this inheritance?"

"Oh, I doubt it. Performing is what she loves. How're they feeling?" Chris considered. "Sheila may be more torn up than Jenny but she's not showing it. Jenny was the closest to Pat, so naturally she's very sad. They're coming over to my place for dinner tomorrow, so I'll see."

"Good." Wendy went off on a collecting trip through the tables. Chris unloaded the glass-washer and filled it up again.

Monday morning. The phone on her desk rang. "Jenny Muir Pedersen."

"Hello. Is that the editor?" A loud, male voice.

"Yes—the non-fiction editor."

"But you're a woman."

"That's true."

"Hm. Well, the non-fiction editor is what I want. I'm looking for a publisher and I'm told you do good books."

Jenny's heart sank—he's told? Does this mean he doesn't read himself?—but she said politely, "We do."

"My book is about my life. I've had an extraordinarily interesting life, and my friends all tell me I should write it down."

"Ah." They would.

"I was born on a farm in Saskatchewan," the voice boomed

on, as though Jenny had asked. "My parents came from the Old Country, we had a very hard time, it would be a good lesson to these soft young people today to read about how we survived, they just want governments to give them handouts. Anyway, my early life was very fascinating, churning the butter, walking to school" (yup, thought Jenny, absolutely riveting) "the winters were very harsh, sometimes our cattle died, but we were plucky, we made it . . . Are you listening?"

"Oh yes, I am."

"Good. Then I left school at fifteen to help support the family, later I married a beautiful girl but she turned out to be a bitch so I left her, then I put myself through university by doing a lot of interesting things, and then I became a lawyer and I was extremely influential, then I ran for Parliament and I have great insights into politics in our fair land, and now I've retired to Vancouver."

Whew.

"I met Peter Gzowski once" (he pronounced the G, and rhymed the rest with "how-ski," which meant he had never listened to "Morningside" for all the years the late, great Peter had hosted it. Or maybe he just had a very bad ear) "and I'm told that when the CBC interviews an author, the books sell very well. So you could get me on a CBC show, of course, and what I need to know now is, how big of an advance do you people give?"

Even Jenny, who thought she had heard everything, was stunned into silence.

"Miss?"

"Yes. Um—we don't give advances until we're familiar with an author's work, and in this case . . ."

"Well, how could you be familiar with my work? I haven't written anything yet. I want the advance before I start. I'm told that's how Peter Newman works."

"I don't know anything about Mr. Newman's financial arrangements, but he has a track record. That is—he's a well-known writer. He's had many bestsellers."

"He had to start somewhere, didn't he? Now, I want to start with my childhood. Don't you think that's a good angle? My whole life will probably take four volumes. It would make an excellent TV series."

"It might, but we aren't the publishers for you, Mr. . . ." Jenny realized he hadn't introduced himself. "You might want to contact one of the Prairie publishers . . ." She felt guilty saying this, but who knew? Maybe he really had been an influential lawyer.

"No. I'm in Vancouver. So you don't want to give me my advance?"

"Thank you for calling us, but no, actually, I'm afraid we don't."

"That's a big mistake, young lady." Click.

Goodness. That was one of the worst. Jenny glanced at her watch. She had time for a quick look at the mail before the weekly meeting. When she didn't come in every day, it piled up. What have we got? Sometimes it seemed as though everybody in the country reckoned he or she had a book that needed to be written. Their own lives or family histories. Books of jokes. Humour was considered non-fiction so those queries sped straight to Jenny's desk. Accounts of trips—across Canada by bus, across BC in a snowstorm, across the Pacific in a sailboat. Every second person in Vancouver had already done that one. Books on the philosophy of life, by twenty-two-year-olds. Fixing up country houses—these authors all said they had written a book "just like *A Year in Provence*." Jenny wasn't jaded, exactly, but she was getting tired of that line. Nobody but Peter Mayle can write books "just like" *A Year in Provence*. Biographies of unknown people who deserved recognition. Yes, they might, but people rarely buy books about individuals they haven't heard of. Unless they're wonderfully written, of course—look at *Angela's Ashes*. I do try to make every manuscript we publish into the best book it can possibly be, but as a famous editor once said, an editor can only get out of an author what the author has in him. Or her.

Enough musing, Jenny told herself. Start opening. Twice in her career as an editor Jenny had opened letters that began, "I have wrote a book . . ." Not for us, you haven't. At least she didn't deal with the children's-book proposals. Beth Chandler, who was the "kids and YA"—young adult—editor, as well as the publisher and owner of the firm, often said she thought that anybody who had ever been a child felt qualified to write a kids' book. And they all had a friend down the street who would do wonderful illustrations.

When she had begun to work as an editor, Jenny had naively assumed that perhaps one in every four or five proposed manuscripts would be good enough to become books. Now she reckoned it was more like one in fifty, or perhaps a hundred. Sometimes the problem was the subject—the author had chosen to write about something or somebody that not enough people would be interested in. Sometimes the problem was that they couldn't write. Jenny believed that almost anything could be made enthralling if the writing was beautiful—and conversely, that even intriguing subjects could be ruined by bad writing.

You need both, she often said, in talks to groups of students or local historians or retirees: both an appealing subject and good writing, to make a successful book. It's a rare combination. But she knew they didn't believe her. Look at all those books out there, they were thinking, their eyes fixed on her as she spoke. My idea/proposal/finished manuscript is just as good as anything already published. Mine is that rare, successful combination that you're chattering on about, editor lady. Too bad about the rest of the people in this room.

She went on with the mail. A collection of potted biographies of BC musicians. Okay, who is this author including? Valdy, Gary Fjellgaard, Bill Henderson, Randy Bachman, Bob Ruzicka, Diana Krall . . . Does she have Sheila?—yes, Sheila. Good! I think I'll ask to see this one.

At this, Jenny put her elbow on the desk and rested her chin on her hand. Sheila. Why is she refusing Pat's final request? All the people who think Sheila is so wonderful and adorable haven't run into this steely layer of hers, this—this carapace. She never, ever wants to do what I want to do. She still thinks I'm just some kid who got inconveniently stuck into her life. Chris was always so much nicer to me. Sheila never wanted to babysit me, even if I was asleep! She checked her watch again.

Oops—time to go.

The editorial meetings were a notion of Beth's, a great enthusiast for the team approach. This was fine with Jenny, who worked alone, often at home, and liked hearing how the other segments of the business were doing.

They all sat around an old rectangular table on mismatched, straight-backed chairs in what, for want of a better name, was called the meeting room. In fancier firms, the furniture would all be matching oak, and it would be called the boardroom; Jenny had been in some of those. She had also been in conferences in basement offices with a close-up view of the furnace, and in little cabins on the Gulf Islands with sweeping views of sea and sky. To one side there were three ancient, overstuffed easy chairs and a sofa around a low coffee table for informal sessions, often with emotional authors ("the weeping-poet syndrome" as someone had said unsympathetically) and a kitchenette in the corner—sink, toaster oven, stained coffee cups, small fridge and 1950s Formica green-and-chrome table.

Everything overflowed with books—the shelves along both long walls, the coffee table and, at this point, one of the deep easy chairs, which was full of the books and papers swept off the conference table as Beth had swept in. She continually tried to ensure that the table was clear. "Couldn't we keep just this one small corner of the office neat," she would moan, particularly when some high-powered author was due, only to be told that since she was the publisher, she was responsible for the problem in the first place.

"Right. That's the poetry titles well in hand," said Beth. "Thanks, Amanda. Okay. Non-fiction. Jenny?"

Jenny had been tapping her ballpoint pen gently against her front teeth and gazing absently across the room at the comfortable old brown sofa. She was not fond of the kind of poetry Amanda favoured, and her mind had drifted back to the urn, standing bossily on her coffee table at home.

"Oh. The fall titles are all at the printers, as you know" (she had told them this last week) "and I've seen the digital proofs so they should all be in the warehouse on schedule, by the middle of September. For the spring, I've got one final manuscript in my hot little hands at the minute—the one about climbers in the Rockies—but the others are in good shape. We'll have five for sure and maybe six. That's about it for now." She looked questioningly at Beth, who was busily making notations on her scheduling sheet.

"Good, Jenny," Beth carried on. "Okay. Promotion. Ken?"

"I've got the press releases ready for everybody but" —he consulted his list— "Terry Ringer, a poet, and the novelist George McDonald, because I haven't got bios of either of them yet." He looked expectantly at Amanda and at Bob, the fiction editor. "And is this Terry a man or a woman? So many people have these androgynous names, like Robin or Dale."

"I know, and Morgan and Hilary," Amanda agreed. "But Terry Ringer is a woman."

"I have friends—a hetero couple—whose names are Terry and Gerry," Bob put in.

"Okay, okay, let's get back on track. I'm being Chairperson Beth here. Ken needs those bios. Amanda? Bob?"

Jenny felt pleased with herself. Sometimes it was she who was late getting the author bios to Ken, and she knew the squirming sensation of being called to account in a meeting. Amanda and Bob were giving the usual explanations—the authors hadn't filled out the questionnaire at the beginning, they had gone away on holiday at the precise moment it should have been handed in, they were too busy with proofs to think of anything else, etc., etc.

We should just have numbers for these explanations, Jenny thought idly. Number one would be the author hasn't delivered whatever it was—manuscript, corrections, bio, photograph, mailing list. Authors blame family commitments, health problems, community obligations. No matter the reason, things are always running late in the publishing business. Cover art isn't ready, illustrations in the text are taking longer than anticipated, new information has turned up so an epilogue has to be revised—people are either madly working late into the night or waiting around and going for long walks.

Her attention swam back into the meeting.

"What's the PIA factor on McDonald?" Ken asked.

"Oh, he's nice. Very co-operative—no pain in the ass at all. You'll get along fine with him," Bob answered.

"Oh!" Jenny said quite loudly. Heads turned. "Sorry. I just remembered. I've got to go back East. I have to take the ashes to Ontario." Kindly nods around the table.

"Okay," Beth said, looking at her calendar. "When do you want to go, Jen?"

"Soonish, I think." Jenny visualized the urn again, and made an effort to organize herself. "Let's say the end of September."

"Right," and Beth drew pencilled brackets. "For a week?"

"Shouldn't take longer than that."

"I've got an idea," said Beth. "Come see me when we're finished here."

Shortly after the meeting, Jenny knocked at Beth's open door. She was sitting sideways behind her desk, chair back, feet up on a pulled-out bottom drawer, chewing on a pen and flipping pages.

"You had an idea, you said. About my trip."

"Oh, yes. This family farm of yours is near Ottawa, isn't it?"

"Yes."

"Do you have people to stay with in Ottawa?"

"No."

"That's what I thought. Why don't I call my Aunt Maggie and see if she's going to be around when you're there. You could stay with her."

"Thanks," Jenny responded, "but I couldn't possibly impose on one of your relatives. And Chris might be coming too."

"Good. How's he doing with all this?"

"Okay. Chris's the calmest, of course. It was worse for him when Sandy died."

Beth nodded. "Well, Maggie would love to meet any of you. And you wouldn't be imposing. She's got this great big house on Dow's Lake, her husband's dead, her kids are grown up, she's retired, and she loves me to send her interesting people. You'd adore her. Just let me give her a call."

"Well, if you're sure." Jenny was still doubtful.

She could hear Beth's loud and merry greeting as she walked down the hall.

"Hi, Mags, it's Beth."

The briefest of pauses. "Hello, dear. How nice to hear your voice. Is everything all right?"

"Yes, fine here, but you don't sound too chipper. You sound faint. Are you sick? Did I wake you up?" Beth checked her watch. "I mean, from a nap or something?"

"No dear, I'm fine. I was just sitting here, looking out at the lake."

Beth frowned. "That doesn't sound like you. Are you sure you don't have a bug of some sort?"

"No, no, I never get sick."

"Well, what's the matter then?"

"My, you *are* a persistent child. You always were."

"I'm not a child, Mags. But I certainly am persistent, so you might as well tell me what's wrong."

"I suppose so." A pause. "It's Danny. He's gone off in a huff again, and we don't know where he is. I'm sure he'll get in touch, sooner or later, but it's worrying in the meantime."

"Oh, no," Beth groaned. "What's it about this time?"

"He quit his job because he said he couldn't live in Ottawa anymore. It's too claustrophobic, with family and people he's known all his life, and he was going to get into his car and keep going till he found a place he liked and see if he could find work, wherever it was. And then, at dinner, Eileen—she was in Ottawa for a meeting—got mad at him, as usual, and said he was an ass and he was too old to be acting like this and when was he going to grow up and accept who he was. So Dan stomped off and that's the last I've seen of him."

"He could just be sulking at home," Beth suggested, remembering her cousin.

"He could be. I've phoned a couple of times but I just got his machine, and I decided not to go round. If he's so fed up with family, the last thing he'll want is his mother at the door."

41

That was a little more lively. "Clutching a pot of chicken soup to her aged breast." Then, remembering Dan again, "No, I guess it would have to be a pan of brownies, or a pecan pie, wouldn't it?" Beth was pleased to hear a chuckle.

"Yes. And leave my breasts out of it. They don't look at all bad for my age. Now, what did you call me about? I don't suppose Danny's turned up in Vancouver?"

"No. I was calling because my friend and editor, Jenny Muir Pedersen, is going to Ottawa soon for a family funeral, and I was wondering if you could put her up for a night or two around the end of September. Are you going to be home? You'd like her."

"Yes, I'll be home and of course. I'm sure I'll like her. I depend on you to send me only people I'll like and so far your record is perfect."

Auntie Mags sounded a bit more like her usual self by the end of the call, Beth thought, relieved. She left her office and stuck her head into Jenny's, just down the hall. "That's okay. Maggie'll be home, and she'd love to have you. So let me know your exact dates in Ottawa as soon as you've got them."

FOUR: Meeting the Queenmother

In a quiet house in the pleasant Fairfield neighbourhood of Victoria, a woman sits reading a manuscript.

Memoirs of Gerald Hatley-Thorpe
The Gold Coast—An Expedition Upcountry

Early in 1952, I undertook an interesting trip north into the colony, to look into the Brong affair. A number of Chiefs, formerly subject to the Asantehene (the Paramount Chief of the Asante or Ashanti people), had seceded from the Ashanti Confederacy and had come together in what they called the Brong-Kyempen Federation; the Government had set up an inquiry to investigate the dispute. I will not go into the morass of legal and technical details that we all had to wade through—the Chiefs' petitions to the King (of England) etc.—because it would make boring reading indeed. However, my interest in anthropology was greatly quickened every time I could get away from Accra, which, being the capital, was where we lived, and this excursion was particularly rewarding because Helen came with me. She did not join me on every trip upcountry, but when she did, my enjoyment was always increased.

Our first stop, Kumasi, was the second-largest city, about 130 miles northwest of Accra. The Ashanti people have lived in and around Kumasi since time immemorial. Their legends of the founding of their nation date back to the seventeenth century when a golden stool was called down out of the sky by Okomfo Anokye, the Fetish Priest of the first king of Ashanti, Osei Tutu I. The stool is the symbol of chieftaincy to this day, much like our throne; it is also considered the primary spiritual symbol of their nation and is never allowed to touch the ground. Another legend explains the choice of the location for their capital city. This came about because two "kum" trees were planted in an effort to find the optimal place. One died and that town is still called Kumawu, meaning "where the kum tree died." Kumasi, of course, is "where the kum tree lived."

We left Kumasi early on a typical tropical morning, while the air was still fresh and cool, and the light misty; we always found it wise to travel as much as possible before the heat grew intense. We had come the previous day from Accra and spent the night in the Kumasi resthouse. I did not see the Asantehene, Sir Osei Agyeman Prempeh II, during this brief visit, as others of my colleagues were assigned to work on his side of the case. Since I was going to the region of his "enemies," he may well have refused me an audience anyway.

Our driver was Yeboah, a splendid fellow whom I liked very much. He had driven me upcountry before, when my regular driver in Accra, Ayettey, was down with fever. Ayettey was a Ga, and since his attacks of fever usually coincided with my trips to the interior, I suspect he disliked leaving home. (The Ga people are indigenous to the area around Accra.) Yeboah was from a village near Sunyani, which town was our next stop on this trip, and he was delighted with the chance to see family and friends. He had served in Burma with our Army during the War, fighting in an anti-tank regiment, and his English was good. He was particularly solicitous of Helen, hovering near her whenever she was out of the car.

The highway from Kumasi to Sunyani, built in the 1920s, was a typical narrow road, with a rutted, laterite (hence red) surface. It wound through thick forest to begin with, which thinned slightly as we approached Sunyani. By then we were beyond the true tropical rainforest, all entwined with vines and creepers, that one finds farther south. The extreme northern part of the Gold Coast is savannah—wide, grassy plains dotted with trees—so we were in fact moving into something of a transition zone. As this was the dry season, the trees were coated with red dust, which gave everything a curiously dull appearance. After the rains came, the leaves would again be a beautiful green, but of course, the road might be impassable. Then, the contrast between the glossy green leaves and the bright red soil is quite striking, but during our trip, the whole countryside was somewhat monochromatic, a strange reddish-green, under the hazy sky. (One rarely sees in the tropical sky the intensely bright blue that, we later learned, is taken for granted in the Canadian summer.) Occasionally, round, rocky hills were visible above the forest, but the main relief from the endless march of trees was the villages we passed.

Poor as many of the smallest of these seemed, with their low houses built of clay bricks the same colour as the soil (and the road), loose-looking, thatched-grass roofs and presumably no amenities, their residents looked cheerful and content. The men wore sweeping robes with one shoulder bare, much like a Roman "toga," and were often to be seen walking at a relaxed pace between the houses or sitting in shelters, conversing amiably and contemplating the scene before them with that calm demeanour that Africans and the peoples of the Middle East seem to share. It appears to stem from the ability to be at ease with one's surroundings. Perhaps we Europeans have progressed beyond this stage, or perhaps we have lost the knowledge and do not remember that we could ever do it. Helen remarked that the women seemed more active, moving purposefully along the roads and around the villages, though rarely did we see anyone truly hurrying. Frequently, people would nod at us, and the almost-naked children that one sees frolicking everywhere often flocked together to point, laugh, and wave wildly as we drove slowly past.

The road was busy, though not with motor traffic; it was people, goats, and sheep. These last animals were the most pathetic creatures I have ever seen, with bony faces, stringy coats, and drooping ears, plodding along slowly with their heads down. The goats, by contrast, were always amusing, leaping about alertly with inquisitive expressions and pricked-up ears and tail. The people, both men and women, walk back and forth daily to their "farms"—small plots of land—because in their system, they do not build houses on their land but close together in villages. This surprised me when I first witnessed it, but by the time of the Brong trip, I took it for granted. Helen, however, had not been out of Accra as often as I had, and still wondered at it. She commented on the amount of time it must take out of every person's day, to go between their homes and their work sites. I reminded her of the people who travel to work in and out of London daily, by train or underground, and she quickly grasped the parallel.

We had a pleasant lunch with the Senior District Commissioner in Sunyani, a chap who had been there for some time and was sympathetic to the position of the Brong, or Bono, people. His wife was in England with the children, and he was alone. This was the conundrum that faced many of us in the Colonial Service. When the children were small, they could be schooled locally, but as they reached public school age, there was no viable alternative but to send them Home. In some instances, they went to boarding schools; in others, the wife went back to provide a home for them. The SDC gave us a good meal of roast beef, boiled vegetables, Yorkshire pudding, and tinned fruit with Bird's custard sauce, his wife having trained the cook well. The beef, which of course came from the skinny, long-horned cows one saw being herded down from the North, was tough, but quite tasty nevertheless. The tsetse fly, which preys upon cattle, had not been entirely eradicated, so the beasts could not live long this far south.

Sunyani was the largest centre in this region, and had almost the appearance of a European town; this may have been in my eyes only, and perhaps someone new to West Africa would not have agreed with my impression. However, compared with the villages we had passed, it looked quite modern, with clean, two-storey buildings, painted in various pastel colours. There were banks, stores, schools, and a hospital, with a few resident Europeans, such as the bank manager, and some Lebanese shopkeepers, though we did not meet any of them.

After lunch, Helen had a lie-down while the SDC and I reviewed the business at hand. The Tekyiman people (the "ky" is pronounced as "ch") appeared to be the ringleaders in this Brong-Kyempen Federation; the Chiefs had assembled in Tekyiman town to issue their manifesto and the Tekyimanhene (the suffix "hene" indicates "Chief") had long been a thorn in the side of the Colonial Government. He had been suspended from office by the Government three times, though his people remained fanatically loyal, and since 1935 he had been accusing the Asantehene of stealing nine villages from his state. As we went over the squabbles, the petitions, the refusals to pay local taxes, etc., it came to me that, idyllic though village life looks as one drives by, it generates quite as many petty feuds and disagreeable arguments as any English parish.

Making sure Helen was safely out of earshot, the SDC said, "I hadn't realized you were bringing your wife along. I wonder if you'd like her to stay here while you go to Tekyiman?"

"Why?" I asked. "I thought there was a resthouse there. I believe it has been booked for us."

"Oh, there is," he assured me. "But Tekyiman has been regarded as an unsafe area for Europeans for some time, and there was rather a nasty incident only couple of years ago, when one of our policemen, who was merely passing through Tekyiman on his way to Wenkyi, was stopped and threatened by a mob."

I remembered the report of that incident, and said to the SDC that I understood the crowd he referred to was under a misapprehension, that the white policeman was coming to arrest their Chief, and that no damage had actually been done. He acknowledged that this was true, but suggested that people could become inflamed, and a scene could turn dangerous.

I told him I would be careful not to make a scene. Privately, I thought he was unnecessarily worried, no doubt due to the presence of Helen, because, though I had witnessed many an altercation between the Native residents of the Gold Coast, such disputes seldom went beyond the shouting of insults. Actual violence was rare.

"And Mrs. Meyerowitz spent quite a lot of her time in Tekyiman during the period you mention. She obviously felt perfectly safe," I commented.

"Oh yes, the good Mrs. Eva. But she was very clearly working on behalf of Tekyiman, and even supposedly was made a Queenmother there."

I had met Mrs. Meyerowitz once. She was German born, a sculptor and anthropologist, who taught art at Achimota College, a highly regarded boys school in Accra. She had become convinced that the Brong people were the last vestiges of the civilizations of Ancient Egypt and Carthage and had written books on the subject. Whether true or not, this was a fascinating theory, and Mrs. Meyerowitz was a tireless researcher, spending weeks at a time upcountry, all by herself with only her steward, driver, and interpreter. She would stay in the smallest of villages, and visit every Chief and Fetish Priest who could provide her with information on rituals, beliefs, and oral history. Somehow, she had got caught up in the Tekyimanhene's problems with the Asantehene and the Government, so perhaps she was not as completely unbiased as one might wish in a researcher of such vigour. In any case, I felt quite sure that, given their affection for Mrs. Meyerowitz, the Tekyiman people should present no threat to another white woman, namely Helen.

After the SDC and I had completed our discussions, Helen was fetched and we said our farewells, with many thanks. He was a kind and lonely man and we would not see him again, as we would be returning to Kumasi by another route. The forty miles from Sunyani to Tekyiman passed quickly, though the road had been repaired less frequently than the previous section. The country here was somewhat more open, so our vision was not always bounded by the endless forest, and Helen preferred this leg of the journey. She was always interested in landscapes and land use, and the march of tall trees beside the road had been frustrating for her, cutting off, as it did, her view of the wider area. We crossed several creeks on rather dubious-looking bridges, but all went well.

Tekyiman was a larger town than any, save Sunyani, that we had seen so far, built around a crossroads in the centre, with a long line of fine, handsome trees shading the north-south artery. We arrived from the west and, with Yeboah inquiring, found our way easily to the resthouse, which was on the edge of the town along the road to the east.

It was a pleasant bungalow, similar to many others in the interior, with a veranda running around it and three rooms, the sitting room, dining room, and bedroom, inside. It was surrounded by a garden of sorts, with cropped grass and some shrubs and trees. The kitchen building was on the opposite side of the drive, rather than behind the house, as is often the case, and the resthouse-keeper and his family lived in two small houses nearer the road. Altogether it was perfectly adequate and even could be said to have a certain charm, though perhaps more to Helen than to me. These resthouses were always associated with whatever current imbroglios one was involved in, and perhaps it was this aspect, rather than any physical attributes, that gave them less appeal in my eyes. To Helen, it was all part of the adventure and she was highly satisfied. I believe she was also pleased to know the location of the latrine, in case, as happens in tropical climes, it became particularly necessary. We unpacked and, after arranging with the keeper about the evening meal (one hesitated to call it "dinner"), we set off back into town.

As the distance was not far, Helen wished to walk, but that would not have done. We needed to call upon the Chief, or at least his office, and as representatives of the Government could not be seen wandering on foot like mendicants. Yeboah knew where the "Ahenfie" (the Chief's House) was and we drove directly there. (Mrs. Meyerowitz always referred to this Chief's House as the "palace," and insisted upon styling the Chief as "King," but since she is the only person to use this nomenclature, I believe it was part of her Egyptian thesis. At least she did not refer to him as "Pharoah"!) People we passed showed little interest in me but were plainly intrigued by Helen's presence. Some children began calling, "Mrs. Eva, Mrs. Eva" and others took up the chant. Presumably they found that all white women looked alike. By the time we reached the Chief's House a crowd was beginning to collect, the word having gone out that their beloved Mrs. Meyerowitz had unexpectedly returned.

Helen, who had not met the woman, turned to me and asked, "Do I look like Mrs. Meyerowitz?"

"Not at all," I told her. "She was much older, and shorter. They'll realize that when you get out of the car."

Which they did. When Helen stood upon the ground, the shouts of "Mrs. Eva" faded and died away, but the people remained, as if entranced. Yeboah moved quietly around to her side of the car while I looked for some sort of official.

A man who introduced himself as Nana's secretary ("Nana" is a chief's honorific, much like "Your Majesty" or "Your Highness" in English. It is pronounced with equal emphasis on both syllables and is used for both men and women) soon approached and, as is the custom, asked me what was my mission. He spoke English, so we were able to do our business expeditiously, and I arranged to meet with the Chief and his Council of Elders the next morning. In the meantime, Helen had been making friends.

When the people understood she was not Mrs. Eva they were disappointed, but then a voice suggested perhaps she was "Queen Victoria." Helen had laughed, shaking her head, and said she was "Mrs. Helen." Though this was not correct by our lexicon (Helen was by no means a widow, with me hale and hearty and nearby), it was clear to the crowd, and the children, pleased, began calling over and over "Mrs. Helen, Mrs. Helen" and dancing around the car. Yeboah was very protective of the vehicle, equally as protective as he was of Helen, I should say, so he snarled at any child who tried to lay a hand on it. This made them laugh and shout all the more.

Having concluded my discussion with the secretary, I said we could go. However, a small boy was now produced, literally shoved into the space in front of Helen, to cries of "Mrs. Eva's husband." He was about six or seven, so the meaning of the cries was not clear. He was not at all bashful, but bounded up to Helen, grabbed her hand and gleefully shouted something in Twi (the local language, which is pronounced "chwee"). The crowd roared with laughter.

"What did he say?" Helen asked Yeboah, still shaking hands with the tot.

"He says he will marry you too," Yeboah explained, smiling, and then to the child, "Ha!" followed by a long exchange in Twi. At the end of it, he said "Hm," and seemed uncertain, turning first to me, then to Helen, and then back to me. "He says he is a son of the Queenmother and he wants to take Mrs. Helen to greet her." He fired a question at the crowd.

"Yes, yes," they all nodded enthusiastically.

"They say it is true. He is the Queenmother's son."

"If he's the Queenmother's son," asked Helen, who was now being tugged insistently by the child, "isn't he the Chief?"

"No. It doesn't work that way in their system," I said, "but it's too complicated to go into now. Shall we go?" and I opened the car door.

"But I'd like to meet the Queenmother," Helen protested, to my considerable surprise.

I paused with one foot on the running board. "Pardon?"

"I should like to meet the Queenmother," Helen repeated with some asperity. "I would find it fascinating." The little boy was still pulling on her hand.

I looked at Yeboah. He gazed impassively back but lifted his shoulders slightly, as if to say, "What harm can it do?"

"All right," I said, withdrawing my foot and closing the car door. "If you don't think we will be transgressing any custom by seeing the Queenmother before the Chief," and I started around the rear of the car.

At this the urchin shook his head decidedly several times and said, "No, no. Mrs. Helen," making it clear who he wanted.

I was taken aback. Was I to allow Helen to go, out of my sight and unaccompanied, to visit an unknown woman in a strange village? She had never gone off on her own before. (I was to learn, later, that this was not entirely true, that she had done some visiting in Accra.) "But she doesn't speak any Twi," I protested, though to whom I am not sure, as the boy did not appear to speak English. "Yeboah, you had better go with her."

He was quite willing, but then a young woman in the front row of the circle surrounding us said courteously, "I speak English. I will go." She was nice looking, neatly dressed in the traditional women's three-piece outfit in a modern, bright print. She smiled reassuringly at me and turned to Helen. "I am a teacher," she said. "I will accompany you to greet the Queenmother."

"Lovely," replied Helen. She cast me a smile over her shoulder and allowed the child to take her away. They made an odd picture; the little boy in a long, brown-striped cloth tied at the back of his neck in the children's fashion, Helen in a light blue summer frock that reached her knees and the teacher in layers of red, green, and yellow print that covered her to her ankles. The crowd opened to give them passage and closed behind them, then began to break up as the adults drifted away. Several children stayed, hopping around in the dust and mischievously trying to touch the car.

"Well," I said, feeling at a loss. "I suppose we just wait here. It all seems most peculiar."

A reminiscent smile crosses the face of the reading woman, part amusement and part sorrow.

FIVE: To Courage and Curiosity

Chris pressed a number on his phone to unlock the front door, and then opened his own door, on the third floor, to listen down the staircase. Were they all here? Or just Sheila, whose voice had said, "Hi, Chris" over the intercom. Voices, not just feet—more than Sheila then. As they clattered up, Chris recognized all three—Sheila, Jenny, and Nick.

"Hi, hi, hi." Greetings, jackets, into the living room.

"Oh, you didn't bring the ashes, Jenny," said Chris wickedly.

"You really are grisly." She grimaced. "I remember about your friend, but I'm just not that comfortable with the idea of lugging the urn around."

"I bet Pat would like to be here, especially since we're going to be discussing all the furniture and things."

"Well, if there's an afterlife, I'm sure Pat's spirit can get here by itself—and Sandy's too—with or without the ashes," Jenny said crisply.

"Fair enough."

Nick went straight to the front window, as usual. "I love this view."

"But, Nick, your view is spectacular. All over the city."

"Oh yes, it's terrific, but I like being almost at tree level. You feel like you're part of the neighbourhood, instead of just gazing over it."

"Yours is probably quieter, though. You're farther from the racket of happy children screeching in the street. Now—drinks? I've got everything."

"Wine please, Chris," said Jenny. "White."

"I've got a California sauvignon blanc and a Frascati."

"The Frascati," Sheila suggested, walking across the living room to look at Chris's newly arranged furniture. "It goes with Pat's chesterfield. It's Italian leather, as I recall."

"I think so."

"Looks good here, Chris," Sheila perched on the chesterfield's wide arm and crossed her legs, swinging one foot. Her snug black jeans and turtleneck accentuated the rich, buttery brown of the leather. "It's a bit too long, really, but I've always liked it, and since you two didn't want it I'd have hated to see it go to the auction. Frascati okay with you, Nick?"

"Perfect." He sat on the chesterfield, at the end away from Sheila's swinging foot. Jenny took one of the straight chairs and drew the side table over in front, arranging her papers.

Chris opened the wine in the kitchen area. When he had bought the Victorian house, it was already divided into three apartments, one per floor, and, apart from painting everything and retiling the bathrooms, he had left the lower two essentially as they were. The top floor, however, he had gutted and rebuilt to his own taste for openness. The kitchen had no upper cabinets to contain it—just a curved counter—so the main room now stretched the length of the house, front to back, with windows overlooking both the street and the back garden. The bathroom, the only enclosed space, was off to the side, and a winding staircase led up to the sleeping loft above it, topped by a skylight. "How much longer do we have the storage unit?"

"For as long as we want to pay for it," Jenny answered, "but the rent goes by the calendar month."

Glasses were already arranged on the sideboard beside the chesterfield. Chris poured and handed.

"Cheers," all round.

"Now," Jenny began, "I made a list of everything we put into storage. How shall we go about this? Do you want me to read down it, and you say if you want something?"

"Fine." They unconsciously sat up straighter, ready to concentrate. Sheila got off the arm and went to lean a hip on the kitchen counter, wineglass in one hand and a twist of her hair in the other. She kept pushing it behind one ear and pulling it forward again, long pink fingernails shining through the glossy black. "You say too, Nick, if there's anything you'd like," she offered.

Jenny smiled her thanks at this but said nothing. Nicky will be glad of Sheila's support, she thought. Sheila wants him "properly" in the family. She's funny that way—she likes her relationships clearly defined: who belongs and who doesn't, who's us and who's not us. It's understandable in her case, but I don't feel that way. Why should we get married? Nicky and I are together whenever we want—we can love each other without the approval of any outside authority. Fear of commitment, Sheila calls it, and she's right. Well, look at the failed marriages around me—Sheila's (she has two to contribute to this sorry little list), Chris's (he hasn't been married, but he had a partner for a long time)—what would make me jump into an arrangement like that? Nicky and I have reached this impasse so often that we hardly ever talk about marriage anymore . . . She remembered where she was.

"Okay. First, the carpets. The big Bergama. You know—it was in the bedroom. Blues and reds." She looked around. "Don't be shy. Remember, if nobody wants these things, they're going to the art students' gallery. They're having an auction to raise funds."

Silence. The other three nodded.

"It's a beautiful carpet, but . . . Maybe because it was in the bedroom . . ." Sheila trailed off, and shrugged, tugging strands of her hair forward and across under her nose.

"I don't have space for it. You don't really either, Nick, but would you like it?" Jenny looked across the room.

"I don't think so, thank you."

"And it certainly wouldn't look right in here," Chris concluded.

"Okay." Jenny ticked her list. "The Bergama goes. What about the Hereke? The one with the rose pattern."

"From the end of the dining room?"

"Yes."

"I'd like that. It always reminded me of the tour I did in Turkey."

"Anybody else? No? Okay." Jenny wrote "Sheila" on her list. "Next, the Chinese silk one."

"It's enormous. None of us have rooms that big."

"True. Nobody? Auction."

And on they went, through the carpets ("I didn't realize there were so many!") and the furniture. ("Too bad about the dining-room suite, but who can use a marble table that size, and ten Ultrasuede chairs!"). The last section, the artwork, took the longest time to divide. Opinions were stronger.

"I don't think you should have both the Batemans, Sheila," Chris protested.

"But they always hung together. They go together." Sheila crossed the room again and swung round, hair bouncing, to stand with her back to the window. She shoved her free hand into a pocket.

"I don't think he painted them as a pair."

"Maybe not, but Pat bought them together. In his studio in Milton, a thousand years ago."

"I think you should each have one." Jenny, distressed as always by any conflict between Sheila and Chris, tried to be even-handed. "How do you want to pick?"

"I like the one with no animals. It's so untypical of what people think of as his work."

"Okay. I like the bird one better. So that wasn't too hard." Sheila smiled at Chris, resting her shoulder against the window frame.

Relieved and pleased, Jenny carried on. "Now some photographs. There're two Vanderpants, one of grain elevators like his most famous ones, and one of a cabbage. I don't think they have to stay together, either."

"I'd like the cabbage one," Chris said.

"Okay with everybody? Then I'd like the other one . . ." Jenny surveyed the room, "because I remember it hanging in my bedroom at one point."

"Funny thing for a little kid's room," Nick commented.

"Pat and Sandy believed in educating our eyes at an early age," Sheila explained. "If it was good, we should be exposed to it." She left the window and picked up the wine bottle on the sideboard. "Anybody else ready for a refill? No?" She poured for herself.

"Now the Varley," Jenny said. "Comes from the time when he was teaching at the art college here. It hung in the living room near the piano the last few years, in case you don't remember it. The sketch."

"I liked it a lot," Nick ventured, "but I'm not really an heir."

"Sure you are," Jenny said warmly. "Anybody else? Okay—the Varley to Nick."

"But if you two ever split up, it should come back to us, don't you think?" Chris grinned. "Not that I want that to happen."

"Okay—that's fair. I hadn't realized what an amazing collection this was," Nick remarked. "Maybe because the house was so big. Or maybe it's just seeing the list with all the big-name artists. How did they do it?"

"Sandy was very well connected, you know," Sheila said. "And a lot of these works are from before the artists got to be famous. Varley, Vera Weatherbie, Jock MacDonald, John Vanderpant. They were all pals in the arts scene in Vancouver, way back, and Sandy was young and attractive and on the fringe."

"And Pat had a good eye too," Chris added. "I remember—"

"We're just about finished here," Jenny announced. "Let's not wander off on tangents."

"Hasn't she got bossy," Sheila stage-whispered to Chris. "It must be because she's the executrix."

"Yes," he answered in the same tone. "She was *so* much nicer as a child!"

Finally, it was done.

"Good work, Jenny," Chris made another circuit with the wine. "That was a lot of stuff to keep track of."

Sheila raised her glass. "End of business. To Jenny! Congratulations on your efficient disposal of the assets." She sat down on the chesterfield beside Nick.

"Thanks. Makes me sound a bit cold, though," Jenny winced. "I didn't think of it as disposing of assets. Well, the people organizing the auction will be thrilled. And the other thing we've got to decide is when to go with the ashes."

Sheila jumped up again. "Can you wait a sec on that? I've got some stuff for you all."

"Sure," Chris agreed. "But where've you got them? Those jeans aren't hiding anything much!"

"In the car. I'll be right back." And she hurried out of the room.

"Did you notice how antsy she is, Jenny? She hasn't sat still since you all got here," Chris said as soon as the door closed.

"You're right. I wonder why."

"My guess is she's fussed about this thing with the ashes. And she's wearing fake nails again. She must be chewing her own to ratshit."

"Why won't she come with us? You've always been able to see her more clearly than I can—what is it?"

"I think she's afraid."

"Afraid of what? That's ridiculous! She's gorgeous, she's talented, her career's going well—what could be frightening about going to Ontario?"

"Change. She's torn—she wants things to stay the way they are—because as you say, she is doing well—but also, at some level, she also wants to know her background. She's never been introspective—she's all about getting on with her career, and the kind of success she's had helps her to ignore a lot of issues. But now the possibility of learning the whole story is hitting her in the face. She may not even realize that it's basically fear."

Jenny thought about this, looking from Nick to Chris. "You sound like a counsellor. Have you said any of this to Sheila?"

"A little. She's very stubborn."

"I know all about that." Jenny made a face. "But how . . ." she began, when the door opened and Sheila reappeared with her arms full.

Out in the street in the warm evening, Sheila had been leaning on the roof of her blue Honda Civic, head bent onto her forearms. She could hear her heart pounding in her ears and wondered briefly if she might be having a heart attack. Don't be ridiculous, she told herself. You're being melodramatic. You're just bothered about this bloody trip with the ashes that Jenny's hell-bent we should go on. All the people closest to me think I should go. Chris, Jenny, Kate, Sally—everybody. A wave of resistance swept through her.

Kate had asked Sheila what she was so afraid of. "I'm not afraid of anything," Sheila had retorted. And Kate had said, "If you aren't, then you should be perfectly happy to go, and if you are, you should face it, whatever it is." "Maybe I don't *want* to know what I'm afraid of." "Probably you don't," Kate had agreed, echoing Chris. "Doesn't mean it wouldn't be good to winkle it out." And left it at that.

Now Sheila admonished herself. Let's think calmly about this, as Chris would say. Why am I so determined not to go? She tried hard to peer into herself. I don't want to lose the life I have. But do I really think that whatever we learn there could hurt me? Yes, I do. What's the worst thing that could happen? But she couldn't begin to imagine that. She stared up into the trees, sighing deeply. Could I live with myself knowing I wouldn't even give it a try? I'm such a coward. But I can't chicken out on this for the rest of my life. She felt tears beginning to sting her eyes and then, seeing someone walking along the sidewalk, she quickly unlocked the car and sat inside.

" I j u s t played Vancouver Island so I brought you back some yummy local things. Bread from Qualicum, chocolate from Courtenay, wine from the Cowichan Valley, cheese from Cowichan Bay . . ." Sheila unpacked bags as she spoke.

"My goodness—you've got *tons* of stuff," Jenny exclaimed.

"I know. And it's all wonderful!" Sheila concentrated on setting the goodies on the coffee table. "You pick what you'd like—I won't assign anything."

"This is almost like dividing up Pat's things," said Chris, examining the wine labels. "Thank you very much, princess."

"Yes, Sheel, thank you!" Jenny echoed.

Sheila sat, cross-legged on the floor, hands loose in her lap, and smiled around at them. "I had great fun foraging for all this, and wondering who would like what."

When they had finished handing the treats back and forth, Chris got up. "Time for dinner?"

"We've had more meals together since Pat died than we've had for years," Sheila said. "It's an unexpected result, isn't it?"

"Nice, though, don't you think?" Jenny asked in hope. "Let's try to keep on doing it. Some families get together a lot. My boss Beth's does. They even have cross-country reunions every few years. They sound terrific."

"Well," and Sheila took a deep breath, "I guess we're going to find out."

Jenny blinked at her. "Oh! Are you going to come? That's wonderful—I'm so glad!"

"Yes. I decided I can probably schedule time to go with you," Sheila said casually, feeling as though she had just jumped off a cliff. She was committed now.

"Good for you," Chris said, nodded in approval, very aware of the storms that lay beneath the calm.

"Fabulous!!" Jenny crowed. "It'll be so great! We've never done anything like this, the three of us. Just think—we're going to see The Farm!"

"This will be the first time I've been on an actual farm since Denmark," Chris said with some surprise. "Do you remember that, Jen?"

"Of course I do. That trip was the highlight of my young life. I wonder if the Ontario farm will be anything like it. Sandy's farm seemed like paradise."

The farm, where Sandy was born, had been in the family for generations, a large spread of gentle, flattish land, like most of Denmark, with elegant old buildings, a cobblestoned courtyard, and ancient trees. It was on the peninsula of Jutland, far from any big city, in a rural area undotted by houses of commuters. Sandy, Pat, Chris, and Jenny had spent three weeks of a glorious July in one wing of the sprawling house where Sandy had been born. It was a working farm, producing sugar beets, potatoes, rye, and pigs, but what had won Jenny's heart was the horses. Her cousins had three horses and two ponies, which they rode every day, following paths and quiet lanes on the farm and around the district. The Canadian visitors had spent their time meeting relatives, consuming vast quantities of smoked eels, delicious butter, and beer, and heading out on exploratory trips. From Skagen—where Jenny stood gleefully with one foot in the North Sea and one in the Baltic—to the German border, with a trip to

Legoland—Chris had outgrown his Lego sets by that time but was still secretly thrilled by their possibilities—they saw most of the western part of the country before moving to Copenhagen for an urban week.

"You know," said Jenny, "we should go again. And Sheila should see it. I know it's not technically family but still—you loved Sandy. And we heard skylarks. That was *really* thrilling. Little, tiny birds twittering away in long, long songs."

"So you think I should go all that way just to hear skylarks?"

"Partly." Jenny grinned.

"I've got other places I want to go first."

"No doubt. But I'm so glad you're going to come to the farm." God—I hope this'll turn out to be all right, Sheila thought.

Still standing, Chris said, "Again. Food?"

"Yes, please," Nick exclaimed.

"Absolutely. And more wine." Jenny was feeling celebratory. "I'm so relieved that we've done all of Pat's stuff. I didn't realize how much it was worrying me till we finished it." Would this be a good time to talk about the other part? No—it was a party now and she was bound to cry. She would do it later.

"What's for dinner?" Holding her glass up, Sheila twirled into the kitchen.

"Dinner is Jenny's favourite," Chris opened the oven. "Roast goose, with all the so-called trimmings."

"Mm," Sheila sniffed the air. "It smells yummy."

"And ratatouille. And Greek-style potatoes, all lemony. And salad. And chocolate cake for dessert." He took the bird out and set it, dark and fragrant, on the stove top. "Would you scoosh some of the pan juice over it, Sheila? I'll check on the potatoes."

"What all's in the juice?" Sheila spooned carefully.

"Oh—wine, olive oil, lots of garlic and rosemary. And it's a free-range goose, so its own juices should be tasty. The stuffing is bulgur with prunes and pine nuts." He straightened and turned off the oven. "The potatoes are fine. They can sit for a bit and so can the goose. Letting a bird rest after cooking brings out the flavours, Sheila. You probably don't know that but it's a useful tip. I'll serve the soup." Turning to the refrigerator, he withdrew a white Wedgwood tureen, and placed it gently on the counter. "This is herbed summer squash soup." Chris ladled it into bowls, and drew an initial in cream on the top of each serving.

"Very impressive. So we won't fight over them, I suppose," said Sheila.

Spoonfuls.

"Mmmm!!"

"Decadent!!"

"Well, there's a certain amount of whipping cream in it, of course."

"Here's to your trip back East," Nick proposed.

"To courage and curiosity," Chris added.

Sheila gave him a wry smile.

SIX: An Upcountry Town

The woman picks up the manuscript and resumes reading.

Left with the car in front of the Chief's House, I got out my cigarettes and offered one to Yeboah.

"Thank you," he said. "Mrs. Helen will have a fine time. And," after a slight pause, "probably it is better that you" (with slight emphasis) "did not greet the Queenmother before you see the Chief."

As there was nowhere else to go, we leaned against the car, smoking, and trying to ignore the band of cheery little imps before us. At one point, they began to chant, "Mr. Helen, Mr. Helen," which gave me the odd sensation that I had lost my own identity. Yeboah finally shouted something that silenced them, and in the end they too lost interest and wandered off on other concerns.

The life of the town went on around us. The Chief's House faced the main road, with a wide, open space of beaten red earth in front, bordered on north and south by other houses, and shaded on one side by a large tree. Men and women criss-crossed the square and walked at a leisurely pace along both sides of the road, exchanging greetings and laughing, although they frequently, particularly the women, carried heavy burdens of yams, firewood, or vegetables. I was struck again by the peaceful currents of village life.

"Did you see some of your family while we were in Sunyani?" I asked Yeboah. This proved a happy choice of topic, as he told me in some detail about all the relatives and friends he had met, and this occupied us until Helen reappeared.

Still accompanied by her small guide and the teacher, Helen approached us with a spring in her step and her eyes shining, looking altogether happier and more alive than she had for some months. I was astonished at the change. She had always been a pretty woman, even when, in Accra, she had seemed somewhat listless, but now she positively sparkled. She looked again like the student she had been at Cambridge, when I had fallen in love with her.

"Gerald," she called excitedly, "I've had a most wonderful time." And as they came up to us, she said, "Constance, this is my husband, Gerald, and our driver, Yeboah." Constance smiled and nodded shyly. "And this," swinging the hand of the assertive little tyrant, "is Kwabena. His mother is indeed the Queenmother of Tekyiman, and her name is Nana Afua Abrafi." She glanced at Constance for confirmation that she had pronounced it correctly, and Constance gave another smiling nod. "Did you know," Helen spoke again to me, her voice quick with enthusiasm, "that these names depend on the day you were born? Afua is for women born on Friday, and Kwabena is the male name for a Tuesday. Constance is Ama, for Saturday. What is your day-name, Yeboah?"

"Kofi, madame. I was born on Friday."

I had never thought to inquire into the issue of people's names, though I could see that Helen found it fascinating.

"Kwabena was a great favourite of Mrs. Meyerowitz's, and when he was only about three he told her he was going to marry her. He's still jokingly called 'Eva's husband,' so when people started saying that she was back, Kwabena came rushing to see her and, alas, found only me."

She smiled fondly down at the boy, holding his hand in both of hers. He beamed upwards, not understanding her words, but certain of her emotion, then looked across at me and made a distinctly challenging face. He next delivered what was clearly a smart remark in Twi, because both Constance and Yeboah shushed him and looked embarrassed. I did not ask what he had said.

"Shall we go?" I asked Helen.

"Yes." She beamed at me. "In just a minute." She turned to say goodbye to her companions and I got into the car, which was now stiflingly hot.

Yeboah held the door for Helen and she bounced in, full of delight in her little expedition. "Aren't they lovely, Gerald? Constance is so pretty and helpful, and Kwabena is adorable."

Yeboah started the car and we headed slowly back to the resthouse. Few cars came through town, so the people habitually walked in the middle of the road, and sometimes it took a while for them to notice that they were impeding our progress. Unlike some drivers, Yeboah disliked using the horn, or perhaps it was because we were almost on his "home turf" and he did not wish to be rude to anyone who might know him.

"I think Kwabena is an indulged and annoying little boy," I responded, finally, "but Constance seemed helpful. What was the Queenmother like?"

"Quite young. Attractive. Not as tall as Constance. She doesn't speak English, but we had a nice chat through Constance. I think she might have expected Mrs. Meyerowitz, but she was very polite when she saw that I was a stranger. Then she wanted to know if I knew Mrs. Eva, as they call her. I said you had met her and that caused a ripple of interest." She dimpled at me and reached over to clasp my hand. "I don't suppose you ever expected you'd be a person of note from having had contact with Mrs. Meyerowitz."

"No," I said shortly. "And I only met the woman once."

"That's all right," she soothed me. "It's only a nice connection. She was made a Queenmother here, by the way. Did you know that?"

"Yes. The SDC in Sunyani mentioned something about it. Extraordinary. Why ever would a white woman want to become a Queenmother here?"

Helen did not answer, and when I looked over at her, her face bore a thoughtful expression, as if she were pondering my remark. Then she said lightly, "Perhaps I will find out. I've agreed to go back for another visit tomorrow."

"What?" I was astounded. "I thought you were looking forward to reading in the garden at the resthouse?"

"I was. But I can read anywhere. I don't get invited to talk with a Queenmother every day of the week. I find it awfully interesting." She seemed about to say more, but subsided.

"Well. And for what time did you arrange this rendezvous?"

"When you go to see the Tekyimanhene. I'll just ride along with you. That'll be all right, won't it?"

"I suppose so." I was surprised at how easily the word Tekyimanhene rolled off her tongue. "But you didn't hear what time I am to go. How will they know when to expect you?"

"I imagine they'll ask someone in the Tekyimanhene's household," she replied calmly.

"Ah. Of course." After that we were silent until we reached the resthouse.

"Now I think I'll take advantage of the garden," Helen told me gaily, "as you probably have some paperwork to do."

I agreed. I wanted to review the background of Tekyiman's case, so that all would be fresh in my mind for the meeting the next day. Helen kissed me warmly, pattered into the bedroom, humming to herself, picked up her book and almost skipped out to a chair on the grass. I settled myself at a table in the sitting room and began the tedious task of studying the dispute from the beginning.

I will include just a little on the history of the issue, as it touches, briefly, on a colourful connection with Canada. The nine villages originally belonged to Tekyiman, and were taken over by the Asantehene following a regional war in the 1820s; later, Tekyiman and Asante were at war from 1877 to 1897, during which time the original Tekyiman town was destroyed, and the Chief and Council moved to the Ivory Coast, the French colony to the west.

The Asante were apparently terrific fighters and determined not to succumb to British rule, but in the Anglo-Asante War of 1874, Sir Garnet Wolseley's forces overwhelmed and burned Kumasi. This was the same Wolseley who served in Canada during the Riel Rebellion, and later engaged several hundred Canadian canoemen for an expedition up the Nile in 1884 in the doomed attempt to rescue General Gordon in Khartoum.

The Asante made peace with Tekyiman and agreed to the return of the villages when the third and final Anglo-Asante War broke out in 1895, because the Asante could not battle on two fronts at once. Unfortunately for Tekyiman, in 1896 the Asantehene, Prempeh I, was exiled to the Seychelles Islands before the suzerainty of the villages was transferred. The British, with our policy of indirect rule, naturally wanted the Asante Confederacy to be as large as possible and, not being cognizant of all this history, forced Tekyiman to rejoin it. Unrest had plagued the area ever since.

I wrestled with the material, making notes and attempting to sort out the confusion, while Helen read outside in the quiet garden until darkness fell at six o'clock, as usual. There are no lingering sunsets in the tropics.

The next morning we left the resthouse at eight o'clock for the short drive to the Chief's House. Our presence did not excite the same attention as yesterday, though some onlookers were idling about as we drew up and parked in the same place. I was greeted again by the Chief's secretary, and Constance immediately came forward, smiling, to lead Helen away.

"Have fun, darling," I said to Helen, but again, I felt most peculiar watching her disappear around the corner of an earthen-brick house.

Nana Akumfi Ameyaw III, the Paramount Chief of the Tekyiman State, was a handsome man in his early forties. Illiterate, of course, as were most of the hereditary Chiefs, because education had not reached most upcountry towns. Nana and eleven of his Sub-Chiefs were gathered to meet me and I greeted them all, shaking hands around the semicircle from right to left, as is the unwavering custom (so that one never presents the back of one's hand to the greeted person). Then I sat down, and the men all came round, shaking my hand again, to greet me. Then the Tekyimanhene's Chief Lingust (the "Okyeamehene") asked me my mission (there is a strict and unhurried protocol for all such meetings), and we began our discussion. The secretary, as I said, spoke English quite decently, and as far as I could tell, did a good job with the translation.

Suffice it to say that nothing was actually resolved—indeed, I had no power, myself, to resolve anything—but I had a much clearer picture of the situation, and ideas of what might be done, when we concluded after a couple of hours. I foresaw then, and was eventually proved correct, that their Brong-Kyempen Federation would never rejoin the Asante Confederacy but would remain a separate entity.

The meeting closed with all the usual, formal salutations, then bottles of beer and schnapps were brought out and the atmosphere became more social. When we finally broke up and the secretary and I went back out into the courtyard, I was surprised that Helen was nowhere to be seen.

Yeboah was sitting in the car, with the driver's door open beside him, smoking peacefully. He uncoiled himself, got out and stood up straight when he saw me.

"Madame has not returned?" I asked.

"No, sir," he replied. "I have not seen her."

I was not best pleased about this because, having finished my meeting and been bowed out with many polite farewells, I did not think it seemly to hang about with my driver, waiting for my wife.

"I will go in search of her," Nana's secretary offered, obviously knowing where she was, which I did not.

"Thank you," I was saying, when Helen, with a considerable escort, reappeared. She was holding hands with children on either side of her, one of them the ubiquitous Kwabena, while several others were skipping about, and three or four women, including the faithful Constance, were strolling behind. Again, her face was alight.

"Hello, darling! I hope you haven't been waiting long. They said your meeting had just ended," Helen called cheerfully.

"Not long, but it is time we left," I responded. "I must get back to the resthouse to make a record of my meeting while it is all in the front of my mind," and I opened the car door.

"Oh dear." Helen's face crumpled in distress. "So quickly? I need to say my goodbyes." She brightened. "I know! You go ahead with Yeboah and write your report, and I'll walk. It's not far, and my friends" —she waved at the group around her— "will walk with me."

"I really think you should come with me," I protested, but weakly, because I knew she could do what she wanted in this case. Her walking would not disrupt our schedule in any way.

"No, no," she dismissed my preference happily. "I would just be reading there while you work, and I will enjoy the exercise." She nodded to Yeboah, as if to say, "Take him away."

Feeling out of sorts, I got into the car and Yeboah carefully backed up and turned. I put a pleasant expression on my face and looked out the window at Helen, but she did not notice, being engaged in animated conversation with Constance.

Back at the resthouse I settled to my papers and was almost finished when Helen and her entourage came in with much jolly chatter. Two children still clung to her hands, though Kwabena had disappeared, and I could not say if the other was the same one she had started out with. There were now even more children and women, wrapped from shoulder to toe in their bright cloth, milling about on the grass.

"Well," I said and smiled at her as I began piling my files together. "Had a nice time?"

"Absolutely lovely, Gerald. I'm so glad I walked. One sees so much more on foot than from a car. It's an enchanting town. Did you know that it's considered a town because it has a Paramount Chieftaincy?"

"I thought it was due to its size. It's bigger than most villages."

"Perhaps that too. Also there's a big market once a week, when everyone comes in from the villages and from even farther away. It's bound to be very lively, but it's only on Fridays." She sounded wistful. "Are we still leaving today?"

"We must. I'll just put my work away, and we can be off. We're due in Wenkyi this afternoon."

"All right, dear. My things are packed so I'll just go out and take my leave of these wonderful women," and she plunged back into the midst of the throng. Yeboah had loaded the car and started it before Helen finished, and her last words were to Constance, "I will write to you as soon as I am back in Accra."

Flushed and smiling, she got into the car and waved back at the little crowd until we rounded a bend in the road. Then she leaned back with a sigh. "My, that was splendid! I feel quite sad to be leaving already."

"Whatever are you going to write to them about?" I asked.

"They need schools, Gerald," she replied, turning to me with great vivacity. (To explain the situation: the schools in Tekyiman, of which there had been but two small ones until 1945, did not go beyond Form Five; to continue in school, students had to travel north to Wenkyi, a distance of some twenty miles, and few could do so.) "They tried to build a school themselves, a few years ago, for the higher forms. In fact, they did actually build it, everybody pitched in, but the District Commissioner refused to let them put a roof on it, so of course the bricks all dissolved when the rains came."

"Why did the DC refuse them a roof?"

"They say it was because they didn't ask his permission before they built it, and because the DC listened to the people of Wenkyi, who were jealous of the Tekyiman people. I don't think I understood it all, but the main thing is that they need a school, and I said I would try to help them."

I must admit that I became somewhat annoyed. "Helen," I said, "wives of Government officials are not meant to get involved in local issues."

"I know that, Gerald," she said patiently, "but this is not politics—it's education. I have no intention of taking sides in any historical arguments, but the fact is, this town needs another school, and I mean to help them get it."

I could think of nothing to say—I did not wish to quarrel with Helen in Yeboah's presence—and an uncomfortable silence fell briefly upon the car. However, Helen felt no such constraint. "Think of the conditions in Tekyiman, Gerald. Most of the people are illiterate, they have no doctor or dispensary, their local police force was disbanded, but they're still fighting for their rights. They have great spirit, but they'll never get any development without education. I won't embarrass you in any way. I'll just see what can be done from my position in Accra. They *must* have schooling."

Seeing that the wisest course was to co-operate, I said, "Well, let me know if you find that there is anything I can do."

"Thank you, darling," and she glowed at me. "I knew you'd agree. And when I need to come back to Tekyiman, I hope Yeboah will be able to drive me."

"Come back!" I echoed, stupefied. "I don't expect to have to come back."

"Not you, dear. Me."

"Why would you need to come back?" This was going too far. "White women don't just bolt around the Gold Coast by themselves, Helen. It may not be safe."

"Mrs. Meyerowitz did, and you know very well she came to no harm," Helen answered calmly.

I was heartily sick of hearing about that woman. "That is not the same thing at all. She was older, and a widow. And she had an official position, of sorts." I realized my voice was getting louder, and went on more quietly. "It simply wouldn't do, Helen. You see that, my dear, surely?"

She smiled sweetly at me, and my heart sank. I knew the determination behind that expression. "I do see your point of view, Gerald, of course." I began to relax. Then she added, "But I don't see the situation in the same way. Tekyiman has a serious problem that I might be able to help with. I'm an educated woman and I need something to do. It's not that I don't like our life there," she said earnestly. "I do. But seeing to the house and reading and visiting the other wives just isn't interesting enough. It was fun at first, but now I'm ready to do more."

I was forced to admit that she had a point. Expatriate society in Accra was indeed limited, and wives were not allowed to work. Perhaps if Helen had been able to do some teaching in the capital, she would not have become so inconveniently entranced by this upcountry village. Now there would be no convincing her that she could focus her pent-up energy on building a school in Accra, where they probably needed them just as much, because she would be failing her new friends in Tekyiman. Once she gave her heart, there was no shaking her; I myself was contented evidence of that.

"Very well, Helen," I said, yielding ground. "When we are back in Accra, I will, as I said, be pleased to help, however I can." Privately, I resolved that she would not be visiting Tekyiman on her own, whether it was with the excellent Yeboah or anybody else.

The woman sets the pages down, again smiling fondly.

SEVEN: The Centre of Her Country

Jenny hung up the phone and returned to the kitchen. "That's all set," she told Beth's Aunt Maggie. "He told me how to get to Juniper Farm and how long it should take, so we'll plan to leave Ottawa after lunch tomorrow."

"Fine," Maggie replied. "More coffee?"

"Yes, please. That's great coffee." If Jenny was surprised that an older woman brewed rich, hearty coffee, she didn't show it. Maggie had lost none of her taste for the good things in life. "You could open a B-and-B with such good breakfasts." Jenny had just finished a granola-yogurt-fruit parfait and two eggs scrambled with herbs.

"Perish the thought. I only do this for my friends. I wouldn't want to cook every morning." Maggie sat down again with her own full cup and added cream. "It would interfere with my life."

"Yes, I guess it would. Beth said you're away a lot."

"I used to be. I do like to travel, because Walter and I stayed put in Ottawa for enough years while the kids were growing up and we were working. But now that we know flying is the worst thing we do to the planet, I'm staying home a lot more. And travelling by train, instead of plane. More toast?"

"No, thank you. It was all wonderful."

"I try to give my guests a good foundation for the day. Now you shouldn't need much of a meal till dinner. I'll take you on a bit of a tour as soon as we're finished here, and drop you downtown. You can look around and then either walk home along the canal or hop a bus, depending on how you feel by that time."

"I'll probably walk. That walk by the lake" —she gestured toward the front of the house— "was really lovely."

"It's a nice place to live," Maggie agreed comfortably. "I'm far enough back from The Driveway that I don't notice the traffic, and I love the view across the lake to the farm."

"And I guess the city takes care of all those flower beds."

"They do. That's where the tulip festival is in the spring. Different colours of them, all along the canal. Sometimes they'll plant a colour I don't particularly like in the beds in front of me—I think of them as 'my' beds, of course—but who am I to complain? Not about that, anyway."

Jenny had understood from Beth that Aunt Maggie had "complained" about—or loudly opposed—many an issue in her life, and had not stopped yet. She asked, "What kinds of things do you complain about?"

"Aha! My little niece Beth has been telling you about me, has she? I complain—well, that's the wrong word. I object, I criticize, I protest—when I see," ticking off on her fingers, "one, stupid disregard for the future and two, injustice." She stopped again and considered. "Of course, those two basic ideas can involve a lot of related issues."

"What do you do?" Was Maggie a Grey Panther? A Raging Granny?

"Write letters, go to demonstrations, boycott products, give money. Nothing very unusual, just what everybody does. Whatever's needed. Vote. Go to meetings. That's the worst part, in my opinion. I hate meetings. They take so much time." Checking her watch, she said, "We'd better get going. What time do Sheila and Chris arrive?"

"I'll look in my Day-Timer."

Jenny finished her coffee and ran up the back stairs to her room. The wide, formal, front stairs swept up around the entry hall; the other, narrower set rose straight up from the kitchen.

Teeth brushed, she joined Maggie downstairs. "Sheila and Chris's flight gets in at four-thirty."

"Fine." Maggie led the way into the garage. "We'll pick them up, take them to their hotel and go out for dinner. They could have stayed here, you know. I've got plenty of room for all three of you. It's silly for them to spend money on a hotel."

"Well, they didn't feel right about it. They don't even have the tiny connection with you that I do."

Maggie backed the MG briskly down the driveway. "We'll take the other car to the airport. You probably wonder why a widow like me has two cars, when I go on about climate change." Without waiting for a reply, she went on, "It's pure sentimentality. This," gesturing at the dash of the sports car, "was Walter's. He adored it, and I can't bear—yet—to part with it. I know it's a silly car. I can't drive it in the winter, it's getting hard to find parts, I can only take one passenger—but on the other hand, it's small, it doesn't use much gas, and I keep it very well tuned. And it's bliss in an Ottawa summer, when it's ninety degrees with ninety percent humidity and I have to go somewhere too far to walk."

Maggie threaded her way expertly through the traffic, zipping from lane to lane north along Bronson Avenue, concentrating. "When you live in a place as long as I have, you tend to think the traffic patterns are carved in stone, but every now and then the city, bless its weird little council, changes the directions of streets. Now I have to think about the best route to the bridge."

Jenny took this to mean "don't talk," so she didn't. She concentrated too, on looking around at her first daytime views of Ottawa.

She had arrived the day before, not knowing what to expect of Beth's aunt ("She's different, you'll love her"), to be met by the slim, crisply coiffed, grey-haired Maggie in jeans, holding a sign with her name on it and a bouquet of autumnal flowers.

"Welcome to Ottawa, the nation's capital," she had declaimed, shaking Jenny's hand warmly. "I'm Maggie, your tour guide for this evening." People standing around cast curious glances at the pair of them, but Jenny was immediately delighted. She beamed at her hostess and accepted the flowers. "Thank you! Should I curtsey?"

"I think it's the giver who curtsies but I didn't. This way," and Maggie whisked her off.

"Here we are." She turned into the driveway of a large, square, brick house. "Your home away from home, whenever you come to Ottawa."

"What a lovely place to live." The house faced a park, a sleek roadway and then a sheet of smooth water. Broad green lawns, with scattered trees, huge and impressive—Jenny didn't recognize many species—bordered the little lake; joggers thumped along paths in the late-afternoon light and two canoes were silhouetted darkly against the bright water.

"Dow's Lake. It used to be Dow's Swamp, till they dredged it ages ago," Maggie explained. "That's the Rideau Canal coming in," waving, "and those buildings are Carleton University. Over there," to the right, "is Carling Avenue and those beigey-brick buildings are government offices."

"And what's that big park right across the lake?"

"The experimental farm. But it is sort of a park—you can walk around in it, and go tobogganing in winter. I practically lived over there when the kids were little. But come on in. We can sightsee tomorrow."

The house felt spacious, with big rooms and high ceilings, but different from what Jenny had expected. Why is that? she wondered, hanging her one dress up in the closet. There were four bedrooms and two bathrooms upstairs—Maggie had given her the tour—and all the usual rooms downstairs in a simple, classic arrangement. So what seemed odd to her?

Joining Maggie in the living room for a drink, Jenny finally understood what had surprised her. "Your house is so uncluttered," she blurted. "I love it. Oh, yes, a sherry would be great, thank you."

"Sweet or dry?"

"As dry as you've got it."

Jenny looked around. No Royal Doulton shepherdesses centred on doilies on small, round tables. No doilies, in fact. And no small, round tables. She realized that, given Maggie's age, she had expected some sort of elderly lady's house, filled with the memorabilia most people collect, and over-furnished with polished antiques. In contrast, Maggie's rooms were not only spare and open but—perhaps "well-used" was the right term. The chesterfields and chairs were large, comfortable and not new, the floor was bare wood, and the light-coloured walls were hung with few, but large, paintings.

"Uncluttered? Yes. That's a good word." Maggie handed Jenny a generous glass of very pale gold sherry. "Cheers. And welcome."

She clinked with her glass of Scotch. "Some of my friends think my house is awful. The ones who are my age. They like to have their things around them, and they reckon my furniture is a disgrace. Well, it is, a bit."

"I like it," said Jenny. "It's like the houses I grew up in. I find most people's places too full."

"I used to have a house like that."

"What happened?"

"Years ago, after the children had all grown up and left, Walter and I suddenly took a look around and thought, 'God! What a lot of stuff!' Four children do bring things in, you know, and then of course they don't take them all away again. You get to the point where your things own you, instead of the other way around. Alarm systems, insurance, getting people to come stay in the house when you go away."

Jenny nodded. "But most folks live like that."

"They do. And I really don't know why we changed. The voluntary simplicity idea wasn't around then. We just felt suffocated, all of a sudden. So we gave the kids ultimatums—or should that be ultimata?" looking at Jenny, "to come and get their things, gave loads to the Salvation Army and places like that and in a few months, we were free!"

"How do you mean, free?"

"That's how we felt. Free. I remember we were quite giddy with the relief. It was like being reborn, almost. You know what? I actually felt thinner!" Maggie laughed heartily. "You might wonder why we didn't go the whole hog and sell this big house as well, and we did think of that. But it was paid for, and we loved being here, near the lake. And the kids wanted us to keep it. In fact, they had fits at the idea of our selling, the bossy brats. 'You can't sell it—Max is buried in the backyard!' Our dog. I guess they would have felt uprooted if we'd sold it. Is your family like that?"

Jenny smiled at her. "No. But my family's different. And we moved around a lot. Living in the same house for fifty years must be some kind of a record. Isn't that how long you said?"

"Yes, but it's not a record. Maybe people in the East stay put longer than you do in the West. A friend of mine who lives not far away has been in her house since she was eleven, and she's ninety-five now."

"That's amazing! Why has she never moved?"

"She married during the war, so her husband moved in with her and her dad—her mother had died years before—and then her husband died suddenly, much too young, and she and their daughter stayed in the house. Then her dad died, her daughter got married and moved away, and there Bets is. Perfectly happy. Now, tell me about your trip. What's the name of these cousins you're going to see?"

"Muir. They live on a farm near a town called Calabogie. They've been there—I mean, the family—since the year dot, it seems. Generations."

"Ah. Muir." Maggie took a sip. "It rings a bell. I'm just thinking back." There was a pause. "George. That was his name." She nodded, to herself rather than to Jenny. "I just dredged up an image from the bottom layers of my memory. Thank god it still works sometimes! And his father was Andrew. Then he—Andrew—would have been your grandfather, I guess."

"You knew my grandfather?"

"No. I knew your—um—uncle."

"My uncle!" Flesh-and-blood family! She had only vaguely been aware that there were uncles, in much the same way she was aware that Captain Vancouver had charted the West Coast. But suddenly, they were real people. Practically here in the room with her.

Maggie was eyeing Jenny speculatively. "I gather from your expression that you're surprised. Not a close family?"

What an understatement. "Not a close family, no," Jenny managed to repeat. "I've never met any of these people. I've hardly ever even heard of them. Do you remember much about my grandfather? He's always been a sort of mythical figure to me—long dead, as far as I know, and never talked about."

"Not a lot. Well . . ." Maggie focused somewhere in the middle distance and thought back. "He was strict, I know that. George wouldn't consider not going home at the weekends, even though he really wanted to stay in town for the parties. He was a lot of fun—very lively and entertaining and handsome. The only time he stayed, that I can recall, was for a formal graduation party out at the Royal Ottawa, I think it was. He was like Cinderella." She fell silent, smiling to herself.

"How do you mean?"

"He had—blossomed. It's the only word for it. He was wearing a very fine dinner jacket because the family—your family—had plenty of money, you know—and he danced beautifully, and he just looked like a prince. We'd only ever known him at school, of course, in classes, or in his football uniform. We'd all liked him before, but I think that night every girl there fell in love with him. And maybe their mothers too." She smiled again, back in a vista of swirling gowns, long gloves and wide verandas. Jenny studied her in wonder, trying to imagine what she was seeing.

Maggie shook her head briskly. "But that was the only party your grandfather let him stay for. And I suspect that that was only because it was given by a couple of the big families he did business with."

"So he wasn't really a farmer?"

"Oh yes. He had a farm, but he had other businesses too. Something to do with lumber, I think, but then, a lot of the old Ottawa money was in logging and lumber. Maybe he was a partner in some retail stores too. Animal feed? Clothes? I can't remember."

"Why did they live out on the farm then?"

"I think it was because," Maggie started carefully, "he had a religious fundamentalist side, and he wanted to keep his family sheltered. Away from the sins of the city, that sort of thing. No fun on Sundays, long church services, no mixing with the damned and all that."

"Then how did George get to be a good dancer?"

"I would imagine because dancing was a useful skill—at least back then—in society and business. Like golf today. There are lots of believers who won't let anything stand in the way of making money."

"Hm." Jenny was not impressed. "So he was a hypocritical funda-mentalist."

"Not necessarily. There are passages in the Bible that read as if they encourage business and capitalism, so probably your grandfather didn't see any conflict."

"I'm getting a pretty clear picture of this man."

"Remember that I didn't know him myself. I'm just giving you my impressions, and they're a lifetime old."

"Yes, but still, they're valid, and this is all a total revelation to me."

"Are you ready for dinner?" Food was an excellent way to ease someone through a shock. And comfortable conversation. "Now I come from a family that's always been pretty close." Maggie decided she would just natter on while Jenny got hold of herself. "Except for Beth's branch, we're all still in Ontario, and family's family, so everybody turns up for weddings and birthdays and anniversaries." She wondered if Jenny was collected enough to be probed gently about her family, because another memory was surfacing. Maybe not—she'd only just met her, after all. Better to check around with a few friends first. Ottawa had been smaller then and people still remembered the old days.

Now, nipping through traffic, Maggie interrupted Jenny's contemplation of last night's conversation. "That's the Peace Tower. You'll see it better later, but here's your first glimpse of it."

Her first glimpse of the centre of her country. A high, handsome, stone clock tower, pointing upward above, as she knew from her reading, the Centre Block of Parliament. Built from 1860 to 1876. Burned in 1916, except for the library. It was like a maypole, the provinces twirling around it on shorter or longer ribbons. How old everything was here—buildings, families, reaching back centuries. It all seemed so solid, so centred, so different from the West Coast, and she wished she knew more history of the area.

One of Jenny's favourite things about editing a wide variety of books was all the different subjects she dealt with, but it was one of the shortcomings too, and she occasionally wished she were an expert on something. Like Chris, whose speciality, before he quit so surprisingly, was Canadian literature. I have a brain full of snippets— I never delve into anything. Maggie pointed out a part of the city,

New Edinburgh, which had been planned before 1800. Even though it was her own country, it felt foreign.

And now they were crossing a bridge into Quebec. "I've hardly ever been to a place that doesn't speak English." The Ottawa River lay broad and sparkling in the morning sun below the medieval-looking Parliament Buildings, high on their impressive cliff. Growing up with tides, Jenny found lakes and rivers a little strange. They always looked the same—no daily up and down, no mud flats revealed and then slowly covered again. Upstream, the Chaudière Falls roared and crashed, as lively as the lower river was calm.

Maggie was amazed. "You've hardly ever been to a place that doesn't speak English?" she repeated. "Of course, in Quebec they do, as well as French. But you mean you've never been to France? Or Italy?"

"Not yet. I went to Denmark once with my family, when I was little, but I'm really reluctant to fly now. As you said earlier, it's the worst thing we do to the planet."

"Yes," Maggie sighed. "My generation didn't realize the harm we were doing when we started to travel so much. It seemed like a good idea, to get to know other parts of the world."

"It's not just your generation. Nobody seems to be making any changes in their lifestyles. I did check into coming here by train, but it's unbelievably expensive. That's what governments should be subsidizing." Jenny was indignant. "Trains are so much less damaging as a way to move around."

"They certainly are, and a lot more comfortable, as well. But it seems odd to me that your family went to Denmark and you've never been to Ottawa before."

"The last thing we were encouraged to do at home was to go looking for our Ontario background."

Maggie let that slide, her curiosity tightening up a notch. "That's the Museum of Civilization."

"I've seen pictures of it, but I didn't realize it was so big. What a contrast to the Parliament Buildings." Jenny swivelled to peer back. "But I guess that's what the architect had in mind." The smooth and sinuous lines of the museum almost shouted across the river at the spiky Gothic presence.

Back across a different bridge, through Rockcliffe and Sandy Hill with the tall, old, brick houses of the early wealthy families, then the Byward Market to the National Gallery.

"I'll drop you here, Jenny, so you can have a wander round on your own. There's Parliament Hill, the Rideau Canal locks are down in that cut, that's the Château Laurier. If you want a nice walk back, you can follow the canal. It's longer than coming through the streets, but prettier. And" —Maggie smiled— "it was built between 1826 and 1832, by Colonel By and the Royal Engineers. That should please your craving for history!" And off she went.

Left to herself, Jenny had much to think about. She decided to look at the locks.

EIGHT: A Memorable Housewarming

In the quiet Victoria house, the woman continues with the manuscript.

The rest of the trip was much less eventful. My meeting with the District Commissioner in Wenkyi took longer than I expected; he was not at all happy about the Brong-Kyempen Federation, regarded the Tekyimanhene as a rabble-rouser and thorn in the Government's side, and expostulated on all this for some time. He was due for annual leave, and it would clearly do him good to see England again.

Soon after our return to Accra, we moved house, to a somewhat larger dwelling, one which we had been waiting for, and this occupied Helen over and above her normal daily routine. I continued to go to the office while she enjoyed herself arranging the new furniture and draperies. These "bungalows," as they were termed, were pleasant, given the climate. They were built up off the ground by several feet, to allow air to circulate beneath the floor, and surrounded by wide, screened verandas that shaded the inside rooms. All the windows were louvred, to admit any possible breeze, and with the ceiling fans turning gently, the rooms were as cool and attractive as one could expect in the tropics.

Accra, where settlement had begun in the early seventeenth century, was by this time a city of perhaps one hundred and fifty thousand people, and the residential areas occupied by Europeans and the professional classes of the Gold Coast, such as "The Ridge," where we lived, were green and rather pretty, with hedges, flower beds, and trees. The central core of the city, where the Government and businesses were located, was less appealing, although, being right on the ocean, it had an openness that some colonial capitals lack. The major buildings were sturdy, sparkling-white structures, mostly not over two or three storeys, with roofed verandas on each floor. It would have been more attractive if more trees had been planted, as the French did in their African colonies, but in the case of Accra, the spaces between the buildings were taken up by haphazard streets, beaten earth and some sidewalks. It was all very clean, as everything was swept at least once a day, and no litter was allowed to remain. There was a huge, always bustling market, where one's servants bought food and other household necessities. It looked very colourful and sounded lively when I was driven past it each day. I was fond of Accra: it was a smallish, friendly city, the clubs were inviting and my work interested me.

While Helen busied herself with the new house, and hiring and training a new steward, the previous one having been let go because of some disagreement with the cook, she never mentioned Tekyiman, so I had some hope that her fascination with the place had blossomed quickly and as quickly died away. However, one evening, as we sat with our before-dinner drinks on the front veranda, she produced a letter.

"Gerald, darling," she exclaimed, waving the pages in the air and smiling, "I've heard from Constance!"

"Constance who?" I inquired, taking a sip of my gin, though I feared I knew quite well who she meant.

"Constance Amankwaa, in Tekyiman. The pretty teacher who was so nice to me."

"Ah, that Constance. And what does the admirable Constance have to say?"

Helen shot me an amused glance; something in my tone may have alerted her to my frame of mind on this subject. "You probably remember that when we were in Tekyiman, I was distressed by the lack of education. I mean" —she rethought her words carefully— "modern, European education, especially in a town of that size and importance. It seems to me that unless the people are at least literate and can speak English, they will never be able to govern themselves and be part of the Empire. And perhaps," she considered, tilting her head, "the older ones don't care about that, and are perfectly happy with life as it has always been. But this is the twentieth century, and the younger people will have to deal, willy-nilly, with a bigger world. How can they do that if they haven't been educated?" It was clearly a rhetorical question. She then fixed me with a very level gaze. "The Government should undertake a program of improving the standards of schooling over the whole colony."

"Well, of course, that's a wonderful and worthy idea, my dear," I began, but Helen interrupted me.

"But you don't have the budget, and it's not a main part of your mandate. I know. Also, good schools are being founded by some of the missionaries. My point is simply that unless and until there comes to be a Government plan for schools, individual initiatives will have to do. And since the very interesting contact I made is in Tekyiman, that is where I would like to concentrate my initiative."

"It's deucedly inconvenient and far away, Helen," I grumbled. "Couldn't you have got enthused about a village closer to Accra?"

"I'm sure I could have." She smiled. "But as it happens, I didn't. And it's a town, not a village."

"Yes, yes, I know," I acknowledged in some impatience. She certainly seemed to have taken the place to heart, much like the never-absent "Mrs. Eva." What was it that so attracted them? "And what does your initiative consist of?"

"Well." She shifted in her chair in evident delight. "I wrote to Constance and asked her to continue the discussions we had had with the Queenmother and to broaden them to include others in the community, and the Tekyimanhene and his Council, of course, about what should be done and in what order." Helen was very good at organizing things and had a tidy mind. "There's no point in rushing half-cocked into a long-term project." My heart sank lower at her blithe use of the word long-term. She went on, "Because of their bad experience of trying to build a school without official approval, that's what they want first, the approval, and I think it's very sensible. So I" —she levelled that look at me again— "shall work to get it for them."

That's not too bad, I was thinking to myself. She will write a few letters and the process will take some time . . .

"Now, Gerald." Helen picked up a notebook. "Whom do I see about permission for building schools? No doubt there are several offices involved." Her pen was poised.

"See? Why don't you just write to them?"

"Because we both know what happens to letters. They get put aside for someone else to answer and the whole thing takes forever. No, I shall make appointments and go to talk with the relevant people. Who are they?"

Resigning myself, I gave her the names of everyone I could think of who might be involved with schools and education. Quite a few of them we already knew, of course, and Helen gave a satisfied nod when she had completed the list.

"Good. Thank you, darling. I'll start tomorrow." She finished her drink. "Ready for dinner? Augustine has done us a nice chicken tonight."

I was indeed ready for dinner.

Over the next weeks I finished my report on the Brong-Kyempen Federation and dealt with some routine tasks that necessitated a few shorter trips away from Accra, west along the coast to Cape Coast and Takoradi. These towns are both sites of old slave-trading castles such as Elmina, built by the Portuguese in 1480. The coast of the Colony is an anomalous dry area, due, apparently, to an upwelling of cold water offshore, so as one travelled, panoramas of grassy landscape opened up. In many ways this was more appealing than the endless, enclosing forest of inland journeys.

After the various normal irritations of the move to the bigger house, we settled back into our pleasant life among the other expatriates; they were mostly English, with a few Danish, Dutch and French citizens as well. There were also quite a number of Lebanese merchants, but they kept largely to themselves. We attended frequent parties at the homes of other Colonial officials and went to Saturday-night dances at one or other of the clubs, and eventually Helen decided we should give a housewarming celebration ourselves. Helen, as I have mentioned, had a talent for organization, and since I was busy at work, I left all the arrangements for our party, after we had fixed upon the date, in her hands. The usual drinks and buffet, it was set for around Easter, and I looked forward to the role of host in the new house, which had more commodious dining and sitting rooms than our former residence.

On the evening of the party the house looked most inviting, with bouquets of flowers (there were no florists in Accra, of course, so Helen had arranged them herself), our new furniture set attractively about, the buffet spread enticingly and banks of glasses sparkling. Helen had engaged the services of some of her friends' stewards, as hostesses usually did for such occasions, and several smiling, white-coated waiters stood at the ready.

I put my arm around my dear wife's shoulders as we surveyed the scene, and congratulated her. "It looks magnificent."

"Thank you, darling." She smiled up at me. "I hope it will be a memorable party." Which indeed it was. Helen anticipated that it might be "memorable" but did not expect that it would be quite such a turning point in our lives. From the advantage of age, I look back with amazement on how often a small event can effect major changes, intended or not.

Most of the guests had arrived when I received my first surprise, as three elegantly dressed Native Gold Coast men appeared in the open doorway. Helen must have been unobtrusively keeping an eye out for them because she materialized immediately to greet them. She then smiled and nodded at me—she had clearly also marked my position—so I excused myself and moved toward her. A hush had fallen upon the room when eyes noted the black faces, but the hum of chatter quickly started up again, as though people realized they should not show any unbecoming interest. High-ranking Gold Coast Natives appeared at political events, of course, and at Ambassadorial or High Commission occasions, but it was less common for them to be invited to house parties of officials at my level.

"Gentlemen, this is my husband, Gerald Hatley-Thorpe. Gerald, my dear, may I present Mr. Boateng, Mr. Adu and Mr. Kyeremeh?"

We all shook hands, then one of the waiters appeared, beaming, with a drinks tray, and we began to converse as if there were nothing at all strange in the situation.

"Mr. Boateng and Mr. Adu are working in education and teacher training, and Mr. Kyeremeh is with the national Chieftaincy Secretariat. We met during my explorations on behalf of schooling in Tekyiman," Helen informed me brightly, though I had assumed as much. "Since there are several colonial officials here tonight, I felt it would be a good opportunity for some informal talk about speeding up the expansion of education." Helen had been associated with Government and the Colonial Service long enough to know that many fruitful connections are forged, and much useful business done, at social occasions; however, at that time the actual recipients of the Government's services were rarely included. "I thought you might introduce Mr. Kyeremeh to Michael Smith"—one of my colleagues—"while I take Mr. Adu and Mr. Boateng over to have a chat with Arthur." Arthur Trethewey and his wife, Emma, were our closest friends in Accra, having been fellow students of ours at Cambridge.

As I obediently led Mr. Kyeremeh through the crowd in search of Michael, I learned that he was a graduate of the London School of Economics and had spent a lengthy period of time in Italy. His uncle was a Paramount Chief in Ashanti, which state is of course wealthy from cocoa and gold, and this probably explained both his job and his beautifully tailored suit.

We reached Michael, and the three of us had an extended conversation, I not wanting to abandon Mr. Kyeremeh right away. He proved to be friendly and informative, socially poised and polished. He obviously knew that he was in an unusual position and equally obviously was determined not to show it. His courtly manner was such that I began to have the odd impression that he outranked me. Eventually, others of the guests came up to be introduced, which made me pleased and proud, and I was able to slip away on my further hostly duties.

The next surprise was not long in coming. I did not recognize Constance when a regally clad woman arrived some time after her compatriots. In contrast to the three men, who were wearing European clothes, Constance had opted for Native dress, though in the very height of formality. This meant the traditional three-piece outfit, but in *kente* (the local, strip-woven and expensive fabric) in rich colours of gold and blue. She came alone, and in the wide, open doorway with the black night behind her, she was a stunning sight. This time the hush was markedly longer, due as much, I thought, to the woman's striking appearance as to the colour of her skin.

Again, Helen was instantly at her side. "Constance, my dear," she said warmly, her voice somewhat raised for the benefit of anyone who might be listening, which, I judged, was the whole party. "I'm so glad you could come! It's such a long journey from Tekyiman." Again, she looked unerringly toward where I was standing. "And you remember my husband, Gerald?"

I approached, hoping my smile was more welcoming than amazed.

"Yes," Constance nodded shyly at me, her smile dimpling her round cheeks. "Good evening."

"Good evening, Constance. How nice to see you again. Thank you for coming all this way. May I offer you something to drink?" I turned to the tray that a delighted waiter was presenting at my elbow.

"Mineral water, please," Constance replied softly. "I do not take spirits."

The waiter had anticipated this, and had placed glasses of orange and cola drinks among the Scotch and gin.

We got Constance organized with a glass of orange in her hand and, as Emma Trethewey and another woman had appeared smartly at Helen's side, I faded, still smiling, back into the crowd. After the lull, the noise level had risen again, so much so that the background music Helen had chosen was completely drowned out. I was looking about, checking to make sure that everyone was having a good time and that there were no lonely stragglers standing in corners, when one of my superiors came up.

"Splendid party, Gerald, and congratulations on the new

house." (Although this had been Helen's ostensible reason for the party, I was now beginning to wonder.) I thanked him and he continued, "Any other remarkable guests on their way?"

I had to confess that I was not sure, at which his eyebrows arched upward, but he went on to say that he had found Mr. Kyeremeh an agreeable and interesting conversationalist. "We should talk to some of these chaps more often, what?" He clapped me on the shoulder and moved on toward the food. It occurred to me that he must think Helen and I had agreed on the guest list, which left me in a quandary. If I let him continue to think that, I might be considered rash by my colleagues; if I confessed that I had in fact not known about our unconventional guests, I would be seen as not being in control in my own household. I decided to remain silent, and let the chips fall where they may.

I went over to Arthur Trethewey.

"Good-looking girl, that," Arthur said, nodding at Constance. "Emma tells me you met her on your last trip upcountry."

"Yes," I said, a little surprised that Emma should have been discussing Constance. Then I realized that this was to be expected, as Emma and Helen saw each other frequently. "It was Helen who spent time with her, actually."

"Of course," Arthur agreed. "Meeting the Queenmother and so on. Must have been quite an adventure for her."

Again I was, stupidly, somewhat taken aback at Arthur's knowledge of our journey. "Oh, yes," I allowed, trying to make it sound like an everyday occurrence. "The people were very hospitable in Tekyiman, as they are everywhere." This was true, the Gold Coast Natives being famed for their joie de vivre and gracious welcomes.

"Helen's got quite the bee in her bonnet about educating them now, hasn't she?"

"She has," I allowed again.

Arthur must have picked up something in my tone, for he said, "Well, she's a bright and energetic girl, Gerald, like Emma, and being the wife of a Colonial officer doesn't always suit a bright girl. I reckon I'm lucky that Emma's got the children to occupy her."

"I think you are too," I told him. Emma was formidably intelligent and direct, but also good company, as she was attractive and had a wonderful sense of humour.

"It's always an option," Arthur grinned at me and held up his empty glass to gain the attention of a steward. "Complete the family and so on."

"Indeed it is," I agreed and then, because I was not inclined to pursue that subject with Arthur, I said, "Helen's right about the importance of education, you know. If the Gold Coast is to become an independent and democratic country—and it's bound to, sooner or later—the entire population should be literate. The chaps here tonight" —and he knew I meant our Native guests— "are obviously members of the elite, because they've been to universities at Home, and are probably capable of running a government, but they're only a small fraction. And the farther north one goes, the more the schools peter out." I had not planned this little speech, but felt I owed it to Helen to support her good intentions.

Arthur sighed, and I wondered if he had already heard these views from Emma, who appeared to be acting as Helen's lieutenant tonight. "That would presumably involve building schools all over the bloody Colony," he said, "and I don't know if the co intends to do that."

It was, of course, exactly what Kwame Nkrumah, the first prime minister, did when the Gold Coast became Ghana a few years later; the Ghana Educational Trust secondary schools sprouted in towns hither and yon. We were long gone from West Africa by then, but Helen was gratified to learn that one of those schools was in Tekyiman.

Arthur continued soberly, "Mustn't upset our masters by pushing too hard, you know, even if it's a worthy cause," and I understood that he was, however obscurely, issuing a gentle warning.

Another of our colleagues and his wife joined us at that point, and our conversation drifted off onto other matters. I noticed Constance being capably shepherded by either Emma Trethewey or Elizabeth Peel when Helen was attending to other guests. The rest of the party followed the usual course—a few people drank too much and shouted, the food was consumed and enjoyed, one glass of liquor was spilt down the front of a light-coloured frock (by another guest, not one of the sure-footed stewards), one couple began to have a row—and the hostess provided no further surprises. I did my best to speak, at least briefly, with everyone there, and I think I succeeded. As the crush began to thin out, Helen came up to me with one of her new acquaintances in tow.

"Gerald, dear, Mr. Boateng would like to come see you in your office one day soon."

"Of course," I said. "I should be delighted. I don't have my appointment book here at home, but please ring me at the office and we'll set something up."

"I will do that." He smiled, shook my hand, bowed elegantly and thanked me very much for the party, so I assumed that he, too, thought the invitation had come from both of us. I was reminded of the adage about "damned if you do and damned if you don't" and simply told him I looked forward to seeing him again.

Our guests trickled away and the rooms became quieter. Near the end, I heard, with a slight sense of alarm, Helen inviting Constance down the hall toward the bedrooms and wondered if the novelty included Constance staying the night in our home. However, they soon emerged, smiling, and Helen asked one of the stewards to go out and flag a taxi for Constance. (Although The Ridge was a quiet neighbourhood, there was a major road a short distance away that was busy late into the evening.) After she had left, with many prettily phrased thanks, I asked Helen if she knew where Constance was going, thinking she might be a stranger to the city.

"Oh, yes. She's staying with a cousin in Christiansborg" (this was a residential area around the old slave-trading fort of the same name, built by the Danes in 1659). "She went to school here for a few years, so she knows her way around. Otherwise, I doubt that she would have come all this way for the party."

"I wonder that she could afford the trip," I remarked, and Helen blushed slightly.

"I helped her a bit with the fare," she said offhandedly, and I remembered their disappearing down the hall. She began picking up empty glasses as we spoke, although there was no need for her to do so. The last guests made their rather unsteady departure, and we were left facing the monumental mess that follows such affairs. However, the pleasant advantage of giving parties in the Colonies was that one could rely upon all the well-trained household staff, and these now swung into action. I drew Helen away.

"You'll just be in the way if you try to help. Come have a drink on the veranda and tell me how you thought it all went." Helen rarely had any alcohol at her own parties because, as she said, she "got quite excited enough just with all the company." We retreated, glasses in hand, to our favourite chairs, Helen with a light wrap around her shoulders; by contrast with the warmth of a room full of people, the air outside felt quite cool. After a long sip, she leaned back, looked up at the sky and sighed happily. "Well, that *was* fun. I'm glad it's over, and we're back to peace and quiet, but it was a lovely party, wasn't it?"

We proceeded to review the event as if nothing unusual had occurred until Helen, who may have been feeling a little anxious, said, "I hope you didn't mind my inviting Constance, Gerald, and the three men. I know it was a surprise to you, but I thought it best not to worry you in advance." Which was an admirably diplomatic way of putting it.

"It certainly did surprise me, but they were all quite—interesting—and I don't *think* it did any harm."

"Oh no, dear, it did a great deal of good. Mr. Boateng and Mr. Adu said they had some useful conversations about schooling with your colleagues, and—my, but Mr. Kyeremeh is a charmer, isn't he?" with admiration. "He's like a prince—so well travelled and sophisticated. Isn't this an amazing colony, with such extremes of people!"

"We have the same extremes at Home, Helen," I pointed out. "Think of the difference between, say, a farmer who has never left Shropshire, and our High Commissioner here." The HC was the second son of a Lord.

"That's true, of course. I don't know why it impresses me here so much. Perhaps foreign places just always seem more intriguing." She fell silent and seemed to ponder this conundrum.

Wide divisions from top to bottom in society apparently occur everywhere, as we were to find the same thing among the coastal peoples of British Columbia, to say nothing of the gulfs within our own race; perhaps it is human nature. At the time, however, I was a little worried about a different aspect of human nature, that of dislike of the unexpected or, as Arthur had put it "upsetting our masters." I did not mention this to Helen, as I did not wish to put a crimp in her pleasure over her party; her strategy had certainly accomplished what she intended.

I finished my drink. "Shall we go in? It sounds quiet, and you had better see to the boys." Although our steward and the "borrowed" ones were on salary, it was the custom to give them an additional amount—perhaps it was a few shillings—for serving at large social occasions.

Helen smiled at me as we went back into the house, and that was the end of our discussion about the party that night.

The next morning being Sunday, we had our usual leisurely weekend breakfast before going to Church. It was a lovely, fresh morning, quieter than on weekdays when activity began as soon as there was light, and I was enjoying my eggs—our cook at the time, James, was excellent—when Helen calmly dropped another "bombshell."

"Constance is staying several days in Accra," she remarked, "for her Easter holidays, and when she goes back to Tekyiman I thought I might go with her, for a short visit."

I froze with a piece of toast in mid-air. "Go upcountry by yourself? What are you thinking of, Helen!"

"I wouldn't be by myself, Gerald," Helen responded mildly, "and I am thinking of schools."

"Yes, yes, I know you're thinking of schools. But you can't just traipse off upcountry on your own, Helen! It isn't done!"

Unfortunately, this statement was the proverbial red flag to a bull, as Helen said frostily, "If it 'isn't done' now," (her disdain was audible) "it soon will be. This is the 1950s after all, and I am not a Victorian memsahib, though I admit that some women of our acquaintance are. I shall only be away a few days," and she calmly proceeded with her breakfast.

Of course this was the twentieth century, and one did not require one's wife to ask permission to do things. In the Colonial Service, however, the things wives did were largely of a social nature; they did not work, nor did they travel, unaccompanied, upon their own pursuits. I pondered for some minutes to decide on my best course of action, knowing there was no point in trying to dissuade Helen from her purpose.

"If you must go, I shall arrange for a car and driver, and see if the resthouse is available," I said, half-hoping it would already be engaged.

"Thank you, darling. That's very kind. I'm sure Constance will appreciate going back by car, rather than in a lorry."

"Oh. Yes, she would be welcome to travel with you, of course."

"And if the resthouse is booked, Constance will find me a place to stay."

"There are no hotels in Tekyiman, Helen."

"No, no, I know that. I meant someone would put me up. The houses are large, as you know, and the women are very friendly and generous."

The vision of my wife dossing down in a mud hut appalled me for an instant, though I knew it was unfair, as the houses were commodious and extremely clean, if underfurnished. "I am sure the resthouse will be free. Tekyiman is not a busy spot for travellers."

"No, I thought not." She smiled. "Still, it would be enormous fun to stay with Constance." My face must have reflected my feelings about this inappropriate idea of "enormous fun" for she quickly said, "But the resthouse would be fine."

"It certainly would. I hope you won't become *too* carried away by your project, Helen. I'm afraid there have to be limits to one's enthusiasms in the Colonies."

"Yes, dear," she responded soothingly. "I do realize that, and

I'll be careful not to embarrass you." (Though in fact, she had already done so.) "More coffee?"

I may have sounded stiff, but I was beginning to have concerns about the direction Helen's energy was taking her. I was still involved, at least tangentially, with the Brong-Kyempen business, and did not want her accidentally getting in the middle of it, or even being perceived as such, because it might interrupt the orderly progress of the political matters.

Dr. Kwame Nkrumah had by then been agitating for "Self-Government Now" for the Gold Coast for some years; in fact, in December–January of 1949–50 the activities of the Colony had been halted by a general strike to press the issue. It seemed that most of the upcountry Chiefs were on side with Nkrumah, and negotiations were proceeding. This was not necessarily easy in a Colony that had, according to a 1946 survey, 108 different states.

In the event, I probably need not have been anxious about Helen's trip interrupting the political process, because all went well, and in 1957, the Gold Coast peacefully became the first independent country in sub-Saharan Africa. We were no longer there by then, but we were very pleased to know about it.

Helen's acquaintance, Mr. Boateng, did come to see me in my office early the next week, and we had an amicable discussion about the state of schooling outside the major centres. I agreed to facilitate his efforts in any way I could, but warned him that education was outside my bailiwick, I being on the political side. He quite understood, and we parted on cordial terms, shaking hands in my doorway as Arthur Trethewey came down the hall. They remembered each other from the party, and exchanged greetings.

Arthur followed me back into my office. "He's the education chappie, isn't he? Not the one from the Chieftaincy Department."

"That's right."

"Helen still keen as mustard on this place in the interior?"

"She is." I debated mentioning her plan to revisit Tekyiman and, deciding he was bound to hear about it anyway, said, casually, "She's going back up to check on the situation."

Arthur merely said, "Ah," and began to discuss the papers he had brought in with him.

Helen returned from her adventure (luckily, the faithful Yeboah had been able to take her) in fine fettle, and I carried on with my work, which now included some consideration of drafts for a possible future Constitution. Being thus busy, I did not inquire into the finer details of the five or six days she had been away, other than to establish that everyone had been very warm and pleased to see her, the resthouse was agreeable and her friends were still keen on increasing the number of village schools. Clearly, she had enjoyed herself immensely, felt her efforts were worthwhile and was fonder than ever of Constance and some of the other women.

Our busy and fruitful life might have gone happily on but for the unexpected illness of my mother. An active and seemingly healthy woman, she wrote that she had been feeling tired and out of sorts for some time, and when she went to her doctor for tests, it turned out, to everyone's shock and horror, that she was suffering from a terminal cancer. I was the youngest in the family and the only one with no children, and although I could not leave immediately, Helen volunteered to go Home. She was a great favourite with my mother, and felt she could be of real assistance in the house. I was given compassionate leave shortly afterward, so Helen and I soon found ourselves in the unfamiliar condition of being ordinary citizens in England. It was a sad and stressful time, especially for my mother, which I will not dwell upon.

I kept in touch to some degree with what was going on in my work, as though I were on a normal leave, but was disconcerted to be the subject of a transfer. The new post was in southern Nigeria, near Port Harcourt in Iboland. Although my suspicions were never confirmed, I believe that when our "masters" had both Helen and me out of the Gold Coast, they saw it as providential, and decided that we would not return.

Poor Helen, who had not had any inkling of this possibility, was quite devastated. "But we *love* the Gold Coast," she wailed, "and we didn't like Nigeria nearly as well when we visited there. Ask them to change their minds. Turn it down!"

As the new post was a promotion, I could not very well turn it down without tacitly ending my career in the Colonial Service. I did have some polite, uneasy conversations in London, but my superiors were not to be budged: I was not going back to the Gold Coast.

Helen and I then had long and serious discussions about our future and the upshot was that I resigned from the Colonial Service to join the Department of Indian Affairs in Canada. We did not regret this rather sudden move, and spent many fulfilling years on the West Coast, but we both felt, always, a little under-lying ache for our pleasant life in the Gold Coast, for the heat, the exotic beauty, and the effervescent friendliness of the Native people.

The woman sets the pages down with a little sigh and reaches for a handkerchief.

NINE: Unknown Territory

"With Sheila at the wheel, The Three head out into unknown territory," Jenny carolled as they drove west out of Ottawa. The sky was high and bright blue, the trees still mostly green, splotched with soft yellows and brilliant reds. The wide river ran invisibly on their right. "Do you remember those Enid Blyton books about The Five?"

"Sure," said Chris from the back seat, and Sheila nodded.

"So we're The Three. Off to solve a mystery that has haunted us all our lives," dramatically.

Sheila cast her a glance, part amusement, part annoyance. "Let's not get too carried away."

"I know." Jenny grinned. "'Haunted' is overdoing it. But the closer I get, the more I wonder. How's 'wonder,' Sheel?"

"Wonder is okay. I'm wondering myself, about a whole lot of things. I'm wondering if this'll turn out to have been a good idea. And will Ben and his wife be pleased to see us."

"He sounded perfectly friendly on the phone. Are you wondering too, Chris? And if so, about what?"

"I'm wondering what Ben and—is it Grace?—will be like, of course. And I'm wondering if we'll meet any more of Pat's relatives."

"Good question." Jenny twisted round to look at him. "I'm a bit nervous, actually. What about you, Sheila?"

"Nervous? Oh, my little heart is pounding away. But I'm also wondering if those hills over there are fremlins," pointing to change the subject, "because I promised Kate I'd pay attention to the landscape."

"What? Oh, drumlins, you mean. Fremlin is a street in Vancouver." Jenny looked across the river at the forested heights she was indicating. "And no, those hills are not drumlins."

"How would you know?" Sheila scoffed.

"I've worked on some books about geomorphology. Enough to know about drumlins. They're sort of oval, with one steeper side, and they're separate from each other. They're called a 'basket of eggs' topography. That, over there, is the edge of a plateau. An escarpment or '*massif*,'" she pronounced and slid a sideways look at Sheila. "And it's bedrock. Drumlins are gravel and sand, left by glaciers. Which is called 'till.'"

"Enough!"

"*Bedrock* is an interesting word, isn't it?" Jenny continued cheerfully, paying no heed. "Bed, embedded, grounded—it's all about being secure and settled. I must look up the etymology of that. Your hills are the Gatineau Hills. This flat land in between is sedimentary lowlands."

"Wonderful. You can tell Kate all about it. I'll just look at the buildings and people."

"There are some very old towns along the rivers—settled before the city of Vancouver was even thought of. And the Gatineau Hills are Canadian Shield, the oldest rock in the world. It's Precambrian, so it's—I think—over six hundred million years old."

"I thought the Canadian Shield was way up north."

"It is. But some of it comes down here."

"What a repository of information you've become." Chris gave Jenny a playful swat. "Have you worked on any books about fishing in this part of the country? Is there anything practical stuffed into that head?"

"Click, click, whirr. I've worked on a couple of fishing books, but they weren't guides, or how to catch things. I know there are muskie in the Ottawa River and I gather they're a big thrill to catch. Did you bring your rods?"

"No. I figured that if any of your new-found cousins were fishermen, they might lend me some gear. I've never caught a muskie. How long are we staying?"

"A couple of nights, I'd guess. We'll have to find a nice place to take them out to dinner."

"They live in the country, Jenny," Sheila reminded her. "There aren't going to be five-star restaurants at every crossroad."

"I know. But maybe in one of the little towns."

"Don't get your hopes up. I've played in a lot of little towns where the food is ghastly."

"Speaking of playing, did you bring any of your CDs?"

"I always lug a few around. Why?"

"You could give some to Ben and his wife. As a hostess present."

"We don't know if they like my music. Or if they even know it. It could be like Chris giving me a fishing rod."

"I'm sure they know it, Sheel. How could they not?"

"Look at that maple tree," Chris interrupted. "What a colour! Do they all go that incredible crimson?"

"Not all," said Sheila, who had seen eastern autumns before. "Some go yellow, like those ones." She pointed to a grove of poplars that had already turned.

"But those aren't maples. I've never seen a red like that before, especially against such a deep blue sky. It's spectacular. Would you call it blood red?"

"I'm sure there are better terms than that," said Sheila. "What about flag red?"

Jenny was peering around. "As farming country, Denmark is much tidier than this, isn't it, Chris? Not that I don't think this is attractive too." They were passing old houses, thinned woodlots, big, silver-sided barns, black-and-white cattle bunched near troughs in muddy corners, occasional solitary elms towering over fence lines and small, yellowing fields dotted with thistles and small cedars. "I like it because it all looks old and lived in. I like the little farms. They're a bit scruffy. I suppose this is what our family farm is going to look like. I've never visualized it before."

"Me either. Funny how Pat wouldn't talk about it, and yet, given the will, it must have been there inside all those years. I wonder if it'll be the same house."

"What do you mean?"

"Well, look at the ones we're going by," Sheila gestured. "A lot of them are new. Maybe when the next generation inherited they tore down the rotting, gloomy old mansions and built modern ranchers."

"Now you're getting carried away. Your 'mansions' were more

likely log houses," Jenny said, "with the beautiful dovetailed corners. That's what the first houses were like. I wonder if there's one on the farm. I'd love to see that."

"Well, don't expect too much. It may be a stucco bungalow."

"What time did you say they'll get here, hon?" Grace asked, running a soft cloth over an end table.

"Mid-afternoon. Whatever are you doing?" Ben stopped in the doorway in amazement.

"Making sure the parlour, as your grandfather called it, is presentable. It gets so dusty, now that it's hardly ever used." Grace straightened up. "It's actually a lovely room."

"It's a nice size and shape, but we should have got rid of all this bloody dark old furniture." Ben turned to gaze out the window that faced the highway. "I like the view better at the back. Who wants to look at the road?"

"Your grandfather, for one. From this very chair." Grace ran her dust-cloth over its straight, ornately carved back. "Watching the neighbourhood go by."

"He didn't do much else, in the end, did he?" Ben came over and put his arm around Grace, nuzzling her ear. "I think he'd really lost interest in everything. Funny, when he'd been so active and involved all his life."

"'Interfering' was your mum's word," dryly.

Ben grinned, his chin on Grace's head. "The classic patriarch. How about if I sat down in his chair and shouted for my tea, the way he used to?"

"You'd go hoarse, for one thing." Grace chuckled. "And hungry, for another. Now unhand me, my sweet, and let me get on with my womanly tasks."

"It's a treat to watch, I tell you." Ben let go and jumped clear. "Anything I can do?"

"Make sure I put out towels for everybody. I know I made the beds, but I don't think I did the towels."

Ben saluted. "Right-o. Consider it done." Grace heard him leaping up the stairs two at a time, whistling.

She stood still in the quiet room for a moment, duster in hand. The formal chesterfield and chairs, the dark wainscotting and the large, polished corner cabinets had never welcomed her. They were too reserved. Echoes of the Victorian era, presumably. Ben was right—they should have sold or given away the furniture when they moved into the house. She remembered that, oddly, she had been the one to protest, to say they should keep everything where it was. It seemed part of the fabric of the house, not theirs to dispense with. And she had wanted a sense of continuity for her children, suspended between two cultures.

She looked out through the formal bay window as Ben had done, across the county road and over the neighbour's fields, but she was seeing again the landscape of her childhood, where the trees never changed colour, and the red was in the soil. These scenes seemed to be popping into her head more often than usual, lately. Was it something to do with the approaching relatives? They were bringing Pat's ashes back to rest, in familiar earth, the family earth. Does it give a person a sense of confidence to know that their ashes are going home, even if they never did in life? Pat could have come back any time, especially after the old man died; Ben's generation certainly bore no ill will. But then, we didn't get in touch either. I guess estrangement works both ways.

Ben ran back down the stairs. "Towels all neatly laid out. Anything else?"

"I was just wondering if the word *familiar*—in the sense of, you know, not strange—has the same root as the word *family*."

"Probably."

"So—*familiar* and *strange* being opposites, maybe *strange* originally meant specifically 'not family.'"

"Mm-hm. Foreign. A foreigner wasn't a member of your family. What started you on this?"

"Pat wanting to be buried in family soil, even after all this time." Grace gave the china cabinet a final swipe with her cloth. "Good enough. I don't suppose we'll sit in here anyway. Aren't people from the West Coast very informal?"

"That's the PR."

They walked down the high hall to the kitchen, the old wood floor creaking comfortably underfoot.

"I thought we could have tea around four, depending on what time they get here, and I made cheese scones, a lemon loaf, and brownies. Heavens, I've turned into your grandmother!"

Ben sniffed. "Wonderful! There's a delicious lemony smell in here. Although I suppose it could be some product, since you've gone into this cleaning frenzy."

"It wasn't exactly a frenzy." Grace laughed. "But do you think I should make some sandwiches as well?"

"No—they'll only have been sitting in a car, after all, and we'll be having dinner in a few hours." Ben looked around. The lemon loaf was sitting on the cooling rack, the pan of brownies waited to be cut into squares, the old biscuit tin was full, he knew, of Grace's wonderfully crumbly and rich scones, the good teacups were arranged on the counter. "It's just like the old days, when I was little, and we used to come over to visit every week. Nana always baked up a storm, and the kitchen smelled so good. And there were lots of cousins running around." He sighed.

"It's a big house for just two," Grace extended his thought. "This house is happiest with a crowd of people in it."

"That's what it was built for. If houses have spirits, this one must be wondering why everyone went away."

"Sounds a bit sad. You think it misses the patter of tiny footsteps and all that?"

"Maybe it's just because you and I miss them."

"Don't tell me you want to turn into a head-of-the-family like your grandfather, with children hovering respectfully around your knees every Sunday?"

"I don't think so. But you might learn to hover a little more respectfully."

Grace let out the hearty, exuberant laugh that Ben loved. He had admired that laugh from the day they met. Nobody he had known in his Canadian farming community enjoyed a laugh the way Grace did.

"Where'll we have this wonderful tea?"

"Outside, don't you think? It's a lovely day, and plenty warm enough." Grace began to cut the brownies.

"Good idea. They'll enjoy looking over the farm from there."

"Outside" meant the flagstone terrace on the brow of the hill that sloped down to the creek, in front of the kitchen windows. It was Ben's most-loved spot. They had built the terrace after his grandfather, who had not approved of eating outdoors, died. When it wasn't too hot, too cold or too insect-ridden, Grace and Ben lived on the terrace, which was "about two weeks out of a year," Grace had observed to a visitor who admired it. Ben had said she was exaggerating.

"I'd better put out the other chairs. Make it look welcoming."

"And maybe give the table a wipe."

"I will, oh Queen of Clean."

"What about the dogs? Are you going to leave them out?"

"Sure. Unless one of the cousins turns out to be a dogophobe. But I'll keep them off the terrace."

Grace did not feel the way Ben did about the dogs. She understood their importance to the farm, and quite liked some particular individuals, but she had never developed the automatic and unconscious connection that Ben felt with them.

"Of course, your cousins may have grown up with dogs too."

"They may. It's so peculiar, not knowing anything about them."

"You're not going to start fussing about this again, are you?" There was an unusual crispness in Grace's voice.

"No, no." Ben kissed her forehead and went out to the terrace. He moved the furniture—wicker chairs with brightly patterned cotton cushions and a glass-topped wicker table—dusted the glass, put the table back in the centre and swept the flagstones clear of a few leaves. Leaning on his broom, he contemplated the pond below, its blue and silver surface ruffled by a light afternoon breeze. Placid and quiet, the little stretch of water looked lonely. In his mind's eye, Ben saw it filled with noisy children, splashing and laughing, practising their swimming strokes. His own two and their friends and cousins had spent all their waking summer hours, for years, it seemed, in and around the pond. And though at times the racket had driven Ben and Grace to the veranda on the quieter side of the house, now he found he missed it.

So does the pond, he thought—it's lying there alone, waiting for some company. Grace doesn't swim, isn't especially fond of water other than bathtub-size, but I could go down now and then. Swim back and forth a few times. Good grief! I'm thinking of ways to keep the pond happy. He shook his head. I'm a practical farmer, and that's just a wide spot in the creek. He took the broom back indoors and went to get the other wicker chairs.

A while later, Grace heard a car slow down and turn into the driveway. Traffic on the road usually whizzed past the house with a high-pitched hum, and a car moving at a different rate instantly caught her attention.

"Ben," she called, drying her hands on a tea towel, "they're here."

Ben had heard the car too, from the terrace where he was half-reading an Ottawa newspaper. He circled the side of the house and reached the lawn as Grace appeared on the front veranda. A chorus of barks came from behind the house. "I shut them up," said Ben to Grace. "Just in case." They smiled at each other, and then at the car.

Sheila pulled on the parking brake. "Oh," she exclaimed in surprise, at her first sight of Grace.

"Here we are!" Jenny opened her door and stepped quickly out. "I'm Jenny," and she advanced on Grace, hand outstretched. "You're Grace."

"I am," Grace responded warmly, shaking hands. "Grace Asamoah. And this, of course, is your cousin Ben."

"Cousin Ben." Jenny beamed, with another vigorous handshake. "I feel like I should give you a hug, except that I don't know you!"

"Yes," he chuckled down at her. "It's very strange, isn't it?"

Chris and Sheila were out of the car; handshakes and greetings followed in friendly confusion. Sheila and Grace shook hands for a long time, smiling, feeling an instant connection. Grace was thinking that Sheila was lovelier in real life than in her photographs, and then, realizing that the cousins hadn't known what to expect, she said, "I'm Ghanaian. Ben and I met when he was with CUSO."

Sheila peered around carefully, almost fearfully, at the ancestral land she had never wished to see. "The home of the pure, the land of the weak," she remembered Pat calling it, in scathing tones, on the rare occasions it was mentioned. "Now, now, Pat," Sandy would say. "Let it go." But obviously, Pat had never let it go. Or else why are we all here, on this pilgrimage with the ashes? Sheila looked at the ground—the driveway, the bushes, the neat lawn—at the hills beyond, anywhere but at the house. Finally, she let her gaze flicker on it, then away.

Evergreen trees stood in a line down its left side. She glanced back, lightly, and away again, to the right. The forest came up to the road, a little farther along. Back at the house. What was I expecting? Hate-filled faces in the windows? Sheila's heart was pounding. Calm down. It's only a house, and the people who lived in it back then are long gone. Just these two pleasant, youngish cousins, one clearly more of a stranger in this land than I am. And anyway, why am I feeling so nervous? I'm not guilty of anything. She shook herself and looked the house straight in the eye. She saw an old, tall, handsome farmhouse, drowsing in the sunshine, front door open, comfortable chairs on the wide veranda.

The windbreak of evergreens cast shadows on the rich green lawn and the flower beds, but where the bright sunshine touched the house, its dark-brown siding lit up, looking velvety and warm.

"Come in, come in. Let's bring your bags up and get you settled, and then we can visit. Are they in the trunk?" Grace asked, moving to the back of the car.

"What a beautiful place," Jenny was gazing around. "How old is the house?"

"A little over a hundred years. The exact date's in the family Bible, but I think it was built about 1900."

"Wow. So it's a true Victorian."

"Has it always been in these colours?" Chris asked. "The dark brown with lighter trim? It's very attractive."

"Yes. It may have varied slightly, with different paints and stains, but basically that's what Granddad chose, and nobody's had the nerve to change it. So far, at least." Ben grinned.

Chris stood on the walk, admiring the turned veranda posts and neatly fitted sills. There was not much gingerbread—the facade seemed too serious and sober for any excesses of curlicues and cut-outs—but all the details were beautifully finished and the proportions elegant. "Two floors and an attic?" he asked Ben.

"Yes. That little window in the peak is the attic. Standing room under the ridge. It's mostly storage, although the idea of storing things in attics is beyond me. Lugging trunks and boxes up and down all the stairs." He shook his head. "It's because an attic's nice and dry, of course, but what a lot of work."

"Is there a basement as well?"

"Oh yes. Goes on and on. But come in. Is this all the bags? You travel light."

"It's not a very long trip." Chris trotted behind him. "And Sheila's particularly good at not bringing much luggage."

"Because of all her travelling, I suppose."

"Probably. I noticed there's a stream running through the fields. Any fish?"

"A few, but there are rivers and lakes nearby that are stocked. Do you like to fish?"

Jenny, mounting the inside staircase behind Grace and Sheila, looked around with pleasure. The tall spaces and shining wood walls were such a change from her own condo. A bit dark, perhaps—the narrow hall, the deep-toned wainscotting—but that was the style of the era. All the upstairs doors stood open and sunshine poured into the hall, lying in angular, honey-coloured patches on the floor and reflecting up the walls. It'd be different on a winter's night, when all the doors were shut. Maybe even a little spooky. But airy and light today. She followed Grace into a bedroom halfway along the hall, where a dormer window gave the view to the east, over a field and then the always-present woods.

"I've put you both in here, if that's all right." Grace looked from Sheila to Jenny. "This is my daughter Elly's room."

"It's perfect," said Sheila quickly. "What a pretty room." Twin beds, one along each wall, with matching, brightly patterned blue-and-yellow bedspreads. A dresser and vanity, painted white, with a chair upholstered in the same fabric as the beds. Posters from fashion shows and art exhibitions on the walls—Elly seemed to be fond of Matisse. A full-length mirror on a smaller door, presumably to a closet. What sort of person might this girl be, Sheila wondered, a mixed-race child like me.

"What's this lovely cloth?" Jenny was patting the bedspread. "It's so intricate and swirly. It's not paisley, though, is it?"

"No. It's what we call market cloth—the kind of cotton you can buy all over West Africa. The patterns used to be wax prints, from Indonesia, but now they're made everywhere. The colours are usually so rich I can't resist buying some, whenever I go back."

Ben peered in the door. "I've got Chris settled in TK's room. Do you want me to put the kettle on, or shall we go walkies first?"

"Walkies?" Jenny echoed. "Do you say 'walkies'? So do I! How funny!"

"From that Englishwoman? What was her name—she used to ride a cow. We saw her on TV and we've been saying 'walkies'"— Ben exaggerated a British accent—"ever since."

"Me too! Isn't that great? We picked up on the same word, thousands of miles apart! I'd love a walk."

"Done." Ben withdrew his head. "Walkies first. Would you like to go up and see the place Pat specified for the ashes?"

"That's a good idea. Do you know the exact spot?"

"Oh yes. It's quite a commanding corner."

Sheila cocked her head. "Commanding how?"

"It's high, and there's a grand view from there," Ben explained. "I don't know why the word command came out."

"'Command' does have a meaning of overlook," Jenny offered. "Probably comes from hilltops being good positions for defence and control of territory."

When they were all gathered on the back veranda, Ben asked, "How do you feel about dogs?"

"Adore them," Jenny was prompt. "Have you got lots?"

"Three. Sheila? Chris? Do you mind if the dogs come with us?"

"No—that'd be fine."

"They're very friendly," Ben said over his shoulder, heading for the pen where the dogs were bouncing around in glee.

"They're also very quiet," Jenny observed. "Just look at them. Leaping around with great enthusiasm, but not saying a word. Most dogs would be yelping their heads off."

"That's Ben's training. They only bark as a warning. They barked when your car turned in, but they quit as soon as they could hear that we were out there with you."

Freed, the dogs gambolled around Ben, and then raced over to investigate the newcomers, tails wagging wildly.

Jenny squatted to greet them "Hullo, darlings!" The others smiled down and gave the occasional pat. Ben strolled back in the dogs' wake, enjoying Jenny's reaction.

"Which way do we go?" Chris asked, caressing one smooth black head.

"Down that path and across the dam."

"Great." Chris fell into step beside Ben.

They crossed the lawn between the house and the terrace, Sheila and Grace following, Jenny, behind, talking to the dogs.

"That's a nice spot." Sheila gestured at the terrace. "You must use it a lot. Are those chair cushions more of that wonderful African cloth?"

"Yes. Some that I actually managed to make up." Grace laughed. "I'm not a seamstress, and I'm just too busy to take time to sew."

"With the farm?"

"No, no—Ben does most of that. Were you visualizing me bottling hundreds of pounds of green beans, or stirring tubs of chutney?" Grace's dimples showed.

"I probably was," Sheila confessed. "Wrong?"

"Wrong. Ben's mother and grandmother did all that, and I learned how, but I didn't turn into a good farm wife, the way they might have hoped. Also, we do contracts overseas from time to time, so that takes me away."

"What kind of contracts?"

"Ben's an agricultural consultant with a special interest in irrigation—I think it comes from playing in that creek all his life." Grace was smiling indulgently. "Just look ahead."

The men had reached the dam and were standing on it while Ben waved his arms and talked.

"He's probably telling Chris all about the creek—where it rises, where it ends up. There's a spring, up in those hills to the west."

Sheila turned toward the steep green hills upstream, past where the fields ended, and tried to imagine a spring. "Is it in a mossy little glade, with ferns around it?"

"That sounds pretty, but I don't remember it that way. The water just came out of a pipe in the earth and ran downhill. There were stones around it, but I think Granddad arranged them."

"Like a shrine?" A song idea was stirring in Sheila's head. A spring that fed a stream, a stream that was the lifeblood of a farm, a farm that nourished a family, a family that honoured the spring . . .

"No. Probably just his sense of order, to keep it from getting too muddy. Animals go to drink there."

Gazelles and unicorns flitted through the ferns, shafts of sunlight fell upon the clear waters of the sacred pool, the kinship of using the same waters . . .

"Mostly raccoons."

Oh. "Right—they like to wash their food, don't they?"

"I think actually they like to make it soggy and squishy, so it's easier to eat. Like dipping biscotti in coffee."

The song idea dwindled to the back of Sheila's mind. "So Ben does irrigation consulting. What do you do while he's thumping around in his gumboots?"

Grace laughed at the description. "I usually get involved in local development, particularly with women's groups. I did an MA in public administration at Carleton a few years ago, and I work for a sort of umbrella organization called the Seeing Beyond Foundation."

"A lot of networking?"

"Yes—you could call it that—both in Canada and internationally. I know people doing a lot of different projects in a lot of different countries, and we can all help each other."

"So if, say, women in India want to start a business raising chickens, and you know a group in Nigeria that did the same thing, you'd connect them."

"Exactly. And with the Internet, people can discuss anything around the world without having to get together physically. Much cheaper and quicker, and much better for our kids' future."

"Oh, you mean in carbon emissions?"

"Yes." Grace was now ahead of Sheila on the dusty path curving down the hill, but she turned. "I meet the most wonderful people. And I do the same work here, when we're home, helping to co-ordinate programs."

The path led onto the dam, where Ben and Chris were pointing and chatting. "And eventually," Ben said, waving downstream, "into the Ottawa River."

"See?" Grace murmured to Sheila. "The life story of the creek."

The ferns and unicorns did another little dance in Sheila's head. Later.

Ben leaned over, rested his forearms on the railing and gazed over the pond.

"Did you build this railing to keep people from falling into the pond?" Sheila patted it.

"More to keep people from falling off the downstream side."

Sheila turned to look down at the creek bed where a thin line of water trickled away. "Oh, I see. It'd be a fall of—what?—five or six feet, wouldn't it?"

"Onto rocks. And at some times of the year this creek really roars. If anybody fell in at the spring freshet, they'd be in serious trouble."

It was hard for Sheila to imagine the peaceful little tinkle swelled into a rush of white water, but she realized that was what Ben meant.

"Does it ever flow over the dam?" Chris asked. "We seem to be a good three feet above the level of the pond."

"My—our—grandfather used to talk about one huge spring flood, when the whole bottom of this valley was covered."

"So you knew him well? Our grandfather?" Sheila asked.

"Sure. I grew up with him. I mean—he lived in this house till the day he died, and my family came to Sunday dinner every week, without fail. It was like a command performance—all his children appeared. Well, not all, of course." He glanced uncomfortably at Sheila.

Sheila was not ready to delve into the past. "Tell us about your own children. We know you have two."

"TK, our son, is studying music," Ben began.

"Oh! Terrific!" Sheila exclaimed. "What kind of music?"

"I think it's called 'world music.' He grew up with the highlife, of course—that's the West African music—and drumming, and also all the North American stuff—rock, heavy metal. I don't even know what to call it all. He's in Toronto doing a degree in ethnomusicology, and we're not quite sure what that might include."

"I don't know anything about West African music, but I've heard some wonderful choirs from South Africa. Is it the same?"

"No. The highlife is a very lively sort of two-step dance music that started, I believe, in Ghana. We'll play you some when we get back to the house."

"And what about the drumming?" Sheila was pleased with this line of conversation.

"There are lots of different kinds of drumming. You've probably heard of the 'talking drums'—they're small drums that imitate language. And then there were the message drums, that could be heard up to five miles away. They were used to send information from village to village, before telephones. They were a very effective way to communicate."

"Like signal fires, in Europe," Jenny put in.

"Probably."

"How old are TK and Elly?" Jenny asked. "Isn't that awful—not knowing anything about my own—what? They're not my niece and nephew, are they?"

"No—I think they're your first cousins once removed. Or is that the same as second cousins? I can't keep your system straight," Grace replied. "Anyway, TK is twenty-four. The initials stand for Thomas Kwame. And Elly's twenty-two. Her full name is Eleanor Abenaa. Their second names are Ghanaian, from the days they were born. Kwame is the male day-name for Saturday, and Abenaa is Tuesday."

"They flow very nicely, especially Eleanor Abenaa. Very musical."
And Sheila repeated the names.

"So TK's in Toronto. Where's Elly?" Jenny asked.

"She's in Ghana, actually. She's doing her MA in art history. She's there for a year. She's living in residence at the university right now, but when she travels around to other parts of the country there are dozens of relatives who want to see her. She's been having fun."

"You and your kids have been all over the world. What about to Vancouver?"

"We've gone through the airport, but we've never stopped. TK spent a summer there a couple of years ago."

"No!" Jenny said, unbelieving. "He was there a whole summer and didn't get in touch?"

"Well, there'd been no contact with your branch for all these years. We had no addresses—we knew vaguely there were relations in BC, but not who or where you were. Except Sheila, of course. We knew Sheila was a cousin."

"TK could have found me easily enough," Sheila said. "Especially if he was interested in music."

"Yes, but it's probably expecting too much of a kid to phone up a stranger—a famous stranger at that—and say, 'Hi, I'm your cousin.'" Ben looked inquiringly at Sheila.

"Especially 'Hi, I'm your black cousin.'" Grace laughed. "Because you didn't know Ben had married a Ghanaian, did you?"

"Nope." Sheila shook her head. "But wouldn't TK have known I'm not all white either?"

"I don't imagine that made any difference to him. I've always thought it a terrible shame—a crime, in fact—that a family could be split apart like yours has been. It's bothered me for years."

The path led off the dam and joined a wagon road, two gravel ruts with grass in between, one of the farm tracks that led from field to field. It sloped uphill as the valley floor narrowed, and higher ground began to close in on both sides. The fields were bordered by stone walls, lined with trees and shrubs. Chris recognized thickets of blackberry bushes, their leaves turning maroon, and birches and old apple trees in their pale yellow fall colours.

By unspoken consent the topic of family was dropped for the time being. A spur of the track turned off to the right, to a silvered old wooden gate standing open between two stone gateposts. In contrast with the loose, tumbled-looking walls, the pillars were squared and cemented.

Ben went through the gate. "The place Pat wanted to be buried is up in the far corner. This was one of the early fields cleared for the farm."

Trooping behind him, Sheila, Chris, and Jenny squinted up in the direction Ben was pointing. It was a large field of cropped green grass, with scattered tufts of thistles and spiky yellow flowers.

Sheila stopped to contemplate the impressive gateposts. "These are pretty fancy. Did they do all this work on the pillars when they cleared the field?"

"Oh no. Years later. In a slow period, when there wasn't much to do. Granddad had them built as a sort of commemoration of the original work on the farm."

"There're plenty of stones around, to be sure." Chris grinned.

"Yes, and cheap labour." Ben nodded. "My father had three brothers, and Granddad believed in keeping them busy. 'The devil finds work for idle hands' and all that."

They climbed diagonally across the sloping field and everyone but Ben was puffing slightly when they reached the top corner. He plucked a blade of grass, stuck the lower end in his mouth and settled himself on the stone wall. "See this great view? It's the only place in the fields where you can see right off the farm."

"I didn't realize we'd come up so high." Chris folded his arms and leaned on the wall beside Ben. "I see what you mean. The forest pretty well surrounds around everything else down there."

The old field fell away in front of them, down to the other stone wall bordering the wagon track. Across the track the land rose again, but not as high, and the mosaic of forests undulated off to the north.

"I count five rolls. Or ridges," Jenny said, "to the horizon. So Pat would have known this view? Just like this?"

"More or less. This field was certainly here. And probably the posts."

"Maybe Pat helped to build them," Chris suggested.

"Could have done. I don't know."

"And we're to plant a sugar maple here, with the ashes." Sheila leaned on Ben's other side. "We were wondering why."

"Whatever the reason, we'll be the ones who enjoy it."

"Enjoy it?" Chris inquired.

"Sure. It'll turn bright red in the fall—like that one." Ben pointed to a spectacular crimson splotch at the edge of the forest, partway down the stone wall to his right.

"Oh—that's like the one we noticed on the drive up from Ottawa."

"And if we wanted to tap it," Ben continued, "we'd get maple syrup from it. We probably won't, because it's a bit far to lug buckets of sap."

"How do you tap a tree?" Chris asked.

"You stick a spigot into it, in the spring, when the sap's rising, and then you boil down the liquid you collect—it's quite thin—into a thickish syrup. Do you not have maple syrup out West?"

"I don't think so." Chris looked at Sheila and Jenny.

"I sort of remember having some when I was little," Sheila said. "And I've seen maple sugar in moulded maple leaf forms, usually in stores at airports."

"We always went to sugaring-off parties when we were kids." Ben had a reminiscent look in his eyes. "They pour the hot syrup onto snow and when it cools, it's chewy and oh—so delicious!"

Sheila was studying the brilliant tree. "I suppose that's what Pat had in mind. Standing bright red on the top of the hill."

"You mean like 'Here I am, I came back in the end'?" Jenny hoped she was following her thought.

"Ye-es. Something like that, and 'You can't avoid seeing me.' I can imagine those ideas in Pat's mind, can't you? Attention-demanding but also generous? With the syrup. Just like in life."

Ben and Grace watched this exchange with interest.

"I'm beginning to see the point of this tree business, now." Chris peered into the distance. "When Jenny read us the will, I thought it was just weird. Plant a tree in the corner of some field? I couldn't believe Pat even remembered where the farm was. But being here, I think you're right, Sheila. It's a statement, maybe on several levels."

"Yes, but the main statement's for our grandfather, and he's long dead," Jenny objected.

"But maybe the will was made years ago, before he died, and Pat was thinking, 'So there! You can't keep me away after all' and never changed it." Chris warmed to his theme.

"Or liked the idea anyway, even after he'd died. I can see Pat enjoying the mental picture of a huge, bright-red tree up here, against the blue sky. It would dominate the hillside," said Sheila, "and maybe little rootlets will even get into the ashes."

"I wonder if Pat knew that one of the first products of the farm was ashes." Ben pushed himself off the wall.

"Just ashes? What for?" Jenny asked.

"Potash. They cut down maple trees and burned them, and then boiled the ashes down to make potash to export to Europe."

Chris stood up. "It seems an awful waste of wood."

"Yes, but in those days, the trees seemed to go on forever. They were more like an enemy, and ashes were a quick source of cash," Ben explained. They all solemnly surveyed the ocean of green before them.

After a few minutes, "Shall we go back to the house and have tea?" Grace suggested, and they started down the field.

TEN: Family Pictures

"How's it been, leaving your home country and living in Canada all this time?" .

Sheila and Grace were doing the dishes after dinner, Grace washing and Sheila drying. This felt like a return to childhood for Sheila and she was enjoying the chattiness of working with another person. Jenny, Chris, and Ben sat around the big oak table with more wine, talking about food.

"Well," Grace began, rinsing a soapy plate and placing it in the rack for Sheila, "that's a big question! It's been interesting and challenging and painful and wonderful. I wouldn't change anything, looking back—or not much, anyway—but it hasn't been the life I expected when I was growing up. Surely everybody thinks that, though. Did you expect to be a singer?"

"I did want to sing, by the time I was sixteen or so. I didn't know if I'd be able to make it an actual career. But that's nothing like as unexpected as moving halfway around the world for the rest of your life."

"Maybe not. I suppose when I was sixteen I thought that after I'd got my degree at Legon—that's the University of Ghana—I'd marry some professional Ghanaian, a lawyer, say, and live in a nice house in Accra. Have children, travel overseas, go back to my village often. Have my nieces and nephews come to live with us, and go to school, if they wished. That's our custom. We have very large extended families." Grace grinned. "It took Ben years to figure out all of my relatives."

"Did you live in Ghana, then, after you were married?"

"Yes. Ben extended his contract, and we did have that 'nice house in Accra.' It was really lovely—I was teaching, Ben was working with one of the ministries, we had lots of friends, both Canadians and Ghanaians, and our social life was very busy." Grace gave a happy little sigh. "We had a marvellous time, and I think it was the best thing for our marriage."

"How's that?"

"I've known other Ghanaian girls who married expatriates— usually volunteers, Brits, Americans, Canadians—and when their tours were over, they went right back to their home countries. Sometimes they got married just before they left, and it all seemed very romantic—sprinting to the plane as soon as the wedding toasts were done. So the marriage had hardly begun, the girl was alone in a new culture, the man's loyalties were torn, and most of them broke up, eventually. But Ben and I had those first years in my culture, which he was already pretty familiar with, so when we came to his culture, we had a good foundation. And we had TK too. He was born four months before we came here."

"So he's grown up Canadian."

"Oh yes—he and Elly definitely think of themselves as Canadians. Ghanaian Canadians, because obviously they look different. But they're as obsessed with hockey as any pure Canadian like all of their friends."

"If there is such a thing. Did they experience any kind of— racism?"

"Some. It's very pervasive, you know. Canadians are so polite, but it's here. What about you?"

"Me too. More when I was young. Less now, but who knows if that's because people are getting more broad-minded or if they're just used to what I look like."

"Elly and TK's worst times were when they were young teenagers. The little kids they grew up with around here took them for granted after about ten minutes, but when they went farther away, to the high school, a lot of people were—let's say, disconcerted— to find that an Ontario farm had produced two black kids. It hasn't been entirely easy."

"I'm sure it hasn't. But do your kids feel connected with both sides of their family?"

"I think they do. We tried really hard to give them the sense of roots in two different places. But that's a danger too, you know.

Depending on the person, you could end up in a sort of permanent confusion between your two sides, and never feel totally at home in either."

"Did that happen to you?"

Grace thought about this before she answered. "It did for a while. I was excited about living here and exploring all the new and amazing—to me—things to do and learn. Getting comfortable with the climate and the food, living with Ben's family, meeting his friends, going to Ottawa. I think I'm a pretty open person, and I like new experiences. That all worked quite fine, actually. But when I went back—home—I felt very odd. The sounds and the smells and the air were all so familiar I slipped back into my Ghanaian skin in a second. But it wasn't home anymore, so I felt as if I were split. Or wrapped in an invisible layer of something. I couldn't totally connect with life there." Grace stopped, hands in the dishwater. "Suspended, I guess, is the best way to put it. That's why it was hard with TK and Elly. I wanted them to feel the richness of belonging to two races, but without being stuck halfway between. Did you feel that sort of two-way tug?"

"No, because I grew up in a totally Caucasian household. There was absolutely no mention, ever, of my other half, and it certainly wasn't seen as 'richness.'"

Grace nodded but made no comment.

"I'd have liked to meet your children," Sheila said impulsively, surprising herself. "I'm not interested in people's kids normally, but yours sound really interesting."

"You'd have a few things in common, that's for sure. Well, I'm sure you'll meet them one day, now that your overly estranged family has linked up, finally."

Jenny looked up as Grace said this and turned to Ben. "Yes, thank you very much for letting us descend on you like this. We're a bunch of strangers, even if we are related."

"To be honest, it was Grace who was really keen on it. She was adamant that you must come."

"So the reconnection of our family went through Africa, you might say?"

"It did. The continent where all our ancestors came from in the first place."

Seeing Grace pull the plug, Sheila shook out the dishtowel and hung it on the rack.

"Finished over there? We were just talking about Ghanaian food." Ben stretched an arm toward Grace. She pulled out a chair and sat down beside him.

"Yes. Do you ever make it? And what is it?" Jenny asked her.

"From time to time I do. Particularly groundnut stew. That's peanut butter stew, in Canadian terms. But our main dish—our 'national dish,' which is called fufu, I can't make properly here. It's usually made from yams. They are big starchy tubers, not what you call yams here, pounded for a long time with water, till it turns into a kind of thick paste and you shape it into balls."

"It takes two people, very labour intensive, and in the end it doesn't have any real taste."

Grace wrinkled her nose at Ben for this but agreed. "It's true. It's a base for whatever soup or stew you serve with it."

"Like mashed potatoes?" Chris was trying to imagine the finished product.

"Like a lump of very gluey mashed potatoes," Ben explained. "It's really good once you get used to it, but it takes a while."

"It is an acquired taste," Grace assented. "But when you grow up on it, you love it forever."

"And the sound of the pounding—it's very rhythmic—is a constant background household noise. One of the kids will be standing, pounding, with a slim pole, into a wooden base, sort of like a big bowl with a flat bottom, and the mother or grandmother will be sitting, turning the fufu with her right hand. Not even looking, because the rhythm is so regular, although if the pole landed on her hand it could break her bones." Ben wondered if he was getting the picture, so clear in his mind, across to his cousins.

Listening politely, and understanding from his expression that he was visualizing something important to him, Jenny asked, "Do they do this in the kitchen?"

Grace chuckled. "There isn't a kitchen, as such. It's usually done in the courtyard. The typical village house, you see" —she drew on the table with a forefinger— "is a square, around an open courtyard in the middle. The house is one room deep, with a covered veranda around the inside, facing into the courtyard."

"Oh." Sheila was charmed. "I see. It must be lovely."

Grace nodded. "And everything takes place in the courtyard. Pounding fufu, cooking, doing laundry, visiting with your friends."

"What if it rains?" asked Chris. "Or is this in a desert? I'm sorry— my African geography isn't too exact."

"No, in the rainy season it rains every day but it doesn't rain very long, so you just move inside, or onto the veranda, while it rains, and then back into the courtyard when it dries up. They're really wonderful houses. Very suited to the climate."

"Not a lot of privacy, perhaps," said Chris.

"You can go into your room and shut the door, if you like. But no—not privacy as in your houses. Everybody can see who's going in and out. So if this kitchen was a courtyard, say in my granny's house, we could be sitting here having a chat—except if it was my granny's house I'd be a child over there in the corner, pounding fufu." Grace laughed heartily. "So the grown-ups are here, somebody's hanging the laundry on clotheslines in that corner," pointing, "little children are playing a game over there, somebody's sweeping the veranda here, another child's being given a bath by his mum there, some old men are coming in the door, there, to discuss something with my grandfather—he was a chief, the Nifahene—and I'm still pounding fufu over there." She laughed again. "Pounding fufu takes up a lot of time in every child's life."

"What part of the country are you from?" Chris asked.

"I'm from a town called Techiman. It's on one of the main roads to the north, almost in the middle of the country. It has a huge weekly market that's been going forever, and a secondary school and . . . I'll get our pictures. That's easier than describing it all." Grace went into her office, reappearing with an armful of photograph albums and a map of Ghana.

Chris spread the map out on the table and peered at it. "Here's Techiman." He put his finger on the spot and leaned back so the others could see where it was.

Ben was turning pages in an album. "We should look at these more often, Grace. They bring back great memories."

"Now," Sheila, beside Ben said, pointing at a group of young people in bright cottons, black and white faces beaming together, in front of a tall green hedge. "Who are all these people, and where?"

"That was our school staff, at a party at somebody's house. There's Grace, that's me. Gosh, we all look young and eager, don't we?"

"And drunk, probably," from Grace. "My, how we did drink in those days. Mostly beer. And it came in quart bottles."

"And the custom is, when you're sitting around a table in a bar or somebody's house, that whenever your glass gets down to half-full or so, somebody fills it up, so at the end of the evening, you have absolutely no idea how much you've drunk. It's not like here, where everybody has their own bottle. We had so much fun." Ben's tone was filled with nostalgia. "Especially visiting in the villages and small towns. The bars were so basic, sometimes—just a cement floor and tin walls, no roof. I can remember looking up into the night sky from one of those little places, in a crowd of friends around a rickety metal table, and thinking I'd never been happier in my life. I thought I'd stay forever." Grace smiled at him, seeing the same scene.

Gazing at another photograph, Sheila asked, "And who is this?"

A handsome woman stood on the roofed cement veranda of a long, low building facing onto an open, grassy space, against a backdrop of handsome trees. "This is the elementary school I went to, and that's my Auntie Constance in front of her classroom."

Another page. Jenny snuggled close to Grace. "So these are the typical village houses you were talking about? All these reddish-coloured buildings?"

"Yes. You see that some have metal roofs and some thatch, and often they're plastered and painted white, but they're all built with red clay bricks. Sometimes people will build two sides of the square first, so it's like an L, and then add on as they get the money. Even a lot of the tall apartment buildings in the cities will be the same, with balconies all opening into the middle. Now, here's our secondary school." The picture was taken from one corner of a quadrangle of cream-coloured, two-storey buildings, connected by red gravel paths edged with knee-high, green-grey plants. "The paths were all lined with that ice-plant by the first Peace Corps teacher there."

"It's quite pretty," said Jenny.

"The school buildings are exactly the same, all over the country," Grace explained. "The Ghana Educational Trust schools. They were built in Nkrumah's time, in the early 1960s. He was very aware of the importance of education, although I don't think he emphasized it enough for girls. Schooling for girls is the most important element for development."

"More important than for boys?" Chris had always taught in mixed schools.

"Actually, yes, because with girls, there are three main benefits that don't apply to boys." Grace began ticking off on her fingers. "Studies upon studies—by the UN, for instance—show that when women are educated, the birth rate drops, and that is huge, because overpopulation is still an awful problem in many places. Not just in Africa but all over the planet. Second, it's women—mothers—who are mainly in charge of health and nutrition in the home, so if they have better understanding of those issues, the well-being of the whole community is improved. And third, if a woman is educated, her daughters are likely to stay in school as well—more than if the mother hasn't been to school—so there's a widening upward spiral throughout the country. Any country."

"I've never considered any of those ideas before. I just figure all education is a Good Thing." Sheila could make it clear when her words began with capital letters.

"And you're right, of course. I apologize for my little lecture—it's a topic that really concerns me. It's not a matter of educating girls *instead* of boys—just that it should at least be equal, and that isn't happening everywhere."

"No." Jenny sighed. "Look at Afghanistan, or Saudi Arabia. But we can't do very much to help girls there."

"We can do a lot for countries in Africa, though, especially through small NGOs." Ben had been listening.

"What are NGOs?"

"Sorry, Sheila—jargon. Non-governmental organizations. They can get the funds and benefits straight to whatever they're working on because they don't spend a lot of money or energy on administration. The Stephen Lewis Foundation, for example."

"Oh yes—Grannies to Grannies. I've seen them on TV."

"That's one. There are many other little private, focused grassroots projects that are very effective. They just don't get a lot of press. But back to the school." Grace put her finger on the photograph that had started her off. "Sometimes the buildings are arranged differently—they're not always in a square, like this. These two," pointing, "are classroom blocks, that's the dining hall and this one is the offices."

"Everything with louvred windows, I see," Chris remarked. "For maximum breeze, I expect."

"Yes. The rooms stay fairly cool." Grace turned the page. "Here's the main street of Techiman, looking north, with the *ahenfie*—the chief's house—on the right. The market's just downhill, on the other side of the road."

"So this" —Jenny touched the photograph gently— "is the chief's house?"

"Yes."

"It doesn't look very big or fancy."

"No—the chief's houses aren't palaces. They're like the ordinary ones, with maybe a few extra rooms. Here are some pictures of the house I grew up in." White walls, blue window trim, flower beds beside the doors, red-floored courtyard.

"It looks very welcoming," said Chris.

"It is." Ben smiled.

"And here's the hospital," said Grace, going on with the tour. "The Holy Family Hospital, it's called, near the north end of town. It was run by American nuns." A screened building beside a tree-shaded lawn with a group of women smiling in front. "And that's the road that goes on north, up to Wa and then Tamale."

Chris was following the route on the map. "Oh, is that the way you pronounce it? It looks like the Mexican word *tamale.*"

"Yes, it's spelled the same, but the accent is on the first syllable," Ben explained.

"I think there are older pictures of Techiman in Mrs. Meyerowitz's book too. Let me see if I can find it," said Grace. She disappeared into her office again and returned with *At the Court of an African King,* by Eva L.R. Meyerowitz. "The photographs are mostly of people, so they don't actually show the town."

"Who was this woman?" Chris asked. "That doesn't sound like a very African name."

"No, it isn't. It's Polish. She was an artist, who had a wacko notion that one of the Ghanaian peoples was descended from the ancient Egyptians. She spent a lot of time in Techiman around the 1940s," Ben explained, "and she always referred to the paramount chief as a 'king.'"

"The men are all very good-looking." Sheila was examining the photograph section. "And they're all wearing a sort of toga thing, with one shoulder bare. Do they still do that?"

"In the villages they do, especially the older men, and for special occasions. It's called 'wearing cloth.' But for everyday life in the cities, the men usually wear pants and shirts."

"The author spells the town 'Tekyiman,'" Jenny said, "but it's 'Techiman' on this map."

"Oh, the editorial eye never rests, does it?" Chris teased.

"That was the old spelling. In our language, which is called Twi, 'ky' is pronounced with a 'ch' sound," Grace explained. "But nowadays, everything is spelled the English way."

"Here's somebody bathing a little kid in the courtyard, just like you were saying, Grace," Jenny said, reading the caption, "'The Queenmother Nana Afua Abrafi washing Kwabena.' He looks like a cheery little chap, doesn't he?"

"No doubt he was." Grace gave the photograph a glance. "I didn't know him till he was much older than that."

"And this looks like a work party at a school. Look at the little brooms."

"Oh yes, sweeping is the first thing you hear every morning. Even in the cities, along the streets. As soon as it's light, somebody's out there, swish swish swish. It's a lovely sound."

"What do they sweep?"

"Leaves, little branches, whatever blew in during the night. Dust tracked in the evening before. We've still got one of those brooms." Ben went to a cupboard near the door. "You bend over to use it, with one hand." He showed them a bundle of stiff fibres, about two feet long, with a woven top.

"Interesting." Jenny jumped up. "May I have a go?" She bent over and tried a few swipes with either hand. "Do you suppose they invented this because they're quick to make?"

"Probably. Just tie the dried reeds together and there you are. No muss, no fuss."

"And no dust," added Sheila.

"That's for sure," Ben said. "I've never seen such clean houses in my life. Ghanaians have never heard of dust bunnies."

"I'm afraid I'm all too familiar with dust bunnies myself," Sheila admitted.

"Dust bunnies," Jenny scoffed. "Dust cows, in your case," with a big grin at Sheila.

"Oh, now we're in Accra. Here's our house. And here again are the young Grace and Ben, laughing on the veranda. This is in a part of the city called 'The Ridge.'" Grace sat back to give the others a view.

Sheila examined the picture. "It's different. I thought it was going to be like the village ones, but it's quite a modern bungalow."

"Yes, the word bungalow comes from India, I believe. From the British Colonial Service there," said Ben. "It probably means a kind of tropical house. You know—'one-storey building with screened veranda' or something like that."

"So the colonial chaps didn't use the African-type houses? They built these Indian ones all over Africa instead?"

"I never thought of it like that, but yes. The Ghanaian-style houses could have been adapted perfectly well, but maybe Europeans prefer to look out, not into a courtyard."

Sheila was still focused on the picture. "This house looks like it's quite high off the ground."

"They all were. About four or five feet. For coolness, and to keep the bugs out."

Grace turned to Ben and said, "But shouldn't we be looking at the family pictures, instead of these ones of Ghana?" She and Ben had dug into drawers and closets and produced many old albums in preparation for the visit.

"Yes, they're all here." Ben moved a pile of leather-bound volumes and a large box from the wide windowsill onto the table.

Chris leaned back in his chair and looked at the room, thinking that the kitchen itself evoked a sense of family: the old-fashioned, high-ceilinged space of it, the years of polish on the wood. Maybe it was because kitchens are the source of food, the sustenance of any group of people.

Sheila glanced around at what Chris was admiring. She considered what Grace had said about their "overly estranged" family and felt more ready to start exploring. Perhaps it was the wine. "Did people in the family talk about Pat?"

"No. I don't think I even knew I had relatives out West till I was—oh—maybe eighteen or twenty. It was a big surprise."

"It was to us too."

"Didn't you ever wonder about your family?" asked Grace in disbelief. "Who they were or where they were?"

Sheila looked at Chris and Jenny. They shook their heads, and all three peered at Grace, solemn as owls.

"Not really. We knew Sandy had family. But Pat never talked about any and actually refused to discuss it if we ever asked. So we didn't." But Sheila didn't intend to be the spokesperson. "What about you two?"

Jenny blinked. "No. I must have been an oblivious child. I guess I just accepted things the way they were."

"Chris?"

"Me too. Pat could be really fierce and stern about some things, and it wasn't anything to do with me—directly, anyway."

"You Anglo-Saxons," Grace said, shaking her head. "So self-contained. I grew up in a house, as you saw, with family in and out constantly, visiting for the day or sleeping over, and dozens of cousins, aunts and uncles. I just can't imagine your lonely little lives."

"But we weren't lonely," Sheila and Jenny said in unison, and Sheila continued, "That's just the way things were."

"I know, but it seems chilly to me."

"Yes, well, there were chilly aspects, particularly in this family, weren't there?" Sheila took a sip of wine, her expression guarded, and surveyed the jumbled pile of albums—black, light brown, blue—that lay in the middle of the table.

"The early ones each have a date on them," Ben said, following her gaze. "The family was very organized in the beginning, when the photographs were really all portraits, or pictures of special events. But the more everybody got cameras and took snapshots, the less time anybody took to put them into albums."

"And by the time we got here," Grace added, "the photos were loose in boxes. And still are."

Ben reached for a dark-brown book with cracked binding. "This is 1918 to 1930." The pages were thick, sturdy paper with alternate sheets of thin, crisp onionskin, to keep the pictures from touching. The sepia photographs had been glued on in perfectly straight, symmetrical rows, marching in precision across the creamy background. The captions beneath were in neat hand printing that must have been done against a ruler, the bottoms of all the letters ending in matching level lines. Each caption concluded with an exact date: "August 12, 1919," "Christmas Day, 1922."

"Photographs were a big deal then." Chris leaned forward to scrutinize the opening page. "Look how serious everybody is."

"Don't get your nose on it, Chris," Jenny protested. "I can't see through you."

Chris sat back. "Sorry."

"We've never seen even one picture of any of these people," Jenny explained to Ben and Grace.

"Weren't there any pictures in Pat's things?" Ben asked.

"No. We went through everything after the funeral, but we didn't find any pictures or letters or anything like that."

"So this is the famous granddad? Here, in the middle?" Chris pointed at a handsome, dark-haired man, sitting very straight, unsmiling.

Ben put on his glasses. "Yes. And that's Nana beside him, with the children arranged around them. This is my dad," he said, pointing to a slender boy cross-legged on the floor in front of his parents, all blond curls and serious expression. "And this is Andrew, and George, and Tom, and . . . and Pat, of course."

"What was the occasion? Why are they all dressed up?" Jenny couldn't see the caption from her angle.

"'Robert's Wedding Day,'" Chris read. "Who was Robert?"

"One of Nana's brothers. He lived over by Arnprior. Here's the whole wedding party, with Robert in the middle and—gosh, I can't remember the bride's name." Ben checked the handwriting. "Oh yes—Alice. I only met them once or twice, when they were much older."

"Look at all these people. I'd never thought about family on our grandmother's side. They'd be our cousins too, of course. There are probably dozens of them." Sheila looked inquiringly at Ben.

"Oh yes," he said, nodding, "there are. They're spread all over Ontario."

"If there's a huge family event we see them," said Grace. "The son of this Robert and Alice, for example, had his fiftieth wedding anniversary a while ago, and we went to that. It was biiiiig." She smiled happily.

"Grace wore her kente—she was the star of the day."

"What's your kente?" Chris asked.

"It's fancy cloth that Ghanaians wear for special occasions."

"Like those gorgeous pieces we saw earlier?"

"No, no—that's printed. Kente is woven in strips, in traditional patterns. I'll get it out and show you." Grace went upstairs this time and came back draped in materials of rich gold, green and maroon.

"Oh, my goodness!" Sheila reached out to handle the fabric. "What glorious colours."

Grace showed how the long strips, created on a narrow loom, were sewn together. "For women, our customary outfit is in three pieces, like these. A blouse, a floor-length skirt and a wrap—what you might call a stole. You can wear that however you like—around your middle or over your shoulder, for instance."

"It's heavy material. Isn't it hot?" Jenny asked.

"We don't work in kente. It's only for parties or ceremonies."

"When people just walk around looking stately." Ben grinned. He slowly turned the page in the photo album. "Shall I keep going?"

"Yes," Jenny and Chris chorused.

"Why don't you sit in the middle, Jenny, and turn the pages. I can answer, if there's anything you want to ask about, but the captions are pretty thorough in these early albums." Positions were shuffled, more wine poured, the cluster hunched around the table grew closer.

The later albums were frustrating.

"Where do you think this was?"

"Who's that?"

"Is there any date on this one?"

"God!" Sheila exclaimed. "This is a lesson, isn't it? Why save all these pictures with no notation? It's infuriating!"

"We-ell," Grace reminded her, "somebody probably meant to do captions, and just never got around to it."

"I'm sure you're right. But it's so sad, not to know who these people are."

"I'm beginning to recognize some of the faces," Chris remarked. "I can see them getting older."

"This is our heritage here" —Sheila waved an irritated hand— "and we can't decipher it. I can see our uncles, like Chris, but the faces don't tell us much, do they? It's like getting your hands on just part of something."

When they had perused all the albums, in more or less chronological order, Ben reached across the table and pulled the box of photographs over in front of Jenny.

"Now these will annoy Sheila even more because they aren't even pasted into books," he said, smiling, and lifted the lid.

"Oh, no!" Sheila clapped a hand across her eyes in mock distress.

The box, about twice the size of a shoebox, was half full of loose photographs of various shapes and sizes, mainly in colour.

"But we were around for a lot of these," said Grace, "so they won't be mysterious, like the earlier ones. Or as interesting, probably."

Weddings, corn roasts, babies, family trips ("There you are at the Grand Canyon, Grace—I know that's not Ontario"). Many snapshots of two little café-au-lait faces: atop bright padded jackets, grinning beside a snowman; still grinning, on either side of a palm tree, with a white wall in the background ("That's at my mother's house, in our town").

"Isn't it amazing," Jenny said, turning to Sheila, "to think that now we have family in Ghana!"

A broad smile spread over Grace's face.

"What's this?" Chris's hands were scrabbling around in the bottom of the box, and he lifted out a large, old, leather-covered book.

"Oh, there it is! That's the family Bible," Ben explained. "I was looking for it the other day, because I thought you might like to see it, and I couldn't think where it had got to. It's got the record of all the Muirs since, let's see, 1875. It starts when they were still in Scotland." The thin paper whispered as Ben flipped gently, finally flattening out a two-page spread, and passing it to Jenny. "Here's our batch."

The precise printing, in thick, rusty-black pen strokes, gave details of milestones, mostly births, marriages, and deaths. Just names and dates—no descriptions.

"Oh, no," whispered Jenny. "Look at that. Every mention of Pat's been crossed out."

Date of birth, first communion, partially obscured by two neatly ruled, parallel, heavy black lines.

They all stared in silence.

Sheila shivered. "The lines are so controlled. It's almost worse than if the dates had all been scratched out in a rage."

Ben nodded solemnly. "Granddad could be pretty icy."

Grace shook her head gently. "Unbelievable," she murmured, gazing at the straight lines. "I don't see how anybody could hate his own child so much."

"Remember," Ben said, "he was acting according to the dictates of what he saw as his god. His religion was a big part of his life."

"I realize that, hon. It doesn't mean it's okay."

"No, but that's the big appeal of religions, isn't it?" Sheila said. "If you believe there's a god, you just do what it tells you, and that absolves you from thinking for yourself."

"Certainly that's one reason. But look at the damage your grandfather's beliefs have done. Those lines have been shaping the generations."

Jenny studied Grace. "Keeping us apart, you mean?"

"Yes. What could be worse than cutting off your family? Ugh. Close it up. It makes me feel sick." Grace rose and crossed the kitchen to scrub in the sink.

Sheila continued to stare at the page, her lower lip held in her teeth. "Yup. Grace's right. Let's close it. Past history," she said with a toss of her head. "More wine, anybody?" She lifted the bottle.

"Fill 'em all up, Sheila," Ben said. "There's lots more. Come on back, Grace—we've closed the book."

Grace hung up the dishcloth. "Good." She returned to her chair, raised her filled wineglass and said, firmly, "To the future."

"To the future," they echoed and a reflective little pause enfolded them.

Diffidently, Ben asked, "Do you have any sort of ceremony in mind for burying Pat's ashes?"

"Oh," said Sheila in surprise, "no, we never talked about anything like that."

"We didn't make any plans, because we wanted to see what you intended, but we'd thought about having a family gathering. People know you're here, of course."

"Pat might have liked that idea, don't you think?" Chris asked Sheila. "A bit of a send-off?"

"Hard to say. But I think we should do what we want, now. I'd like to have some relatives. What about you two?"

"Well," Jenny looked uncomfortable, "no. I was visualizing just the three of us."

"That's fine, that's fine. We really didn't mean to intrude. Whatever you want." Grace reached out to pat Jenny's arm. "It can be as private as you wish."

"But, Jenny," Sheila protested, "it would be a way to bring the family together, after all these years. We can make something good come out of Pat's—death."

"We could get the family together sometime anyway. It doesn't need to be when we're burying Pat."

Chris and Sheila exchanged astonished glances.

"You like people, Jenny," Chris said. "You're probably the friendliest person I know."

"That's different. Pat had only us in life—I mean, besides Sandy—and it should be just us to say goodbye." Jenny's mouth was settling into a rare, stubborn line.

"Well, this isn't hard to solve," Grace offered. "How about if you three bury the ashes, and then we have people here, separately, in Pat's honour."

Sheila and Chris peered at Jenny. "Yes," she allowed, after a moment. "Our own little farewell first, and then a family one."

"Good." Sheila pressed on, in case Jenny changed her mind. "When were you thinking of having this gathering?"

"I think we'll have to give people a couple of days' notice," Grace replied, "although most of the relatives are prepared. How about the day after tomorrow?"

"Is it all right with you to have us stay that long?" Sheila asked. "We don't want to impose."

"Of course, of course, why do you even ask?" Grace sounded almost cross. "You're not imposing. This is your home."

Ben glanced at his watch. "Do you want me to phone round, hon?" And to his urban cousins, "Country people don't stay up late."

"Yes, thanks. For four o'clock, don't you think? Then people can have drinks or tea, whichever they'd like."

"Right." Ben disappeared.

"And you can do your own little ceremony tomorrow. I'll leave you to decide about that together. It's a private thing and you're probably ready for some time alone." Counter-clockwise, Grace shook hands all round. "I'm truly thrilled to have you here, and so is Ben. Stay up as long as you like, and I'll see you in the morning."

"Well, we are truly thrilled to be here, too," Sheila blinked quickly, "and thank you so much for having us. What time do you and Ben get up?"

"Oh," Grace laughed. "Ben gets up early. If you hear him, don't feel you have to jump out of bed. Take your time—we'll all end up here in the kitchen sooner or later, and you can tell me what you'd like for breakfast. The coffee will be on," and she gestured at the machine. "Good night, and sleep well." She gave them each what Jenny described later, marvelling, as "the most loving smile I've ever seen," and left.

"Well," Sheila said, eyebrows raised, "you certainly surprised me, Jenny, about your private goodbye."

"I surprised myself. But when I started to picture a whole crowd of strangers, I realized that I'd wanted it to be just us three."

"It's going to work out fine, having it both ways," Chris soothed. "What would you like to do?"

"I don't know, exactly. I'd just pictured the three of us up in that corner of the field, looking down at the ground."

"In which we'd just deposited the ashes?"

"I assume so, Chris."

"Shall we each say something? I can't believe none of us have any ideas on this." Sheila frowned. "But of course, we've never done it before."

"Maybe Jenny and I just assumed you'd have planned something."

"Why?"

"Because we look up to you as our leader?" Chris grinned at her.

"As if!"

"Come on, you guys. We're organizing a ceremony here."

Curious, Sheila asked, "Are you seeing a major event, Jen? If it's only us, there won't be chanting choirs and incense."

"No, I know that." Nonplussed. "But I think we should do some-thing. Not just bury the urn, brush our hands and walk off."

"There's the tree too, remember," Chris put in.

"Oh! The tree!" said Sheila. "I had forgotten it, for a minute."

"Here's a thought. What about if we three bury the ashes tomor-row, with a little private ceremony that Jenny'll like. That we'll all like," Chris amended. "And then, when the rest of the family is here, we'll plant the tree."

"Good." Sheila nodded. "I like it."

They turned expectantly to Jenny, who pondered. "Yes. So for tomorrow" —she was enjoying the unexpected position of planner— "let's each think of some little goodbye. Something to say and maybe something to put in the ground with the ashes. That's all. No chants or incense. Then we'll cover it up and that'll be that."

"And will that be enough for you?" Chris asked.

"Yes. I'd never thought of a great big huge deal. I just wanted it to be only us three saying goodbye. But for the tree, I think it's a great idea to have the relatives there."

"What time do you want to do this?" Sheila asked, yawning. "Not the crack of dawn, I trust."

"No, but how about sunset? That'd be appropriate. When day is ending, and all that."

"'Sunset and evening star,'" Chris quoted.

"Yes! One of us could read a poem. I'm sure Ben and Grace have poetry books. Do you want to sing something, Sheel?"

"Maybe. I'll think about it."

"And I'll do something too," Chris said quickly. "I won't sing, but I'll think of something significant."

"Great. We're going to have a nice, quiet, private farewell to Pat."

"Whether or not Pat would have wanted something this quiet is another question, of course," Sheila muttered. "But then, we'll have the tree planting. We know that would be approved of."

"How do we know that?"

"Because it was in the will, Chris. When a person asks to have a memorial tree planted, it's obviously a desire to be noticed."

"Or at least, not forgotten," Jenny added.

ELEVEN: Meeting the Publisher

A woman appears in the doorway of Beth Chandler's office. Tall, white-haired, slender, she is carrying a cardboard box, a white jacket and a briefcase. She knocks gently on the frame, smiling. Although the day is warm, her pale yellow blouse is crisp and smooth, tucked into a white linen skirt. Beth envies the woman her tiny waist. She probably would have been considered "willowy" in her youth.

"Come in, come in." Beth shoots out of her chair, almost coming to attention. "Mrs. Hatley-Thorpe?" and she rounds the desk, hand outstretched.

"Hello, yes, I'm Helen Hatley-Thorpe. Thank you for seeing me." Her voice is soft and her accent English. She folds herself neatly into the chair, the box on her lap, and looks interestedly at Beth. "How nice to see a young woman running a publishing house."

Surprised, Beth says, "Oh, it's not just me. I couldn't do it all alone."

"No, that's not what I meant." Helen Hatley-Thorpe smiles. "I meant how refreshing that the head of your company isn't a man. It's my age, I suppose, but I somehow think of publishing firms as being a male preserve."

"They used to be but not anymore."

"Good. Now," leaning forward, "I shan't take up much of your time. Thank you very much for your letter—I would have just dropped the manuscript off at your front desk if you hadn't suggested a meeting. I realize that until you have read it, you won't know if you want to publish it, so there's nothing for us to discuss at this point, but I will quickly give you a bit of background." She pauses to look out the window.

She had arisen that morning in her pleasant Victoria neighbourhood, made herself tea and toast in the silent house and noted with satisfaction that the day promised to be fine. She'd be able to do her various Vancouver errands on foot and not worry about downpours, a raincoat or taxis. She put on a linen jacket and comfortable shoes and placed the box containing the manuscript in a briefcase with a shoulder strap. The briefcase was big enough to hold her wallet, glasses, keys and a book as well, so she could dispense with carrying a handbag, an urban habit she disliked. She locked the door of the small, pretty house, which still felt strange after all her years of never-locked homes in remote areas of the coast, and set off toward the bus station. It was a walk of a mile or so, a pleasure on a fresh morning because most of her route lay along residential streets with tidy lawns, colourful gardens, and generous, shade-giving trees.

Lovely, she thought, and realized it was the first time in months that she had been aware, through the haze of grief, of the calm beauty surrounding her every day. She stopped suddenly and took a deep breath. The air was mild and faintly floral, with an under-tone of fresh coffee from someone's open window. How lovely, Helen thought again. It occurred to her that perhaps the mourn-ing process had evolved naturally to a different stage; perhaps she had survived its depths and this was the beginning of healing. She mused for a moment and then went on, almost sorry when she reached the bus station. It was all hard edges, noisy with people and smelling of exhaust, a contrast to the fragrant streets.

The bus took her comfortably to the ferry, an easy, worry-free trip and a pleasure on a bright day. On board, Helen didn't even open her book, finding that the boat offered her time. A special kind of time, suspended on the ocean, away from the empti-ness of the house with all its attendant, ironic busy-ness—legal details, financial issues, meetings, letters, phone calls—and not yet plunged into the maelstrom of Vancouver's downtown. A surprise respite, a small treat. The wide blue channels between the islands were dotted with small vessels—powerboats ploughing purpose-fully, sailboats dancing on angles; the forested shores shone deeply green, and the summer sky was clear to the horizons. It's gorgeous, she said to herself in wonder.

"My husband died a year ago." She nodded at Beth's expression of condolence. "Yes, thank you. It was a shock. But the reason I'm here is that he had finished writing his memoirs, as I told you" —she placed both hands on the cardboard box— "and had been planning to seek publication. I don't know which publishers he intended to approach, but I started with you because your firm has an interest in West Coast history, and Gerald—my husband—was for many years an 'Indian agent' as they were called then. We lived on a number of reserves up and down the coast, and I think his manuscript gives good insights into that era and that way of life. I read the whole thing through just recently, and although there are a few places where I might have disagreed with his account if he were still here to talk about it" —she smiled— "I have resisted the urge to change anything. These are his memories, after all. So—here it is."

As she handed it to Beth, she explained, "The early chapters are about his life in England and our time in the Gold Coast—it's Ghana, now—but most of it is about British Columbia."

"Thank you." Beth placed the box on the left side of her desk. "You're right that we're interested in coastal history, so we'll certainly read the manuscript and tell you what we think. I'll give it to my non-fiction editor as soon as she gets back."

"Don't be afraid to be honest. If you don't think it's good enough, you may tell me. I'm aware that publishing is a difficult business and that a memoir like this might not sell."

"It depends a lot on the quality of the writing," Beth told her candidly, "but the subject could be terrifically appealing. One problem is that your husband—well, that he isn't here to do promotion, and book sales are really boosted by author appearances. But you lived it all with him. Maybe you could do the book tour. I mean, if we decide to publish it."

"You're being very kind to suggest it." A hint of delight in the blue eyes. "And what would a book tour involve?"

"It depends on the author and the book, but interviews on radio and TV, book signings in stores, giving readings or talks or maybe slide shows, if they're relevant to the subject. It's all about getting the authors out in the public eye."

"But what if they're shy?"

"Yes, that can be a problem. I mean, the whole idea is ridiculous, in a way, because writing is such private, quiet work—just the writer and a computer, or a sheaf of paper, before that—and then the first thing we ask writers to do, when a book is published, is stand up on their hind legs and talk to people."

"It's an extra connection, I suppose, between the reader and the author."

"Must be, although I myself never go to hear people read," admitted Beth. "I can read perfectly well myself, and that's why the author wrote the book in the first place. I go to listen to them talk about how the book came to be, because that can be fascinating. And if the author's a good speaker—witty, you know, and entertaining—all the better. I've seen people literally run to buy books after an author's given a good talk or shown great slides."

"It all sounds a bit daunting, though perhaps it could be an adventure. Let's see how you like the manuscript before I go shopping for travelling clothes. And—I don't know if this is appropriate, but—if you think you might like to publish the book and there is a shortage of funds—I am not a wealthy woman but I would be able and happy to contribute. I'm sure Gerald would have made the same offer."

"That's very nice of you, but it's not something we do. We publish books that we think will make it in the marketplace on their own two feet, so to speak. But thank you."

"I hope that wasn't an insult, my offering financial help?"

"No, no—not at all. It's just that there are some firms—we call them 'vanity publishers'—that make their money off their authors, and we like to keep a clear distinction between them and us."

Helen looked at Beth inquiringly and appeared to be waiting for further clarification.

"Trade publishers make their money by selling books—lots of books, we always hope—and pay royalties to the authors according to the numbers of copies sold. So we work very hard to sell as many books as possible."

Helen nodded, as if this were all a given, but continued to listen intently.

"But in the case where the authors pay them, the companies have already made their money, so they don't have to work at selling the books."

"Ah," Helen's face cleared. "Now I see what you're saying. That's when the author ends up with a basement full of books that he has to sell himself."

"Exactly. But we have a marketing network of promotion people, sales reps, distributors, wholesalers and so on, to the individual booksellers, so it's way more exposure for any book than an author can get by himself. Usually. There are exceptions, of course."

"No doubt. There always are," and Helen smiled again, a merry smile this time, that lit up her eyes. "Thank you. This has been most interesting, but I have taken up quite enough of your time. It was extremely good of you to see me." She extended her hand. "My address and phone number are with the manuscript and I'll look forward to hearing from you, whatever you decide."

"You do have this on disk, don't you?" Beth asked. "Because if we decide to publish it, we'll need to email it back and forth."

"Oh yes. Gerald made sure we were up to date on such things." And, gathering up her jacket and briefcase, she made a brisk but graceful exit.

What a nice lady, Beth thought, picking up the box. And if this turns out to be good, who knows—maybe we could send her out on a book tour.

TWELVE: Greetings from Africa

"Would you like to read some of Elly's emails?" Grace asked Jenny, pointing to a sheaf of printed pages on the table. "I dug them out because you sounded interested in Ghana last night."

"But won't she mind?" Jenny asked. "She was writing to you and Ben."

"No, no." Grace laughed, shaking her head. "She sends them to all her friends too. They're more like newsletters than personal messages."

As the maple leaves above their heads bobbed gently, shifting shadows played over the terrace and the empty lunch dishes. Everything in the valley below was still, except the water chuckling down the creek; high above, a hawk swept in silent circles. Peace on the farm.

Grace reached for an oatmeal cookie and leaned back in the white chair. "Unlike Elly, I didn't write many letters to my parents when I was at university because they couldn't read. But I do remember writing to tell them about Ben."

"How did they read it?"

"Oh, there was always some schoolchild in the house who had learned to read."

"Was this to tell them that you'd met him? Or that you were going to marry him?"

"I think I said I liked him and wanted to bring him home to meet them."

"How'd it go?"

Grace thought, head to one side. "Very well, I'd say. When you consider that it had never crossed their minds that I'd get involved with an oboruni, a foreigner. There were lots of teachers from America and Canada and England—volunteers, you know—on one- or two-year contracts. They came and went, and hardly any of them got into real relationships with Ghanaians. Many short-term relationships, mind you." She smiled. "We were used to white people being in our country, from the colonial days on, sort of like a tide, always there at the top, washing in and out but never staying. So when Ben came to meet my parents, they thought he was just one of my fellow teachers, somebody who maybe wanted to get a bit closer to a Ghanaian family than most of the expatriates."

"Did they like him?"

"Oh, yes. By that time Ben had been in Ghana for more than a year, so he could say a few things in Twi and he knew what the food was like and the way families worked so it wasn't hard for him to enjoy himself. And my parents—like all Ghanaians—are very hospitable. Even if they hadn't liked Ben they would have been polite. But they did like him—they thought he was easy and fun." Grace fell silent, seeing once again the central courtyard of her family's house filled with smiling, teasing, chatting relatives and neighbours, curious about the man she'd brought home, the old women in head scarves inspecting Ben and making sly, rude jokes amid gales of laughter. And Ben, bless him, knowing perfectly well that he was the object of intense interest but ignoring it, warmly greeting everyone who came up to him, answering endless questions, occasionally smiling at her across the sunlit space, eyes crinkling: "See, I can do this. No problem."

The problem had come later, when Grace announced to her astonished family that she intended to marry Ben and move to Canada.

As if she had been following Grace's thoughts, Jenny asked, "Did your parents mind that you did turn out to have a permanent relationship with Ben? And that it meant coming here?"

"Yes. They minded."

Jenny was awed. "I just can't imagine doing that. You must have loved Ben an awful lot to give up everything you'd ever known and go with him to a foreign country."

"We didn't leave right away. We lived in Accra for the first couple of years, partly to show my family that the marriage was good. But by the time we left we had TK, and they were surely not happy about losing a grandson."

"Weren't you scared? What if you got here and then the marriage didn't work? And you had a child. Did you ever worry about being a single mum in a strange place?"

"I don't remember having that worry. I did love Ben very much—and I still do—and I suppose I had faith in that love."

Sheila had been half-dozing, listening to the conversation. Now she stretched, arms above her head, and smiled. "You were lucky."

"Probably I was. More tea?"

"Yes, please. Jenny's right. You could have had an awful time here." After a pause, "I was terrified of coming here myself. I refused to, for ages."

"Why was that?"

"I'm not exactly sure. Not rocking the boat? I'd got my life pretty well organized, finally, and I didn't want any complications. I think I was afraid of—well, finding out something unpleasant. We didn't know what you'd be like—that you'd be so welcoming and friendly. And also, I suppose I'd absorbed Pat's animosity toward anything to do with the farm. All of that."

"Yes, I see. It must have taken quite a bit of courage to come."

Sheila considered. "It did. And perhaps my courage has been rewarded, just like in all the old fairy tales. I conquered the dragons and lo! I won a family! That stretches all the way to Africa!"

Jenny began leafing through the papers.

Hi Mum and Daddy and TK and everybody,
Sorry I haven't written till now but it's been a *totally* frantic time. First surprise: we arrived in Accra just after six PM and it was pitch dark! I'd forgotten about that, especially after the two weeks in London, where it was light till almost ten. What a shock, going out of the airport into black night! Beatrice and Ama met me—wasn't that sweet of them? I knew they were coming but second surprise: they said I must stay with them before I move to the university. I think they felt the family would have failed me if I'd gone straight into residence. So here I am, in a nice room in Beatrice's quite fancy house in Nungwa. It's a big house, two storeys, with a gorgeous garden, fish pond, outbuildings, and a wall around

the property. The houses out here are all pretty posh.

Everybody sends you their greetings. I'm not exactly sure how I'm related to all the people I've met so far. I know Ama's your sister and Beatrice is your cousin, Mum, (except they both call you their sister) and Beatrice's husband is Uncle Alex. Their kids are grown up, but they've been dropping by to meet me with their friends or families, and there's a nephew of Uncle Alex's living here as well, taking a course in auto mechanics, and Ama's youngest daughter and her kids just arrived for a couple of days and then they'll all go home with Ama. It's so much fun—everybody's friendly and chatty—but a bit confusing. I can't always remember who I've told what to, and I'm afraid of repeating myself and maybe they'll think I can't tell them apart because I'm so new. (You know—like some people say all Asians look alike.) But I can.

They're looking after me so well I'll be totally spoiled by the time I move to the campus. I keep saying "make Ghanaian food, I want to taste everything," but they're still having mostly British-style meals, since Beatrice and Uncle Alex lived in England for a few years and they figure they know what I'm used to—things like meat and veggies, roast chicken (actually it was guinea fowl—much like chicken). I'm dying for some fried plantain—I remember how much I liked that before—and I'm sure the cook usually makes Ghanaian dishes, but no luck so far.

We went into Accra my second day—Beatrice and me and the driver. Nungwa (for those of you who don't know) is east of the city, and my god! the traffic!! It's bumper-to-bumper and you sit stock still for ages. There's countryside between Accra and Nungwa and only one main road connecting them—along the coast—and is it terrible! We got caught in "rush"—ha—hour coming home, and it took us an hour to go ten miles. How do people stand it!? They just know it'll take forever and resign themselves. This year will either kill me or calm me down!

There don't seem to be any pollution laws, so all these little old cars and vans are visibly belching black exhaust into the air—yuck! My lungs! There are also municipal-looking buses so I don't understand why there are still so many cars—and zillions of taxis—on the road. They're going to have to do something about the congestion and bring in emission controls or everybody will die of lung cancer. I know that's my fresh-air, farm-raised self talking, but health is health, after all.

Accra is huge—around two million people. It goes right out past the university. Mum, you said when you were there, there was countryside in between (separation of town and gown), but not anymore! Beatrice and Ama took me out to see the campus. The original part is beautiful!! That main avenue leading up the hill to the Great Hall with the elegant buildings on each side—you must have loved it there, Mum—such a classic idea of a college—paths across lawns, lots of trees, colonnaded walkways. The red tile roofs look a bit more Spanish than African to me, but they're very pretty on the white buildings. The Great Hall is incredibly gorgeous—palatial. Then, when you get away from the central road, they've changed from that white-and-red theme so the newer university buildings are sort of ordinary looking.

I didn't remember much about Accra. The old colonial-style buildings are very graceful but the newer, taller ones aren't—they're blocky and not architecturally interesting. (Says I, the great architecture critic!) We went past the old Parliament House—pretty, in the old style—and Independence Square on the waterfront—enormous, with Kwame Nkrumah's tomb—very imposing. We saw Christiansborg Castle—an old slave-trading fort. (I hadn't realized that Ghana was a Danish possession before it was English. I'm sure ignorant about this side of my family background.) I can imagine that the centre of the city was probably very nice in the old days, when it wasn't so full of cars, because there are lots of overhanging trees and they look quite lovely with the red earth. But the traffic is incessant, and they all honk their horns, just for fun, it seems—it doesn't do any good—and the office buildings are mostly dingy with grey streaks running down them—no doubt from all those exhaust fumes—so I can't say, really, it's a beautiful city now. It could be, though, because it's right on the ocean and if they would reduce the traffic and plant more trees, it could be wonderful. But in a way, it doesn't matter that it's not lovely because it's so full of life. People walk everywhere in a relaxed way—they're quite stately, swinging along gracefully. They hardly ever hurry. They might run a few steps to catch up with a bus or something, but mostly it's an I'm-at-peace-with-the-world pace. The streets are teeming, everybody's laughing and talking, the women's clothes are brilliant and colourful, people are calling to each other and high-fiving—it looks like one big constant street party. There are some beggars, especially around the department stores, but of course we have beggars in Canada too.

And we went to the market—the main Makola Market. I adored it right away. I've always liked bustle and action (as you all know!!), and the market is even *more* like a party than the downtown streets. I'm sure some Ghanaians must have bad moods and be grumpy, but I haven't seen one yet. Even when they bargain about prices, they're pretty jolly. I was a bit unnerved to see so many vultures lined up on the roofs of the buildings in the market—they're so big. And not pretty. But part of life here. And I wasn't quite prepared for the smells—not all bad but strong. I guess any bit of fruit or whatever that gets dropped starts to decompose right away in this heat and the market isn't as tidy as the houses. People here are compulsive sweepers! Every morning, somebody, usually a kid, is out in the compound, sweeping up any leaf that's had the nerve to fall down in the night.

Nobody pays any particular attention to me because I don't look like a *total* foreigner and I'm with my cousins. I can pass! We bought cloth—oh, the cloth stalls are so gorgeous! I'm going to wear nothing but local wax-prints. The colours and the patterns are just fabulous and I almost wish I hadn't brought any clothes with me. Beatrice has a seamstress that she always uses so we bought lengths of four different prints. Beatrice was determined to pay for all of it and we almost had an argument but eventually we settled that she bought two and I bought two. She's so generous—I think she sees me as her own daughter, and wants to provide for me, but I said I had money from my job and my grant, and I couldn't sponge on her. She didn't really understand "sponge"—I think they all do so much for their families that it isn't a concept here—but she put it down to my Canadian upbringing and was quite gracious in the end.

So off to the seamstress tomorrow. More later.

Lots of love, Elly

Hi Everybody,

Am installed on campus! I've got a nice room—small—in one of the nondescript new residences I told you about. I walked by Mensah Sarbah Hall where you stayed your first nights here, Daddy. It's lovely—I wish I could be in one of those gracious old buildings. I didn't know who Mensah Sarbah was till now—he graduated as a lawyer in London in 1897! Amazing to realize there were Ghanaian lawyers here back then, way before it was a country, or even called Ghana.

Everybody is very friendly. As soon as I say something they realize I'm a foreigner and they're all so helpful with everything. When I tell them I'm a Ghanaian-Canadian they're thrilled to bits. Canadians are very much liked here (your legacy, Daddy!). One man I'd just met bought me a little print for my wall because he had appreciated some Canadian teachers at his school. People want to know about you, Mum, and where's my village and who's my family. Somebody I was talking to is related to Uncle Alex— isn't this a funny little country? So interconnected.

I think I'm going to just *love* being here. I don't know if this is genetic (!?), but I like the heat and the noise—it's such an exuberant country. Of course, I haven't seen all of it yet. The humidity isn't bothering me—people tell me Accra is, oddly, in a dryish section of the coast—I like the feel of the moisty air on my skin and it's not that different from summer days in Ottawa.

Jenny skimmed over the pages that described Elly's classes and professors—the girl was certainly enthusiastic, and determined to tell her family and friends every detail of this experience.

The trip to Kumasi was amazing. I'll be going again, often, but I know I should write down my first impressions before I get used to everything. I decided to try the government bus service. They use big modern buses like ours and I thought that would be more comfortable (for a soft Canadian) than the little Benz buses that always look to be incredibly overcrowded. Also, the government buses are supposed to run on schedule. The others don't—you get into your chosen bus at the lorry park and when it's full, it'll leave.

So I got to the terminal and bought my ticket and then sat for three hours! I never did find out what the delay was—the lady on the loudspeaker kept saying to "our dear passengers" that the bus for Kumasi would be leaving soon. You know how antsy I get waiting for anything—well, you'd all have been proud of me. I found a bench and opened my book and just willed myself to be calm. All the other would-be passengers sat and chatted or daydreamed or dozed, seemingly perfectly relaxed about having hours taken out of the day they'd planned. I wasn't perfectly relaxed, but I concentrated on my book and looked around at all the bustle (other buses came and went) and actually enjoyed myself a bit. I'm trying to learn to let things happen.

When we finally got going, the trip was lovely. A nice woman who spoke English (a lot of the women don't, or maybe won't because they're too shy with a foreigner) sat beside me so I could ask her things. About halfway there's a rest stop and we all piled off to go to the bathroom (they need to work on those) and buy food. Mostly the countryside is flattish, rolling, with sometimes hills in the distance, very green, all little farms, with a few patches of tall trees. I thought there was going to be thick forest, but it's pretty well all open. At Nkawkaw there's a range of spectacular cliffs, perhaps sandstone?—a nice change in the scenery. The bus stopped in all the towns and people stood around talking, so it took us about six hours to get to Kumasi. No problem! I just gazed and gazed at everything, and pestered the poor woman beside me with questions. "What are those trees?" (silk-cotton trees), "What's that boy selling?" (balls of fried sweet dough), "What's that procession?" (a funeral), "How can you tell?" (they're wearing funeral cloth). We went through Konongo-Odumase where there's a big underground gold mine—this wasn't called "the Gold Coast" for nothing, was it?

Ama met me in Kumasi with another huge crowd of relatives—
I feel like I'm related to half the country—all looking so delighted
to see me. They're dying for you to come back, Mum—at least for
a visit. Barbara Antwi (a cousin of some sort—don't ask me how)
said you should build a house in "our" village so you'd have a
home here to retire to. I said that you're not likely to retire from
the farm but apparently a lot of Ghanaians do work abroad for
their careers and then come home—to be closer to family, I suppose, and also it's nice and warm. No heating bills!

Kumasi is called the "Garden City"—it's very hilly and green—
lots of trees and indeed gardens. But it's the second biggest city in
the country, nearly a million people, so the downtown is busy and
crowded, and the market is even bigger than the one in Accra!

This is a very ancient city and that's what interests me. It's
been the seat of the Ashanti kingdom since nobody knows exactly
when, because it goes way back into prehistory, before there
were (of course) any written records. The myths are right here—
the Golden Stool, the symbol of the Ashanti nation that came
down from the sky, and Okomfo Anokye's sword and all that. I
can remember you reading us those stories when we were little,
Mum.

It's so frustrating—all the thousands of years of history here
that's not written down. I'm used to being able to read about what
happened in say, Italy, a thousand years ago, but think of all the
interesting things that were going on here—people were making
art and talking about it and developing their governments and
rituals and laws and teaching their children—and we can't know
anything about it. And West Africa is one of the places in the
world that may have originally developed agriculture. Wouldn't it
be nice to know about that!

Love, El

Hi Mum and Daddy and everybody,
I have to tell you about my trip to Techiman—it seemed as if my
life just clicked together. I was in the compound of the very house
where you brought Daddy to meet the family, Mum, and there

was the usual crowd of people coming to say hello, and a boy pounding fufu in one corner with, I suppose, his mum, and a girl giving a little kid a sponge bath—everybody laughing and talking and joking and just carrying on with their lives—and it was so warm and I looked up at the blue sky and the tops of the trees past the roof and realized I just *love* it here. Not that it's totally home—I think the farm is home—but it's *sort of* home. I'm going to learn to speak Twi, I've decided. I don't need it for my studies, but I want to really fit in here, and you can't do that without the language.

But to begin at the beginning, as Daddy always says so calmly. Ama and her daughter Margaret and I left Kumasi early in a taxi and went out along the road northwest to Sunyani. The scenery is much the same as coming from Accra—basically flattish with distant hills or rocky knobs, green farms, two-lane paved road, tall grass, the odd big tree, villages, etc. The houses are whiter in the villages than in the cities, probably because of less pollution from cars. Sunyani is quite big, with a lot of "storey buildings," as they say. It looked very busy. After Sunyani we went east and after forty miles, there we were! I got out and looked around and thought, "Here I am"—as if I'd completed a circle or something.

As soon as the taxi stopped at the main intersection, the usual crowd of little children gathered round, and when Ama spoke to them, a couple of them rushed off, presumably to say we'd arrived—you can't drive right to the house because the lanes between the houses are too narrow. We started walking slowly and more kids and adults joined us so by the time we met Granny coming to greet us, we were quite the procession. Granny was both laughing and crying and gave me a huge hug, rattling away in Twi, and then she held me off with her hands on my shoulders and inspected me and then hugged me again. Then we all carried on to her (our) house.

It's built like all the others, with the central courtyard, but more tiddly than some. The roof is new, the doors and trim are painted a nice bright blue, the courtyard is cemented and there are flower beds beside the main door. Margaret and I shared a nice room—a corner one, with two windows. I never did find out who got moved to make space for us, but of course we were hardly ever in the room. We were either in our courtyard greeting people or going to greet people in their houses. I met the chiefs and the queenmother and the fetish priest and the teachers and everybody who's anybody here. I felt absolutely like a princess.

Until now, I never wondered about you wanting to leave Ghana, Mum. I just thought, "Of course, anybody would rather live in Canada, because it's the best," but now that I've experienced just a little bit of life here, I can't imagine growing up and then going away forever. I love the warmth and the relatedness—everybody *belongs* somewhere. They've all got a home village (even if they don't live there) and a zillion relatives, not to mention friends, and everybody seems to know everybody. (I know this isn't strictly true, with twenty million people, but it feels like it) and they're always greeting each other. Maybe it's because they've lived here for thousands of years and they know who they are, and in Canada the Europeans just got there two or three hundred years ago.

I'm going to spend a term or so in Techiman, staying in our house. It's quite a contrast to see TV aerials or dishes on the roofs of the earth-brick houses here and there, and people in the market talking on cellphones, when a lot of the villages don't have electricity or running water yet—I guess that's true of some parts of Canada too. But there so many wonderful aspects of life here—things move more slowly, they don't fuss about having a bunch of unnecessary stuff, they're almost always cheerful. Even with aids (which is here, like in every country), the campaign to get people to use condoms is witty. There are billboards that just say, "If it's not on, it's not in." If there really is such a thing as a national characteristic (like Canadians being polite), for Ghanaians it's *having fun!* I can relate to that!

Love, Elly

"Elly certainly sounds like a cheery young person. And observant— you really get a picture of the country from her descriptions." Jenny put the pages down in a tidy stack on the table.

"We told her to write her experiences down right away, because after a while, the things that seem new and amazing get to be part of your normal life and you don't notice them." Grace offered the cookies round again. "And yes—she's very cheery. We say she got most of the Ghanaian genes and TK got the Scottish ones."

"How so? Wears a kilt? Plays the bagpipe? Loves haggis?" Sheila asked.

"No, no," laughing. "He's more serious. Quieter. Elly always sees the bright side, makes jokes. It's no wonder that she's the one who's gone back. She was drawn to the art and the music and the history, the idea of being half-African, and wanted to explore it all."

"Good for her." Sheila put her cup down. "She got to that point a whole lot younger than I did, didn't she?"

THIRTEEN: Lullaby at Juniper Farm

"About here, d'you think?" Jenny cast a measuring glance at the corner in the old stone walls above her. "Then the maple tree can be a few feet higher up."

"Fine." Sheila was carrying the box with the urn and put it down as soon as she reached Jenny. "Oof. This hill is steeper than it looks. Clever of you to carry this on the flat." She shrugged out of a shoulder bag and laid it on the grass. "It feels a bit weird, lugging Pat around like this."

"I know."

Chris, a spade angled across one shoulder, was trudging up the field behind them. "You both seem to be in better shape than I am. You could have carried this bloody thing," he panted, setting the blade on the ground and leaning on the handle. "And now I suppose you want me, as the only male present, to dig the hole."

"No. We'll take turns." Sheila reached for the shovel. "I'll start." She examined the ground, placed the blade, pushed with her foot and with several strokes carved a neat square in the turf.

Chris was surprised. "When did you get to be so good with a shovel, princess?"

"I don't know. I think the motion's coming back from all those little gardens we had as children." She began to push deeper. "Like riding a bike—maybe you don't forget how to dig."

After a while, "Here—my turn to do the next layer," and Jenny took over. As she dug, she wondered, Is this the right time to bring it up? Maybe it is. No—maybe I should wait till after we've finished the actual burial. Hard to talk and dig.

When Chris completed his stint, the hole was over a foot deep, several large rocks having been dislodged and removed. "How much deeper?"

"Maybe a bit more. We don't want frost heaves bringing the box to the surface."

"Frost heaves?" Chris and Sheila echoed, blinking at Jenny.

"Ben told me. The ground freezes and thaws here, and rocks and things in the ground get moved around."

"Gack—we don't want that. Well, we can put these rocks back in, on top of the urn. That should help to hold it down."

Eventually, Sheila pronounced the hole deep enough, and tidied the four steep sides. "There." She straightened up and leaned back, hands on hips, breathing quickly. "Working out at the gym doesn't prepare the body for digging. Have you got your ceremony planned, Jen?"

"I do."

The sun was still high and the sky bright, but with the softened, golden glow of the coming evening. A few streaks of cloud moved slowly eastwards; at ground level it was quiet, and the scents of leaves and grass, warmed throughout the day, hovered in the air.

"Gosh. It seems a lonely place to leave Pat, doesn't it?" Chris gestured at the fields and hills. "Not a house in sight, for such an urban person."

"It does. But this spot was described very clearly in the will. And you know, seeing all this," Jenny said, looking at the gentle landscape, "makes me realize why Pat loved the place on Saltspring. It would have felt like home, if this was home for the first part of your life."

"You're right, Jenny," Sheila agreed. "And also why Pat never liked the old Ruckle House at Beaver Point. It's too much like the house here."

"Do you suppose it was put in the will so that we'd come here— come home—and figure it all out?" Jenny asked.

"Good question." Sheila was noncommittal.

After a moment they turned as one, to look at the urn.

"Okay. What are we doing, Jen?" Chris asked.

"I worked on a book of rituals once, and I remember a few of the ideas. Let's all place the box into the earth." Jenny knelt, picked up the urn, and held it over their square little excavation. "Hold the other sides, and we'll lower it together."

Sheila got down on her hands and knees on the grass, crawled to the edge and reached out to grasp part of the rim. Chris eased himself into a crouch and took another part.

Silently, they set the urn onto the bottom of the hole.

Jenny patted the metal. "Goodbye, Pat," she said quietly. "Thank you for everything."

"Goodbye, Pat," Sheila echoed after a moment, "and yes, thank you—for many good things."

"Goodbye, Pat." Chris's turn. "I'll miss you. And I'm grateful to have had you in my life."

Still kneeling, Jenny fumbled into one of her pockets. "Do we all have a little something to leave here? I brought a picture of all of us. Remember this?" She handed it to Sheila.

"Ye-es," Sheila said slowly. "I don't remember the year—it was one of our Christmas cards, wasn't it? Sandy and Pat on the balcony in West Van, and the three of us with the dogs. You look to be about five, Jenny. And those are Buffy and Jonothan, aren't they?" She passed the photograph to Chris.

"It's Buffy," Chris agreed, examining the dogs, "but is the spaniel Jonothan or Jake? Didn't one of them die young and we got the brother?"

"It's Jonothan." Jenny reached for the photograph. "Jake was the one that died. Anyway, it's a nice memento, don't you think? Pat looks so happy." She smiled, searching the scene. "And that was such a gorgeous view, across to UBC." She stroked the picture with one finger and placed it gently on top of the urn. Then turned to Sheila.

"We don't have to go in any particular order. What have you got, Chris?"

"I didn't think ahead to bring anything, like Jenny, so I went down to the creek to look for a nice pebble. I'm sure all the generations of children who grew up in this house played there, like Ben and Grace's kids did. And the creek running through the Saltspring property was one of Pat's pet places. So here's a pretty little rock," and he held up a smooth, flattish, pink-and-white pebble that fit in the palm of his hand. "Smooth like that, it's been worked in the water a long time, so it was there when Pat was in and out of the creek. And it's Canadian Shield granite—you can't get more grounded than that."

Sheila and Jenny nodded, and Chris set his small offering on top of the photograph.

"Well, I didn't bring anything from home either, I'm afraid. Not very foresightful, are we, Chris?" There was a twist to Sheila's mouth. "But the creek said something to me too. Isn't it funny that it seems important to both of us. Something about continuity, I suppose. I didn't think of a stone, though—I went rootling around looking for flowers and I made this little bouquet from plants growing along the banks. Some actually in the water," and she took a plastic bag out of her pack. The stems of the feathery fronds were wrapped in a clump of wet tissue. "Look at the elegant leaf arrangements. I tried to pick things Pat would have approved of." And Sheila laid the little bundle crosswise over the photograph and the pebble.

"Let's hold hands now," Jenny said, getting up and stretching her arms out, so they stood joined. In a lower voice, she said, "We have brought the ashes of Pat to their original home, and we now give them back to the mother of us all, the Earth. May they enrich this piece of earth, as Pat in life enriched us. Anybody else want to say anything?"

"I think I'll sing," Sheila offered. She cleared her throat and, still holding hands, began Brahms' "Lullaby," changing the words slightly to fit the situation.

"'Lullaby and good night,
'With maple leaves bedight . . .'"

Her voice poured down the quiet field, and tears began to slide down Jenny's cheek. When Sheila finished, she mumbled, "I have to let go and get a tissue."

"What a sweet choice, Sheila." Chris blew his nose. "I'd never have thought of a lullaby."

Sheila smiled faintly. "I didn't either. It just popped into my head and wouldn't go away. It's not really a goodbye song."

Wiping her eyes and grasping Sheila's hand again, Jenny sniffed. "It was perfect. Chris?"

"Yes. This isn't a goodbye poem either, but in the circumstances I think it's appropriate," and he recited "Fire and Ice" by Robert Frost.

"'Some say the world will end in fire . . .'"

At the end he added, "I hope that, now the ice in this family has melted away, the new connections will be maintained."

Sheila looked at him soberly. "It's a chilling little poem, isn't it?"

"Like you said, it came into my mind last night and stayed. It felt like it might be an invocation of some sort, to banish the ice if it was said out loud."

"It was perfect too," Jenny declared. "Well," she said after they had all gazed down for a few moments, "we should cover this up now."

Sheila gave a little sigh and reached for the spade. "Shall we take turns again?" She carefully lifted some soil from the pile beside the hole, held it over the offerings, wavered, then emptied it beside the urn and handed it to Chris. He held his shovelful out, murmured, "Mm," and also emptied it into the gap between the urn and the side of the hole.

The shovel went round, and the urn was securely nested before Jenny said, "Somebody's got to be the first to put soil onto the ashes. Don't you think it should be you, Sheila?"

"I suppose so." Sheila shook the shovel gently so that the soil filtered down in a layer onto the photograph, the pebble and the plants. After that, the hole filled up steadily, with the rocks returned near the top and the surface smoothed.

"I wonder if imagining this—I mean, the urn being buried up here—made Pat feel complete again." Sheila stood up.

"I wonder," Jenny repeated. She climbed up to the stone wall, searched the top for a moment and brought back a medium-sized, rough, greyish rock. Placing it firmly onto the fresh earth, she said, "I know you didn't want a marker, Pat, but I think we need this *and* the tree." She stood up. "Well, that's it. For today."

"This was good, Jenny," said Chris. "You were right that we should do our own ceremony. Thank you."

Now I'll tell them the whole thing, thought Jenny. It's the perfect time. And she opened her mouth to speak.

"One last thing." Jenny's mouth closed. Sheila held up a bottle of cabernet sauvignon. "One of Pat's favourite bottlers. I'm going to open it, and pour a little libation on the—do we call it a grave?—the spot—and then we'll drink the rest. To Pat's spirit, wherever it is." She unwrapped three wineglasses from a tea towel. "I borrowed these from Grace. I couldn't see us passing a bottle around and taking swigs of it in honour of Pat, who always insisted on the correct glasses for every kind of wine. It would have been an insult. Would you open the bottle, Chris, since you're the expert these days?"

"Sure. Got a corkscrew?"

"Yup. Here."

The cork came out easily, and Chris handed the bottle back to Sheila.

"Okay. Let's all hold the bottle for the libation." Six hands were wrapped around, and Sheila poured a small amount of wine onto the grey rock. The red liquid splashed briefly and ran off onto the dark soil. "I sort of want to say, 'Rest in peace,' but it sounds so corny."

"Say it anyway," Jenny urged.

"Okay. Pat, rest in peace."

"Rest in peace," the others echoed softly, and there was a moment of silence.

"Now, here're the glasses. Hold them steady."

Chris, with two, and Jenny, one, obediently held the glasses out toward Sheila and she poured carefully from above. "I know you're only supposed to fill glasses about a third full, but what the hell?" She stooped to set the bottle on the fresh earth, working it down slightly so that it stood straight.

"To Pat." They all clinked and drank.

"It should have been opened longer, of course, but then I couldn't have carried it in the bag. Remember how Sandy used to make sure the wine for dinner parties was opened in the afternoon? For the big reds?"

"Yes. And I remember Pat and Sandy having a never-ending argument about how cold the whites should be served. I think of it all the time at the bar. But none of the customers ever mention the temperature."

"We should be talking about Pat, not wine," said Jenny.

"They're sort of synonymous, in my mind. When I think of growing up, one of my main impressions is of all the good food and wine. And good paintings. Except I didn't know it was all so good at the time." Chris drank again.

Jenny reached over to clasp his hand. "We were so lucky, weren't we? When you think of it now. It wasn't so easy then, moving around a lot and growing up in an odd family—for the time, I mean. But there was always interesting conversation and people, there was lots of great food, and we grew up surrounded by beautiful things. And they loved us."

"We were only slightly odd—but don't all kids want their families to be the same as everyone else's? And we've turned out okay," said Chris comfortably.

"Some people might disagree with that," Sheila scoffed. "Failed marriages, odd relationships and—except for Jenny—no career paths. God, we could be the Royal Family!"

"Don't be silly," Jenny protested. "How can you say you don't have a career?"

"It's not a steady career path. That's what I meant. I sing this, I sing that, I write songs, I do a little acting—I'm not going ever upward toward some specific goal. And look at Chris. All that education, all the books he's taught, and now he's a bartender."

"I like being a bartender."

"I know—I think it's fine. I'm just showing Jenny what I meant by a career path."

"I do see what you mean, Sheel. I just don't think the word path has to imply linear. I think lateral hops, like Chris's, count too."

"I'm not sure that hopping from a classroom to a bar is even a lateral. It might be downwards," Chris said with a laugh.

"Depends which side of the bar you're on," Sheila pointed out. "You're on the right side, Chris."

"Yes, but sometimes I think I'm just contributing to marriage breakdown and liver failure."

"Maybe it's a fallow period for you, and you'll have another hop somewhere. Shall we finish the bottle?" Sheila went round again with the last of the wine. "Done."

"I think we should have a toast to Sheila," announced Jenny, "for bringing this wine. It was the perfect touch."

"And for coming," said Chris, "when she really didn't want to." Clinks.

"Aren't you glad you came, Sheel?" Jenny examined her over the rim of the glass.

Cautiously, "Well, I'm glad we've met Grace and Ben. I think they're terrific, and I hope we'll all stay in touch. And I think the farm is quite beautiful in its way."

They looked around again, appreciating Pat's choice of a final resting place. The sun, lower than when they had set out, was still bright in the paling blue sky. The air was motionless and soft, the green and red hills marched away, ridge on ridge, and closer up, a cricket shrilled in the warm corner of the stone wall.

"I feel better now, about leaving Pat here," Jenny said, her voice low. "It doesn't seem so lonely. It seems quiet and lovely, instead."

"It's probably always been quiet and lovely," Chris said. "Maybe Pat came to this corner as a kid, to get out of the house and admire the view."

"Not the kind of thing our grandfather would have approved of, it sounds like. Sitting still and looking at something beautiful." Sheila drained her glass.

"He might have approved of music," Chris said thoughtfully. "There's that old piano in the front room, and didn't families do a lot of singing around the piano together?"

"Some did. We'll have to ask Ben about that."

"You got your musical talent from somewhere, Sheila."

"Mm. Well, I feel as if we've finished here." Sheila looked at Jenny. "Ben and Grace will be expecting us."

"Okay."

Shovel and bag were slung over shoulders. The three stood for a moment, for a final caressing view of the marker stone, and turned away. Halfway down the field, Jenny, in the rear, cast a glance back for a few seconds, sniffling, then caught up with the others. Well, I messed up that chance to tell them, idiot that I am, but it'll come. I'll just have to be more determined.

"How'd it go?" Ben got up as his cousins trooped into the kitchen. "Can I offer you a drink before dinner?"

Grace, observing the three faces, flushed from what—emotion, exercise, wine?—decided that they looked happier than when they had left the house. The private farewell had been good for them. Another plateau in the process.

Sheila stopped beside the sink. "Thank you for the wineglasses, Grace. They were perfect. We all remember how Pat hated plastic."

"You're welcome. Your ceremony seems to have made you all feel better."

Sheila considered, glancing at Jenny and Chris. She too saw a difference. "I think we all have a sense of something—closure? Jenny was right—it felt really appropriate to say goodbye to Pat on our own. And the place, that corner of the field, is quite—comforting."

Ben was busy pulling a cork. "I've always liked that corner myself. You can tuck yourself up against the stone wall and see for miles over the ridges."

"We were thinking it might have been a place Pat liked as well," Chris suggested. "It was so specific in the will."

"It could have been. Everybody has special spots. My father's favourite was right out there, where we built the terrace. I can remember him, years before anybody thought of a terrace, taking a chair out to sit there in the evenings. In the summers, of course. He loved the way the light fell on the creek at the end of the day."

"He always called it 'sweet,' I remember," Grace smiled fondly. "The sweet light."

Jenny eyes were on her face. "He sounds like a nice man."

"He was. A bit too controlled by your grandfather, though."

"Granddad sounds like such a tartar."

"It's funny to hear you say 'Granddad' like that, Jenny." Sheila accepted a glass from Ben. "It almost makes it sound like you knew him."

"I certainly know more about him now than I ever did before, and so do you. He doesn't exactly feel like a real person yet, but he's sort of getting filled in. Like colouring a cartoon figure."

"Except cartoons are usually funny," Sheila objected.

FOURTEEN: Little Connections Shooting Out

"So you're Pat's daughter," said the beaming elderly woman, shaking hands. "How wonderful that you've finally come home. It's been far too long."

"It certainly has," Jenny agreed. "But it wasn't that we were holding off from coming. We truly weren't aware that we had so much family. Pat never talked about any of this."

The back lawn and terrace were full of people, chatting in knots, strolling, greeting, laughing, hovering under the maple tree around a long table laden with wine, juice, tea and coffee, sandwiches, cheese and crackers, fruit, cookies and squares.

"We'll let everybody help themselves," Grace had told Chris earlier, as they shook the tablecloth out and draped it over the table. "Then we will just keep an eye on the drinks. Refill the teapot or bring out more wine."

"It sounds like you know how to throw a party."

"We've done it a lot, here and there, so we've figured out pretty well what everybody likes and what's easiest for us."

"I'll be happy to play bartender, if you like. It's my current trade, you know."

"I do know. Well, you can help Ben with that. Sometimes he likes to go round with the bottles. It gives him a good excuse to talk to everybody." Grace wiped her hands on her apron and looked around critically. "That's fine. Thank you for scattering the chairs about. I expect people will mostly stand and mingle, but the older ones will appreciate being able to sit down."

"How many people do you think will come?"

"Oh, thirty or forty, perhaps. They're all dying to get a look at you." Grace winked at him. "There's nothing like a mystery to add spice to a family gathering."

"Will they all be family?"

"Mostly. But a few old friends. People who have always lived around here, the way Ben's family has. It's going to be wonderful. I think this is what life is all about. It is such a thrill to me to have you here, and connect you with the rest of your relatives. When I came into this family I was quite nervous, as you can imagine. But now I really do have two sets of relatives—one here and one in Ghana. I am a lucky woman."

"You're a woman who sees the bright side."

"I do that. But" —the dimples showed— "I appreciate the good luck too. It's not all my doing. Now, as soon as the tree is planted, I will zip back here and start the tea and coffee."

"I'll zip with you."

"No, no—you must stay and wander back with the rest of them. You're part of the main attraction. If there is anything to be brought out by the time you get back here, I'll let you know."

But there hadn't been. When Chris, meandering back as ordered and chatting with the new acquaintances, reached the terrace, the white tablecloth was almost invisible beneath platters, cups and glasses. The late afternoon lay like a charm upon the scene— warm, slanting sunlight, the tiniest of breezes barely moving leaves, brightness overhead. This, he thought, standing off to the side for a moment, looks like a movie—the deep greens and reds of the tree above the murmuring throng, the pretty colours of the women's dresses (nobody had worn black, thank goodness), Grace in her spectacular kente, the trimmed grass, a few children frolicking. The Garden Party, he titled it. And now I'll plunge into it.

Ben was standing beside the table with a bottle of white wine in his hand. "What did you think of the tree planting?"

"I thought it was exactly right. The little tree is perfect. I'll always think of it there. Particularly in the snow—poor wee stick."

"It'll be fine. Up in the corner of the stone wall it's more sheltered than you might think. And they're tough." Ben slapped the thick trunk beside him. "Built to last."

"So." Chris craned his neck. "Pat's tree will be like this?"

"Yes. Not for a while, obviously, but it'll really stand out, up on that hill."

"I guess that's what Pat had in mind."

"I'd say so. They can grow to almost a hundred feet, you know. It's bound to be a landmark, eventually."

"Will you be able to see it from here?"

Ben peered speculatively off to the east. "Probably. When it's mature, and we're old. We should be able to see the crown, especially from the upstairs bedrooms."

"Too bad nobody will know what it's a landmark for, by then. Because by the time it's that big, everyone will have forgotten the whole business."

"I wouldn't be too sure about that. Some family stories persist down the generations."

"You're probably right. Do you want me to go round with the wine?"

"Sure. It's a great way to meet people. Oh—you're a professional. You know that." Ben handed him a bottle of red wine.

Though Chris had been introduced to most of the guests as they arrived, before the tree planting, he couldn't remember every name. But they all know who I am, he thought, approaching a trio of women.

"Hello," he said, raising his bottle. "Would you like some more?"

One woman was drinking red. "Yes, please. Chris, isn't it?" She held out her glass. "It's very exciting to meet you all. My husband and I are big fans of Sheila's. What do you do? Are you in show biz too?"

"No, I'm a bartender," and seeing her smile begin to fade, Chris added, "but before that, I was a teacher."

"Ah," she nodded, uninterested.

One of the other women, older, dressed in a lovely shade of pink, from shoes to hat, was curious. "Now why did you make that switch? I was a teacher for thirty years and it never occurred to me to become a bartender." She laughed heartily. Drinking tea, Chris noted. "I'm Cousin Pearl, by the way. I'm sure you can't remember who we all are from one meeting."

"You're right. Thank you, Pearl. I'd be happy to tell you why I quit teaching, but first I've got to go round with this," waving the bottle. "I'll find you later."

The noise of conversations had risen slightly, to what Chris thought of as First Drink Level, and occasional loud laughs, usually male, rose from various parts of the lawn. People were beginning to relax: memorials, however casual, created a certain strain. He could see Sheila, in the centre of the biggest group—that was to be expected—and Jenny, chatting animatedly to a man much taller than she was. She'll get a kink in her neck, he thought, lifting his bottle with an inquiring look at two men whose glasses were empty.

They instantly offered their empty glasses, like twins.

"For the heart," said the bigger one, with a ruddy, outdoor face.

"Cheers, Chris. Welcome," said the other, saluting with his glass. "A sad occasion, in a way, but it brings everybody together."

"It does that," Chris agreed. "I've been told that funerals bring people together more than any other family event."

"I don't call this a funeral," the bigger man objected. "A tree-planting, I call it. There wasn't a service of any kind." He sounded vaguely accusing.

"No. That's what Pat wanted. No religion, no typical ceremony."

"You West Coasters. No respect for tradition. Lotus Land." He drank deeply and frowned off into the crowd.

"Now, John," the slighter man remonstrated mildly, and to Chris, "His youngest son joined a commune on one of those islands—the Strait Islands?"

"Gulf Islands."

"Thanks—Gulf Islands. Grew his hair long, wore earrings, made drums. It was just a stage, perfectly harmless, but John here didn't like it much."

Chris nodded understandingly. "Mm. And is he still in it? The commune?"

"Oh, no. It folded but some of them, including Steve—John's son—started doing graphic design. For computer software, I gather. It's been hugely successful, and that's the real problem." He grinned mischievously at Chris. "The success, I mean."

"It is not," spluttered John. "I think it's just fine that they're successful. You don't know what you're talking about, Earl."

"Oh yes, I do. I've known you too long, John. You'd have preferred that boy to come slinking home with his tail between his legs, saying, 'You were right, Dad,' but instead he's ended up rich."

"Hmph."

"Are you cousins of Pat's? I've forgotten the connections, I'm afraid."

"No. Our families all settled here around the same time, and we've lived down the road for generations. Our fathers were friends of your grandfather's."

"His sisters' grandfather, you mean," John interjected.

"Oh yes."

"Do you remember him?" Chris asked.

"Indeed I do. I understand your lot never knew anything about him." Earl sounded surprised.

"That's right. What was he like?"

"Quite the old tyrant, in point of fact."

"Now, Earl," said John warningly. "Don't you go speaking ill of the dead. He was a good man. Just a bit stern."

Earl's eyebrows shot up. "A bit stern? Read 'inflexible.' Yes, he was a good man," he reassured Chris, "in a lot of ways. A good farmer. A good neighbour. But rigid, if you see what I mean."

"I do. It's the picture I've been getting of him." Chris topped up John's glass again. "Well, I'd better press on into the thirsty throng. Nice talking with you."

Earl smiled warmly. "See you again."

John nodded briefly.

This was more fun than staying behind a bar, Chris realized. You can pick and choose your conversations. He waved his bottle at a couple standing on the fringe and edged over to join them.

A little distance away, Sheila was answering more questions than she was asking about her family. "But I'm here to learn about you," she finally protested. "Your side of the family. My uncles, for instance. What can you tell me about Pat's brothers?"

But the young people surrounding her were a generation too far from the men Sheila was talking about. They murmured, "Don't know" and "Which ones were they?" and "Where's my dad? He'd know," until a voice from the outer ring of the circle cut in.

"I remember your uncles well—one in particular." A short, very erect old lady was speaking. The younger fans eased out of the way, like the Red Sea, and the woman marched toward Sheila. A friendly handshake. "I'm Norah O'Shaughnessy. I used to live around here, ages ago. I didn't walk over for the tree planting. I'm too old." She smiled up at Sheila. "You're wondering about your uncles? I was very fond of your uncle Andrew, for quite some time. You know which one he was, do you?"

"The oldest brother."

"Older than me too, but still. He was fond of me."

The young people began to drift quietly away across the lawn. Ancient history. But Sheila was entranced. "What happened?"

"Do you think we could find a chair? I've been standing a long time and my knees are getting tired."

"Of course." Sheila scanned the lawn. "Over there."

When Norah was settled comfortably in one of Grace's white wicker chairs, Sheila found a footstool to perch on. "Now you're lower than me," Norah laughed. "That doesn't happen often. Now—Andrew. What do you want to know?"

Hugging her knees, Sheila answered, "Anything. Everything. I've just seen a few pictures since I've been here. Pat never said a word about him. About any of them."

"No, well, I'm not surprised. Andrew sided with your grandfather, in just about everything. That's mostly why it didn't work out between him and me. Just as well, the way it turned out." She was quiet for a moment. Then, rousing herself, "Andrew was very handsome. They all were, to be honest." Another little pause. "I'm trying to put myself back into those days, you see. It's been a long time." She shifted her small self in the chair with obvious enjoyment. "I was living along the road here when I was in my teens. My dad was hired to work for the McDowells—they had a big farm a couple of miles away. Andrew was—oh, six or eight years older than me, and in line to inherit the farm. He was a good catch, I guess you'd say. And I was pretty, in those days, though you wouldn't think it now."

"Yes, I would."

"Thank you, dear. Aren't you a nice, polite girl. So Andrew and I, naturally enough, started keeping company. I was quite pleased about this, and so were my parents. But Andrew's father—oh, that man." Norah shook her head ruefully. "His precious son wasn't going to link himself with the daughter of somebody's hired hand! So as soon as Andrew seemed to be seriously interested in me, the old man quashed it."

"What?" An outraged squawk.

"Oh yes," Norah nodded calmly. "He told Andrew not to see me anymore, and that was the end of that. So, as soon as I finished high school, I left. I went to Ottawa and had a different life. It was fine. We all survive these heartbreaks, you know, with no lasting scars. Or most of us do."

"But what a wimp Andrew was! Imagine giving up a relationship just because your father said so!"

"Now, now—your grandfather was a powerful man. And maybe young people were more obedient in those days. I don't think it was possible for Andrew to go against him. They were too much alike."

"And what happened to Andrew? He didn't inherit the farm—I know that much."

"No. He fell in love with a girl your grandfather approved of, and she didn't have any brothers, so they took over her father's farm. Everybody was happy."

"What about you?"

"Oh yes, dear, I was happy too. Am happy. I had a nice job with the government and then I married Ted—he worked for the government too. In those days you didn't work after you were married, so of course I stayed home with the children. They grew up, Ted retired, and here I am. And I've outlived Andrew—he died several years ago. I've had a very good life, and to tell you the truth" —she tilted her head closer to Sheila's and lowered her voice— "it was much better than if I'd married Andrew and stayed on this farm the whole time." A conspiratorial wink. "But don't tell the family that. They all think Andrew was the best thing that could have happened to me."

Sheila grinned at her. "I won't tell, but I don't suppose anybody in this generation thinks that."

"No. You're right. I'm dating myself." And Norah went off into peals of laughter at the thought. "I kept in touch with your grandmother till she died, though. She was a nice lady, and we got on well. I think she'd have liked to add me to the family, but I was better suited to living in the city than to baking pies in that kitchen all of my days."

"I can understand that. I'm not much of a pie baker myself."

"No, you travel so much. I see you on TV sometimes, and I'm so proud. I almost feel related to you, knowing the whole story, you might say."

"Do you mean Pat's story?"

"Yes."

"But you must have been in Ottawa by that time."

"I was. But anybody who knew your family knew what had happened. Your grandfather might have thought he'd kept it a secret, but he couldn't control how the word spread. I came back often to see everybody, so I was still like a neighbour. And people talk." Norah shrugged. "Even somebody like your grandfather can't cut that off."

"He certainly tried."

"And considering that you young folks have never come back till now, he did a pretty good job. And Pat must have inherited some of that stubbornness."

"That's for sure," Sheila agreed with a little twist to her mouth.

"Now, which one is Jenny?"

Sheila stood up and glanced around. "She's over there, with the curly red hair, but you won't be able to see her from where you are. I'll introduce you, if you like."

"Yes, but later. I'm enjoying this chair now, and I've reached the age when I don't have to dart around at parties anymore. Eventually, everybody comes by. And here's Ben, just to prove my point. Yes please, dear," holding up her glass.

"How've you been, Norah?" Ben poured carefully. "And Ted?"

"I'm very well, dear, but Ted isn't quite so good. He had a little stroke in the summer, so he doesn't go out as much as he used to.

He's fine, but" —Norah's voice trailed off— "this crowd would have been too much for him."

"I'm sorry to hear that."

"We're getting on, Ben. It's only to be expected."

"Age doesn't seem to be bothering you much, though."

"Oh, it does, dear, it does. But I look after myself. Eat my vitamins, take a walk every day, all that."

"Well, whatever it is, it's working. Keep it up." Ben saluted with the wine bottle and carried on.

"Nice lad, that. He always has been."

"I gather Ben caused another upset to my grandfather when he brought Grace home from Ghana."

"Oh, you have no idea! But he was old by then and Ben's parents had taken over the farm. I heard that he sat by himself in the front parlour a lot."

Sheila shivered, visualizing an old man, upright and ferocious, in that formal room, hands rigid on the arms of the ornate chair, gazing fixedly out the window. A commander put aside, a ruler no longer.

Seeing Sheila's reaction, Norah said, "But he came round in the end, you know. He was very fond of Grace by the time he died. Of course, it was probably only Grace, because she's such a wonderful girl. Not all foreigners."

"He didn't like foreigners?"

"No. That is—I don't think he minded if they spoke good English. And were white."

"That limits it, doesn't it?"

"It does. He only really liked other Scots, I believe."

"It figures."

"Don't dwell on it too much. He couldn't help the way he was. He was a product of his time and place and beliefs, and there were many men like him, then. Women too."

"You sound amazingly forgiving, considering that he wrecked your life. At least, you must have thought that at the time."

"Oh yes, I'm sure I did. But he gave me a better life, overall. Of course, he didn't give a fig about my future, and I suppose I could resent him for that. But you know, one thing I've learned, being old, is that resenting people is a waste of time and energy." She cast a speculative look at Sheila. "It sounds like Pat never stopped resenting him, though."

"I think you're right. I suppose it was that stubbornness you mentioned."

"Do you have it?"

"Absolutely." Sheila smiled up at Norah. "You have to be stubborn in my business."

"Well, perhaps you could thank your grandfather for that stick-to-it-iveness."

Sheila's eyes widened. "You know, that never occurred to me. I've just been thinking of him as a horrible old ogre, but you're right. Being stubborn *can* be helpful."

"Nobody is all bad, you know."

"Well, maybe you've just given me the silver lining. Thanks, Norah!"

"There you are, Sheila!" Jenny's voice broke in. "No wonder I couldn't find you, way down there. Sorry to interrupt, but Grace was wondering if you'd say a little something. Hello," she addressed Norah, extending her hand. "We haven't met. I'm Jenny."

"Hello, dear," a vigorous handshake, "Norah O'Shaughnessy. I've just been having a lovely chat here with your sister."

"Norah used to go out with one of our uncles. Andrew." Sheila got to her feet. "What do you think? About saying something. Wasn't the tree planting enough for the formal part?"

"I think she means just a thank you to all the people here, for coming today. And you're the obvious one to do it."

"It would be nice, dear. I think you should do it. I've monopolized you quite long enough." Norah waved one small hand. "Off you go."

"Okay. I'll see you again. And thanks very much, Norah."

"I'll come back in a while, for my chat with you," Jenny said to Norah and when they were a few feet away, "What were you thanking her for?"

"I'll tell you later. Basically, for a new slant on our grandfather. Where's Grace?"

"Over by the food." And they nudged their way gently through the crowd.

"Good," said Grace when they reached her. "I feel we need a few words. Everybody would like it. Otherwise, the party will feel unfinished."

Ben, standing nearby, said teasingly, "At least it would to Grace. It's that Ghanaian speechifying tradition. Every gathering has its little formula."

"And very useful it is too." Grace's words were clipped. "As you have admitted."

"I have indeed." Cheerfully. "I've come to like it myself."

"What would you like me to say?"

"Perhaps something about coming home, you know. You can imagine what would be nice."

"Sure. When? Now?"

Grace looked a question at Ben. "Now would be good. Some folks might be thinking about leaving." She clinked a spoon against her wineglass and a circle of quiet widened through the buzz. Into the stillness, she said, "Thank you, everyone. I would like to have your attention because Sheila is going to say a few words."

"Hop up on this," Ben said, moving an upturned wooden crate from under the table, "so people can see you."

Up Sheila hopped. "Thanks, Ben. I'm not going to make a speech, you'll all be glad to know, but on behalf of Jenny and Chris—my family—and for myself, I'd like to thank you for being here today, to witness the planting of Pat's tree and, in a way, Pat's homecoming, after so many years. It's amazing to us, visiting this farm for the first time, that we have so many—and such marvellous—relatives. You all take it for granted, but I can assure you that the three of us find it absolutely wonderful to be connected with you, and to be here. We never knew about this part of our background. It seems terribly sad to me, now, but when Pat left, the links were cut off. I'm just extra-ordinarily glad—and so are Jenny and Chris—that we've finally met you all and sad as Pat's—death—was" —she swallowed— "this is truly a great good that's come of it. So we thank you, more than you can ever imagine, for—for—giving us our family."

Several people were blinking rapidly as Sheila concluded and stepped down, amid a hearty burst of applause. Jenny blew her nose. "That was lovely, Sheel."

"Before you take that soapbox, or whatever it is, away, Ben," rumbled a low voice, "I'd like to say something."

Grace's face lost its happy expression.

"I'm the oldest of the cousins," said a very tall, greying man, moving forward to stand beside the box. "I'm Andrew Muir, if anybody doesn't know, so I think I'm the one to respond to Sheila's kind remarks. I'm sure I speak for all of us when I say that we're glad that you've come from your West Coast to meet us and to lay Pat's ashes to rest in family soil. We've all got a link here today and that link goes back to the first Andrew Muir who settled this very land. Now, some of you here may blame my grandfather and the grandfather of many of us here, for the split in this family, but there's much to be said for preserving traditions and bloodlines the way they were meant to be. To each his own—we all have our place. Granddad stuck to that and it's not a bad rule. Anybody who is old enough will remember that he was a man who knew what was right and did his best. We do honour to him, as well as to Pat, by our presence here today. I welcome our BC cousins, and I thank Ben and Grace for inviting us to be here on this occasion."

Andrew inclined his head graciously toward Grace, unsmiling, clapped slowly and walked forward into the crowd, nodding as he went. A few claps had sounded but most people shifted uncomfortably, shook their heads, and gave each other disgusted looks.

"There's lots more of everything," Grace called out with determined brightness. "Food and tea and wine. Come help yourselves." But the glance she shot at Andrew's departing back was black. She turned to Ben. "The old horror. He can't pass up a chance, can he?" And to Sheila, "If I had realized he might do that I would not have asked you to say anything. I'm so sorry."

"What on Earth was all that about?" Jenny was perplexed.

"That was our dear cousin Andrew, seizing yet another opportunity to spout off about one of his pet themes," Ben answered wearily. "I didn't think he would either, hon," to Grace.

"The pet theme, it seems, Jenny," Sheila said quietly, "being racial purity. Right? Keep the white race white?"

"You've got it," Ben put his arm around Grace's shoulders and hugged her to his side. "So you can imagine that Grace and I aren't exactly his favourite relatives."

"But we have lived with this for a long time and it hasn't hurt us yet. In fact, I believe most of the relatives think Andrew is a perfect ass, and it only diminishes him."

"He's a dinosaur," Jenny fumed. "I can't believe that anybody could even think that way in this day and age."

"Oh my, you've led a sheltered existence, young Jenny." Chris moved closer. "There're still lots of reactionary old jerks in Vancouver. I hear them at Jason's all the time. People who don't like all the Asians coming in."

"I guess so. But to find it in your own relatives! And I had such a nice talk with him earlier. I had no idea he'd be like that."

"Oh, he's nice enough," Ben agreed. "He's polite and sociable and hardworking and successful. People look up to him, no joke intended. But I overheard him once, saying, 'Nobody gives a rat's ass for brown people on the other side of the world.' And that's his mindset."

"Sounds like our grandfather all over again." Sheila gazed at the departing grey head.

Grace nodded. "That's exactly right. A carbon copy. So was his father. Some things don't change."

"It's so stupid." Ben was getting angry. "Because you know, we're all family. Not just us—the whole human race. And the sooner we realize that, the better for everybody." His voice rose. "If we felt we're all brothers and sisters, how could we let anybody live in a garbage dump, or die of starvation, no matter how far away they are? We're all family," he repeated, glaring in Andrew's direction.

Grace put a calming hand on his shoulder. "You're right, hon, but I think you should go circulate again with the wine now."

"Good idea. I will too." Chris picked up an almost-full bottle.

Jenny looked around the lawn. "Just think of it, Sheel. These people are *related* to us. Isn't it the most astonishing feeling?"

"Yes, but some of them are actually family friends, like Norah, the old dear I was talking with when you found me."

"Oh yes, Norah," said Grace warmly. "Isn't she lovely? She was engaged—or maybe not quite—to Horrible Andrew's father when they were young. Good thing for her that Granddad stopped it. The man she did marry is a sweet fellow."

"So she was telling me. That seems to be one case where our grandfather's rigidness had a good effect."

Grace registered Sheila's expression. "But you know, maybe it did in your case too. Would you have liked to grow up on this farm? It appears that Pat was never forgiving, but maybe Vancouver was a better place for you."

Surprised again, Sheila said slowly, "You're right. Much as I love being here and seeing this place—and it is beautiful—I'd rather have spent my life in Vancouver. I blended better there, for one thing. What an interesting angle, Grace—I'd probably have turned out a completely different person if I'd been a farm child."

"You'd still have had all your talents, but living here might have restricted you."

"That's true. And, in fact, you wouldn't have known me at all!" Jenny exclaimed. "Just think how dreary and sad your poor life would have been without me in it!"

"But also how peaceful and quiet!" Sheila laughed.

"How boring!"

"How tranquil!"

Grace stood grinning at this exchange.

"What are they getting so giddy about?" Chris was back for another bottle.

"It started with what if Pat hadn't moved to Vancouver, and then Sheila wouldn't have had Jenny in her life."

"Quite true. Or me either, for that matter. Definitely boring, Sheila." Chris raised his voice to join in.

Sheila held up both hands, laughing. "Okay, my life would have been one of endless emptiness without the two of you."

"That's better!"

"Here you all are." A tall young woman smiled as she approached. "The Lost Family."

"Hello, Muriel. I didn't see you before." Grace stepped forward to give her a hug.

"I couldn't get here for the tree planting, I'm sorry. Now, I know which one is Sheila," holding out her hand, "so you must be Jenny. I'm Muriel Howard, your first cousin once removed. I mean, one of them." She glanced around the lawn. "My mother was your first cousin—she was your uncle Tom's oldest daughter, Elspeth, who became Elspeth McIntyre."

Jenny shook her hand enthusiastically. "So Bob McIntyre is your brother. I had a chat with him earlier. And this is Chris."

"It's so too bad that my mother died before you came. She was the one who always called you 'The Lost Family,' and she'd have been so pleased to see you here."

"'The Lost Family,'" Jenny repeated, feeling the words. "It sounds so—mournful. And romantic. We had no idea anybody back here thought about us at all."

"Oh, we did," Muriel affirmed. "We do. We know everybody else, you see. All the cousins—of my generation at least—are still around. Well, between Montreal and Toronto. You were the mystery."

"We were the mystery, Sheel," Jenny chuckled. "And now we've turned out to be just ordinary. People must be so disappointed."

"No, no," Muriel shook her head. "Real cousins are better than a mystery any day."

Sheila considered the phrase. "'The Lost Family.' It gives me little chills."

"It could be a song," Jenny suggested.

"It could."

Muriel looked pleased. "Let me know if you do write a song about it, would you? I'd be so honoured to have given you an idea."

Sheila turned her most brilliant smile on Muriel. "Of course I will. And thank you for telling us. It's truly a gift."

Observing the effect on Muriel, Jenny realized, yet again, how dazzling Sheila could be.

Guests began to leave, coming up in twos and threes to thank

Grace, shaking hands with the "West Coasters," collecting handbags and children.

"Lovely to meet you . . ."

"Come and see us . . ."

"Hey, Jeremy, we're going . . ."

Shadows lengthened over the greens of the grass and leaves as the lawn gradually emptied, and eventually the five were left, regrouped by the food table.

"Gosh, there's hardly a scrap of anything left." Jenny viewed the table in dismay.

"Never mind," said Grace comfortably. "There's dinner in the house, whenever we want it."

Sheila sank into a chair. "How about not quite yet. But I'd like another glass of wine. I hardly had any—I was talking so much."

"This is the best part of a party," Grace said, beaming. "Sitting around afterward, doing the post-mortem."

"So many people," Jenny marvelled. "And so nice."

"Well, most of them." Sheila caught Grace's eye.

"Yes. You can't expect everybody in a family to be open-minded, kind to animals, and earnest about recycling," Chris said. "But they were mainly a good bunch."

"So, do you feel like you have a family now?" Ben handed Sheila a bottle.

"Oh yes," Sheila answered, as Jenny nodded vigorously. "I can feel little connections just shooting out of me."

FIFTEEN: A Walk in the Woods

In the kitchen the next morning, Sheila stood up and stretched her arms over her head. "I think I'll go for a little walk. It's such a nice day."

Jenny and Chris gaped at her as if she had suggested a junket to Mars. "A walk?" Chris asked. "Little Ms. Call-Me-A-Cab is going for a walk?"

Sheila pirouetted, arms still up, and crossed her eyes at him. "Yes, a walk. I do know how to do it. One foot in front of the other," and she tiptoed an imaginary tightrope across the floor, arms out for balance. At the door, she twirled again and with a "See you in a bit," disappeared.

"Well," Jenny said to the closed door. "Imagine that."

"Do I gather," Ben asked, "that Sheila is not one for exercise? She looks pretty fit."

"Oh, she exercises, but at a gym. Aerobics classes and such. I've never bumped into her out walking in Vancouver, and I'm out a lot."

Sheila ambled down the pathway to the pond and over the dam, breathing deeply of the warm breezes and noticing the scents they carried. Meadow grasses, some moist plants on the banks of the pond, sun-warmed wooden planks, dusty gravel on the track through the fields. She considered going up into the "maple field" as she now thought of it but decided she'd been there enough and continued along the track. The grass between the tire ruts was tall, the heavy heads nodding left and right, bouncing gently when Sheila's knees brushed them. A faint path led off to the left and after a moment's pause, she turned up it into the forest.

The winding trail, soft and smooth, led her between the trees until she could no longer see the fields behind her. She stopped. It was quieter in here, no insect buzz or bird song, though the breeze seemed brisker high above. The tops of the tall pines swished and swayed but their trunks barely shifted, a slight, dignified motion, like statesmen bowing stiffly after church. She glanced around in some awe at the pale grey bark dappled in sun and shadow, the greens and browns of the forest floor, brightened in spots by shafts of golden light, the shreds of blue sky overhead. It's so peaceful, but it's all alive, she thought. Everything around me is growing steadily, on its own timetable, totally separate from anything humans might be doing. This is nature's time, and in the city we live on human time. We scurry through our twenty-four-hour days and our eighty-year lives, building roads and condos and power plants, and this forest goes calmly about its own business, the trees getting taller and bigger around, these bushes and mosses thriving. The cycle of growth, death, decay and nurture is going contentedly on, unregarded by our restless eyes. And the energy for all this activity is the sun. If we didn't have light coming down, we wouldn't have plants; all this life around me is nourished from way out in the universe. That's amazing. I must try to remember this.

She stood, not focusing on the scene but absorbing impressions. Then a tiny movement to her right caught her eye, a sudden jerking among the dried needles on the forest floor. There it was again. She concentrated. A very small creature, a mouse—long tail, big round ears—came pattering out onto the firmer surface of the pathway and halted. It was only about six feet in front of Sheila and she kept still, breathing very quietly, touched by its little presence. The mouse looked around quickly and turned to its right, trundling along the path in the direction Sheila intended to go. Silently, she followed, amused by the delicate, narrow back feet angled widely out to each side, lighter in colour than the fur on the mouse's back, paddling hurriedly up and down, up and down. She closed the distance between them till she was only a foot or two behind, but the mouse didn't appear to notice. It has absolutely no concept of anything as big as me. It's probably wary of hawks and foxes and weasels, but humans just aren't part of its awareness. The mouse stopped, picked up something tiny—a seed?—and sat back on its haunches to munch on it. Sheila squatted, very slowly.

The mouse was turning the seed in its paws, nibbling. When

Sheila put one hand carefully on the ground to steady herself it stopped eating, glanced at the large pink intrusion into its world, wiggled its nose and turned back to its meal. When it had emptied the seed, it tossed the husk to one side and headed over to investigate. Sheila flinched—what if it bites me?—but kept her hand flat on the ground. The mouse sniffed her thumb just beside the nail, appeared to consider briefly, and then clambered aboard. Its tiny feet were cool and ticklish on her fingers and the back of her hand as it explored. Then it stood and stretched itself up her arm, its small body narrowing, its forefeet reaching almost vertically above her wrist. Perhaps this new avenue was too steep. It turned around, sniffed her skin again in a couple of places, pottered along her third finger and slipped off. Back on the ground, it scurried ahead on the path for a few feet, head down, then paused, turned a sharp right again and darted back into the forest.

Sheila waited, still squatting, hoping it would come back, but there were no more little movements. Quiet prevailed. Astonished, feeling as if she had experienced a benediction of some sort, she gradually straightened up. She regarded her hand, remembering the gentle pressures of the feet. What a brave little animal! She walked a short way forward and stopped to look where the mouse had disappeared, but the forest gave no sign of anybody.

Sheila had never spent much time in forests. Although the family place on Saltspring Island had included several fully treed acres, she had preferred the veranda, the lawn, and the seashore. Little wild things did not interest her, and following a path alone, among tall trees, would have been alarming. When did I change, she wondered. When did I get to be Our Lady of the Animals and want to go exploring in the dark woods? Now, the gentle curve in the path ahead beckoned to her; it invited, rather than repelled. Isn't that odd, because this forest is much more strange to me than our own forest was. It's a total mystery and I don't seem nervous at all. Is this a sign that I've grown up?

"I'm a grown-up," she said to the nearest pine tree. "Imagine that!" And she walked on, her feet making no sound in the dark dust. Around the bend the path dipped slightly into a hollow, where in spring there might be a stream, then twisted away again through the trees. A faint brightness began to show ahead.

The brightness grew as she walked toward it until she could see colours between the trunks, yellow-beige at ground level and green, with blue above. Then the trees stopped—suddenly, like a regiment on parade. They didn't thin out gradually; they were as dense as before but in a couple of paces, Sheila stepped from shade into sunlight. To her left and right stood the abrupt face of the forest; in front, grass. It wasn't extremely tall grass, so even urban Sheila understood that it must have been cut for hay not long before, and it was dry, the stalks whushing softly against each other in the light air. From the forest behind her, a shadow grew out onto the grass, darkening the yellows.

She walked farther out, appreciating the warmth of the sun as a contrast with the cool forest. Feeling conspicuous, she sat down and, with legs straight out in front, leaned back on her hands, crushing a small patch of grass. "Sorry," she murmured to the heated stalks prickling her palms. After a little time she lay right down, not quite believing herself. Lying down flat in the middle of a field?! Who knows what could be lurking in those woods?! But she felt so at peace she couldn't frighten herself. There's nobody in the woods, she scoffed at the part of her that was fussing, except mice, and I already know that they like me just fine.

The sun was very bright. She closed her eyes. A bee droned by. Warmth poured like mercy out of the sky. Amazed, Sheila felt cradled, exposed in the open though she was. Supported, not vulnerable. Mother Earth, she thought wryly, just before she fell asleep.

Later that day, "May I come with you?" Sheila asked as Ben was putting on his gumboots. "I haven't been into the barn yet."

"Sure, but you'd better put on some boots. The barnyard's a little gooey and those shoes of yours are too nice. There's bound to be a pair here that'll fit." He opened the big closet beside the back door. Many layers of multicoloured coats and jackets were hung on pegs, and the floor was covered in running shoes and boots, neatly arranged in pairs.

"Goodness. Whose are all these?"

"Oh, the kids', Grace's, mine. We tend to wear socks or slippers in the house, so most of the shoes end up here. Another holdover from Granddad's rules, I guess, but it's also what you do in Ghana. Here—these red gumboots are Elly's. They might fit you."

Sheila shoved one foot in experimentally. "Yes, they're perfect, actually. Cute too."

As Ben opened the door, the dogs bustled around on the veranda. "Do you mind the dogs? I can tell them to stay here."

"No, no. I may not adore dogs as much as Jenny does, but I like them fine," and Sheila patted one black head to prove it. "We always had a dog when we were growing up. Pat liked dogs. I suppose it was from being here, with the forefathers of these very dogs." She considered the dogs with new attention and followed Ben down the steps. "They're all directly descended from the first ones, didn't you say?"

"Yes. We've got a book with the dogs' family tree, I guess you'd call it. Every time we have a new litter, we still faithfully record it."

"I'm sure the dogs would love it, if they could read." And after a moment, more seriously, "It's the kind of thing I'd like to know."

Ben turned to her. "But you do now—oh, I see."

They walked on a few yards. Then Sheila, feeling very brave, asked, "Do you know anything about my father, Ben? Did the family ever talk?" She lowered her head and grabbed distractedly at the waving plume of a tail beside her.

Recognizing the gravity of the seemingly casual question, Ben did not answer right away. They continued in silence while he thought, and had reached the barnyard before he spoke. He slid back the clasp and opened the gate for Sheila. "It must have been a forbidden topic, because I don't remember anybody mentioning Pat when Granddad was around."

"I'm sure not, given that black line through her name in the family Bible," with an edge of bitterness.

"And by the time I was old enough to understand anything about a 'scandal,' it was old news. I'm afraid I don't know anything. I'm sorry."

"That's okay." Sheila was both regretful and relieved.

They proceeded across the barnyard, past a knot of calves who eyed them with mild curiosity.

Close up, Sheila could see that the siding on the barn was weathered; the recent red paint made it look newer from farther away. She stepped carefully up onto the cement floor in the open doorway. The central aisle stretched ahead to a matching set of great doors, with box stalls on one side and a row of milking collars on the other. She looked up at the ceiling, wide old boards on huge, roughly squared timbers. "And you store hay up there?"

"Yes. Can't you smell it?"

Sheila sniffed. "I think I can. That sweetish, dryish smell?"

"That's it. I've loved that smell all my life. As soon as I was big enough to climb up there, I used to go and play on the bales. It's such a—a *good* smell."

"It probably means security, or continuity, or plenty—stuff like that. Food for the animals equals food for the humans."

"Could be. When you think of other smells that everybody seems to like, like freshly cut grass, or baking bread . . ."

"Meat on a barbeque . . ."

". . . ripe apples, wood-smoke—maybe we're hardwired somewhere to enjoy smells that imply survival."

They walked slowly along in the cool dimness.

"How do you get up to the hayloft?"

"There's a ladder there," Ben said, pointing into one shadowy corner, "for people, and there's a ramp for the wagons going straight in from the uphill side."

"Oh, of course. The hay has to be brought here by trucks, doesn't it? Can we go up?"

"Sure."

"Heavens," Sheila exclaimed, emerging from a square hole in the floor and gazing in awe at the high, neat stacks of bales. "What a lot of hay!"

"Remember that haying season is just over, and we haven't started feeding yet, because the grass is still good. So this is about as full as it gets."

Sheila looked around and her nose twitched appreciatively. "It's so quiet. The hay must deaden noises, somehow. No wonder you liked it up here. It's calm and quiet, and smells absolutely delicious."

Ben smiled slowly. "You've got it. The perfect retreat. And when it rains, it's even better. You're snuggled down warm in the hay, the raindrops are pounding on the tin roof—you can't imagine how cozy it feels. I used to spend hours tucked up here, with my books."

"Were you escaping from your chores?"

"Oh, no. I didn't mind doing my chores. I just liked being by myself sometimes. Do you want me to bring you up some books?"

Sheila laughed, giving him a friendly look. "No, let's go down. But I might come back myself, with those books."

When they were back on the cement floor, Ben jerked his head over his left shoulder. "I was going to do some monkeywrenching on the tractor, over in the shed there. Did you want to come see that too?"

"Of course. I don't get up close and personal with tractors that often."

Ben opened the door to the shed. "This is Tracy."

"Tracy?"

"Tracy the Tractor. Elly named her. She's always naming things, and nothing but a female name would do for this tractor."

"Hello, Tracy." Sheila put her hand on a gleaming fender. She watched Ben for a few minutes as he arranged his tools on the workbench and opened the hood. His movements were unhurried. "You certainly seem like a happy person, Ben. What's your secret?"

Ben straightened up, leaned one hip against Tracy, looked first at Sheila and then pensively out the door. "You know, years ago I came across a quote from Pascal—the French mathematician?" He looked the question at Sheila, who shrugged. "Well, he lived in the seventeenth century and one of the famous things he said—it gets translated in different ways—was 'All our unhappiness comes from man's not knowing how to sit quietly in a room.' That really spoke to me, somehow." He paused. "But I wondered why it was put in that negative way so I turned it around. 'Happiness is being able to sit contentedly alone.' And I believe that. If you can be happy by yourself, all the other good and nice things that happen to you are icing on the cake."

"God, I never do that. You mean not even watching TV or listening to the radio, don't you?"

"I do."

Sheila tried to imagine herself in her current apartment, sitting alone on her chesterfield, the living room quiet, perhaps some dust motes drifting in the silent air. "I don't think I could. The idea scares me."

"It might seem scary at first. Because part of sitting quietly can mean facing whatever problems or worries you have, and we all want to avoid that. But I think if you can do it—I mean, face your worries—you can face anything, and that's the other side of being happy. You can deal with anything life throws at you if you can go off and sit contentedly by yourself. At least, that's what I've found." Ben had surprised himself with his wordiness. "Sorry—I didn't mean to carry on about it."

"You didn't. It's very interesting. I've never thought about happiness in that way before." Sheila revisited her mental picture. "The main feeling I get when I imagine sitting quietly alone is guilt. Like, there must be something I should be *doing*."

"There always is. Especially on a farm. But I've learned to put it aside for short whiles. Everything'll get done, even if I take half an hour to go sit on the terrace."

"But you're looking at a lovely view from there. What about people who might like to try sitting contentedly alone and they'd have to look at a wall?'

"I hate to keep quoting Frenchmen at you but Matisse—the painter?"

"Yes, I do know who Matisse is."

"He said something like 'There are flowers everywhere, for those who wish to see them.' In other words, you can find beauty in everything. Or you could close your eyes. It's not what you're looking at that's important—it's that you're paying attention to just being alive." Ben pushed himself away from the fender, feeling that the conversation had gone on long enough. He couldn't remember talking to anyone but Grace about personal topics like happiness or fear. But Sheila was family too, and she'd asked. And now she persisted.

"So is this meditation?"

"I don't think so. I've never studied any meditation techniques."

"Do you close your eyes?"

"Not necessarily. Sometimes."

"Hm. Thanks, Ben—you've really given me something to think about. Maybe next time we get together, I'll be as peaceful as you are."

"You mean at supper tonight?" He smiled down at her.

"You never know." Sheila laughed. "I'm a quick study. Well, I'll let you work. Thank you for this little chat."

"You're welcome. And" —Ben put both hands on the tractor and leaned toward Sheila— "about your—um—father. Are you going to try to find him?"

"I don't know. Would you, if you were in my place?"

"Yes. I think I would."

"You do, eh? Well, I'll see."

"You might ask Grace about it. She and my mum did a lot of talking, because Grace wanted to learn all about the family as soon as we came here. I wouldn't be surprised if she knows more than I do."

"Oh. Good idea. Thanks, Ben," and Sheila went thoughtfully out into the sunshine.

SIXTEEN: Finding the Spring

"Grace," asked Sheila tentatively, "did Ben's mother ever tell you anything about my father?" She kept her gaze fixed on the path they were following, though the walking, so far, had been easy.

Grace was leading the way. "Not much. Let me think now." The path began to slope uphill. "He was Chinese—well, you knew that. Did I ever hear a name?" she asked herself. "I don't believe I did. And where did Pat meet him? In Ottawa, as I recall. Maybe they were at school together?"

They were climbing along the sidehill across the valley from the farmhouse. Thick trees broke up the view of the creek below into intermittent flashes of mid-morning sunlight on water. The little trail meandered around boulders and large trees, sometimes soft with pine needles, sometimes on bare rock.

"Are there many Chinese in Ottawa? Growing up in Vancouver I went to school with lots of Asian kids, but I don't know about this part of the country."

"There were certainly Chinese in Ottawa when I came here. And I believe there have always been, at least a few. Have you tried to find out about him before?"

"No. I've thought about it, off and on. I asked Pat, oh, once or twice when I was young, but we just ended up in a fight, and I never got an answer. She would never talk about her life back here, as we were telling you the other night, and I can sort of understand that. But maybe she just didn't want me to know who he was. Or maybe" —Sheila paused briefly— "she didn't know herself. I've wondered about that."

"Oh, I don't believe that was the case. I'm sure the family knew who he was."

Sheila grinned. "So I'm illegitimate but not from some one-night stand."

"Yes."

"Ben didn't know anything about him at all. It's funny how both parts of the family clammed up, isn't it? I suppose nobody talked about it here because of Granddad, and maybe Pat never would because she was still mad."

"Or because it was too painful for her to think about?"

"You didn't know Pat. I think fury is more likely than pain."

"Another thing I remember is that Pat was expected to come home. She was supposed to have the baby, give it up for adoption and come right back here. And she refused. So that was more defiance of Granddad, and think how brave she was, staying in Vancouver alone with you." Grace stopped. "Let's have a little sit down. This is a good spot."

Beside the trail, someone had flattened the top of an ancient log—the adze marks were visible—and pushed it against an outcrop of granite.

"It's quite comfy." Sheila leaned back and wiggled her shoulders against the rock. "Did Ben fix this up?"

A wide opening in the trees just below the trail offered a view of the farm, from the creek immediately below, over the fields, the barn, outbuildings and house to the road, and on to the dark-green humps of the hills beyond.

"No. Granddad. He liked to sit up here and look out."

"Granddad did? I thought he was such a total dynamo. Work work work."

"He was. At least, till he got old. But he loved this farm, and he took time to see it, you know?"

Sheila thrust her feet forward and examined her sneakered toes. "Stopping to smell the roses."

"Something like that."

"That surprises me. But," lifting her head to look farther, "it is a lovely scene."

"It is. He mostly came up here at sunset. He liked the evening light, and watching the shadows creep across the fields. I wasn't used to the idea of landscape as scenery—we didn't think of admiring the countryside, at home—but he had a couple of places he went to, to sit and look around."

"This was when he was old, did you say?"

Grace cocked her head. "Well, he was slowing down by the time I came, but it seems he'd always had the habit of disappearing off by himself now and then. Your grandmother would say he'd gone 'to have a think,' and maybe he did. But when I talked to him about it, he said he just liked to smoke his pipe and watch the light change."

"Not the one-dimensional old bugger I've been visualizing. Did you like him?"

"Did I like him," Grace repeated slowly. "I came to appreciate him for what he was, but I can't say I ever actually liked him. Though I believe he quite liked me, in the end." She grinned. "I was just Ben's little African wife. Being polite and cooking what he wanted to eat was all he ever looked for in a granddaughter-in-law. I was an awful shock to him when we arrived, but eventually he got over the colour of my skin."

"You'd think then, he'd have got over the colour of mine, so to speak."

"Maybe he did. Maybe, even in the beginning, he was enraged at Pat not so much because she was pregnant, or even because her boy-friend was Chinese, but because she'd been disobedient. His kind of Christianity, you know, was all about obedience to his god. And then, when she stayed away, maybe he was sorry but he was too proud to say so."

"Because it seems weird to be perfectly happy with a Ghanaian granddaughter-in-law . . ."

"I wouldn't go so far as 'perfectly happy'!"

"Okay—accepting—of you, and still not accept a half-Chinese granddaughter."

"Ah, but there's the blood thing."

Sheila turned, eyebrows raised at Grace.

"The family tree. You were related to him, I wasn't. Pat had brought alien blood, so to speak, into his immediate family."

"But so did you. Your kids are half-Ghanaian."

"Yes, but if you keep the analogy with Pat, it would be Ben he was cross with, not me."

Sheila nodded. "For going outside the family norms."

"But you see, I come to it from a different viewpoint, because my people traditionally reckon descent from the mother, not the father."

"How does that work?"

"You always know who your mother is, right?—because people literally see you pop out of her. But your mother could have slept with someone other than her husband—without DNA testing, there is no way to be one hundred percent sure, unless the girls are all kept locked up. And they aren't. So the bloodline comes through the mothers. It was the custom for your uncle, your mother's brother, to look after you, because he knew he was related to you."

"Then what did your father—I mean, your mother's husband—do?"

"He'd look after his sister's kids. This wouldn't be for daily needs, like food. But paying school fees, or if a young man wanted to buy a taxi or some other kind of business, and didn't have enough money, he'd go to his uncle for help. That system is breaking down now, in the last couple of generations, but people will still call their mother's younger sister their 'junior mother.' And what we here call first cousins would be sisters and brothers."

"So Ben," Sheila said, figuring this out, "would be my brother?"

"No. He's your mother's *brother's* son. Who knows what his mother'd been up to? If he was your mother's *sister's* son he'd be your brother."

"Heavens. It must get awfully complicated."

"Not at all," Grace laughed. "It's whatever you're used to. I found your system very limited, because our families go on and on. As we" —she stood up— "should do. If we're ever going to see the spring."

"Yes. Thanks, Granddad," and Sheila gave the bench a little pat. "Great spot. Ooof. My legs are definitely not in shape for living on a farm."

"All the ups and downs, I expect. You're used to walking on city streets."

"I'm not used to walking much at all. But I'm determined to see this spring."

"My, my, when I think of how my grannies walked! In and out from the villages to the farms every day, carrying water, getting firewood, going to the market, everywhere."

Sheila felt a twinge of envy. "So you knew your grannies?"

"Of course. Both of them. They were a big part of my growing up."

The path edged around the shoulder of the hill and up the side of a narrow, V-shaped ravine where thick ferns, their graceful green fronds spread wide, hid the ground. In the bottom of the V ran a thin trickle of water, caught here and there on its way down behind fallen branches.

"And here's the spring," Grace announced, as the trail angled down into the ravine. An iron pipe protruded from the bank. Someone had scooped out the bottom of the channel and banked the sides roughly with stones, so the little stream of water fell from the pipe into a pool before running down the ravine.

"You said Granddad did this?" Sheila asked as they stood at the edge of the small sheet of water.

"Yes."

No ferns close around the pondlet, Sheila observed. No filigree of fronds reflected in the silver water. Not the spring as I visualized it. Very plain—water, rock and an old pipe. Still, there was something touching about it: an endless supply of water off in the woods, tinkling on and on, whether anybody came to see it or not.

"But is this the source of your creek? It's so tiny."

"No, no—it's just a tributary. It flows into the creek at the bottom of the hill, down there." Grace waved vaguely. "I don't know where the creek actually starts. Farther west somewhere. But it's probably the only source on this farm," she offered, feeling obscurely that Sheila was disappointed.

"I'm glad we came to see it. It's very sweet." Sheila knelt and cupped her hands under the pipe. "Hiking uphill is mighty thirstifying." She gulped a few handfuls. "Mm—nice."

"I guess I'd better have some too." Grace stepped around to the other side of the pool. "It doesn't come as easily to me. Even after all these years in Canada, I'm still a bit nervous about drinking water outdoors. There could be so many things in it."

"I'm surprised," Sheila said, glancing around, "that with the work Granddad did on this spring there isn't a cup. For drinking."

"There used to be. A tin cup. It sat on that flat rock beside the pipe. I wonder what's happened to it."

"If nobody comes to use it anymore, the human scent probably wore off." Sheila pointed to the many marks of little pads and claws in the moist soil. "See all the footprints? Some raccoon must have made off with it."

"Whatever for?"

"Curiosity maybe. Or to serve soup to their children."

"I can just see it." Grace stood up again, smiling. "Baby raccoons sitting round a table and mum dishing out soup. Chicken soup—made from one of our chickens."

"Do raccoons take your chickens?"

"They would if they could get into the henhouse, but they don't manage it very often. The dogs run them off. The chickens squawk if they hear anything sniffing round at night, and then the dogs tear over to check it out. Sometimes it's a mink, Ben says, not a coon."

"How does he know?"

"I have no idea. Ben speaks dog. There are things he's just absorbed through his life here. We had a dog in Ghana too—he can't be without one—and he communicated with He Who too, so it's not just the Juniper Farm dogs."

"He Who?" Sheila echoed.

"Yes. His whole name was He Who Wishes My Downfall Shall Never Prosper. It's one of the slogans you see on lorries or buses. He Who was a great dog. He was just a bush dog—sort of nondescript—that we got as a puppy, but he was so smart and interesting that I liked him a lot, even though I wasn't used to the idea of dogs as pets in the house."

"Jenny's the great dog-lover in our family. In our part of the family, I mean." Sheila turned to look down. "Goodbye, little pool." And after a moment, "Thanks again, Granddad." As they started away, she said, "Considering Ben's so rooted to this land, it's amazing that he ever went overseas in the first place."

"He had a great interest in the outside world, even as a kid, or he wouldn't have joined CUSO. He loves this place very much, but he loves working in other countries too. He truly feels he's part of a global village, maybe more than anybody else I know."

"You're the one who typifies a global villager, I'd have thought."

"That's because I'm the obvious transplant. But in his head, Ben's world view is really wide. He sees the unfairness—people not having clean water, or working horribly long days for a pittance— and he simply feels he has to do something to fix it. That it's our responsibility, as humans, to make the world a better place."

"Good for him. I know I don't think enough about people without clean water."

"Nobody does, really." A sigh.

"Thank you for bringing me up here. It's beautiful." With a final glance back along the ravine, Sheila thought of the conversation she had had with Ben, about sitting contentedly alone, and wondered how he managed to do that if he felt that he had to fix the world. She posed this to Grace as they walked back to the house.

"Where's Grace?" Ben came into the kitchen while the dogs flopped disappointedly on the veranda.

Jenny turned from the counter where she was beating eggs in a bowl. "She's gone off with Sheila, to show her a spring. In the hills, somewhere."

"Really? She hasn't been up there in years. Hope she'll find it."

"She sounded perfectly confident. Isn't there a trail?"

"There is, but it might be a little overgrown by now. What are you making?"

"A pound cake. For dessert tonight. I wanted to do something to help Grace out with all these meals."

Ben smiled. "That's very sweet of you, but she's loving having you here. A house with only two people in it isn't a house, for Grace. And she likes cooking, so the more people around her table, the merrier. And where's Chris?"

"Down at the pond, with that fishing rod you lent him. Gosh, I feel like action central." Jenny grinned at Ben. "And it's not even my house."

"You're doing a great job of keeping track. Maybe I'll wander on down and see how he's doing. Unless I can do anything to help you?"

"No, no, thank you. I'm having a wonderful time. I never make dessert at home so this is fun."

And off Ben went, to the delight of the dogs, who had been expecting a much longer wait. He whistled a little tune as they all clattered down the steps, realizing it wasn't only Grace who enjoyed a house full of company. He picked up a stick and hurled it far ahead for the delirious dogs to chase and, with long strides, followed them down the path.

"Hi, Ben," Chris said as he reeled in slowly. "This is a lovely rod. I'm surprised you'd lend it to somebody you hardly know. I might have been a total klutz with it."

"Didn't sound like you were." Ben sat on the grass beside Chris, elbows on knees, and plucked a long blade of grass to chew.

"The archetypical farmer." Chris cast again, laying a graceful arc of line out into the middle of the pond. "I'm not having any luck so far. Maybe Ontario fish like a different movement in their flies. But who cares—it's a treat. I can't just walk out of my house in Vancouver and start fishing like this." His movements were understated and smooth, his eyes fixed on the speck of colour that was the fly.

"It's soothing to watch such elegance. You're a much better fisherman than I'll ever be."

Chris laughed. "But isn't the true test of a fisherman whether he catches any fish? I'm batting zero, here."

"Oh, well." Ben leaned back on his elbows and squinted up into the blue. "Who cares, as you said before. Fishing's really just an excuse to get away by yourself." He lay down, folding his arms beneath his head, and closed his eyes, knees still bent up.

Ben looks so relaxed, so comfortable. He knows every inch of the ground he's lying on, Chris thought. What must it be like, to feel so connected to a place? He's part of all this, and it's part of him. I can almost see little white fibres growing down from his head and the soles of his feet. He felt a ridiculous urge to warn Ben to roll over before it was too late. Then he looked around at the golden day.

Small insecty noises, buzzing and jittering; just enough air movement to set the bulrushes jostling gently; sunlight streaming from a cloudless sky; the dark green hills sitting protectively around the little valley. Paradise, he thought. It's beautiful, it's warm—and he felt the pang of an outsider. But don't I feel connected, like Ben, to my own bit of paradise anywhere?

Saltspring was the only country place he'd lived, and that wasn't for more than a few weeks at a time. What about the homes in the city? Sifting through his memories, Chris decided no, he had never in his life experienced the calm at-oneness that he saw in Ben. After Dad married Pat they were restless; they liked to move, to see the city from different vantage points, and to clean out clutter with each change. Maybe their rootedness was in each other. Chris had not thought about their relationship from this perspective, and felt a comfort: perhaps a person doesn't need a physical place. "I envy you your sense of belonging. I don't have the kind of ties that you do."

"Maybe you never know how strong your roots are till you go away. When I went to Ghana I never gave a thought to coming back. I just wanted to see the world and keep on going," Ben reflected. "It might be a function of getting older too."

"Makes sense. When we get to this point in our lives—and I refuse to call it middle age—we think ahead more." Chris curled another loop of line out into the middle of the pond. "But still, I might get a case of itchy feet before I settle down cackling in an old folks' home."

"It's probably never too late."

Up in the kitchen, Jenny took off her apron, hung it on the back of a chair and sat down. "That was fun," she remarked to the house plants by the window. She checked the time. The cake wouldn't be ready to poke for half an hour, and she had washed up all the bowls and utensils. I should do something else, she thought, but she remained in the chair, looking out over the terrace. Nothing moved. The big house settled comfortably around her, and outside the day was bright.

What a release it was, being away from home. Even though she wasn't really on a holiday, she didn't feel the usual pressure of work. "The big problem with the book business," she had explained to Norah at the party, "is that you're never *done*. As soon as you get a book off to the printer, there's a whole bunch more waiting on your desk. I'm normally working on quite a few manuscripts at different stages, and they all want attention *right now!*"

"I see. It's not the kind of job where you close the door on Friday and not think about it till Monday."

"No, it surely isn't!"

Quiet descended on Jenny. Odd that this house should feel so peaceful, given its history. She swung her feet up onto the next chair. There's a different kind of sound in the country—no traffic, no sirens, no seaplanes or helicopters, no leaf blowers. I can hear little wee voices—crickets or something—and a dog, far away, and a bird tweeting. I suppose on Sundays you might hear a faint church bell. I should really be doing something. But she stayed as she was.

"Ben has a great capacity for peace," Grace said, after Sheila had described her chat with him.

"How do you mean?"

"He doesn't fuss. When something needs doing he does it and when it's done, if he has the time, he's perfectly happy to sit on the terrace and look at the pond. It's not that he doesn't work hard, because on a farm there's lots of hard work. It's that he" —Grace searched for a word— "he *balances* better than most of us. I've often seen him out there, not reading, just thinking, I suppose. About what, I have no idea. The farm? Me and the kids? The world?"

When they returned to the house, Sheila went upstairs with that image of Ben in her mind—comfortably in a chair, ankle on knee, perhaps arms crossed behind his head as she'd seen him sit in the kitchen, in calm contemplation of . . . life. That's what it is, she thought, as her gaze strayed out the window of the bedroom. Maybe that's what he'd been trying to tell her, that if you don't stop now and then, and consider where you are, how do you know you're alive? Sheila sat down on her bed in a sudden moment of panic.

If you don't pay attention to your life, it passes you by. Oh my god—it's true. That's how I got to be this old so fast; I didn't notice! I was so busy—working, partying, travelling—that I never thought about it. Viewed from where I am now, my life looks like a mad scramble: lively and fun but a kaleidoscope without a pattern. It's a shock, this standing aside and observing it. What have I been doing?

The five words started a rhythm in her head. Where was the beat? *What* have I been doing? What *have* I been doing? What have I been *doing*? And more pictures came. She saw herself as a waterbug, zipping around on the surface, rushing back and forth; am I afraid I'll sink if I stop to think? And musical notes came.

When a song began to take shape, Sheila played with it in her mind, noting the words and images, hearing the melody, letting it loose to shift and sway, seeing colours. Away in a different dimension, she often didn't know how long she sat or, if she was at the gym, walked on the treadmill. Her focus turned inward and her good friends had learned to recognize the expression on her face. "Listening to her inner piano," Sally termed it, but it was more than a tune. It was scenes and anecdotes and paintings in art galleries and snippets of emotions and conversations bubbling up, as Sheila saw it, from the rich storehouse of her subconscious when some trigger was pulled. She was grateful for the wealth of material that flooded in, and her job seemed to be to make order of the treasures, to pick and choose, to send some elements back into the vault for another time, to find the melody. Only when it had jelled in her head did she jot it down, and that first draft was usually, though not always, reworked several times as she sat at the piano, "plinking." Playing with the notes, thinking about their effect, combining chords with lyrics, finding the right tone, expressing the ideas.

Now she sat still in Elly's bedroom, seeing herself and the people she knew engaged in a merry dance, dashing from work to amusements, changing partners, buying furniture, trying on clothes, talking on cellphones, whirling, swirling . . . And then Ben, relaxing on the terrace, alone, quiet, happy. A structure began to emerge—the stanzas loud and complicated, the chorus simple. Balance, Grace had said. That's what it was actually about. Not that you should *stop* the whirling and swirling but that you should take equal time to stop and think about what was going on. A vaguely recalled phrase drifted in—something about an unexamined life wasn't worth living. A Greek philosopher, perhaps. She'd have to look it up. But that's good—it was an ancient notion too.

By this time, Sheila was actively thinking again; she'd come out of the gathering stage and decided to go and plink on the old piano in the parlour. She entered the silent room almost furtively, feeling like a trespasser. Its very stillness was a presence. She glanced apprehensively at the stern, dark chair against the back wall and quickly looked away, hesitating. But there was the piano, gleaming and lonely. It wanted to be played. Sheila tossed her head defiantly and crossed the room, seating herself on the piano bench. He can listen if he wants; I don't care. Back straight, wrists up, she began gently touching the keys. They were a little stiff but in tune. Oh yes, TK probably played when he was at home. Her fingers moved tentatively at first while she listened to the melody in her head, probing the order of notes, trying chords, finding the emotional level. What have I been doing? A lament, a realization, a resolution—an upbeat ending, self-knowledge, intention. She played and worked, unconscious of time or place, far away in the space of the bench and the sound of the piano, her eyes sometimes closed to help concentration, her body moving easily from side to side.

The notes grew stronger as she found the song and began to sing. Stop, start, yes, no, this way, a little higher, a neater rhyme, back over it, that's better, that's coming. And again. Happy, she sang out, retrying the verses, repeating the chorus, building confidence—this was a *good* song! Her voice, accustomed to concert halls, brightened the room, the crisp and lovely piano notes floating beside it. Liquid tones bounced in the high corners, polished the furniture and scoured the floor. The parlour rang.

Delighted by the joyous sound, Grace and Jenny sat down in the kitchen to listen. They were too respectful to go down the hall, much as they would have loved to lean in the doorway and watch creation taking place. It had been a long time since such an exultant melody had come from the parlour, and that it was Sheila, the banned baby, making the air dance was doubly exciting. Grace was thrilled and grateful.

When Sheila was satisfied that the new song was firmed up, she branched off. Some voice and finger exercises, then favourite songs, some of her own compositions and some written by others. Rapt and nourished, Grace was profoundly sorry that Ben was out.

Eventually Sheila finished with a quiet folk song, doodled a little longer on the piano and then let her hands fall into her lap. Well! That had been wonderful! A new song, a good workout and the parlour felt—warmer. Something made her turn and contemplate the big chair. Her eyes had not lingered on it before, because she had felt repelled, as if it were brooding in its corner, but this time she observed how elaborate the carving was. Rising, she walked over closer and bent to examine the chair's headrest. Graceful swirls, with a wreath in the centre surrounding a—was it a pineapple? No—a thistle, of course! Sheila laughed—the prickly family heirloom. She patted the chair, smiling, and left the room.

The back door flew open and the dogs skittered in, tails wagging, tongues out, claws slipping on the polished wood.

Hands on hips, Grace exclaimed, "What are you doing in here? You think this is the dead of winter?"

At her tone, the dogs wheeled abruptly, ears down, and crowded back outside, between the knees of the incoming Ben and Chris.

"They were just trying it on," Ben said. "We've had a great hike and they thought they might get away with a little house time."

"I know. But they don't need house time on a warm day like this, especially when we've got visitors."

Jenny, who would have quite liked some smiling dogs in the kitchen, asked, "Do they only come inside in the winter?"

"Mostly. They're fine outside, even then—they've got a dog-house and blankets—but if it's really cold and nasty, we let them in for a treat. They just love to curl up near the stove."

"They're very funny," Grace added. "They'll be still as little mice and you'll think they're asleep but if you get up, you'll see their beady eyes fixed on your every move. It's like they're always on watch."

"As they should be." Ben sank into a chair beside Jenny. "That's what they're bred for."

"You're not fooling anybody with that line, you old softie," Grace laughed. "We all know you adore them and they'd be sleeping on the bed if I weren't here. You sound like your grandfather."

Ben grinned at her. "He was pretty soft on them himself, under all the stern talk. I remember once, when I was quite young, one of them—maybe it was Jill—had a bad cut on her paw, and Granddad fixed up a bed by the stove and fussed around with medication and salves as if she was a sick child."

Sheila came in while he was talking. "Sounds like he preferred dogs to people."

"He certainly found them easier to deal with," Ben agreed.

"As in more obedient, I assume. What's that music?" Sheila noticed the infectious background beat.

"Highlife. I thought since we're having a Ghanaian meal, we should have some Ghanaian music," Grace replied.

Sheila's feet started moving. "I see why it's dance music! It's caught me up already. Anybody else?" Nobody got up but she carried on fluidly.

"You're doing it exactly right," Ben exclaimed. "You must have music in your bones."

"That I do." Sheila grinned at him.

Jenny skirted the dancing Sheila and bent over the stove where Grace was stirring a large iron pot. "This smells too delicious for words. What is it?"

"Groundnut stew. You wanted to try one of our dishes and this is the foreigners' favourite, usually. Groundnuts are peanuts."

"Oh, no wonder it smells so good. I love peanut butter. I could live on it, if it weren't so fattening. I only allow myself to eat it on the weekends."

"Jenny reckons peanut butter is a food group all by itself," Chris said.

"How do you usually eat it?" Grace asked.

"On a spoon, right out of the jar."

"What all is in this stew?" Chris crossed the room. "I need to have a sniff too."

"Basically it's onions, tomatoes, chicken, peanut butter and hot peppers. Only a little of the hot peppers in this one—just to give you an idea. If you like it, I'll give you the recipe. It's very easy. No exotic ingredients and it's flexible. You can make it with beef too. Or goat, or fish."

"And what's in these little dishes on the table?" Chris inspected the array of small bowls.

"We do groundnut stews like a curry, with condiments everybody can add themselves. There's cut-up bananas and oranges, chopped green onions, minced hard-boiled eggs, flaked coconut, raisins. But this is all a special treatment. If a Ghanaian family's having an everyday groundnut stew they won't have all these extras." Grace lifted a spoonful of stew and tasted it. "Fine. I won't fiddle with it anymore." She turned to Ben and Chris. "Sheila played the piano in the parlour earlier. It sounded absolutely wonderful."

"I had an idea for a song and since the piano was there, I didn't think you'd mind." Sheila was still two-stepping around in the middle of the kitchen.

"Mind! I was thrilled. Would you play it for us now? I know Ben would love to hear it."

"Sure."

"This'll be the first time we've had cousins here for a concert in the parlour since Granddad died," said Ben with quiet satisfaction.

SEVENTEEN: At the Château Laurier

"Oh," Jenny exclaimed, throwing her arms around Grace, "thank you for *everything*—having us to stay, getting the family together—it's just been unbelievable!"

Grace hugged her tightly, feeling the warmth of Jenny's back. "Come back any time. Come back soon."

"But you've got to come to Vancouver next."

"We will. I promise." Grace turned to wrap Sheila in another close embrace. This one was quieter.

"Thank you so much," Sheila murmured. "I'm so glad we're related."

"Me too."

"And do come out soon, as Jenny says. The proverbial fatted calf will be waiting. Except that it'll probably be Saltspring Island lamb."

"Marvellous." Ben was waiting his turn in the hug line.

"Thank you very much for talking to me about the family," Sheila said to him.

"Anything you want to know, any time. It's your birthright too."

Chris shut the trunk of the car on the bags and came back to the front steps, arms outstretched to Grace. "Much as we all hate to go, I'm afraid we're ready."

Grace laughed. "You're always welcome. It's your home too."

"That's certainly extending the family, but actually, I do feel it's home, somehow."

"It's that Ghanaian hospitality. Grace could make anybody feel at home." Ben shook Chris's hand heartily. "But it's true—you *should* feel it's your home."

Chris blinked quickly. "I can't offer you any expansive acreage in Vancouver, but I promise to take you fishing."

"Whether there are fish or not. Chris just likes to get out on the water to get away from everything. He won't even take his cellphone." Sheila shook her head.

Chris and Ben grinned, the grin of men who knew perfectly well that the fish were not the main lure. "Which little Ms. Always-Stay-Plugged-In can't understand, of course. Come on, Sheila," Chris said, putting a hand on her shoulder, "we'd better get this show on the road."

Grace and Ben waved until the car disappeared around the bend.

"I hate it when people leave. The house feels so empty," Grace mourned, an arm around Ben's waist.

They climbed the steps slowly, still entwined.

Chris drove this time, but Jenny still played navigator.

"And I'll be Ms. Rich Bitch back here." Sheila crossed her legs and leaned back, arms spread out along the back of the seat. "The role I was intended to play in life. Carry on, staff."

"Find a different route back to Ottawa, Chief Navigator," Chris suggested. "We should see some new country, and we're not in a rush, are we?"

"No," Jenny replied. "We probably can't check in till mid-afternoon anyway." And to Sheila, "Maggie truly would have liked to have us come and stay with her, you know."

"I know, Jenny, and I'm sure it's a lovely house, but I'm just so used to having my own space when I travel, it's a strain to stay in somebody's home. I did it all the time, when I was first touring, and I don't want to do it anymore. But you called her, didn't you? And we're going to see her?"

"Yes. And I told that other nice old lady, Norah, that I'd call her. Do you think you'll be able to find out something about your father?"

"Maybe. After all these years it's not something I have to know immediately."

"He might be in Ottawa! You might actually be meeting him in a few hours!"

"Now, Jenny," Chris cautioned. "Don't get carried away. Sheila's dad must know who she is. He could have got in touch with her any time."

"But maybe he doesn't know. Maybe Pat never told him she was pregnant. She might have just left for the West Coast—you remember how stubborn and silent she could be."

"But people knew. And anyway, one look at Sheila—at her beautiful face, that is" —Chris grinned at Sheila in the rear-view mirror— "and with her surname, you'd think somebody in Ottawa would have put two and two together."

"All I know is that nobody's ever come up to me and said, 'Hi there, I'm your daddy.'"

"But he might have admired you from afar." Unquenchable, Jenny started on another tack. "Not wanting to upset you, he's been going to your concerts and feeling proud, and then leaving quietly, without a word to anyone."

"God, what melodrama. Stop her, Chris."

Jenny turned to look back. "Seriously, Sheila, I'm awfully glad we made this trip, aren't you? I feel so much more Canadian. I know you've criss-crossed the country forever, and you probably already feel this, but seeing the Parliament Buildings was an amazing thrill for me. I didn't expect to be so touched."

"So we're a flag-waver now, are we?" asked Sheila. "Going to learn French? Eat salt cod and drink screech?"

"Well, maybe not all that."

"But speaking of eating and drinking," Chris cut in. "Where do you recommend for lunch? We'll be in the city in plenty of time."

"Why don't you park at the hotel," offered Sheila. "It may be too early to check in, but we could leave the car and walk to the market. There are lots of nice restaurants there."

"Okay," said Jenny. "I'll navigate us to the Château Laurier."

Maggie slowly turned the pages of old scrapbooks, looking for anything she could show the Muirs, as she thought of them, at dinner that night. But were they all Muirs? No. Only Sheila was.

After she had burrowed down through six decades of memories, following a faint trail of recollection, she found that nuggets of information and rumour were indeed stored in the dusty archives of her mind. Bits and pieces surfaced, as if uncovered by the sudden beam of a flashlight. Yes, there had been gossip that Patsy Muir was pregnant. Yes, she had certainly disappeared from the scene. And yes, an even greater scandal: it was said the father was Chinese. But who could he have been? That wasn't in the storage lockers of her memory.

Maggie had asked around among her friends, but since Patsy had not been one of their crowd, only a few remembered anything, and it was just a vague impression. For such an unusual occurrence in its time, it had left amazingly few ripples.

The Chinese boy must have been at Lisgar with Patsy. Where else could she have met him? He wouldn't have lived out near her, because the Chinese who came here were urban businessmen, not farmers. Could he still be in Ottawa?

Maggie shook her head, smiling at the things she had thought important enough to save in a scrapbook. Clippings from the old *Ottawa Journal* about high school football games. Black-and-white snapshots of herself, mugging with friends, pretending to be in pain—or not pretending?—from going barefoot to the Sand Pits "to toughen our feet." An invitation to a Christmas dance hosted by the wealthy parents of one of her classmates; Maggie remembered the dress—white lace, with a red velvet bow—that her mother had laboriously made for her. It must have been an awful job for somebody who wasn't a professional seamstress! Seamstress? That jogged another line of thought. Could Patsy Muir have had a Chinese seamstress with a good-looking son? Her family was well enough off to have their clothes made—their city clothes, at least—but did they? Another impression had pigeonholed the patriarch Muir as puritanical and thrifty. Perhaps a seamstress would have been a luxury he didn't approve of.

Back to the scrapbook. Here's a mention of their handsome uncle in a basketball game: ". . . scored nineteen points against Glebe in the tournament opener." Even after all these years, Maggie could recall incidents, albeit fleeting and disjointed, from her high school years. Scenes swam into her mind: George Muir laughing in a group of athletes near the "boys' door"; another star player, Rich something, carrying his school books under his arm in a different way that instantly set off a new style among his young admirers; Muir again—this was like watching a slide show, or a procession of "coloured stills" as people had called them then—marching purposefully into the wrong classroom to a titter of excitement, before realizing where he was and whirling to leave. Funny how those elite athletes, only two or three years ahead of her, had seemed unimaginably sophisticated and grown up. Think what seventeen-year-old boys are really like! But it didn't change a thing: in her fourteen-year-old vision, they were permanently heroes and properly regarded with awe. She had met the occasional one of those boys in later years; they were usually shorter than she expected, chubby and bald—but that didn't change the shining memories.

Patsy Muir must have been a rebel. She wasn't only having sex, she was having it with someone of another race. If that wasn't rebellion, for those days, I'll eat my scrapbook. Was she really infatuated or did she just want to defy her father? Both, probably. This scrapbook isn't going to tell me anything—it's all my stuff. But it might pry something loose in my mental storehouse. Knock it off a shelf in there. However, by the time Maggie closed the book, she had had a highly enjoyable excursion into her teenage years and had found not a trace of Patsy Muir.

She went into the kitchen to pour herself another cup of coffee and, mug in hand, surveyed the garden. In front of the bronze mums swam an image, one that had been in her mind earlier: that group beside the boys' door. Who was standing beside George Muir? John Evans? Brian O'Connor? Gerry Palfrey? They'd all been on the senior football team . . . Maggie concentrated and to her considerable surprise, the face became clear. It was Derek Clark. And Derek still lived in Ottawa—he'd gone into the insurance business. What an amazing organ the brain is, she thought, putting the coffee down and reaching for the phone book.

There were many listings for Clark, and Maggie didn't know where she lived, but she eventually tracked him to a condo on The Driveway. He's not far from his high school days. But then, neither am I. She dialled.

"Hello?" And a cough.

"Is that Derek Clark?"

"Yes."

"This is Maggie Rath. You won't remember me—I used to be Margie Ballantyne and I was a few years behind you at Lisgar."

"No, I'm sorry. I can't say I know the name. But that was a long time ago." A wheeze.

"That's okay. I'm not calling about me. I seem to remember that you were a friend of George Muir's. Some of his family—a couple of nieces and a nephew—well, the nieces anyway—are in town from the West Coast, and I told them I'd try to find some people who knew their family. They've never had any contact, you see. Till now." Why am I babbling? Am I still overwhelmed by the football hero?

"Yes, I knew George Muir pretty well, back in high school. We were on the football team together, and basketball . . ." Maggie's heart sank at the enthusiasm in the elderly voice. Oh dear—was she going to be treated to a nostalgic listing of decades-old sporting feats? ". . . we had a rifle team, too. But," a brisker tone, "you didn't call to hear all that. Muir's dead. Do they know that?"

"Yes."

"Heart attack, I think. I saw the obit in the paper."

"So did I."

A pause. "From the West Coast, you say?"

"Yes."

"These wouldn't be Patsy's kids, would they?"

A great thump in Maggie's chest. "Yes, they would."

"Well, I'll be damned. I used to wonder, now and then, how she was doing. Such a pretty girl, she was. But you say these are the children, not Patsy?"

"That's right. She died this summer, and they brought her ashes home."

"Ah. I'm sorry to hear that." Another pause. "What are her children like?"

"They're not actually children now. The oldest one is a singer—you may have heard of her—Sheila Muir. She's beautiful." Maggie stopped, not wanting to give anything away, in case . . .

"She'd be the Chinese one, then, would she?"

Bingo!

"Yes. Do you—do you remember anything about her father?"

"Sure."

"You do?" Maggie blurted, amazed. "I've just been going through all my old scrapbooks and yearbooks and I didn't come up with the faintest clue."

"No, I don't imagine you would," a dry chuckle. "It was hushed up pretty quickly. Some of her friends must have known. I think Patsy almost flaunted it, to spite the old man. He was a bit of a Bible-thumping old curmudgeon. I was terrified of him myself, but of course I couldn't show it. Oh, the acts we put on when we were young, eh?"

Fearing another lapse into tender memories, Maggie asked, "Can you tell me who he was? The chap who got Patsy pregnant?"

"Oh, I don't think it was quite as one-sided as that. I think young Patsy was pretty keen on the process herself." Another lengthy chuckle turned into a wheeze. "Well, I promised George I wouldn't tell. I only knew about it because we were drinking beer one night and he said he should go and cut the fellow's balls off. Pardon my language. He wouldn't have done it. It was the booze talking."

"I'm sure you're right."

"I don't know if I can remember his name—Patsy's boyfriend, I mean." Maggie's shoulders slumped. But "Albert? Andrew? It started with an A, I'm pretty sure. Yes—Anthony, I think. And I don't remember the surname, but his family owned the Yangtze Café. D'you remember it? It was on Slater Street."

"I sort of remember a Chinese restaurant on Slater, but I don't know if I was ever there."

"Well, I remember going there a few times, usually after a dance or a movie. We used to eat egg rolls and think we were very worldly."

"How did Patsy ever meet the son? At school?"

"I don't know. He waited on tables in the restaurant at night, but I'm sure he was at school somewhere. The Chinese immigrants have always been dead keen on a good education."

"Do you have any idea if he's still around?"

"Not a clue. The café isn't there, but that's not too surprising, after all this time. So many new places to eat now, all nationalities. Egg rolls aren't the height of sophistication anymore." A raspy laugh. "Well, the world moves on, doesn't it?"

Maggie agreed, thanked him effusively and hung up, as quickly as she politely could.

I wonder if the boy's family and friends have forgotten Patsy in the same way her side has eliminated him? Probably. It's much easier to silence the boy's part—he doesn't end up with the baby. It could be that his parents didn't even know he was going out with Patsy. Well, "going out" was probably not the right term.

Maggie got up from where she was still sitting by the telephone. Ow. Her knees were a bit stiff these days. They'd been better when she'd had Max, who had demanded a walk first thing in the morning. Oh, those lovely summer mornings by the lake: Max chasing squirrels with his tail lashing furiously, ducks following Maggie in hope and always, the cool air, freshly scented with grass and water. Clouds building from the northwest, the Gatineau Hills in the distance. Briskly round the lake, across the locks and home to a hot shower and coffee. Bliss. Maybe I should get a dog again. Keep me active. No—they do tie you down. But there's nothing to stop me trotting round the lake on my own. I don't need a dog, like a visa, to go walking! I've let myself get old and lazy. Old and lazy on the outside, still thirty-five on the inside.

Back to the Muirs. Can I get any further with this thing before I see them tonight? I could possibly find out the name of the boy's dad. If he owned the café, there must be a record. But that's a good lead to pass on to Sheila. Maybe she'd rather do it herself. Yes. Stop trying to do everything. Do I have anything else on today? She went to consult the wall calendar. Because if not, I'm bloody well going to walk around Dow's Lake.

"I like this." Jenny looked around the room with satisfaction. "I would never have thought of staying in this great hotel. Good idea, Sheel."

"I've never stayed here before either, but since this is a special trip, we deserve it." Sheila opened her suitcase and lifted out a dress. "And we can afford it, now."

"The view is marvellous! We can see the locks right below—oh!—there's a boat going through. Those are the Gatineau Hills again, and look at the colours! And the river. You know, I hadn't realized till I got here that the Ottawa was such a big river. It was brilliant of you to make them give us a corner room."

"I didn't make them. But that's at least one useful thing I've learned over the years. You can always get a nicer room in a hotel. If you don't like where they put you, just tell them it's unacceptable. Politely, I mean. They're bound to give you something better." Sheila shook the dress and hung it up in the closet. "What time are we meeting Maggie?"

"She's coming here at six-thirty. And I'll call Norah when I've got this stuff stowed."

Sheila sat down, swung her legs up onto the low table and gazed out toward the hills.

Jenny glanced at her. "Maybe you'd like to ask Norah a few questions?" she asked casually, walking into the bathroom with her sponge bag.

"I know what you mean—don't think you're being subtle! I'm considering it." Sheila folded her arms behind her head. "Overall, I think I'd like to meet him, if he's still around. I'm just not sure that I'm ready. I don't feel like rushing into anything."

"It's not exactly rushing, is it? It's something you've known about all your life."

"Yes, but it feels like rushing, since we've just met all this family. Half of me thinks I might as well add one more new relative to the mix and half says, 'Whoa—let's think about this for a while.'"

"Well, I'd sure like to meet him. Would he be my stepfather? No—that's only after your parent marries again, like you got Sandy."

Why am I so hesitant? Sheila wondered. But everybody must be nervous about meeting a birth parent. Why delay it? I know that basically, I do want to connect. Why am I not raring to get on with it? She sighed. There's no rush. But there is—Pat just died and he might too. Two little voices, one from each side. You shut up, she told them both, and picked up the guide to the city.

Jenny was on the phone. "Hi, Norah? It's Jenny Muir Pedersen. We met at Ben and Grace's farm the other day."

"Yes, of course, dear. I remember. Are you in Ottawa now?"

"I am. At the Château Laurier, no less. I was wondering if you'd had time to think about Pat, and what you said when we were talking at the reception."

"Certainly I have. I looked through a lot of my old things and I think I found an old snapshot of your mother and her friend. Sheila's father."

Jenny shot a look across the room at Sheila, who seemed absorbed. "Really?"

"I believe so. It's a group picture in Ottawa and I'm not sure I remember all the people, but I think it has the—shall we say, relevant?—young man in it."

"That's amazing. Can we get together?"

"Yes. How long will you be here?"

"Chris and I are going home tomorrow afternoon. Sheila's staying a bit longer. What about lunch tomorrow?"

"Yes. Let me think. There's a nice place right on the canal, near where I live," and she gave Jenny the details.

When Jenny hung up she contemplated Sheila's bent head. Shall I tell her about the picture or let Norah surprise her? If I tell her, will she get all flustered and worry about the father thing till tomorrow? If I don't tell her, will she be mad at me? Deciding that the latter was too awful to risk, she said, "Sheila, we're meeting Norah for lunch tomorrow. And, um, she thinks she has a photograph of your father."

Sheila turned calmly. "Oh. That'll be interesting. I've just been wondering why I'm not racing about trying to find him. Maybe this'll be the spur I need." Then, "So are we organized? Shall we get hold of Chris?" Tomorrow I'll see my father's face, Sheila thought. It feels unreal. Part of me wants to rush over to wherever Norah lives and grab that picture right now. But I've lived this long without even thinking about it very much—I can wait another day. And if

Norah has a name, it'll make a search that much easier.

"He'll be right along. And he's got a whole list of things he wants to see."

"We've only got a couple of hours," Sheila protested. "I want to have a bath before we meet Maggie."

A knock at the door.

"What's the program, Chris?"

"First, I'd like to go over to the National Gallery. It's right here. You can see it from your window probably." Chris crossed the room. "Your room is much nicer than mine, by the way. How did you rate a corner?"

"Sheila bossed the man into it."

"I did not!"

"She says she was being 'polite but firm,' but if he hadn't given us a corner room she'd have shrivelled him on the spot."

"Poor guy. That's the gallery." Chris pointed. "And the Parliament Buildings, of course. And then maybe the Museum of Civilization, over there. And the National Arts Centre is behind us, on the canal."

"I expect by the time we trot round the art gallery and Parliament Hill, it'll be time to meet Maggie."

"We're going to have lunch someplace on the canal tomorrow, with Norah," Jenny moved toward the door, "so maybe we don't need to see it today."

"Well, let's get going anyway. Come on girls, show a little hustle."

"God, and you think I'm bossy." Sheila rolled her eyes at Jenny.

EIGHTEEN: Backup Plan

"Oh good." Sheila sat down. "Here's a bench in the perfect spot. Let's just have a little rest."

"Okay, but not for too long. We've still got places to go, things to see."

"Slave driver," Sheila complained, but mildly. "I'm glad we did the Parliament Buildings, Chris—thanks for putting it on your list. So, what are we looking at here? It's like the view from our hotel room."

Backs to the Parliamentary Library, they surveyed the distant golds and reds of the hills behind the office towers across the river; to their left, water pouring over falls winked in the sunlight and then quieted to flow directly below their cliff top; the river burbled away to the right and, over on the far shore, more reds and golds undulated gently away to the horizon.

"Lovely," sighed Jenny. "Yes, it's some of our same view—the Gatineau Hills yet again, the Chaudière Falls, the Ottawa River, the Museum of Civilization. The Fathers of Confederation, or whoever it was, picked a grand spot for Parliament, didn't they?"

"I notice they can't see out from the chambers, though. Good thing. They might all just sit admiring the scenery. Ready to trot on?"

It was now or never, Jenny realized. When would they next all be together, alone? If she didn't tell them now, she'd lose her nerve completely.

"Um, can we wait just a bit? I've got something I have to tell you and this is a good time." She shifted nervously on the bench between Sheila and Chris.

Ah, thought Sheila, here it comes. Finally.

"Okay," said Chris curiously. "Shoot."

Jenny pursed her lips, eyes fixed on the far hills. Then she blurted, "Pat didn't just die. I helped her."

An expectant silence.

"That's it?" Chris sounded surprised. "You're not going to tell us anything more?"

"Of course I will. I just wanted to get the first shock over with."

"Okay. It's over. What did you do?"

"Maybe I should start at the beginning. When Pat understood—I mean *really* understood—that she wasn't going to live, she made me promise—swear, in fact, you know how fierce she could be—that if she asked me, I'd help her to—to go. If the pain got to be too bad, or if she was just—ready. So I swore. What else could I do? We don't keep a dog lingering alive if it's in pain—why do we do it to people? And she coped for quite a while. Much longer than anybody thought, wouldn't you say?" turning to Sheila and then Chris. They nodded, profiles dipping.

"I don't mean she became peaceful and calm, because that wasn't in her nature, but she quit raging. She started reading again, more than she had for a while, and of course she had all those visitors." Jenny stopped speaking and focused on her hands, clasped in her lap. "You know all that—you were there too. I don't know why I'm saying it."

"Say whatever you want. There's no rush." Sheila sent a warning glance at Chris over Jenny's lowered head.

"Well, she got to that point. She didn't want to hang around any longer. It was a Wednesday night. I'll never forget it. She'd had a couple of mouthfuls of meat loaf—she'd asked for it specially but she wasn't eating much by then—she'd lost interest even in food—and she looked at me, very directly, and said, 'That's enough.' I thought she meant the dinner so I picked up her tray, but she said, 'That's enough of living.' And I sort of froze. She said, 'Put the tray down, Jenny,' and I set it on the bedside table, and she said, 'I've figured this all out and here's what we'll do.'" Tears began to wet Jenny's cheeks but she spoke steadily, gazing across the wide river again.

"We tidied up the bed and I got her comfortable with pillows and stuff and we talked. I asked her if she was really, really, really sure, and she said yes and I started to cry and she was quite gentle.

214

She held my hand and explained that the pain was getting worse and the morphine wasn't keeping it down, and it made her mind muzzy so she didn't want to take more and more of it, because what was the point of staying alive if you were in a stupor and she was tired of people trying to cheer her up and she just felt she'd done it all long enough. And I couldn't stop crying but I'd promised, you see, and she said—in a kind way, though, not cross—'You can't fail me now, Jenny,' and I said, 'I know, and I won't.'

"And she sort of grinned at me and said, 'Shall I, for once in my life, go to sleep without brushing my teeth?' So I started to laugh at the same time as I was crying but she decided no, she'd brush them one last time so her breath would be fresh and she laughed too at that. I got her toothbrush and glass and she brushed but she was laughing so hard she nearly choked, and she said, 'That would have been a novel cause of death, wouldn't it?' and laughed even more. I guess we were both a bit hysterical by that time. Then we calmed down and she lay back and said I should go down to the living room.

"She wanted to have a little time alone, and she might read a bit and then she'd give herself a good big dose. And I was to come in again in an hour and if she was still breathing, give her another good dose. She even told me to get a pair of her gloves out of the top drawer to wear, in case of fingerprints. Then I cried again and told her how much I'd miss her and she said, 'Yes, I'm sure you will, and that's very gratifying, of course. I hope everybody will, but it's my life, and I've had enough of it. So give me a hug and off you go.' And I did."

Silence. Chris wondered but didn't think it was his place to ask.

Eventually, Sheila couldn't wait. "Was she still breathing when you came back?"

"She was," Jenny said after a moment. "She was lying on her back, with her arms outside the covers, and her breathing was very sort of raspy and she was twitching and making little gasps. I thought, 'Oh no, I don't think I can do this, I'll wait a bit,' so I sat down beside the bed and took her hand in both of mine. And as soon as I did that," she paused, concentrating on her memory, "she seemed to stop twitching and her breathing wasn't quite as raggedy. And in few minutes, I don't know how long, it—just—stopped. I sat there for a bit, not realizing, but then I did. So," her face began to crumple, "I killed her by holding her hand. I know it's not rational, but it just haunts me and haunts me. You know, maybe I should have done something else—called the ambulance and saved her for a little longer." Her voice quavered.

"No," said Sheila and Chris together and he gestured to her to carry on. "You were exactly right. Think how absolutely furious Pat would have been if she'd wakened up in a hospital. She'd have hated it. We all know that. You just calmed her down and helped her to slip away." Sheila was reassuring, wondering how on Earth Jenny would have coped if she had actually had to give Pat the extra injection. "And you know what? I was her backup plan."

Jenny stared at her with amazement and a beginning hope. "How do you mean?"

"I mean, Pat told me about her arrangement with you, and if you'd turned out to not be able to go through with it—she knew you might have second thoughts—I was supposed to do it."

Relief broke over Jenny's face. "Oh, Sheila! That makes it so much better. You have no idea how awful I've been feeling. Oh, thank you!" she clutched Sheila in an awkward, sideways hug and burst into tears.

With her free hand, Sheila patted Jenny's shoulder. "It's okay, Jenny, it's okay."

"Should I go away for a bit?" Chris silently asked Sheila, pointing at himself and miming a walk with two waggling fingers. She shook her head, still patting, so he stayed put, imagining the scene Jenny had described and trying to understand the burden she had been carrying, alone. Poor thing. And she'd been the closest of them all to Pat, if anybody other than Sandy could be thought of as "close" to her.

Jenny didn't cry very long. It was a quick release of the tensions she hadn't entirely realized she had been carrying. She sat up, found a tissue, blew her nose and wiped her face on her sweater sleeve.

"Sorry, Sheel. I didn't expect to come apart like that."

"It's fine. Really."

"But if you knew all along, why didn't you ask me about it? It would have saved me all this guilt and worry."

"I didn't know. Pat could just as easily have died on her own. And if I'd asked you, I'd have seemed accusing. 'By the way, Jenny, did you give Pat an overdose?' It had to come from you."

Jenny nodded. "I see that. And somehow, now that I know you were standing by, I feel better. Not so totally responsible, maybe. And we don't have to dwell on it anymore. Thank you for listening." After a moment she stood up. "Okay—let's carry on with Chris's plan."

"G o d , I really deserve this drink," Sheila sank into her chair in the lounge of the Château Laurier. "I haven't walked that much in ages. I didn't realize you were going to drag us around for miles, Chris."

"It couldn't have been very many actual miles," said Chris reasonably. "We didn't have much time."

"Hurray for that. We did plenty! You and Jenny can trudge around again tomorrow morning. I'm going to get my beauty sleep."

"You don't need any more beauty sleep—you look just fine. What you need is more exercise."

"I do not," Sheila yelped. "I do weights. I go to the gym three times a week. I take yoga classes sometimes."

"But nothing beats a good brisk walk in fresh air. It's good for every bit of you, including the brain."

"Oh, stop. You sound like a fitness guru, not a bartender. What do we all want?" Sheila nodded at a waiter and ordered a bottle of Sauvignon Blanc without waiting for an answer.

Jenny raised her glass. "Another toast to us! Hasn't this been fun—finding family and spending time together? Cheers."

"Ah." Sheila smiled and leaned back. "There's nothing better after a strenuous day than a comfy chair and the first glass of wine."

"Strenuous my ass," Chris scoffed. "We were just strolling round galleries!"

"It was fun. I'm quite sorry Chris and I are going home tomorrow," said Jenny. "We should all go on holiday together again, don't you think?"

"This wasn't a holiday." .

"I know, Sheel, but still. Not working, seeing new country, meeting people . . ."

"Jenny. My idea of a holiday is to do nothing. Sit by a pool somewhere warm with a glass in my hand. Racing around to meet new relatives is a great thing to do, but a holiday it is not."

"Well then, let's do a real holiday sometime."

"I've had a lovely time with you both—truly—but don't let's get carried away. There was a reason for this trip, and if we decided something else, like let's all go to Hawaii for a week, it might feel forced."

Crestfallen, Jenny took a sip of wine. She could see her vision of the three of them, tramping cheerfully around some European capital, guidebooks in hand, fading. "Oh good—here's Maggie."

Chris popped to his feet to pull a chair out, smiling broadly. "Hello again."

"What would you like to drink?" Sheila asked when Maggie was settled.

"Scotch, please. No ice, water on the side."

Sheila glanced around; the hovering waiter nodded at her and headed for the bar.

Jenny had noticed. "Boy, you get good service, Sheila. I could sit here waving for ten minutes before they'd see that I wanted something, but as soon as you walk in, they're glued to your elbow. The perks of fame."

"I bet it's not. They might not know who I am and could care less. They're just good at their job. They're used to much bigger wigs than me in this bar."

"Did you all have a splendid time with your cousins?" Maggie asked.

"We certainly did," Sheila answered. "They couldn't have been nicer."

"They invited a whole bunch of relatives for a little memorial to Pat," Jenny added. "It was just amazing to find we have all this family back here. And Ben's wife is from Ghana, which we hadn't known, of course, so now we find out we even have extended family in Africa!"

"That's exciting, isn't it? Are you going off to visit that end too?"

"Oh, I doubt it," said Sheila.

"Maybe," said Chris, and his sisters' heads whirled round in astonishment. Looking from one to the other, he grinned at their expressions. "I've been considering a change so I thought I might go to Ghana and see if I can teach for a while. Ben really loved his time there."

Sheila and Jenny exchanged bemused glances. "After all you've said about being sick of teaching and perfectly happy being a bartender—no taking the job home with you and all that—now you might go teach in Africa?" Sheila's voice rose in disbelief.

"It might not be that easy to get a job, but I'm starting to feel ready for something different."

"Gosh, that's a pretty big one, Chris. You've never been more than a few blocks away for my whole life." Jenny's face showed her distress.

"Don't sound so mournful, Jenny—maybe it won't happen. It's just that after talking to Ben and Grace, I seem to be getting itchy feet. And I'd like to do something, again."

"Were you feeling that before we came on this trip?"

"Not that I recall."

"There's nothing like a change of scene to put your life in perspective, is there?" Maggie sipped her Scotch.

"But I thought I had my life in perspective." Chris grinned. "I wasn't expecting to be joggled out of it."

"And you may not go to Africa, in the end, but it's probably healthy to consider it. See other possibilities. I wish I'd done more of that when I was younger."

Jenny contemplated Maggie's face. "Are there things you wish you'd done?"

"Good lord, of course. You can't get to my advanced age and not have a few regrets about things you didn't manage to do or see. But we aren't here to discuss my life. It's your family that's the topic of the moment and I have some news for you. Well, it's especially for Sheila."

A conflicted expression darted over Sheila's face, part alarm, part anticipation.

"Now I didn't mean to pry, but Jenny did say that you sometimes wondered why Patsy never told you anything about her life back here."

"Patsy? Did you know her as Patsy? I can't imagine her as Patsy, can you?" Jenny looked from Sheila to Chris.

"She was never Patsy to us," Sheila agreed. "It sounds much too cute and cheery."

"Let's let Maggie go on with her news," Chris urged.

"About the name—I didn't really know her, but I knew of her, and she was definitely called 'Patsy' in those days. It's amazing how hardly anybody I know remembers this business. You'd think it must have been the most awful scandal, and that people would still recall at least some details, but hardly any did, until I talked with an old friend of your Uncle George's. Apparently George got drunk one night and told Derek who the chap was who'd got Patsy pregnant, but then he realized what he'd done and swore Derek to secrecy. And Derek says he's never told a soul, until I called him today."

"But if it was hushed up effectively, maybe people weren't interested after a few years," said Sheila. "They all started having their own babies and it wasn't such a big deal. So who was he?" I feel pretty relaxed, she thought, though her heart had lurched suddenly at Maggie's words.

Maggie took a folded piece of paper out of her handbag and handed it to Sheila. "Derek doesn't remember the boy's family name, but they owned a restaurant, and here's the name of it. If you want to investigate further."

Sheila unfolded the paper quickly, in case her fingers trembled. "Anthony. The Yangtze Café, Slater Street. That should be easy enough to trace. Is it still there?"

Maggie shook her head. "No. It's long gone. I imagine there's a record of it at City Hall, though."

"Thank you very much." Sheila unleashed the famous high-voltage smile. She refolded the paper. "I'll check into it." And to herself—Maybe.

The bar was busier now, the bright buzz of conversation louder than when they had sat down. In the golden early-October evening, the room was glowing; laughter arose, smiles widened. Light gleamed on burnished blond and well-kept grey heads.

"It looks all very jolly, but who knows what careers are being ruined or plans being hatched," said Maggie darkly, casting a glance around.

"Is that the Ottawa take on any bar scene?" Chris was amused, thinking of the activity at Jason's.

"Particularly here, right next to Parliament Hill. You can't help but think politics."

"This is quite the event, isn't it?" Jenny observed, undistracted by her politically charged surroundings. "Chris says he's off to Africa and Sheila might find her father." She raised her glass. "To turning points."

"What about you? What kind of turning point is this for you?" Sheila challenged.

"Maybe it isn't, for me. Or maybe I'll realize it later. I'll think really hard about my life, like Chris did."

"I didn't. The notion just appeared in my mind. I wasn't sitting brooding about my future, if that's what you're imagining."

"You mean you were wandering along and a voice said, 'Go to Africa'?" Jenny was still taken aback by the idea.

"No," Chris laughed. "No little voices, but when the idea came, I thought, 'Oh, yeah, maybe that would be a fun thing to do.'"

"It's not my idea of fun," said Sheila, "but Ben certainly liked it. And if he hadn't gone, we wouldn't know Grace, or have family in Ghana for Chris to visit. Are we ready for another drink?"

NINETEEN: Turning Points

The telephone rang in the quiet house in Victoria.

"Hello?"

"Hi, Mrs. Hatley-Thorpe, it's Beth Chandler calling, from Chandler House Publishers. We met a month or so ago, in Vancouver."

"Yes," warmly, "of course. How are you?"

"Oh, I'm fine, thank you. I'm calling to tell you that we'd like to publish your husband's memoirs."

"Really! That's wonderful news. I truly wasn't sure if it would make a viable book, as you so graciously explained it to me. You do think people will buy it, then?"

"We do. It's because of his descriptions of life along the coast for all those years and the experiences you both had. We think it'll make a real contribution to our understanding of First Nations and their society. I like the Gold Coast parts too, though. It's all very readable and involving. Your husband was a nice clear writer and he lets us really *see* the scenes he's talking about."

"Yes." Helen cast her mind back over the manuscript. "I think you're right."

"It needs just a little work. There are some awkward sentences here and there, and in a couple of places we need a bit more explanation of who the people are, but I'm assuming you could do that."

"If you'll show me what it requires, I'll do my best."

"Our non-fiction editor, Jenny Muir Pedersen, will be in touch with you about that."

"Good."

"First, we'll send you out a draft contract. Please read it carefully and check it out with your lawyer, if you like. If you want to make any changes, let us know. Then we'll send you the customized contract."

"I'm sure it'll be fine. And thank you again, very much."

Helen sat down. Gerald's book would be published. She felt a jab of pain, physically, in her chest, at the thought that he would never know. He would never hold it in his hands, smell the new paper, admire the cover, see his words on the pages, realize it would be read by strangers. In a way, he hadn't died, because his experience, his ideas, the breadth of his knowledge, would carry on. Oh, poor Gerald, to miss all of that.

Helen doubled over, arms crossed at her waist, and rested her forehead on her knees as a wave of sorrow engulfed her. It had been dwindling away, her mourning, but now it surged back. She could visualize Gerald so clearly, sitting in the glassed-in porch he called his "study," typing briskly on the computer, transcribing the untidy piles of handwritten pages, unaware that he was in a race against cancer. Only after he had finished the manuscript had he mentioned a pain in his side. Darling, darling, your work was not in vain, but I will never be able to tell you. Knowing she must let herself grieve, suffer the hurt, not push it away, Helen remained still and saw again her husband's face as he said, "There. It's done. My deathless prose, captured for all time!" with a wry smile. The pain swallowed her. She wept. Minutes passed.

I need a cup of tea. The kitchen was always bright in the autumn, when the leaves had fallen. Helen looked out at her patch of grass till the kettle shrieked. She thought about the manuscript. Their lives together had begun with Gerald's posting and visions of the Gold Coast—no, Ghana, now—flitted through her mind. Warm, green countryside, smiling people, red houses, the clean streets of Accra, the beach, the houses she and Gerald had lived in, the officials she had invited to their housewarming party, the Queenmother up in Tekyiman, and Constance—enthusiastic, pretty, helpful Constance! It had all been such fun, especially her involvement with the school project. What a pity they had had to leave. Her contacts with the friends she had made in West Africa had lessened to sporadic Christmas cards, but her memories were clear and immediate.

Helen poured the boiling water into the teapot mechanically, her focus far away. What would our lives have been like if we had stayed in Accra? Apparently we were not going to have children, wherever we were, and I couldn't have just played bridge and given tea parties endlessly. Would I have visited Techiman again, maybe with that nice driver? Perhaps I would have gone to the opening of the secondary school.

As Helen sat, both hands clasping her tea, gazing at green grass and seeing terra cotta earth, the wisp of an idea floated past: I could go and see it now! She almost lost her grip on the cup in amazement and sat up straight. For fifty years, she had travelled as a wife—a happy wife—part of a pair, sharing experiences and decisions, letting Gerald (it must be admitted) do most of the arranging. Now she was just one. But a healthy one, with enough money to do what she wanted and no particular duties. Helen's mouth fell open as possibilities filled her mind. Her world view had cracked open; she felt as though she were hovering on a threshold, the door wide open in front. Vistas stretched before her. I could go back to Ghana. I could go to East Africa, to the game parks. I've never been to visit my cousins in Australia. I'd like to see the Himalayas. Oh, we should have gone travelling earlier. It would have been so lovely to have all those adventures with dear Gerald. (The door began to swing closed.) But I can still go. And I will. (And noiselessly to open again.) I'll go back to Tekyiman and visit Constance and see the school.

Resolution made, Helen took a sip of her tea. Cold. She dumped it into the sink and refilled her cup from the pot. Always organized, she began to plan. First, I'll have to do whatever the editor wants on Gerald's manuscript. After that, I'll be free. Free? She wondered at the word, tasted it, felt surprise, a beginning joy, a reaction of guilt, a twinge of fear, then slowly back to growing excitement. Free!

"They didn't think you were a screw-up," Jenny protested, standing in the middle of her little living room. "They were very proud of you."

"Sandy was," Sheila allowed, "but I'm not so sure about Pat. I think she thought I just slept with anybody who'd give me a gig. In the beginning, anyway."

"No!" Jenny turned to Chris. "You don't think Pat felt that way, do you?"

He shrugged. "She might have, in the early years, as Sheila says. She was a very complicated person, your mother. Both proud and envious of Sheila, in equal parts, I'd say."

Sheila leaned over the coffee table and refilled her wineglass. "Envious is maybe not the right word, but I was sort of a living symbol of a wrong turn in her life. If she hadn't had me, she would have carried on in the normal path of girls like her. Like Maggie. Gone to university, probably Queen's, married a doctor, had a big house in Ottawa, partied with her friends, taken the kids out to the farm to see the grandparents, all that stuff. And instead, she was alone with slanty-eyed little me in Vancouver, where she didn't know a soul. And—maybe even worse—where nobody knew her. Who out here cared that she was a Muir from Juniper Farm?"

"Except that she loved Vancouver, and she would have been bored to screams in a big house with all her old friends." Jenny still disagreed.

"Possibly, but when she had me, that was totally closed off to her. It wasn't her choice—that's the point. Up till then the world was hers—she was a smart, pretty, well-off girl in a friendly social scene, and then, slam!—you can't come in here anymore. And her father, who was probably somewhat indulgent with her as his only daughter, was absolutely arctic with rage. It must have been an awful shock to her. No wonder she was bitter about it for the rest of her days."

"But she had a good life, Sheel. She and Sandy had a grand time together and she adored being part of the arts community here."

"I know Jenny, eventually it was wonderful. But her first years in Vancouver, when she'd refused to go home, with just a yowling baby and no friends, must have been horrible. I don't think they ever left her."

"And the yowling baby grew up to yowl very successfully." Chris nodded.

"And have seemingly endless choices, about when and where to perform, when her own life choices had been cut off. I do see that," Jenny admitted. "Did you ever talk to her about all this?"

"No. What was there to say? I couldn't very well ask, 'Are you sorry you had me?' She was enough of a mother that she wouldn't say, 'Yes.' Let's talk about something else." Sheila squirmed restlessly in the recliner.

Jenny was disappointed. Sheila rarely opened up as much as she had in the last few minutes, and her relationship with Pat was a subject that had always been fascinating. But she knew a cut-off when she heard it, and there was no point in asking for more. "Okay. Here's a funny thing. When I got back from Ottawa, Beth gave me some new manuscripts and one of them has a section about Ghana! Except it was the Gold Coast then. Isn't that an amazing coincidence, when we've all just met Grace?"

"It is. But your list is mostly regional. Why would Beth want to publish a book about West Africa?" Chris loyally read the books Jenny gave him.

"It's the memoir of a British chap who started off in the Colonial Service there but then he came here to work for Indian Affairs. I've only just started it but most of it is about the West Coast and the First Nations villages he lived in. The author's dead, actually, but Beth says his widow is willing to do the revisions."

The door was elbowed open and Nick appeared, laden with bags and cartons. "Hello, everyone. Sorry I'm late—there was a big queue at the deli."

"Hi," Jenny went over to help. "What are we having?"

Nick thumped his armloads on the counter. "Lots of stuff. A bit cross-cultural—I hope none of you are going to go purist on me."

"Not a chance," Chris said. "We're a polyglot little bunch."

"Well, we've got a roast chicken, Thai noodle salad with peanuts, Greek salad, dark rye bread, peeled baby carrots, pâté, a good big wedge of brie, and wor wonton soup. Not in that order. It's a picnic."

"All we need is some ants." Sheila opened the fridge for another bottle of wine.

"And I made a green salad earlier." Jenny peeled plastic wrap off the large wooden bowl.

Chris began to arrange the cartons in his idea of the proper order.

The reflections in the window shifted and shimmered as four people busied themselves in the tiny kitchen.

"Do you want a drink, Nicky, or would you rather plunge into dinner?"

"I'd like to sit for a bit first, Jenny, if you aren't all dying of hunger."

"We're not. We've been eating peanuts. Put the soup in a pot to keep it hot, Jenny, and I'll top up the glasses." Sheila waved the bottle.

"What's the latest on the dad project?" Nick asked when they were all seated again.

Sheila, lying back in the recliner, grinned at him. "Well, I have news!"

Jenny and Chris stared at her. "You do? How come you didn't tell us?"

"I was waiting till Nick got here."

"That was nice of you."

Sheila turned to Nick. "You know I tried to find him in Ottawa?"

He nodded. "I know a bit about it."

"Jenny's friend Maggie gave me his first name and the name of his family's restaurant, and Norah gave me a picture. That was exciting." Sheila stopped, remembering the shock and delight of seeing her father's youthful face for the first time. "I phoned and phoned, and tracked down every clue that anybody suggested, but it was just like a wall. I only had two days, and I was disappointed when I came home. But I thought, 'Oh well, I tried. Maybe he's been dead for years.' But also, I wondered why nobody remembered him, even if he'd died."

"So you had the family name . . ."

"Yes, Lee, from the records of the restaurant."

"And the years he was in Ottawa."

"Mm-hm. People certainly remembered the place, and the family—I even talked with a great-grandson of the actual Lee who'd started the restaurant, but he couldn't think of any Anthony among his uncles or great-uncles. Or said he couldn't, anyway. It seems

Anthony is basically a Catholic name—there's a St. Anthony—and this chap said his family were all Protestants. With first names like Andrew and Robert, you know?"

"I've never thought about names being Protestant or Catholic."

"Me either but back then, I guess it was important. Anyway, I left my address and phone number everywhere, in case somebody remembered something. And somebody did."

Sheila pulled an envelope from the pocket of her jeans, smiling broadly, and waved it like a talisman. "It's from an old Chinese lady but written by her daughter. I guess people started talking about my phone calls and trying to figure out who I was and it eventually got to this lady, who's one of the Lees. She says she didn't know anything about Pat but cousins from China used to come to work in the restaurant. You know—the Chinese have these extended-family connections, like Ghanaians, as Grace was telling us, and relatives would come for a year or two to learn English or get a Canadian education or whatever. And she remembered which cousin was there the year Pat got pregnant."

"This is incredible!" Jenny's eyes were fixed on the envelope.

"So his name wasn't Lee, and that's why nobody could think of who you belonged to," Nick said.

"Yes. His name was Anthony Chia, if this lady's got the right person. And" —Sheila paused for effect— "the cousins didn't always go back to China after their stint in the restaurant. Anthony lives in Toronto. He went into business—not the restaurant business, what a surprise!—but food imports, close enough, and the lady gave me the name of his firm. And!"—another pause—"he married a Canadian girl."

Silence, while her listeners absorbed the implications of this.

"So, I called him up." Sheila made no mention of the hours she had spent agonizing and wondering and dithering before she picked up the phone.

"Heavens," Jenny gasped. "I can't *imagine* the conversation."

"Well, it was pretty amazing. I said who I was and who my mother was—had been—and when I was born, and could he be my father? And right away, he said yes. So we had a really long chat.

He sounds so nice! He said he'd been going out with Pat and then she—disappeared. Nobody would tell him why she'd gone away or where she was—or maybe nobody could, because at first probably only her parents knew. But he kept trying to find out, and when he'd finished the time he'd promised to do in the family restaurant, he moved to Toronto, partly because he thought she might have gone there. He was right in figuring that her father had sent her away, but he thought it was just because he was Chinese, not because she was pregnant. Eventually, he did hear she'd gone to Vancouver, but by then he couldn't just drop everything and rush out there. Here."

"But didn't he know about you? I mean Sheila Muir, the singer?" Jenny asked.

"He'd heard my name, but I guess he likes other kinds of music, and he's never actually seen me. Otherwise he might have twigged, I suppose."

"He must be a bit out of it," said Jenny indignantly. "Everybody in the country knows what you look like."

"Apparently not."

"Was he thrilled? Are you going to meet him?" Chris asked.

"Yes, he was thrilled. And so was I. And we're going to get together the next time I'm in Toronto. Which is pretty soon. Isn't it fantastic?"

"If I'd known all this was going to happen I'd have bought champagne," said Nick.

"Yes, after this excitement, dinner'll be an anticlimax. But it's ready. Chris's laid everything out in killingly logical courses. Soup first." Jenny got up.

Chris served the soup and Sheila made her way carefully to the table with a full bowl. "I thought we were going to have a picnic, but you've set the table. It looks quite formal."

"Well, when Nick brought soup I thought it'd be easier to eat at the table. And we don't have any ants, anyway."

Four heads—black, blond, brown, and red—bent over soup bowls in the warm little room.

"Wine anybody? Bread?" Jenny passed the basket. Here we all are at the table, she thought. We're all connected, but with different ties—me by blood with two of them and by inclination with the other. I'm the linchpin here, and before me it was Pat—or else Chris and Sheila wouldn't be in the same family. And now suddenly Sheila has a dad. But really, the true linchpin for the whole family is Grace. She's the one who insisted we all come to the farm. Isn't that interesting—the connecting of all of us had to run through . . . "Chris! What's happening about you going to Ghana?"

"It's coming. I'm muddling my way through the formalities."

"You still want to go? It hasn't worn off since we got home?"

"No. I find myself looking around the bar, and at my customers, and thinking, 'Maybe I've done this long enough.' So I'll go for a visit and if I like it, I'll look for a teaching job for a year or two."

As Jenny filled her plate for the next course, she glanced at the big windows. Look at our reflections. Chris, Nick, and I all knew our fathers—well, that makes only two fathers, of course—and there's no mystery. We know our dads' educational levels and siblings and medical history and everything. But Sheila never did. Poor thing—I never thought about that before. She shook herself and turned back to the room, just as Sheila announced, "You know what? This is a kind of wrap!"

"What?" Jenny, alarmed, stopped with a forkful of noodles in mid-air.

"Pat and Sandy are both gone, Chris's off to Africa, and I'm about to meet my father."

"Oh. I thought you meant it was a last supper."

"No, no—of course not. Only that our lives will be different from now on."

For the last year, they had been meeting fairly often for drinks or dinner, either at a restaurant or one of their condos, talking about Pat and how she was doing, remembering Sandy, helping each other out in small ways—Chris fixing Jenny's leaky faucet, Sheila getting concert tickets for Chris—grumbling about the rain, exulting in the spring flowers. Jenny realized Sheila was right. Now, all of a sudden, everything is changing, she thought. My dear Chris, my childhood hero and then pal and then adult ally, is going away to another continent; Sheila is heading out soon to meet her father; Nicky has moved closer into my life. But we're all still family, wherever we are, and we've added Ben and Grace and their kids.

"Better." Nick grinned. "I'm sure you mean our lives will be better, Sheila."

"Especially Sheila's," said Chris, "now that she's connected with her dad."

"Just imagine," Jenny said, calmer, and helped herself to a chicken thigh. "Sheila will find relatives in Toronto and China. And Chris will meet Elly in Ghana."

Nick, with mock solemnity, raised his glass. "To this suddenly and surprisingly far-flung family."

Three other glasses rose.

"We really should be having champagne," Chris said.

Two days later, Jenny, engrossed in the adventures of Gerald Hatley-Thorpe, exclaimed aloud when she read the name "Tekyiman" and realized he and Helen were travelling to Grace's hometown. And that she had seen pictures of the town, taken at almost this exact time, in the book that Grace and Ben had by the Polish woman. She then came upon Gerald's mention of that very woman, Mrs. Meyerowitz. Truly, the Gold Coast must have been a small colony in those days. Thoroughly excited now, Jenny consumed the pages, delighted by Gerald's detail, until she read about the appearance of Constance, in front of the chief's house.

She stopped and looked out at the North Shore. "Constance?" she frowned. That surely was the name of Grace's aunt—the teacher. Was Constance a very common name or could this be the same person? Well, I can easily find out if it is, and immersed herself again in the hot bright scene: Helen vanishing with Constance, the children leaping and teasing around the car, Gerald and Yeboah smoking in the sunshine. He made it so vivid that she could feel the boundless light beating down, and his dismay in the situation. Poor Gerald—he sounded like such a nice man, though on the stuffy side. She looked forward to meeting Helen.

Jenny emailed Gerald's description of Techiman and of Constance to Grace, asking, "Could this be your Aunt Constance?" And, always alert for errors, "Has the author spelled all the names right?"

"Listen to this, hon," Grace burst into the kitchen, waving Jenny's email. "Jenny's working on a book that's partly about Ghana and it mentions my Auntie Constance!" She read aloud the account of the first meeting between Constance and Helen.

"When was this?" Ben looked up from the newspaper.

"The early 1950s. It must have been in the first couple of years that Constance was teaching. Where did you put that box of photographs? I'll scan the one of Constance and email it to Jenny so she can show the author. But I have no doubt that it's our Constance. Let's ask Helen to come for a visit!"

When Helen saw the photograph that Jenny forwarded, of Constance smiling on the veranda of the elementary school, tears clouded her eyes. It was certainly the same woman. Dear Constance, dear Tekyiman—oh, Jenny says it's spelled Techiman now. What a wonderful time I had there. The people were all aware of my efforts on their behalf, and grateful, and their generosity overwhelmed me. When I returned to Accra in a car laden with yams, groundnuts, chickens, and eggs, Gerald made no comment, other than raised eyebrows, but our cook was happy to have food straight from the country.

Jenny had also sent a photograph of Grace, and Helen scrutinized her, wondering if she could find a resemblance to Constance. No, Grace did not particularly look like Constance, but her beaming face was so open and her smile so generous that Helen decided she would accept the invitation to visit Juniper Farm on her way to Ghana.

Her work on Gerald's manuscript was not onerous, as Beth had predicted. She went through it line by line, answering Jenny's questions, revising a few sentences and double-checking some names and dates. Although her sorrow that Gerald could never know about the publication remained as a little underlying hum of grief, she enjoyed the process of getting the book ready. When she had emailed the final draft to Jenny, she began to plan her trip. She would go in February, because that was often the greyest, wettest month on the West Coast and she remembered that in West Africa, it was the dry season. Sunny days, even though they might be dusty, would be a welcome change.

"I wonder where Jenny is?" Sheila looked around the echoing airport. "This isn't like her. She's always earlier than me whenever we get together."

"Traffic, maybe." Chris nudged his bag ahead of him with his right foot. The check-in line snaked between the stanchions with the usual twitter of nervous excitement before international flights. "She'll be along."

Sheila sighed. "This feels really weird, Chris. I'm not used to saying goodbye to people. I'm usually the one going away, not that anybody came out to see me off very often."

"Well, I guess not. You're always going somewhere."

"I don't think I like being the one abandoned on the ground." Another sigh.

"Oh, come on. Abandoned? All your friends are here."

Sheila's doleful expression remained. "Yes, but Vancouver's going to seem so odd without you. Just knowing you're not here!"

Chris was surprised to hear this from Sheila. Jenny would miss him because they saw each other more frequently, but Sheila had always been focused on her work. "I can't see that it'll be all that different for you. There'll be a new bartender at Jason's, of course. You'll have to train him or her about what you like to drink."

"Will it be Wendy?"

"I don't think so. She doesn't want to work more hours. But she'll still be there. And she does know what you drink." He knew Sheila enjoyed that sort of recognition, of being able to smile and nod when a server asked, "The usual, Ms. Muir?"

"Mm-hm. But I don't mean just Jason's. Everybody's always been in Vancouver—I mean, until Sandy and Pat died—and suddenly there's just Jenny."

"So what are you feeling—un-anchored?"

"I guess so. I could come and go, but you were all always here. Where you belong!!"—with a mock glare. "Maybe it's another kind of loss, now that Pat's gone."

"Sheila, I'm not dying. And you could come and visit me if I stay."

Sheila sighed again. "I'm not coping well with these changes. Maybe it's a sign of age. I'm getting rigid."

"No, you're not." Chris wondered whether departing passengers always had to cheer up their well-wishers. Why were they called "well-wishers" then? "Look at your own changes. You're going to meet your father!"

"What if I don't like him?"

"You're just determined to be gloomy today, aren't you? You got up this morning and thought, 'I'll put on my glum face. That'll teach him to go off and leave me almost alone in Vancouver!'"

Sheila straightened up, threw her shoulders back and gave him a big grin. "You're right. I'm in a bit of a funk. But here's my real face. I won't rain on your parade anymore."

"Attagirl! Positive thoughts. Oh—there's Jenny." He waved vigorously. "And Nick too. I didn't expect him to come out."

Jenny spotted them, nodded and threaded her way through the crowd. "Thank goodness! We got delayed and I was terrified you might have to finish checking in and go on, and we'd never find you."

"I'd have waited at the gate. Till the last second."

"We've got a surprise," Jenny announced, grinning hugely at Nick. She thrust her left hand forward. A ring glittered.

Sheila and Chris locked their gaze on it and then gaped at Jenny's beaming face.

"We got engaged!" she explained helpfully.

"So—so I see," stammered Chris, the first to recover. "I'm astonished. I always thought you were perfectly happy as you were. But that's lovely."

The line moved convulsively ahead a few feet, people near them trying to pretend they weren't listening avidly.

"Hurray!" Sheila flung her arms around Nick, glad of some action to release her strong emotions. "I've been bugging Jenny for years that you should be really part of the family! What made you all of a sudden decide to get married?"

"Don't know, exactly," Nick replied. "I've been wanting to and we talked about it, on and off—Jenny was never very keen—but when she came back from your trip to the cousins, she was more positive. So I quickly slid a ring on her finger and here we are!"

"How come?" Sheila asked Jenny.

"Maybe it was being with Grace and Ben, hearing the family history, meeting all those relatives we hadn't heard of." Jenny shrugged. "After we had that little chat with Grace, I realized that when she married Ben, she faced a much bigger change in her life than I ever will. And I thought what a coward I'm being, what a pathetic wimp. So I decided yes, I'd like to be married to Nicky."

"Wonderful! It'll be so much fun to plan your wedding!"

"Don't get too excited, Sheel. It's going to be small and there's no rush. We're going to wait at least till Chris comes back. And why are you so keen? You haven't had anything good to say about the institution of marriage since Hugo."

"I may not be interested in marriage but I certainly like weddings. Other people's particularly. And it's fine that there's no rush. We'll have plenty of time to find you a dress. I can hardly wait to take you shopping."

"I can just see it." Jenny laughed. "Trooping in and out of stores, getting cranky and tired, just like when we were kids and Pat was buying our school outfits."

"Oh, it'll be much better than that."

Chris was at the head of the line and he stepped up to the check-in wicket.

"Gosh, he's really going." Jenny grabbed Sheila's arm. "I can't stand it."

"Yes, you can. He'll have a grand time and we mustn't be self-ish about wanting him to stay here. We've all had a lot of changes lately—even you, now—and this is only one of them. Can I look at your ring again, by the way? You just flashed it by my nose."

"Sure." Jenny took it off and handed it to Sheila.

"It's very pretty," she said, holding it up in the light. "Where did you get it?"

"A designer friend of Nicky's." The ring was set with small sapphires in a random pattern, connected by curving lines scribed in the gold. "It can double as a wedding ring when we get to that stage."

Chris picked up his boarding pass, thanked the agent and turned. "Okay—all done. Let's go to the lounge. We need to celebrate these two."

"Remember not to drink too much alcohol," Sheila warned Chris as they strolled to the bar. "It's dehydrating. Drink lots of water."

"Yes, Mumsy." He laughed. "I'll make sure not to arrive in London with a hangover."

Jenny listened to them, caught between laughter and a wave of weeping. She slid an arm around Nick and sighed a little.

"I know," he said sympathetically. "Seeing people off always feels like this. But he'll have a wonderful time."

"When are you going to Toronto, Sheel?"

"Next week. I've got a date with my—um—dad for dinner on Wednesday." Her bright expression slipped for a moment and then she smiled. "At a fancy place. So even if we don't get on, we'll have had a good meal."

"Oh, you'll get on beautifully," Chris predicted. "He's bound to adore you."

As they settled themselves at a table, Jenny asked, "If we hadn't gone to the farm and met Grace, would you have gone to Africa, Chris?"

Sheila ordered a bottle of champagne and looked inquiringly at Chris.

"No, I'm sure I wouldn't have."

"What did Elly say when you emailed her?" Jenny was still hovering on the edge of tears.

"She sounded very enthusiastic, and keen for us to get together. She's in Techiman for a few months, but she's coming to Accra to meet me and then we'll go back up there. I'm staying in a hotel there, at least at first. But I'd really like to try living in one of the village houses."

When the champagne came in its celebratory chilled bucket, the silver surface beaded with light-filled droplets, a succession of toasts was proposed: to Chris's Great Adventure, to Sheila's meeting with her father, to Jenny and Nick's engagement.

"We need another bottle," Nick suggested.

"Sheila won't let Chris drink any more." Jenny laughed.

"It's on the *plane* she said I shouldn't drink too much. I can get on with a skinful and then drink water all the way across the Atlantic. Right, Sheila?"

Sheila grinned at him. "It's your headache. And if your flight's called, the three of us will finish it."

TWENTY: Legacy

"I love this building." Jenny craned her neck to look straight up as she and Sheila walked into Vancouver's tall, marble-trimmed railway station. "It's so elegant. I've always admired those paintings way up high. I'm glad it hasn't been torn down, like so many other old buildings."

"It probably has a heritage classification by now." Sheila glanced briefly at the high ceiling. "So it's safe."

"I hope so. After seeing all those old buildings in Ottawa I might be becoming a heritage advocate myself. It made me realize how new everything is here. And I love that statue outside, of the angel carrying the soldier. I'm glad it's still here too."

They positioned themselves with the expectant group inside the bank of glass doors leading to the tracks and had not long to wait before Grace and Ben appeared.

Hugs, hellos, welcomes.

"Thank you. It's good to be here." Ben looked interestedly about. "This is a nice old station. The one in Ottawa is beautiful, but it's very modern—glass and steel."

Jenny started across the polished floor. "Sheila's parked right out-side." As they wound their way through the streets, she played tour guide. "That's BC Place . . . the Queen Elizabeth Hall . . . the Vancouver Hotel . . . Barkley Heritage Square . . . and Sheila's new digs!"

Unlike Chris and Jenny, Sheila had never owned a home. Her income had always been too sporadic for her to consider a mort-gage with any confidence, and although she and Hugo had lived in a large house, it was clearly—especially by the end of the mar-riage—"Hugo's house." Her family and friends had encouraged her to use that divorce settlement to buy something, but she was still uncertain and invested it instead. Sheila was quite content to rent. As she said, "I'm not committed and if anything goes wrong in the apartment, I just pick up the phone and say, 'Hello—this is Sheila in 623. My toilet's stopped working, or whatever,' and they fix it." But a month before Grace and Ben's visit, she had moved into a bright and spacious condominium, which, to everyone's amazement, she had suddenly bought.

Knowing she would have to explain this about-face, she decided it was because her inheritance from Pat had allowed it. This was perfectly true, although Sheila herself suspected it was more than that. But she felt disinclined to engage in self-analysis and was secretly glad that Chris wasn't around to press her on it.

Now she was delighted to usher Grace and Ben into her guest room. "You're my first visitors! I've never had any guest space before—just a pullout sofa in the living room. I hope you don't mind my electric piano in here—it doesn't take up much space. And here's your bathroom."

"Isn't it great that the first people to stay in it are family?" Jenny enthused. "We should pour libation, the way you told us, Grace."

"Not on my new carpets, you don't!"

"Aha—the responsibility of ownership is creeping over you, Sheel. A little white wine wouldn't make much of a mark!"

"Don't even think about it." Grace smiled. "If anything, we can pour libation out on the balcony. But it'll be to welcome Sheila to her new home, not us."

"Sounds good. Libation on the balcony in ten minutes. Jenny, come and help me in the kitchen and we'll let Grace and Ben unpack."

Because it was in an older building that had been turned into condos, the kitchen was a narrow walk-through, not part of the living space with a vast granite counter as in more modern examples. Jenny and Sheila set out glasses, olives, nuts, cheese and crackers.

"This is a really, really nice place," Jenny told Sheila for perhaps the hundredth time. "I'm so glad you bought it."

"Me too. Would you take this tray out?" Sheila asked quickly, in case Jenny began ruminating about why it had taken her so long to put down roots in her home city.

Unlike the kitchen, the balcony was a generous size. Sheila's condo was on the southwest corner of the building, and the balcony ran all along both sides. It was this feature, as much as the large living room and bedrooms, that had drawn her to the condo when she had decided to buy something.

"Isn't this lovely!" Grace sighed happily when they were all outside.

"Okay—the libation. What do we say, Grace?" Jenny held her full glass out expectantly.

"It doesn't matter—there's no strict formal wording." Grace tilted her glass. "To Sheila's happiness in her new home," and let two or three drops fall on the concrete floor.

"To Sheila's happiness in her new home," Jenny and Ben repeated solemnly, offering their own small splashes.

"Thank you very much," and Sheila held her own glass high. "Here's to all of you, for being here."

Clinks.

"Now, what are we looking at here?" Ben asked.

"That's English Bay straight ahead and False Creek going off to the left. The university's out at the far end of that peninsula. And on the right, across the water, those mountains and houses are West Van."

Grace breathed deeply. "The air smells so good, after three days on the train. And I love all the flowering trees we drove through. The petals look like pink snow on the streets. I've never seen such abundance. Is it like this every year?"

"Yes—gorgeous, isn't it?" Jenny answered. "On some streets, when the trees are all in bloom, they seem to actually change the quality of the light. I was so glad you decided to come out at this time of year. What's it like on the farm?"

"Cold and wet. The snow's melting but it's not all gone and the trees look very dark. There aren't any leaves yet, let alone flowers. Maybe we should come out here every spring."

"Well, of course you should. You can always stay here, whether I'm around or not," Sheila offered quickly.

After the reuniting of the family at Juniper Farm, Grace had been eager to plan a trip West, for Ben to connect again on the other home territory, to solidify the linkage. Not for Grace a single, friendly meeting and subsequent Christmas cards. She had chosen the dates to include the launch of Sheila's new CD at the Vancouver East Cultural Centre, and the timing proved to be particularly lucky, not only because of Sheila's generous new accommodations but also this unexpected glory of the urban forest, luxuriant with blossoms.

"If Helen were back from her trip, we'd have gone to Victoria to see her. We had a marvellous time with her on the farm," said Grace. "When is her book—I mean, her husband's book—coming out?"

"In a few months. Thank you again for those photographs of Techiman. We put three of them in."

"I'm glad you could use any. They were taken after Helen and Gerald's time, but some things haven't changed too much."

"I especially liked the picture of the secondary school because it brought the story of Helen's involvement right up to date."

"Oh—that reminds me," Sheila interrupted. "Chris called last night. To wish me luck with the show. He's having a great time at that school you sent him to, Grace. St. Louis."

"I didn't send him. I just gave him the name of the headmistress because I know her, and those kinds of contacts can't hurt. It was pure luck that one of the English teachers needed some leave, and who knows—a temporary job at least gives him an in."

"It isn't the school you went to, is it?" Sheila moved around the little circle, refilling glasses.

"No. I went to Techiman Secondary—TESS, we call it—the one with the picture in Helen's book. But I know St. Louis is a good school and I thought Chris might like being in Kumasi. It's a wonderful city—very alive."

"He sent us their fiftieth-anniversary yearbook, all about the history of the school. It was founded by Irish nuns, in 1952. Just about when Gerald and Helen were there." Jenny was always pleased to see connections.

"I guess that's why it's a girls school." Sheila sat down again.

"No." Jenny had read the publication thoroughly. "Some of the chiefs asked the Catholic Church to establish schools for girls, because only about fifteen percent of them were going to school. This was in the 1940s, amazing to relate! The chiefs were certainly ahead of their time, to be worrying about educating girls, weren't they? Even here, at that time, people would often send their sons to university but not their daughters."

"Yes, but they probably all went to high school," Grace pointed out. "What the chiefs were concerned about was that the girls weren't even getting that far. And they still aren't. Not more than about forty percent of girls go to secondary school, but at least it's better than it was. I certainly hope Chris likes St. Louis."

"It's a big school—nearly a thousand girls—and Chris said he's amazed at how much they do with so little money. It costs less than four hundred a year for each girl. That's everything—room and board, tuition, books. Here, it'd be about twenty thousand dollars."

"The schools are all short of funds, but they can't raise the fees very much because even at four hundred dollars, lots of families can't afford it."

Sheila regarded Grace thoughtfully for a few moments, her lower lip caught in her teeth. "Grace, would you mind talking about that for a few minutes at the Cultch on Saturday? We'll try to raise some money for St. Louis."

Grace's face was immediately alight. "Of course I'll say a little bit. If I'd known, I'd have brought my kente! But what's the Cultch?"

"Oh—sorry—that's the nickname for the Vancouver East Cultural Centre. Where we're having the CD launch. It's a lovely old church that's been made into a theatre and arts centre. The timing's a bit tight for fundraising, but I'll put the word out every way I can—Facebook and stuff. But even if people aren't expecting it, most of them will have an extra few bucks in their wallets."

"That's a marvellous idea, Sheel. I'll let all my friends know too."

"Between us, Jenny, we'll cover the town! I want people to buy my CD too, mind you, but it feels really good to do something beyond that." Sheila was pleased by her initiative.

Ben stood up and stretched until his arm sockets clicked. "Would anybody like to go for a walk? I really need to work out the kinks, and I'd love to explore your neighbourhood."

"Absolutely." Jenny jumped up. "We can go collect Molly on the way. She's my foster dog. And we'll scuff in the petals, Grace,

242

like we do with the leaves in the fall. You'll like that."

"It seems wrong, somehow, to go stepping on flowers."

"You can flutter them in your hands instead." Sheila picked up the empty tray and led the way inside.

The Cultch was sold out for the CD launch and people who had left it too late were hovering outside the theatre in hopes of scoring a no-show seat. Sheila's fans were delighted that she was finally performing again, and the ticket holders looked pleased and triumphant as they passed into the building.

Sally and Dave stood with Kate in the lobby and observed the scene.

"They all seem really excited to be here. They're not just walking in going, 'Ho hum, another concert,' are they?"

"No." Kate had noticed the same little thrill of anticipation on the faces of the people streaming past. "There's a sort of festive feeling. Maybe they were afraid Sheila would never do another CD."

"Remember she said—last fall, I think it was—that people would think she'd been to Betty Ford because she'd been out of the picture for so long?"

"I do remember that. But she just couldn't sing after Pat got sick. Odd, wasn't it? She'd always had a hard time with Pat, but it was like her creativity was connected with that relationship anyway. She picked the date of this launch because it's exactly a year since Pat signed her will."

"You were right to press her to go to the farm with the ashes. After that she got to work with a whole new spirit."

"I know. It freed her up, somehow. But I wasn't expecting that. I just thought if she didn't go, she'd regret it later on."

"Oh, you're a wise woman. Sheila's lucky to have you as her manager."

Kate laughed. "I'm the lucky one! Look at all these people going in. I hardly had to do any promotion—Sheila's name is magic."

"Well, sweetie." Sally turned to Dave, who was smiling silently beside her. "Let's go get our seats before people think they're vacant. See you later, Katie."

Backstage, Sheila was dealing with her usual pre-performance butterflies. Breathe deeply, she told herself, close your eyes, relax. She had learned that she needed to be alone for the final fifteen or twenty minutes before a show, to calm down, to focus on what she was going to say and to sing at the beginning. After that, a comfortable momentum took over as she gained energy from the audience; it was the walking out into the expectant silence that was daunting. She knew she looked good, in a severely simple slim black dress, her hair straight and shaped to just below her ears, with only a pair of huge and dazzling ruby earrings to give colour. A legacy of Hugo, she thought wryly; I wonder if he's in the audience?

"Time, Sheila." Kate stuck her head in the door. "Break a leg, honeybunch—it'll be a fabulous show!"

Tears started in Sheila's eyes at the warmth in Kate's voice. She blinked and nodded. "Thank you, honeybunch yourself."

As she strode out onto the stage, a storm of applause washed over her: whistles, catcalls, shouts of "Hurray!" and "Welcome back!" Honestly amazed, she put a hand to her breast and bowed. The uproar continued. She straightened and smiled, broadly, endlessly, including every person in the hall; from Jenny and Nick, Ben and Grace, Sally and Dave in front, because she knew where they were sitting, to people in the boxes and back rows. That smile somehow welded the house together. The clapping quieted and with contented rustles, everybody sat back, sure of a wonderful evening.

"Thank you very much," Sheila began. "It's lovely to be back here at the Cultch and to spend an evening with you all. I do have a new CD out, as you know, and some of you also know that we're having a fundraiser tonight. But what you don't know is that we'll have a little surprise at the start of the second set." She grinned. "And now that I've enticed you into staying for the whole show, let's have some songs, shall we?"

Another loud wave of approval.

Sheila and Kate had planned the set list carefully, as usual—a mix of old favourites, songs from the new CD and a few covers, sometimes with the piano, sometimes the guitar, many the voice alone, each introduced in a sentence or two. From the stage, Sheila could feel her listeners' concentration, particularly on the unfamiliar material, and their appreciation mounted after every song. She ended the first set with "What Have I Been Doing?"—the song that had come to her in the parlour at Juniper Farm—and the applause that followed seemed thoughtful, as if the audience was pondering her words. Good, thought Sheila; she had placed it just before the intermission on purpose, so that it might ring in people's heads longer.

"Okay, we'll have a short break now—see you back here for my surprise." The house lights brightened and people rose, smiling—at their friends, at strangers—connected, for these few hours, by shared and complex feelings of enjoyment and gratitude, and the awareness that they were, luckily, part of a special event. Suffused with warmth, they flowed gently out into the lobby, where they beamed and exchanged exhilarated comments.

"Isn't this extraordinary?" Jenny heard a young man say. "It's not just that her voice is as good as ever—I have the sense that I'm relating to everything she sings."

"I know," said the woman with him. "Or like she's singing right to me. I'm so glad we got tickets."

Jenny, who had been to innumerable concerts of Sheila's, was almost weepy, holding Nick's hand tightly and saying nothing, stunned by the heightened emotion in the hall.

"My, she's amazing," Ben said. "You'd never guess, when you're sitting around talking in the kitchen, that her voice could fill a concert hall like that, even though I realize it's miked."

"It's filled bigger places than this one." Sally laughed. "And I'm sure it will again."

The CDs sold briskly. Then the lights flickered and the reverse flow began.

When quiet had descended, "Remember my 'little surprise?'" Sheila turned toward the wings. Grace walked out into the light, smiling serenely at the house and Sheila, with an arm around her shoulders, introduced her. "This is my cousin Grace Asamoah, from Ghana."

A murmur swept through the hall.

Sheila chuckled. "And she's going to tell you what we're raising the funds for tonight."

Grace spoke briefly but eloquently about the importance of educating girls, about what a good school St. Louis was and how far a few Canadian dollars could go in countries like Ghana. "And we even have a member of the family at St. Louis right now," she concluded. "Sheila's brother, Chris Pedersen, whom I'm sure many of you know, is teaching English there." She smiled again out into the darkened hall.

"Great, Grace. Thank you very much." Sheila gave her a hug and explained about the donation baskets, speaking long enough to give Grace time to regain her seat. "Now," brightly, "are you ready for some more music?" The response that rang out assured her that they were.

The second set was even more rewarding than the first: Sheila didn't have any jitters and the listeners, relaxed and charmed by the early part of the evening, were receptive on a new level, focused and absorbed.

Toward the end, Sheila introduced one of the new songs with, "This is called 'The Lost Family,'—it's sort of 'How I Spent my Fall Vacation,'" and she gave a short account of taking Pat's ashes to Juniper Farm. "Well, we're not lost anymore, and now our completed family includes Africa!" She had wondered about mentioning her father's side and decided against it. Too complicated for the purposes of this one song.

"Cousin Muriel will be so pleased to hear this," Jenny whispered to Grace. "We'll send her a CD."

"She'll be thrilled!" Grace's eyes were shining.

The song started off as a lament, for a family estranged over time and distance; then a distinct change in rhythm came in, what Grace and Ben, and perhaps others, recognized as the West African highlife beat; after that the tune and the words became more and more upbeat and it ended with a joyful, two-note repetition of "We are all fam-i-ly" and Sheila waved, inviting the audience to join in. They did. "'We are all fam-i-ly, we are all fam-i-ly,'" they chorused, louder and louder, Sheila conducting. A few people jumped up, singing, swaying, clapping in time, then more, until the entire house, electric, was on its feet. "'We are all fam-i-ly,'" they sang and swayed as one, in the cozy darkness, until Sheila made a cutting motion and immediately bowed deeply, her hair falling silkily forward from the nape of her neck.

Shouts, cheers, stamping of feet; the ovation went on for minutes. As it began to die down, Sheila gestured for quiet. "Are you tired? Ready to go home?"

"Noooooooo!"

"Okay. We'll have another one. But this is the encore," she warned them, "and then we will all be ready to go home."

She closed the show with a familiar, quiet song, calming everyone, sending them off into the night happy and satisfied. At the last moment, a stagehand walked out with a huge bouquet.

"Oh! Thank you very much!" Surprised, Sheila fumbled for the card. "Elly and Chris," she read aloud. "It's from my brother Chris and Elly, Grace's daughter. They're both in Ghana," she exclaimed to the crowd, and people clapped again. She buried her face in the blooms and breathed deeply. It was time to calm herself, to come down from the performing high. She was still ringing from the strength of the audience response, awed and exhausted, and she could feel her dress clinging to her back.

People edged slowly out of the hall. "Wasn't that amazing?" they said to each other, and would be saying for weeks. "Fantastic," someone else would sigh in answer.

Offstage, Sheila fell into Kate's embrace. "Gosh, you're drenched! You better change right away or you'll catch cold. That was a show to end all shows!"

"There was really something extra here tonight, wasn't there?" Sheila pulled the dress over her head.

"There was something extra in you. I've never seen you give so much energy before."

"I guess because it's been so long between concerts. I must have been totally charged up."

"Maybe. Or maybe you've morphed into a new phase. Now

put something on. People are waiting for you and you can't stand around chatting in your lovely beige slip."

"Okay, Ma." Sheila laughed.

"It looks like almost nobody's left." Jenny was gazing around the crowded lobby. "People don't want to go home."

When Sheila came out, now in a white silk shirt and black pants but the same brilliant earrings, everyone was eager but polite and patient as they waited to have a few friendly words, to have CDs signed, to offer heartfelt congratulations. Sheila, still wired, glowed even more at the close contact, smiling, nodding, greeting, autographing. Several people came to speak with Grace as well, and the donation baskets that Jenny and Nick were shepherding filled generously. Gradually, the lobby emptied.

The family group was standing in a corner, watching Jenny dump the contents of the baskets into a large bag, when Grace looked up and gave a delighted gasp. Sheila was approaching, holding the arm of a tall, elegant Chinese man. With an expression Jenny had never seen on her sister's face before, a mixture of pride and shyness, Sheila said, "Jenny, Grace, Ben, Nick, this is my dad, Anthony Chia."

Ben was the first to recover. He stepped forward with his hand out. "Mr. Chia. It's an honour to meet you, sir. I'm Ben Muir, Sheila's cousin, and this is my wife, Grace Asamoah."

"Hello," Anthony Chia said, smiling and shaking hands warmly. "But please, call me Anthony."

Immediately the others crowded round, making him welcome.

"Did you know he was here?" Jenny whispered in Sheila's ear.

"No. He just came up to me now. Isn't it marvellous?"

"It really is. I see what you mean when you said how attractive he was. After you met him in Toronto."

Sheila had reported on that dinner with happiness and restrained hope. "He's really tall for a Chinese man, he's handsome, well dressed, friendly, interested—he seems like an extremely nice person. I didn't meet his wife—it was just the two of us" —she blinked rapidly at this— "but he showed me her picture, and the pictures of their daughters."

Now Jenny was remembering her fanciful description, months ago, of how Sheila's father might be coming to her concerts, quietly proud, and leaving without making himself known. "Has he been to your shows before?"

"No. This is the first time."

"Well, he certainly picked a great one to start with!" and Jenny hugged Sheila tightly. "I've never been to a better one. Congratulations!"

"Shall we get going?" Nick looked around the lobby. "I'm sure the staff wants to close up here."

"Yes, we should. Will you join us, Anthony?" Sheila asked. "We're going back to my place for pizza. I never eat before a concert and Jenny and Nick kindly organized a little after party. Just the family."

Anthony Chia bent his head gracefully. "I'd be happy to join you. Thank you very much."

"Ben and Grace are staying at Sheila's," Jenny explained to him as they left the theatre, "and Nicky and I will take you to your hotel afterward. Where are you staying?"

"The Bayshore."

"Great—that's really close. Why don't you go with Sheila now because Nicky and I are stopping to pick up the food."

As Anthony folded himself into her Honda, Sheila was filled with amazed gratitude. This was her father! Right here in her car, beside her!

In Sheila's little kitchen, Ben took over opening the wine. "This seems to be my role wherever we are. And Chris's not here to help me this time."

"No, but his flowers are." Grace had made sure to bring them from the theatre, although the bouquet had almost crowded Ben and herself out of the back seat of Sheila's Civic, and was arranging them in a large vase. "They'll have to represent him. And Elly."

"Would you like to see the rest of my condo?" Sheila asked Anthony. "I just moved in. It's the first place I've ever owned."

"It's very attractive, and yes, I'd like to see it."

While Sheila led Anthony on a tour, Jenny and Nick arrived with the pizza, which was expected, and a big cake, which was not. "Hurray for Sheila!" it proclaimed in icing, with huge pink roses at each corner. "I know it's a bit over the top" —Jenny tilted it for Grace and Ben to admire— "but this was going to be a special celebration, even before Anthony joined us. Aren't they here yet?"

Grace placed the pizzas carefully in the warm oven. "Sheila's taking Anthony round the condo."

When they reappeared, Sheila, flushed and proud, said, "I think my next guests will be Anthony and Marjorie, his wife."

"Terrific! When?" Jenny stood up and offered Anthony her chair. "Would you like to sit here? This was one of Pat's."

"I come to Vancouver now and then, on business," Anthony replied to her first question, "so I'm sure we'll be here soon. Thank you." And he sat.

Sheila pointed to the Bateman painting in the living room and the rose-patterned carpet in the entrance. "Those came from Pat too."

"I appreciate her good taste. I have an early Bateman myself."

A short silence indicated that the implications of this were being considered.

"May I give you a glass of wine, Anthony," Ben offered. "Sheila?"

"Here I am, being waited on in my own house!"

"You've had a big night. Sit down, put your feet up. You deserve it."

"Yes, cousin." Sheila sank obediently onto the chesterfield with a happy sigh and a glass in her hand. She turned to Anthony. "This is awfully informal, for your first visit with the family. I hope you won't mind just having pizza."

"Of course not. I'm delighted to be with you all. I had hoped to have a word with you after the show, but I never expected to meet everyone else. Or that Ben and Grace would be out here too."

"Did you come out to Vancouver specifically for Sheila's event?" Grace asked.

"I was due out around now anyway, but I did time my trip for her show."

"And you really will be coming back?"

"I certainly will." Anthony was at ease in this group of strangers. He leaned back in his chair, legs crossed, one brilliantly polished shoe swinging slightly, smiling at them all as he answered their questions. He was by far the best dressed among them, his polish offset by his low-key manner.

Finally, "Ready for pizza, Sheel?" Jenny was hungry too.

"I sure am. Want any help?"

"Nope. I'll just put it out. There's both vegetarian, with lots of spinach, and meat, with sausage and pepperoni." Jenny was already in the kitchen and Nick set placemats, plates and napkins ("Use the cloth ones," Jenny had whispered) on the dining-room table.

"Okay—come on, everybody. Sheila, you get first pick."

"No, I'm the hostess."

"You're also the one who hasn't eaten since noon."

"You're getting bossy again." Sheila cupped Jenny's cheeks in her hands. "I hope you're ready for this, Nick."

"Oh yes." Nick turned to Anthony. "Jenny and I are getting married."

"Yes, Sheila told me. Congratulations. When?"

"We don't know yet. Jenny wants Chris to be here, of course, and we don't know what his plans are."

"Chris and your daughter are both in Ghana, I understand." Anthony sat beside Grace and shook out his napkin.

"They are. But they're here in proxy, with that gorgeous bouquet they sent. What a nice idea to put it on the table, Jenny."

"I wanted them to be here too." Jenny passed the meat pizza to Ben.

"And I believe you have a son, as well," Anthony continued to Grace. "Where is he?"

"In Toronto, studying ethnology and music."

"Ah. I'll get in touch with him. You must give me his phone number. My daughters will enjoy meeting him."

"That would be lovely! It'll be fun for TK to work out how you're connected."

"I'll simply tell him I'm his father's cousin's father. That's not too distant, is it?"

"No. It sounds quite close, in fact, when you put it that way. We have very extended families in Ghana."

As the pizzas circulated, Sheila apologized again to Anthony for the informality. "I do have knives and forks, if you'd rather."

"No, no, this is fine. The pizzas are very good."

"You're in the food business, aren't you?" Ben asked. "So that's high praise."

"Yes, but not the Italian food business," Anthony chuckled. "As you might expect."

He's starting to feel at home with us, Sheila thought, observing the exchange. A rush of warmth swept through her. That must be a wave of happiness. Or maybe it's the food and wine.

When the pizza was finished, Jenny cleared the table. "Now I know you hardly ever eat dessert, Sheel, but tonight you have to, because it's a special occasion." She took a tub out of the freezer and a small silver tin from a cupboard. "Vanilla ice cream and maple syrup!" she announced with a wide grin. "When you talked about it, Ben, it sounded so delicious I knew we had to try it, and this is the perfect time." She set the ice cream in front of Grace and the syrup beside Ben. "Getting the whole family involved." She then produced the cake, placed it in front of Sheila with a stack of dessert plates, and gave everyone a fork and a spoon.

"Oh my god—this cake is enormous! How many people were you expecting to feed!?"

"Don't worry, Sheila. It'll freeze if we don't eat it all." Jenny was unbothered. And to Anthony, "If we'd known you'd be here, we'd have put your name on it too."

"Oh no," he said. "Thank you, but this is Sheila's night. The show was a most marvellous experience."

"She's just as excited to have you here as she is about the show." Grace handed him a plate with a large slice of cake. "As we all are. You have expanded the family."

"Speaking of which" —Sheila licked icing off a thumb— "Anthony has pictures of his family. Would you mind showing them round?"

"I'd be pleased to. Perhaps after we've finished the cake."

"Good idea. Otherwise we might get sweet stuff all over them."

"Especially the maple syrup," Grace warned. "It's very sticky."

"May I have a little more?" Nick held his plate toward Ben. "It's fantastic."

"It's nice to think of Pat's tree making syrup for the family. Eventually, I mean." Jenny was scraping her plate. "We should keep some in stock all the time, now that we know how good it is."

Later, they clustered around Anthony in the living room. "This is Marjorie, my wife. She was from Wingham, a small town up near Lake Huron, and we met in Toronto. She's of Scottish descent, as Patsy was."

Sheila and Jenny shared a pleased glance.

"And these are our daughters, Katherine and Roseanne."

Katherine had glossy, straight, black hair, a round face and blue eyes; Roseanne curly, dark-brown hair with more angular cheeks and black eyes, a little more slanted than Katherine's.

"Aren't they gorgeous! They're your *sisters*, Sheel, as much as I am. Katherine looks quite a lot like you, except for the colour of her eyes."

Anthony nodded. "I think so too."

"Oh, I wish Chris were here." Jenny sat back on the chesterfield. "He'd have so loved to meet Anthony and see these pictures."

"He will, one of these days. Maybe he'll come through Toronto on his way home. I would like to have him stay with us."

Jenny gazed at Anthony. "Just think of the things that have happened, and it's all because we took Pat's ashes to the farm. We met Ben and Grace, Chris's gone to Africa, Sheila and Anthony found each other, Nicky and I got engaged. It's amazing."

"Some of that might have happened anyway," Sheila objected. "I could have got up the courage to go looking for Anthony, and Nick could eventually have persuaded you to marry him."

"But—maybe not. Isn't it a good thing you came with us, Sheel! It was in Pat's will," Jenny told Anthony, "but at first Sheila refused to go."

"I know. I'm extremely glad she did go, if it was the visit to the farm that prompted her to try to find me."

"Was it, Sheel?"

Sheila thought. "Yes, I guess it was. Something about being on the farm must have got me started—I don't know exactly what it was."

"Pat accidentally made us into more of a family than she could ever have imagined," Jenny marvelled. "It's sort of an unintended legacy."

"Who knows?" said Sheila. "Maybe it is what she intended."

Grace looked around at the four faces, and smiled across the room at Ben.

Acknowledgments

My warmest thanks for this book go to many people.

To my first readers—my husband, Michael Schubart, my sister, Elsa Fraser, my Auntie Bets, Betty Eligh (who is described briefly in the book), and my dear friends Susan Anstine and Alan Stewart (fellow CUSO volunteers in Ghana)—for their love and support and thoughtful comments, and for not saying, "Um, Marlyn—perhaps you should take up knitting instead."

To my brother, Valdy, and sister-in-law, Kathleen Horsdal, for vetting my version of how people might write songs.

To Kathy Page and the Amethysts—Jacqueline Jacques, Renate Mohr and Jane Rusbridge—for their gentle and insightful help in shaping the manuscript.

To Christine Sanders, for talking about her "Lost Family."

To Fu-Shiang and Sharon Chia, for lending their surname to Anthony.

To Pat Touchie, for her affectionate encouragement, and for her faith in this book.

To my editor, Rhonda Bailey, for her meticulous and perceptive input in making this book the best it could possibly be.

To Wendy Hilliard, for generously making the time to take my photograph for the book.

To my publisher, Ruth Linka, of Brindle & Glass, for the care and dedication she devotes to all of her titles, including this one, and to promotions co-ordinator Emily Shorthouse and designer Pete Kohut, for their help and enthusiasm, and their friendly professionalism.

And my warmest thanks for enriching my life go to all of the people I've named above, and many more.

To the late Bill McWhinney and CUSO, for sending me, among

two dozen eager young idealists, to Ghana, and to my CUSO room-mate at Techiman Secondary School, Lynn Taylor Graham, for her companionship on our adventures then and on our trip back to Ghana in 1996.

To all the Ghanaians I know, my students and friends, for their generosity and good humour.

To all my friends and relations everywhere—my own personal branch of our human family tree.

Marlyn Horsdal is a publisher, editor and writer. In 1984, she co-founded Horsdal & Schubart Publishers Ltd., and ran the company with her husband Michael Schubart, until it sold in 2002. She was born in Ottawa and educated at Queen's University in Kingston, Ontario, and the London School of Economics, in London, England. She taught in Ghana as a CUSO volunteer and started a non-profit called Educating Girls in Africa, a program that provides scholarships to girls at St. Louis Secondary School in Kumasi, Ghana. All royalties from the sale of *Sweetness from Ashes* will be donated to this cause. Marlyn lives on Saltspring Island, BC. *Sweetness from Ashes* is her first novel.